SPIT
and
SONG

travis m. riddle

Cover illustration by Amir Zand – amirzandartist.com
Author photo by Jawn Rocha – jawnrocha.com
Book Layout © 2014 BookDesignTemplates.com

Spit and Song/Travis M. Riddle. -- 1st ed.
ISBN: 9781699812150

SPIT

and

SONG

an Ustlian Tale

also by **travis m. riddle**

Ustlian Tales

Balam, Spring

Standalones

The Narrows
Wondrous

Praise for Travis M. Riddle

For myself. Because this book was damn hard to write.

You'll get what you want in time
Just sign on the dotted line
And hold onto the coattails
And pray that your record sells
Until I get what I want
I'll be kicking
I'll be screaming
We've waited too long
For nothing to come

As Tall As Lions, *We's Been Waitin'*

TABLE OF CONTENTS

CHAPTER I

THE NEW USUAL

The city smelled of hot sand and steaming offal. It was a stench that Kali thought she might never grow accustomed to, no matter how many times she traveled to Yspleash.

She slid off the side of the lumbering ayote she had ridden across the desert over the past three days. A smile crossed her face as she caressed the animal's bumpy, banded shell. She unfastened her knapsack that hung from the tack and strapped it over her shoulder before unhitching the saddle. The animal chittered with satisfaction as she scratched its chin underneath the long, pointed snout. Its whip-like tail gleefully flapped back and forth.

"Good boy," she cooed, moving her hand from the ayote's chin to scratch behind a tiny, pointed ear, which was level with her face. "You're gonna sleep good tonight after that long ride, huh?"

The ayote, which was named Bango, was a rental from the stables in her hometown of Seroo's Eye. Truthfully, Kali could technically afford to outright buy an ayote of her own, but at the moment there was no way she could pay the continual costs of housing, feeding, and other general care.

Daily rental fees could also rack up pretty quickly in her business, though, so thankfully her father was old friends with a man who owned one of the city's stables and he allowed her to borrow a mount at no charge. So, whenever she needed to travel, she went to the stable owned by Gregori and rented Bango. She and the animal had become pals over the past few years.

With one hand firmly placed on the ayote to guide him, Kali made her way toward the stable situated on the far outskirts of the Yspleash city wall. As she approached, the owner waved bombastically at her, practically flinging his body back and forth with each swing of the arm.

He was a jeornish man named Lorrne and, together with his wife Zashi, he had maintained the Yspleash stables for as long as Kali had been traveling to the city.

Must be rough, she thought as she waved back, wondering how the man and his family could stomach the incessant smell that emanated from within the city.

The non-centript population of Yspleash was exceptionally small, as was the case in all centript hives. Someone needed to tend to the ayotes that travelers rode across the desert on, though; the animals were natural reservoirs for the mold, so there was not a centript alive that would risk handling them. Hence Lorrne and his family.

"Hey, Lorrne," Kali greeted him as he ambled over to meet her and Bango. "How're things treating you?"

"Not too bad, not too bad," the man replied, his tan jeornish skin glistening in the overbearing sunlight. Lorrne had recently shaved his platinum-white hair nearly down to the scalp. It was now as if he wore a white, skin-tight cap.

"I'm gonna need to buy one of those," she said, pointing at the facemask that covered his nose and mouth, muffling his speech.

Even on the outer rim of the city, the scent was nauseating. She dreaded stepping foot inside, and regretted forgetting to bring her own facemask. It didn't ever completely eradicate the smell, but it at least *somewhat* helped. She was thankful that the stables sold them.

She couldn't blame the city's primary inhabitants; centripts lacked olfactory organs, and therefore had no idea what their bodies smelled like or what ghastly scent was created by their combined masses.

Kali, however, was a faif, and her nostrils were unfortunately working perfectly fine.

"No problem," Lorrne said, running a flat palm down from Bango's forehead to the tip of his snout. The ayote closed his eyes and basked in the sensation. "How long you stayin' for this time?" Lorrne asked.

"I think just overnight," said Kali. She pondered the question for another moment. "Two at most, but I don't think that's likely."

"Not a problem either way," Lorrne said. "Plenty of room here." He gave Bango a soft pat on the head. The ayote blinked open his eyes and gave Lorrne a sloppy lick on the face with his long, skinny tongue.

They both laughed, and Lorrne wiped away the saliva on the back of his arm.

Kali asked, "Where's Zashi today? Off with Caya somewhere?" Caya was their son, a young boy that Kali had only met on a handful of occasions. He was usually roaming the streets of Yspleash with his friends, much too busy to bother mingling with his parents' customers.

"Nah," Lorrne said, leaving Bango to fetch his logbook. "She's running some errands while Caya plays. Leaving all the hard work to me!"

"It sure is rough, having to write down a name and take some money every few hours," Kali joked.

Lorrne cracked a smile. "True, I am the lazy one of the bunch," he said, flipping through pages until he found the one he was searching for. He scribbled her name into the next blank line (underneath two other names; a fuller stable than usual), then clapped the book shut again.

She paid him for a single night, plus an extra crescent for a facemask, and gave Bango a farewell pat. "See you in a bit, bud," she told the animal.

After thanking Lorrne, she commenced her trek toward the entry arches several hundred feet away, slipping the mask over her face.

First things first, she wanted some food. Her stomach grumbled at her in irritation.

It had been over a month since her last visit to Yspleash, located on the eastern end of the Gogol Desert, the largest span of dunes in all of Herrilock. An impressive distinction, given how much of the country was covered in sand.

Yspleash was surrounded by an imposing tan wall built of mudbricks, comprised of sand, water, and the centript residents' own dung. Bricks were stacked atop one another, then plastered over with a sand and water mixture. The perimeter wall towered thirty feet in the air and was painted with intricate, colorful patterns along its entire length.

Not many people milled in or out of the city, so the entryway was nearly empty as Kali approached. The only other person there was the stablemaster's son Caya, no older than eight, who ran up and down, weaving back and forth with a ball at his feet before kicking it into the wall and attempting to catch it on the bounce back.

Kali waved a polite hello to the boy, but he ignored her in lieu of his game. Long hair flopped over his face. It was the same platinum-white color as all jeornish.

A surprising *thwack* reverberated through the air as the child's rubber ball slapped against the adobe wall and ricocheted to the left, in Kali's direction.

It sputtered to a stop in the sand a few feet away from where she stood, and she let out a chuckle as Caya rushed over, spewing apologies.

"Sorry, ma'am!" he squeaked, clearly not recognizing her. "Didn't mean to, I promise!"

"Not a problem," she assured him with a laugh.

"Just playing with my ball, is all!" he said, skidding to a stop and spraying sand out in front of him. "I'm the best kicker here, you know. I can kick it the hardest."

"Oh, yeah?" She couldn't imagine many of Yspleash's other kids were particularly adept at kicking, given centript anatomy.

The boy reminded Kali of her sister Lissia. Both were jeornish and sported loud, boisterous attitudes.

He beamed. "Yup! Wanna watch? I've even kicked it over the wall before," he boasted, though she severely doubted the claim.

"I can't, sorry," she said. "I've got an appointment I need to keep. Plus, I'm pretty hungry. Could you point me in the direction of the bakery?" Despite her semi-frequent visits, she never could memorize the city's complex geography. Caya told her, and she made her way further into the city.

As she entered the city limits, the sight would have taken her breath away if the smell hadn't already. It never failed to amaze her.

Centript construction was fascinating to her, provided how comparatively run-of-the-mill the architecture in Seroo's Eye was (though it too had its share of awe-striking features). Buildings in Yspleash, as well as all centript cities, were constructed from the same material as the outer wall, though the material was simply poured and molded against the mountain range rather than divided into individual bricks. The result gave the impression of a city that was one huge, amorphous mass that virtually melted off the mountainside. Various points had been molded into more distinct buildings, but the interior walls of every building were shared with another, hence the colloquial term for a centript city being a *hive*. Misshapen ovals bore into the sides of buildings to act as tiny windows, and single planks of solid wood shielded entryways.

She navigated through the twists and turns of the narrow streets according to Caya's somewhat vague directions, and was pleasantly surprised to find herself at the entrance to Delightful Desserts.

Kali stepped through the doorway and was greeted with a booming hello by the store's provisioner, a stocky faif with a broad face and a wide smile. Her skin was a shimmery green mixed with bright yellow, in stark contrast to Kali's, which was a swirl of pale blue, violet, and pink pastels. Very few faifs shared the same combination of colors or patterns on their skin, though Kali and the baker both had long, crimson hair.

"How can I help you, dear?" asked the woman with a toothy smile. She wore no facemask; either she had long since grown accustomed to the city's inherent scent, or the aroma of baked goods kept it at bay. She stood behind a glass-plated shelf stocked with cookies, baklayv, sugartongues, and other various sugary treats.

Faifs generally sustained on sunlight and a minimal amount of water, but when they ate real food, it was packed with sugar. It had been over a week since Kali had last eaten, so she was craving something sweet.   Kali scanned the rows of food and had to stop herself from drooling over the multitude of pastries from which there were to choose.

Baklayv consisted of several layers of thin dough, filled with finely chopped nuts. They got their sweetness from being soaked in sugar syrup, honey, or both. Kali did love the dough's fluffiness after biting through that initial crunch, but it sounded a little *too* sweet for her today.

Despite their name, sugartongues were not as cloying as baklayv. They were made by mixing the same type of dough with finely-ground almonds, then baked off and glazed with sugar syrup. Sugartongues earned their name from the shape they were molded into: somewhat cylindrical, but coming to a distinct point on one end. Children loved the novelty of rushing into pastry shops and buying up as many tongues as they could.

Today, a particularly scrumptious-looking knaff on the bottom row of the baker's display caught Kali's eye. Knaffs were a thin, noodle-like pastry shaped into a square (or whatever shape the baker pleased) and soaked in sugar syrup, then topped with a layer of cheese and sometimes nuts to offset the sweetness with some savory flavors.

She pointed at the knaff, with a mild white cheese sprinkled on top, and said, "Just this, please."

The baker nodded and scooped the knaff up off the shelf, plopping it onto a ceramic plate. "Would you like anything to drink with it?" she asked. "We've got coffee, cactus tea, and I even got a shipment of mir tea in last week! You ever had mir tea?" Kali shook her head. "It's delicious. Very strong and sweet."

It sounded tempting, but the sweetness of the knaff would abate her craving just fine. "Not today, thank you," she said. "I would take some water, though, if you have it."

Kali paid, then shuffled over to a small table cramped in the corner of the bakery by the window with her knaff-topped plate and cup of water. She heaved a sigh as she looked out at the streets of Yspleash, dropping her knapsack to the floor, thinking about her upcoming appointment.

There wasn't much time to waste, so she slid the mask down beneath her chin and bit into the pastry. It had a satisfying crunch, a rich sweetness mingling with the salty cheese. Exactly what she needed. This baker's food never disappointed.

"How is it?" the woman asked from behind the counter.

Kali gave her a thumbs-up. With her mouth still full, she said, "Perfect."

- -

The drugs were probably not of the highest quality.

Puk was aware of that.

They never were when he bought them from his friend in Rus Rahl, a scrawny dealer who went by the nickname Pillbug and was, by all accounts, a dipshit.

But that hardly mattered, because drugs were drugs, and Pillbug's prices were cheap due to Puk hooking him up with a discount at Rus Rahl's worst-kept secret: a brothel in the theater district where Puk's pal worked as an accountant.

Connections. Connections were invaluable.

That was one of the few useful lessons his pop Doro had ever imparted. His other four fathers and his mother had been much better role models in general, but unfortunately they had not left as much of an impression on him as Doro.

Puk and a few of his fellow qarms, who together comprised an entertainment troupe known as The Rusty Halberd (not his idea), had made the journey from Rus Rahl to Seroo's Eye as the latest stop on their tour across Herrilock. They hailed from central Atlua, but thought they might make a pretty penny by voyaging across the Loranos Gulf and making their way from city to city in Herrilock.

Personally, Puk was not a huge fan of Herrilock. The entire country was too arid and hot for the qarmish. He constantly felt dehydrated. But he had been there a few times, mostly staying put in Rus Rahl near the coast, and in fact it had been his idea to tour there in the first place.

Which he had already come to regret.

But it was neither here nor there, and now he had a hefty bag of drugs to occupy himself with, so he was mostly content.

Puk was snuggled up in bed in one of the two rooms his troupe booked at Seroo's Eye's dingiest inn, a room that he was sharing with Vick and Dern, though they were both out seeing the sights. There were plenty of fascinating things to see in the city, but Puk had seen them all already, and so he wanted to be cozy while he ingested his fire-spit. His recreational drug of choice back home was marshweed, but while in Herrilock he had to go for the spit.

Fire-spit was a specialty of Herrilock, gathered from creatures called cordols that buried themselves in the dunes. Naturally, given its name, it was a product of gathering the animals' saliva, which contained chemicals that, when ingested, created a tingly, euphoric sensation that Puk was in dire need of at the present. It hit a little harder and faster than marshweed, but the general effects were the same. It came in both liquid and powder forms (Puk was blissfully ignorant as to how either was produced), though he had an affinity for the powder.

The pouch of fire-spit he purchased from Pillbug was likely cut with something else, just like it always was, but it would still get the job done. He harbored no ill will toward stupid little Pillbug.

Puk carefully poured a thin line of the dull gray powder onto the back of his hand. The line contrasted with his blue skin, which was slick with sweat from the desert heat. His eye-stalks twisted to peer at the doorway, and he listened intently for any sign of his companions' return.

Others in the troupe dabbled in marshweed and fire-spit all the time, naturally, but it was generally frowned upon during a tour. The drugs clouded their senses and logic too much to give their best performances, according to Hin.

But Puk was not one for following that rule.

The coast was seemingly clear, so he brought his hand to his face and inhaled the line of powder. A bit of it still stuck to the wetness of his skin, but it didn't hinder the effects of the rest from kicking in almost immediately.

His body sank back into the pillow, propped up against the marred wall with its peeling paint. Even for a qarm, Puk was pretty stout, and so his whole upper body was enveloped by the warmth and fluffiness of the pillow.

For a minute, his mind was completely blank.

He shut his eyes and welcomed the darkness, matching his mental state, nothing registering at all except the softness of the pillow and a gentle rippling sensation throughout his body.

His eyelids slowly drifted open and he rotated his stalks to face the wooden bedside table. On top of it lay the dirtied pages of the script he was supposed to be memorizing for his skit with Dern later that night, after flubbing it during their show in Rus Rahl.

He had hoped against hope that a bottle of gin had materialized on the table, but alas, he was still lacking any alcohol.

"That sure would hit the spot," he croaked to an empty room.

His lips moved sluggishly and his tongue was heavy, like it threatened to tumble out of his mouth and bounce off his prominent belly onto the thin yellow sheets.

That was a new side effect.

Typically, fire-spit was just like marshweed. It would make him feel slightly tingly, a bit more jovial than normal, more carefree. He'd feel like he was going through a timewarp if he took a sizeable hit of either drug, but given that he would be performing soon, he had made sure to be conservative.

This was not a normal reaction.

"Fudking Pillbug," he slurred, tapping the side of the pouch housing the rest of his supply. "So'd me bu-shit."

He struggled to sit back up. His body was being swallowed by the fabric of the pillow and the tangle of the sheets.

Soon he would be lost to comfort. It was a noble way to die.

While he sat there immobile in his bed, his mind was still a blank canvas, with no intrusion of any thoughts or images. Until finally, he heard himself say in his head, *Script*.

Out loud, he mumbled, "I got to read da script. I got to know da script."

There was no mental filter stopping him from expressing every thought aloud. If he had been more cognizant of his current state, he would have thought himself an imbecile. But the fire-spit was hitting him harder than it ever had before, and the few thoughts he had were scattered.

He muttered another jab at Pillbug, then slapped his hand down on the script and crumpled it in his hand in a sloppy attempt to pick it up. Remnants of the spit powder tumbled off his hand and onto the floor.

"Got to read," he said, un-wrinkling the couple pieces of paper he had nearly ruined.

Puk stared at the first page of the script, which was where his previous mess-ups had occurred. He had not even been able to make it three lines into the skit before derailing the entire thing.

Acting had never been his strong suit, but The Rusty Halberd liked to interject short, comedic performances in between each member's act in order to pad out time and garner more tips from patrons. Jit and Dern loved acting and wrote all of the scripts together, but Puk would have been much happier being left alone to his songs.

"Got to read," he said again. With the effort it took to shove three words out, singing tonight was a dicey prospect. His eyes scanned the page, but every word written on it was incomprehensible to him.

At least the bed was comfortable.

Puk eyed the clock adorning the wall by the doorway, ticking away methodically. Only three hours stood between him and their performance across town. His companions would surely be back soon so they could commence final rehearsals and grab a bite to eat.

"Goddu read," he grumbled. "Fudking Pillbug."

- -

The streets were surprisingly vacant as Kali made her way through Yspleash, following the directions she had written for herself so long ago, the first time she'd dealt with Bryieshk.

The scrap of paper she'd written on was now torn and faded yellow, but it was still getting the job done. While finishing her knaff, she had also scribbled down directions to Delightful Desserts for her next trip.

She turned left onto a street called Greshiiks #2, designated by an old, wooden sign with the name carved into it, likely done with a centript's pincer rather than any tools.

The first time she had visited the city, she had made the mistake of wandering up and down Greshiiks #1 for over half an hour, desperately seeking out Bryieshk's storefront. The man had laughed heartily, a skittering squeak of a sound, when she regaled the story to him. She did not make the same mistake twice, though it was beyond her why such a vast city would have multiple streets with the same names.

Kali came to a halt outside Bryieshk's shop, a humble building located at the end of Greshiiks #2 called Bryieshk's

Bazaar, a name that always amused her. The use of Commonspeak and alliteration was a far cry from the naming conventions of surrounding establishments.

She entered the unassuming building to the sounds of Bryieshk haggling with who she assumed was a customer rather than another merchant like herself. The centript perked up at the sight of her and gave her a wave with one of his many hands.

The two were speaking in Carsuak, the native language of centripts, though nowadays almost every centript grew up learning Commonspeak as well. Carsuak vocabulary was incredibly complicated to pronounce, and nearly impossible for those without centript anatomy. Kali could mostly read it, but actually pronouncing the words was somewhat of a struggle for her. The unfamiliar combinations of consonants and vowels was easy for a centript, but not so for others. Very few people could speak it, and Kali's sister was one of those few. She wasn't fluent by any means, but she could get by in a casual conversation.

While Bryieshk wrapped up his business, Kali perused the shop's wares.

Bryieshk's Bazaar housed an eclectic assortment of items, ranging from clothes to musical instruments to potions to whatever else one could imagine. It was truly a one-stop shop, but given its location, the guy did not receive as much foot traffic as he deserved. With his low prices, though, word seemed to spread around town and he received a steady stream of customers.

Parts of the walls had been molded inward to create natural shelving along the perimeter of the store, and every shelf was packed to the brim. There were additional shelves throughout the floorspace, commissioned when Bryieshk had run out of room and started storing items on the floor, oftentimes being trampled by customers. He had kept this going for a short while, hoping that a "broken items must be paid for" policy would generate solid income, but more often than not it led to irate customers, so he eventually relented.

Kali picked up a dusty harmonica, plated with thin red metal and bearing sixteen holes. The device was caked in a layer of dust, and she had to wonder when the last time a non-centript had browsed the store. There was no possible way for a centript to form the embouchure required for the instrument. She might be the harmonica's only salvation.

Alas, she placed it back down on the shelf next to a ragged notebook (marked "free with any purchase" in Carsuak) as Bry-ieshk's customer scuttled out of the store, grumbling a pleased-sounding noise.

"Kallia! My favorite person!" said Bryieshk as she turned her attention to him. It was impossible to tell if he was smiling, but he sounded happy to see her.

He skittered toward her on his twenty or so tiny, sharp feet, which clacked against the hard floor. Bryieshk's body was long in comparison to other centripts she had met, nearly seven feet, which made him tower above her despite his full height being shortened by the S-shape centripts contorted their bodies into.

His carapace was a muddy brown and his crimson-colored head stood out in sharp contrast to the rest of him. In spite of his larger body, the horns on his head were shorter than most, and one on the left was broken after a particularly bad kerfuffle a few years prior.

Bryieshk snapped his bulky mandibles together, a sign of excitement. He said, "I am glad to see you. Sorry for the wait."

"No trouble," she assured him.

"Great," said Bryieshk, carefully turning around and returning to his counter near the back of the store. "How was your journey across the mighty Gogol this time?"

Kali followed him to the counter and placed her knapsack down on the ground. She leaned her elbows on the countertop and cradled her head in her hands.

"It was fine," she replied. "Just hot. Always so hot."

"Is that so?"

"Yep. Turns out the desert is pretty hot."

"I am surprised it took you this many trips across it to realize."

"I'm a slow learner," she grinned.

"Ahh, you see, I already knew that," Bryieshk said with a laugh. Or the closest approximation to a laugh a centript could make. "I know because you decide to keep doing business with me."

Kali stood up straight. "What can I say?" she asked him. "I like you, for some reason."

"One of the great mysteries of this world," the centript said. "Did you caravan with that band of sightseers?"

Kali shook her head. "What band?"

Bryieshk's long line of arms on either side of his body shifted upward, one after another, resembling a shrug that traveled the length of his upper body. "Just people who are evidently visiting the major cities along Vanap's Peaks. I cannot imagine what sights there are to see, but I am jaded, of course." As far as Kali knew, he had lived in Yspleash all his life.

Kali returned his shrug. "Nawa has that huge oasis, so I'm sure they'll be stopping there. I would think that the Repository would be more of a destination, though. Not the mountainside."

He nodded. "That is certainly a much prettier centript accomplishment than this city. We are in dire need of some reconstruction. Or at least another mural somewhere to brighten up the place."

"Some color would certainly spice things up," Kali chuckled. "But anyway, no, I traveled on my own."

"On the back of a trusty ayote, I presume?"

"Yep, same one as always."

"And how is Bango doing?"

"Very well," she answered. "Toughest guy I know. I was told he had a stomach bug a few weeks ago, but he's in top form now." Bryieshk always asked her about Bango; like other centripts, he had no desire to actually encounter the animal in fear of contracting the mold, but he appreciated them all the same.

"I am glad to hear it," said Bryieshk. "And now, I am going to perfectly segue into our next topic. It will impress you. Here we go: were you able to bring what I requested?"

Kali laughed at him. "I did," she said, reaching for her bag.

She opened up the flap and pulled out the duraga that he asked her to obtain. She held it by the neck and gently laid it out flat on the counter in front of him.

The duraga was a small instrument, only a few feet long, with a slender neck and a base that was crafted from dried pieces of ayote shell. It was outfitted with ten slim strings and there was a rough painting of Seroo on its body, with the creature wrapping itself around the sound hole.

Bryieshk lifted the duraga and Kali saw his six eyes all dart back and forth in varying directions, observing every inch of the instrument.

"Breathtaking," he said.

In truth, it was the cheapest one she could commission, but she was relieved that her buyer was still so impressed with it. He set it back down with tenderness and addressed her. "Is the price we previously agreed upon still suitable?"

She nodded. The duraga had cost her thirty crescents back in Seroo's Eye, where ayote shells were plentiful, and Bryieshk had offered one-hundred and twenty if she could deliver one to him.

Bryieshk tittered giddily as he gathered the money. Kali had no idea if centripts could even play a duraga, but perhaps the mere novelty of owning one would be sufficient to land a sale.

"I take it that is not all you brought for me?" Bryieshk asked.

It wasn't. She had not made the three-day journey for only ninety crescents in profit.

"I have more ranneth," she said. The potion was always a guaranteed seller, so she always scouted savannahs for quillis, which her apothecary friend back home had to then distill into a potion that fought the mold. Quillis was used by mercenaries as a poison, but it could be manipulated by skilled white mages into abating the centript disease.

"Local or exotic?" Bryieshk asked.

The question puzzled her. "What do you mean by 'exotic'?"

Bryieshk placed the agreed-upon crescents on the counter-top beside the duraga. Kali scooped them into her pack, clanking against the glass bottles of ranneth as they rained down.

"A white mage in Atlua came up with a new type of ranneth," he explained. "They use some sort of herb that grows in the forests there. It is much stronger than what we have here. It can even *reverse* some of the effects, not just prevent them from spreading. Or so I hear."

Kali was baffled. She had never heard of a potion that could reverse the effects of molding.

The mold was a disease only found in centripts, and its effects were horrific. If a centript was afflicted, their body deteriorated segment by segment. The skin underneath their shell would begin to rot, leading to the carapace cracking and falling off. It was possible for a centript to survive with some of their shell missing, but it could become an issue depending on which segments were exposed, making it difficult to walk or use their arms. The centript then died once the disease reached their head, though it was impossible to know when that would happen—it could be the third segment affected or the twentieth.

If Bryieshk was to be believed, this new version of ranneth could be used to undo the putrefying effects of molding. There couldn't possibly be a way for the centript's shell segment to grow back, but from the sound of it, this new potion could stop the part from rotting and help return it to normal. The ranneth potion distilled from quillis could only delay the mold from spreading to any other segment after it finished with one where it had already been introduced, but in time it would eventually spread.

A new potion would change everything for centripts.

"Judging by your silence and also your lack of knowledge about the exotic ranneth, I take it yours is just local," said Bryieshk.

Kali nodded dumbly. She asked him, "Has someone been bringing in exotic ranneth?"

"I have only seen it sold in one store here," said Bryieshk, "but I have heard talk of it being more common on the coast, where traders come in from Atlua. A majority of their supply is bought up before they can ever make it inland, but Vonoshreb managed to snag a few bottles during his vacation to Restick, the bastard. He got a ton of bottles and is making a fortune."

She couldn't resist asking, "How much does a bottle go for?"

"Forty crescents."

The words struck her across the face. Her mouth hung agape, and Bryieshk uttered a laugh.

Forty? Forty fucking crescents?

The average bottle of "local" ranneth could net her ten crescents, maybe fifteen at the absolute most, which still wasn't a great profit after having to pay her associate to distill it.

"Well…" she muttered, "…I just have local. Sorry."

Bryieshk considered this, then said, "I could pay you five per bottle."

"*Five?* The usual is ten per bottle," she objected.

"There is a new 'usual' now," he said with a shrug. "Nobody wants the local stuff anymore. Not when something considerably better is on shelves somewhere. I have only had two people buy any ranneth from me since Vonoshreb started selling his. The bastard."

"But—"

"I am sorry, Kallia, but it is just not worth the cost right now. I am not selling any. I could do five and take a couple bottles off of your hands, but no more than that."

Kali sighed. There was obviously no further negotiating with him. "Okay," she said. "I can sell you three."

"Two would suffice."

So she grabbed two bottles, leaving the other eight in her bag, and placed them next to the duraga.

- -

A substantial crowd had gathered for the troupe's performance.

Hin, their leader, booked the gig at a run-down theater near the edge of the city (the only venue that would have them), and much to everyone's surprise, it had sold out.

The assumption among the group was that the city's residents were not necessarily starved for entertainment, but had not seen a qarmish troupe perform before. They were a novelty.

Up next was Puk and Dern's skit, which Puk had gained no traction in memorizing due to how high he was. A high which he had not yet come down from, though the slurring had lessened.

Puk managed to throw himself out of bed and stumble through the city to the theater, which he personally felt was a magnificent feat that earned him the right to abstain from performing for the rest of the night.

He stood backstage, swaying mindlessly, the weight of his body seeming to fluctuate. He could still barely process a coherent thought beyond "be on the stage." The amplified effects of the fire-spit would have been cause for concern if he were able to form a concerned thought.

Jit was finishing her act, and Puk's eyestalks twisted together as they rocked back and forth, the room spinning all around him.

"You alright?"

Dern's voice knocked him out of his daze. His friend clapped him reassuringly on the shoulder.

"Mmfine," Puk mumbled.

"You seem a bit out of sorts," said Dern. He was taller than Puk, but only by an inch and a half. The absurd length of his eyestalks gave him an extra half-inch on top of that.

Puk shook his head, untangling his stalks. The sight was not a very convincing retort.

"You gonna be able to perform?" Dern asked.

"Yes."

"You sure about that?"

"Yes."

"You can sit this one out if you need to. Hin will prob'ly be pissed, but if you're feelin' sick, she'd understand."

"Mmfine," he grumbled again.

He did not know why he was being so adamant. He had an out, but was too braindead to take it.

"Okay," Dern said, uncertainty in his voice. He crossed his arms and stood next to Puk. The two watched Jit juggle three balls that had been set on fire, much to the crowd's delight.

After another minute or two, Jit gave Puk a pat as she exited the stage and said, "You're up!"

Puk thought a nasty thought then put one foot in front of the other and slowly ambled out onto the stage.

He stood underneath a blaring lamp shining down from the rafters and his skin felt like it was going to leap off his body and crawl away. He could not see the audience seated before him, which congealed into a huge, dark mass, and for that he was thankful.

Dern dove right into the skit he'd written, crossing his arms and tapping his foot in irritation. His character was meant to be waiting on Puk's, who was late for their meeting.

"I'm late," Puk blurted out, without even taking a step toward his scene partner or turning to face him. He stared out at the blank audience, who laughed at his awkward, unconvincing delivery.

Dern cocked an eyebrow, already disoriented by Puk veering off-script. "...you're late," he said anyway, trying to steer things back in the right direction.

"I'm late," Puk said again, louder this time. He then turned to Dern and yelled, *"I'm late!"* This garnered a boom of laughter from the crowd.

But Dern was less amused. He had never been one for improvisation. He was too proud of the words he wrote to merely throw them out the window in lieu of improvisation.

So he stuck to the script.

"I've been waiting over an *hour* for you!" Dern said angrily. "What do you have to say for yourself?"

Puk glared at him. Silence hung between the two for excruciatingly long seconds.

Script, was all he could think. No actual words came to mind.

"Well?" Dern urged him.

And so Puk said, "...I'm late!"

The rest of the performance lasted another five minutes and went similarly well. The audience grew more and more wearied by Puk's lack of improvisational prowess, and Dern became much angrier as the skit dragged on. He had to go against his own personal values and improvise as well, conjuring up a half-way-believable reason for the scene to end. He was steaming as he stomped off the stage, leaving Puk alone to perform his solo act.

Somehow, he had to sing.

Script, he thought.

He couldn't see their eyes, but Puk knew there were a hundred pairs fixed on him at that moment. All watching and waiting for him to do something. To entertain them. Show them a good time.

The first song he was planning to sing was one he'd learned years ago in a tavern in Din's Keep. A rocyan whose name he'd forgotten over the years taught it to him as they sung over countless rounds at the bar. It was a tune called "Sweet Sheri," detailing a summertime tryst in the woods. A light, breezy song that always won people over with its catchy melody.

Suddenly, he could hear the song perfectly in his head—

I saw her underneath the sway
Of branches twisted a hundred ways
She smiled and the leaves, they fell
And I saw her close her eyes, I pray
Sweet, sweet Sheri, sweet, sweet Sheri,
It's hard to believe, what I can see
The shade of the tree
Left me in peace, somehow

He was filled with newfound confidence. The song was within him. An adoring crowd awaited.

Puk opened his mouth and vomit spewed out onto the wooden stage.

The audience screamed.

He was altogether extremely aware of where he was and what he was doing, and he prayed none of his puke had splashed out onto the people in the front row.

From backstage, Hin began to shout. Dern and Vick rushed onstage and ushered Puk away, bile still dribbling down his chin.

That did not go well, he thought, though he was impressed by the complete sentence.

Two hours later, Puk had finally sobered up and Hin had been railing into him for ten solid minutes.

She paced back and forth in his room while he sat on his bed being scolded like a child.

"It's gotten to the point of ludicrousy," she huffed, unable to tear her eyes from the ground. She couldn't even look at him.

"Is 'ludicrousy' a word?" he asked her, genuinely unsure.

"I don't know or give a fuck," Hin barked. She turned one eyestalk toward him while the other remained focused on the ground. Hin's vocabulary was usually fairly tame, so when she started swearing, things were serious. "You've gotten out of control, Puk. This shit has happened way too many times."

"I've never puked on stage before!" he cried.

Hin halted and faced him. "Yes you have!" she said. "You did three months ago, in Marshwind!"

"Oh," he muttered. "Well, I didn't know that time counted. It was barely more than spittle."

"*Any* amount of vomit is too much vomit!" Hin looked as if a vein was going to burst in her head.

Puk shrugged. "I don't see what the big deal is. You guys get drunk and high all the time too."

"No we don't."

"What are you talking about? I met you all in a bar!"

"Yeah, where *we were performing* and *you were getting drunk.*"

"Well, my point stands."

"The *point* is that we don't indulge when we're about to perform. We have our fun on off days. When we need to perform and be in peak shape, we have fucking self-control and do our jobs so that we can make money and earn a living. Don't you give a shit about that?"

The answer was that of course he did, but Puk was too proud to admit he was in the wrong. He remained silent while Hin stared at him expectantly.

Finally, Hin asked him, "What were you even on?"

"Fire-spit," he answered meekly.

"Did you do your usual dosage?"

He nodded.

"You're massively dehydrated. We all are. Qarms weren't built to live in the desert. That's why your regular amount fucked you up so much. How could you not realize that would happen? Aren't you a *pro* by now?"

It was a reasonable question. One that he did not have a reasonable answer for. He offered her a shrug.

So it was my own fault, then. Sorry for disparaging your good name, Pillbug, he mentally apologized.

Hin looked him up and down then heaved a sigh. "You know what I gotta do, Puk."

His eyestalks scrunched up. "You don't," he said. His pride was slipping away by the second.

"I do."

"C'mon, Hin."

"Don't grovel. You fucked up. You fucked up one too many times and now something actually has to be done. I wish I didn't have to, but you don't leave me much choice. You're bringing down the whole troupe."

"What are you talking about?" he asked. "The rest of the troupe did fine. The crowd loved the song you and Dern closed with."

Hin chortled. "Like you'd know. You were conked out on the floor behind the curtain. I'm surprised you even know we closed with a song."

"Well, I mean, you close with a song every night."

"The tips were at an all-time low. And of course a quarter of the audience left after your little incident. The ones who stuck around loved our song, sure, but—"

"I'm sorry," Puk interrupted, hopping up off the bed. "Really, I am. I dunno what I gotta do to make it up to you guys, but I'll do it. Name it, and I'll do it."

He looked into her eyes, pleading with his own, hoping she could see the sincerity in them.

But it didn't matter whether she did or not.

"You've gotta leave the troupe."

The words sank into him like his body was made of sand. He never imagined he would spend his entire life performing in The Rusty Halberd, but he didn't want to go out like this. Not in some shitty inn in the middle of a desert.

"C'mon, Hin."

"*You* come on, Puk!"

"I'm an invaluable member of this team!" he said, finding some fight within himself. If he was going to leave the troupe, he wanted it to be on his terms and at the time of his choosing. Not now.

Hin irritably rubbed the area between the base of her stalks. "You're not really, though. You never learn your lines, you sing the same three songs over and over again—"

"It's always a different audience! How would they know? Who gives a shit!"

"—and you're always either drunk or high! We can't ever predict how you're gonna behave from one day to the next! Who wants to watch a qarmish troupe throw up on stage every night? What venue would want to book that? We'd never go on tour again."

"This whole tour is because of me," said Puk. "I'm the one who had the bright idea to do our show in Herrilock. I'm invaluable, like I said."

Hin shook her head again. "You're not," she told him. "You're expendable, and it's about time we shed your dead weight."

The room was quiet. They could hear children laughing on the streets outside, the shutting of doors, people conversing. The two stared at each other, wishing the words could be taken back.

"Okay," Puk said. He couldn't think of any other reply.

It had been a long time coming. He knew that.

Even if he hadn't, Hin had just made it abundantly clear. He had been coasting for far too long, living an unsustainable lifestyle, and it had finally caught up to him.

His biggest problem now was that he had nowhere to sleep and probably not enough money to afford a room anywhere. And if he couldn't afford a room, he definitely couldn't afford to book passage back to Atlua. Back to his home in Trillowan.

He turned and gathered his belongings, stuffing them into the burlap sack by his bed. The last thing he tossed inside was the little pouch of remaining fire-spit.

He slipped his shoulders through the bag's straps and made his way to the door. He reached out and turned to Hin with his hand on the knob.

"See you around," he said. He swung the door open and stepped through.

"I'm sorry," Hin said again from the other side.

Puk nodded and shut the door behind him.

- -

Her usual inn was a few blocks over from Bryieshk's Bazaar, on a street called Niesolkm #3, a name which Kali had no idea how to pronounce.

The innkeeper was working the front desk when Kali arrived to check in. The nightly rate stung after her exchange with Bryieshk, but there was nothing to be done. It was already the cheapest lodging she knew of in the city. She reluctantly paid the woman and marched upstairs to her room.

The room was slightly cramped, but cozy all the same. There was a window on the wall, a charmingly misshapen oval, which peered out over Niesolkm #3.

Kali set her belongings down and then spent a few minutes gazing out the window, watching people wander in and out of buildings. It was a much busier street than the one that housed her friend's shop.

She had managed to convince Bryieshk to buy a few more goods—some spices, leather pouches, a cheap watch she had found left behind in a savannah—but the profits did not amount to much. Not what she had been expecting, in any case. None of the items fetched a high price.

Her mind unavoidably drifted to the exotic ranneth from Atlua.

Ever since she was a young girl, Kali had wanted to become a traveling merchant. The prospect of traveling the world, seeing its beautiful and fascinating sights, made her heart race.

She refrained from mentioning it to Bryieshk, but a piece of her envied the band of sightseers passing through Yspleash. Personally, she had only seen a fraction of Vanap's Peaks, and she longed to experience the famous oasis in Nawa. Not to mention the sparkling beaches on the other side of the range, on the coastline.

Forty crescents, she thought again. *Forty per bottle.*

The mage she knew in Seroo's Eye had walked her through the process of distilling quillis into a ranneth potion once or twice before, and it was not especially complex or time-consuming. She had to assume the process was similar, if not identical, with whatever herb was being used in Atlua. Meaning the base cost had to be the same too. The profit margin for a bottle of exotic ranneth was huge.

If only she could afford to sail to Atlua and acquire some.

There was no telling what other goods she could obtain while overseas then bring back to sell in Yspleash, in Seroo's Eye, maybe even in Restick. Glamorous clothes, bizarre contraptions, exotic foods. The list was endless.

Not to mention the items she could grab in Herrilock for cheap and sell in Atlua. Goods that Atluans had no other way of obtaining.

She knew ayotes were only found in desert regions, and Atlua contained no desert at all. She could name a high price for duragas over there. Way more than the hundred-and-twenty she'd gotten from Bryieshk, which was already pretty good, in her book.

Kali tore her gaze from the window and threw herself face-down onto the bed, slamming her nose into the hard mattress. She let out a pained exhalation and continued to fantasize about traveling the world.

She turned herself over and stared at the ceiling, thinking about ranneth potions and duragas.

I need to get to Atlua, she thought.

But she had no idea how.

CHAPTER II

BUY-IN

At home, Kali could sleep until midday without issue. She could wrap herself up in her blanket, sink into her pillow, and be swallowed up in the darkness of her bedroom for hours on end.

While in other cities, though, something itched at her in the mornings and she always awoke early. It was annoying, but she also thought it might be a good quality in a traveling merchant: always getting an early start to make the most of the day.

When she went downstairs the next morning, a centript clerk had replaced the innkeeper at the front desk. He greeted Kali with a polite click of his mandibles. His golden yellow carapace was shiny, as if recently cleaned.

As she approached the counter, he asked, "What can I do for you?"

"Just checking out," she said through her mask. She knew of one or two more places to make some easy sales in the city, but beyond that it didn't make any sense to stay another night. The cost outweighed the benefit. Hardly anyone wanted what she had to offer, apparently.

The clerk gave a displeased click. "We're sad to see you go so soon," he said. He shuffled a few papers around, filing the appropriate paperwork for a check-out, and told her, "All done."

She thanked him and headed out the door, knapsack banging against her back with each step.

The city was aflutter with activity.

Across the street from the inn was a café that Kali had tried once and regretted, but today there was a line almost out the door.

The shop served traditional centript dishes, and their flavor palate was vastly different from her own. They typically blended the usual spices with other substances like rocks and cactus needles that had been ground into fine powders. Centripts caked all of their meats in the concoction (anything from vissian meat to cubed bulloko steaks) and cooked them wrapped in dough to create hearty palm-sized pastries.

Kali had sampled both a vissian pastry as well as a vegetarian option, and she found the flavors ranging from bland to outright bad. Savory foods were not what faifs typically ate, but even so, she found the taste to be quite appalling. Regardless, she was pleased to see how well the café was doing for itself; she remembered the owner to be an exceptionally friendly woman.

Down the street, two human boys (brothers, from the looks of them) were playing a card game with a centript kid who seemed confounded by the rules, much to the amusement of the boys. One of them laid down a card from his hand and the centript loosed a curse word in Carsuak.

Kali passed the children and headed in the direction of her other regular customer, a centript man who operated a shop in a more centralized area of Yspleash than Bryieshk's Bazaar. He sold sweets that appealed to everyone in the city, especially the non-centript population, so Kali's imports from central Herrilock were always a big hit there.

As she walked through the winding streets past the plastered buildings, however, she began to doubt herself. Perhaps the sweet shop's needs had already been met by traders from Atlua.

Dust whipped through the air, stinging her eyes. She shielded her face and ducked into an alleyway to wait out the small sandstorm that was kicking up in the middle of the street.

She leaned against the building and ran her fingertips along the tan, uneven plaster. With her eyes shut, she could almost pretend she was home. Almost.

The wind settled, and she continued along the route to the main shopping plaza. Navigating the winding, narrow maze of the city streets was tricky if the destination was a specific building tucked away somewhere, but it was fairly easy to make one's way into the center of Yspleash.

Vendors had set up small wooden booths with leather tarps to shield from the sun. The plaza was a large square with restaurants and stores all around its perimeter, with the booths set up in the middle of the square twice a month. They sold dried meats, handmade jewelry, leather boots, toys for children, and much more.

When Kali and her sister were six years old, their parents had taken them on a trip to Yspleash. Their father knew a man in the city with whom he wanted to go into business, and so he was making the journey to pitch a proposal to him. It didn't end up panning out; a couple years later, their parents had saved up the necessary funds and started the business together themselves.

But the girls had just begun their months-long spring break from school, and they were eager to travel with their father, so the business trip turned into a makeshift family vacation. The marketplace had been bustling when the family arrived. They were shuffling through the plaza, searching for the inn where their father's friend worked, and the wooden booths with their brightly-colored, hand-drawn signs instantly enraptured Kali.

She had stopped in the middle of the plaza, staring wide-eyed at the multitude of people and goods that were shifting around the square like one huge living organism. She grinned seeing the joy on another kid's face as their mother handed them a cordol hand puppet, then laughed at an irate man who was not getting the price he wanted to pay for a paring knife.

Kali's family had trudged forward without her, not noticing her absence with so many other bodies around. When her father had finally looked back and realized she was missing, he raced through the masses, yelling out her name.

He found her standing in the same spot, watching with fascination as faifs, humans, centripts, and the jeornish all milled around the plaza and went about their day. Seroo's Eye had a large population, but she had never seen somewhere teeming with so much *life*.

"Come, Kallia, we need to go," her father had said, grasping her tiny, pastel purple hand.

"Can we come back after?" she asked him.

She gazed up longingly at his face. He had recently shaved his head, leaving behind so little of his blinding white hair that it simply faded into his olive skin. It made him look more severe, but his rigid face wilted into a sweet smile.

"Of course," he had told her. "We can check out every booth."

"Promise?"

"Promise."

She smiled.

Kali was now less captivated by the marketplace, though she did have a soft spot for it in her heart. She had briefly considered propping up her own booth once, but the prospect of having to transport a booth there, find storage for it somewhere in Yspleash, or move to the city herself all seemed too overwhelming to deal with.

She was about to make her way around the throng of people to reach the sweets shop when she noticed Bryieshk browsing an assortment of jellies.

The sight of him inevitably made her think of their discussion the day before, and the bitterness returned to her. She imagined trying to sell her mother's candies, only to be told "Sorry, we got something better and more expensive in from Atlua this morning! Maybe next time!"

Bryieshk held a can of spiced cactus jelly in his hands, chattering with the purveyor to get the best price possible for it. Once they reached an agreement and he scuttled off, Kali approached him.

"Hello, Kallia!" he said with a pleasant chitter. "Checking out the market today?"

"Not exactly," she replied.

"Shame. I have had this jelly before. You should try it out. She is a master," he said, nodding back toward the faif woman he'd been haggling with. "I find myself enjoying spicier foods lately. I like the burning sensation. Do you enjoy spice?"

"Not really," she said, trying to be polite but push past his questions. "Listen, would you be able to tell me where I can find—" she searched her brain for the man's name "—Vonsheb's shop?"

"You mean Vonoshreb? The bastard. What do you want with him?" Bryieshk asked, obviously still frustrated by the increased business his competitor was receiving.

Kali didn't want to lose the centript's trust and ruin their business relationship. "Nothing, really," she told him. "I just want to ask him some things about Restick, that's all."

"Planning a trip, are you?"

"I wish," she sighed. "I doubt I could afford it, but I wanted to see what he could tell me anyway, just in case."

Bryieshk nodded, though he still sounded annoyed. "I understand. Well…"

He explained how to reach Vonoshreb's shop, called Vonoshrebka Crestihth ("Vonoshreb's Market" in Carsuak), and Kali was off.

As she marched out of the plaza down one of the many streets in the Yspleash hive, Bryieshk called out behind her, "You really should try the cactus jelly! It is sublime!"

\- -

Mornings were none too harsh in Seroo's Eye, which was a blessing because Puk was nursing an incredible hangover and he wagered harsh sunlight might genuinely kill him.

Being qarmish, Puk had been raised following the Waranex Church by his parents. In his later years, he had intermittently maintained his religious duties, though he didn't mind letting them slide when he was busy or simply uninterested.

He was often uninterested.

His mild religious ties had come in handy the night before, though, as he had been allowed to seek shelter within the church located on the western end of the city. It was a wonder a Waranex Church had even been founded there, given the tiny qarmish population in the country, but one of their goals was to expand as far and wide as possible, so they had dipped their hands into most pockets of the world.

The priest had been understandably hesitant yet concerned when Puk had stumbled into the small, elegant building. It was built from the same material as practically every other building in the country, but the priests had coated the plaster with azure paint to put it in line with the color scheme and style of the church. An extravagant chandelier hung from the ceiling, and Puk had to imagine the beauty was what a majority of the funds had gone toward during construction. There were two sets of three rows of pews, divided by a walkway, all constructed of mirwood dyed red.

Puk had slumped into the backmost pew, resting his head on the warm wood, and was soon approached by the priest, a man called Anure Rahk. The Anure was wearing a robe that matched the walls, with red trimming at the edges of its sleeves.

Anure Rahk was patient with him while he rambled on about nothing of value, draped over the pew like a discarded cloak. Eventually the holy man led him to a vacant back room that housed a messy desk and a small, uncomfortable cot. Puk was told he could sleep there for as long as he needed.

When he awoke, the church was empty.

He recited a short prayer after waking, then stepped outside into the muted sunlight and gazed upward at the translucent white ceiling shielding the entire city.

Seroo's Eye was built in the skull of a gigantic, staggering beast called an aeon. The aeons were massive creatures that roamed the world centuries ago, but had long since gone extinct—as far as anyone knew, anyway. If there were any aeons left alive, they were somehow keeping to themselves.

Seroo was the name given to one such creature. It had been a lizard stretching hundreds of feet long and had collapsed at some point and died. Its skeleton was the only tangible proof that aeons ever existed at all beyond the pages of storybooks.

The skull lay on its side, half-submerged in the sands of the Gogol Desert, towering over three hundred feet in the air. One eyehole looked down upon the city, granting it its name, and acted as the sole source of direct sunlight; the rest of the light was filtered through bone. An ornate reflecting pool dubbed the Gaze had been installed in the center of the city where the sunbeam shone down, warming the still waters.

Puk ambled down the walkway from the church leading toward the city's main thoroughfare, which contained the Gaze at its heart. He shuffled toward a bench by the pool, his squat legs carrying him slowly with tired, deliberate steps.

Many people already surrounded the pool's edge. It was a common destination for tourists, as well as a location of meditation, prayer, and relaxation for residents. Seeing the Gaze had been one of his primary goals the first time he ever visited Herrilock. The entire city was a sight to behold, enclosed in the maw of such an awe-inspiring beast.

With great effort, he found an empty bench and hoisted himself up onto it. He drummed his fingers against the stone, staring down at the sand underneath his dangling feet. The Gaze was at his back, and he listened to families exclaiming how beautiful it was and explaining the history of Seroo's Eye to their uninterested children.

A half-heard lecture brought one of his fathers to mind. Of Puk's four fathers, Grut had been considered the intellectual. There was many a time when he had gone on long tangents about this subject and that, boring Puk and his siblings with details of qarmish cultural history, Waranexian beliefs, animal factoids, and much more. Their mother, Mip, had always favored Grut above the other three men that helped her bear children. Those children, however, thought him to be enormously dull. But still, he had turned out to be a better and more-present father than Doro, who likely would have skipped town after the birth of the litter if he'd had any money to his name.

Puk was shook from his reminiscence about his fathers by a splash and booming guffaw behind him. He twisted one stalk around to see that a teenager had pushed his friend into the Gaze, much to the chagrin of everyone else, who shot the boys dirty looks.

Doro would've thought that was funny too, Puk thought, turning his eyestalk back around.

He tried not to think of his fathers, who would have had opposing views on his current state.

Doro would've barely given it a second thought, saying with a shrug that shit happens and he should go where the wind blew him, followed by asking if he had any fire-spit left to share.

Grut, however, would have been immensely disappointed. He had spent a lot of time and money getting Puk lessons with a vocal coach, honing his craft. Grut himself was an alchemist back in Trillowan, and surely would have been thrilled for his son to follow in his footsteps, but he was equally happy to support Puk's dreams of being a musician.

And look where I am now, he thought pitifully, once again staring down at his stumpy feet. His sandals hung loose from his toes, and he slapped them against the bottom of his blue soles.

"Hello," came a familiar voice, cutting through the angry murmurs from the crowd, still irritated by the boys' rowdiness.

Puk looked up and saw Anure Rahk trudging toward him, his bare feet sinking into the cooled sand with each unhurried step.

"Morning, Anure," Puk said with a tilt of the head. He scooted over a tad to give the elderly priest room to sit.

Rahk smiled at him but said nothing. He reached the bench and, after one failed attempt, pulled himself up onto the stone with a heavy sigh. After settling in and adjusting his robes, he turned his eyestalks toward Puk while his body remained facing forward.

"How are you feeling today?"

"Been better," said Puk.

Rahk chuckled. "You seemed very unsettled last night. I imagine you're still feeling the after-effects."

"You imagine right."

The priest nodded and turned his stalks to look ahead, out toward the mouth of the skull, which served as one of two primary entrances to the city. The Mandible Gate was relatively calm at the moment, not receiving many new arrivals or departures. Though Puk knew that in an hour or two, The Rusty Halberd would be loaded up on a wagon riding out through the gate toward their next destination.

"Do you wish to talk about anything?" the priest asked, as if he had probed into his mind's eye and seen the wagon rolling out of town. Out of Puk's life.

Puk shook his head. "Not particularly." His voice was a low croak. His head pounded.

Disappointment tinged Rahk's words. "Are you sure?" Then, after a moment, "Are you of the Waranexian faith?"

Puk instinctively rolled his eyes and then hoped the Anure hadn't caught it. "Sort of," he answered truthfully. "My parents raised me practicing in the church. It's been a while, though."

This seemed to please the priest. He asked, "When was the last time you entered a Spiral?"

It was customary for traveling qarmish to stop at every Spiral they came across, but it took Puk a moment to think back to the last time he'd stopped by one of the numerous Waranex altars scattered across the world. Spirals were plentiful along the roads of Atlua and Gillus, but seemingly less so in Herrilock. The last time he'd used one, he had prayed for a thick hock of meat and a cheap bar in the next town rather than for safe travels or his parents' health.

"Must've been two or three months," he said with some shame.

That estimate was probably generous. They hadn't seen one at all since entering Herrilock, and even while in Atlua, he had not been seeking them out as of late.

Rahk tut-tutted and swung his legs back and forth. Neither of the qarms could quite reach the ground from where they sat on the warm bench.

"It may bolster your spirits," said Rahk. "I do not know what troubles you, but I find that entering the Spiral can be a soothing experience. There is even a cooling effect to the rock

we use to construct them here, which is always a welcome reprieve from this heat." He smiled again.

"You have Spirals here?"

"Of course," Rahk grinned. "The nearest is along the
Ribroad, but there are others as well. We have two along
Vanap's Peaks, a few in the Cascades, and a large amount all
throughout the Gogol."

Puk huffed, impressed that he had not spotted any at all,
even in his previous visits to the country. "I'll have to stop by,"
he said, unsure if he was being honest.

"You should," Rahk agreed. "As I said, I do not know your
troubles—in fact, I do not even know your name—but let me
say this: do not give up on yourself. Do not be lost to your vices
or self-doubt. I will not quote verses at you, because I'm sure
that is the last thing you want to hear right now, least of all
because of your headache." He chortled. "But if you ever need
my assistance again, feel free to return. Just remember that we
are all worthwhile."

And with that, the ancient qarm hopped up off the bench,
pausing a moment to ease the tension in his joints, then sauntered off in the direction of his church.

Puk let out a light laugh at the corniness of the priest's part-
ing words, but he found himself thinking about a Spiral. The
cooling rock sounded intriguing to him.

If nothing else, it would feel good on his dry skin.

- -

The eastern side of Yspleash was the wealthier area of the city.
All of the families who had made their fortunes mining in the

mountains back when the city was first settled were there, as well as the best school, restaurateurs, and merchants.

It was no surprise to Kali that the east side was where Vonoshreb's shop was located. Evidently the man had a penchant for traveling to seek out the most exotic wares that he could then sell for high prices to the city's wealthiest denizens, fueling the cycle of wealth among the neighborhood.

No wonder Bryieshk felt so bitter.

She sidled up to the impressive clay building sporting a sign that read VONOSHREBKA CRESTIHTH and stepped out of the way for people exiting.

Unlike the rest of Yspleash's messy, fluid architecture, everything in the east side was meticulously crafted, even more so than other cities in the country. Centripts were the best builders anywhere, able to mold the adobe with precision, so those with money to spend took great care to hire the best sculptors they could find.

Breaking from the typical hive design of the other neighborhoods, the area in which Kali now found herself housed towering rectangular buildings with unique web-like designs carved into the clay. Each building also had a distinct trim, with flourishes that varied from monochrome flower petals to geometric patterns. Kali knew from when her father was starting his business that sculpting the clay and keeping it in place while it completely dried could be a frustrating endeavor, so the detailed designs were remarkable.

A bell dinged above her head as she stepped through the doorway into the centript's shop. Several individuals were browsing the store, unlike the barren wasteland that had been Bryieshk's shop the previous day.

Another difference between the shops was the organization. The Bazaar was crammed with shoddy shelves lined messily with any object that could fit, while Vonoshreb's market was neatly organized with items in clearly designated sections of the store. There was a section for jewelry, one for weaponry, one for books—the way the shop was laid out was the clearest indicator yet that Vonoshreb was operating on a higher tier.

In the shop was a centript woman examining jewels. Centript jewelry was fairly different from what more humanoid individuals wore. While faifs, jeornish, and others wore earrings or pendants strung up on glittering chains, centripts instead bought gems and placed them into silver or gold inlays, which were then drilled into their carapace. Kali smiled at her as she slipped by toward the back of the building, where she anticipated finding Vonoshreb.

Near the back wall was a counter topped with tens of glass bottles, all differently shaped and sized. Most contained liquids of varying colors—pink, green, one an unappetizing muddy brown—but there were a few repeats, which were encased in similar bottles. The most common of these potions was a dark purple substance in a tall, cylindrical bottle with little glass wings jutting out on either side. An unnecessary feature, but it did look nice and set it apart from the other bottles.

Three centripts were gathered around the collection of winged bottles, vying for them. Two of the centripts, both with shiny, blue carapaces, appeared to be quite healthy. The third, however, possessed a red shell that seemed to be dulling on the segments that still had a shell at all. Several segments of his body were bare, exposing puffy, discolored gray skin underneath. The mold.

A centript man she assumed to be Vonoshreb stood on the other side of the counter, tapping numerous fingertips on the wooden top. It sent a vibration running through the table that lightly shook the glass bottles.

Vonoshreb was a tall, imposing centript with a golden carapace. His crimson head shot back and forth between his three customers, his eyes squinted with glee at the sales he was about to make.

He spoke to the three in rushed Carsuak. *"Kuweat zutih tunyut vurur,"* he chittered, tapping his many fingers impatiently.

Kali would never be as skilled as her sister, but she managed to make out the number "six" in what he said. So the bottles on the counter were all that was left of his stock, if he was telling the truth and not simply trying to encourage a sale. An artificial shortage.

"Quweat tunyut cri!" the sick centript shouted. *"Quvruk ceu pioruhts tunyut lae. Kuyui ghi tunyut vurur. Kujku blonsk!"*

Once again, all Kali could understand was the number he had said, which was "one." The man was clearly upset about something, though she had no idea what. He pounded a few fists on the table in agitation.

Vonoshreb muttered something too rapidly for her to make out a single word, while pointing toward the front of the store. The two healthy centript women exchanged uncomfortable glances. They wanted the interaction to end.

I really need to ask Lissia for some Carsuak lessons, Kali thought to herself as she watched the conversation unfold. She needed to brush up on more than just one-digit numbers and random phrases.

The sickly man slammed a fist on the table again and Vonoshreb said, *"Quyui xhara."* He glared at the man across from him, his tone low and grave.

"Fuck you," the sick centript spat before pushing past Kali toward the exit. She instinctively flinched and scooted away as he passed, though in her mind she knew that the mold was not contagious to centripts, and she couldn't even catch it at all. She hoped he hadn't noticed.

"Kujku hihtsh," Vonoshreb apologized to his remaining customers. Kali could at least recognize that phrase: "I'm sorry."

The two women finalized their purchase of all six winged bottles and shuffled out of the store a few minutes later, chirping excitedly.

With them gone, Vonoshreb turned his attention to Kali. "Hello," he said, tilting his head downward in greeting. "I apologize for that scene. What can I help you find?"

Kali started, "I'm actually not looking for anything. I was wondering—"

"Well, if you're not looking for anything, I see no reason for you to be here," Vonoshreb interrupted her. With a crooked, condescending grin, he said, "That doesn't make a whole lot of sense. Right?"

She blinked, staring at the centript, who stared right back. Her mouth hung open mid-sentence, processing, seeking a response.

Finally, she said, "Right." She swallowed down her frustration, but pressed on. "Okay, well, I was looking for that medicine you just sold. I presume it was the mold cure I've been hearing about?"

This pleased Vonoshreb. He emitted a delighted click. "I see word of my goods is spreading across the city. Even into the more *unsavory* areas, as you unfortunately witnessed." He was referring to the sick centript who had been attempting to buy the cure. "I must be honest, though, and tell you that I'm out of stock. That was the last of my supply that just walked out the door."

Kali feigned surprise. "Well, shoot," she said. "Do you know when you'll be getting more?"

"What does a pretty faif girl like yourself need a mold potion for?" Vonoshreb asked.

"I have a friend back home who needs it. We have ranneth, of course, but when I heard about this more powerful brew, I thought I might try to bring some back for him," she lied.

Not that it's any of your business, really, she added in her mind.

Vonoshreb nodded. "I don't know for certain when I will obtain more. Whenever I visit Restick again, I'll be returning with a bundle and a half, I can assure you," he said.

"Restick?" she said, pretending this was new information. "Can I ask who you bought it from in Restick?"

The seedy centript chuckled. "If I told you that, then you would just buy it from them and not from me!" he said. "And it appears that you'll already not be buying anything from me."

Kali heaved a sigh. Like a true businessman, Vonoshreb's sole priority was his earnings. That was no doubt how he ended up with the largest shop in the wealthiest part of town.

She said, "I suppose that's true. My friend is desperate, though. I really need to get my hands on some."

Vonoshreb shrugged. "I'm sorry I can't be of more help," he said. "I encourage you to check back soon to see if we have anything that catches your eye."

Kali had to stop herself from audibly groaning.

She spun on her heels and scoured the shelf immediately behind her for the cheapest object it held, which turned out to be an old, pathetic dagger with a price of five crescents.

Good enough.

She snatched it by the hilt, surprised by the blade's heft. It did not feel as cheap as it looked.

The blade clattered against the tabletop as she slammed it down before Vonoshreb. "I'll take this, actually," she said, continuing the man's charade.

"Ahh, I'm glad you found something you like!" he said as if she had not grabbed it at random right before his eyes. "That will be five crescents, if you please."

She handed over the money, counting herself lucky that he had not raised the price on the spot. At least he had *some* amount of integrity, however little.

But the thought had come too soon.

"Actually," Vonoshreb said, "I'm noticing now that this is an antique."

The dagger was definitely old, but it was no high-quality antique. Kali wanted to throttle him.

"I'll have to ask for slightly more, I'm afraid. I can't just let go of my valuable vintage items for so few crescents. I'm sure you understand," he smiled.

"I'm not giving you more money," Kali refused. "How about this: I'll throw in two bottles of ranneth."

Vonoshreb laughed. "What makes you think I need ranneth?" he asked her. "Mere minutes ago you saw me selling a potion that renders ranneth obsolete. The people want nox-spring now."

"But you don't have noxspring. You just said it yourself, you sold all of your supply. If *the people want noxspring* but can't get it, then they're gonna want ranneth. And I don't see any on your shelf, here."

Vonoshreb considered her words as she went on.

"You know who *does* have ranneth, though? Bryieshk's Bazaar. I know because I sold him some yesterday. If they can't get any from you, they'll go to him. You'll lose business."

He scoffed. "I don't make much from ranneth anyway," he deflected.

"True, but it gets people in the door. They come in to buy a bottle, and maybe a nice tunic catches their eye..."

Vonoshreb grumbled. She could tell her argument was getting to him. He was going to accept her terms.

Sorry, Bryieshk, she thought with a pang of guilt.

"Fine," said Vonoshreb. "Five crescents and three bottles of ranneth."

"Two bottles. If you want a third, you'll have to buy it."

Vonoshreb waved her away. "Just two," he muttered. He tapped his hand on the counter and clicked his mandibles as if to say *get on with it.*

Kali obliged and rummaged through her bag for two bottles of the potion. She placed them down with a clack on the table beside the dagger she had just reluctantly purchased. It was still an unfortunate loss, but at least it was a loss on her terms and not whatever absurd price hike the man had been plotting.

"About that merchant," she said.

"The one you want to find so you can buy noxspring for your friend? Why not give him this ranneth you just gave me?" Vonoshreb prodded.

"I wanna give him the good stuff," Kali said with a fake smile. The centript was pushing it, but she wouldn't let him get under her skin.

Vonoshreb narrowed his six eyes and nodded. "I bought it from a woman in Restick named Zara. Jeornish woman from Atlua. Small ship, small crew, but good products."

"Does she own her own ship?" Kali asked.

"Seemed like it."

"What's the name of the ship?"

He shrugged. "I do not pay attention to such details. I simply wander the marketplace and buy whatever catches my eye. It doesn't matter to me which bucket of wood it was hauled off of."

The merchant's name would probably be enough. "Thank you," Kali said, grabbing her "antique" dagger and turning to leave.

As she headed for the door, Vonoshreb said from behind his counter, "Could I interest you in a sheath for that?"

Lorrne looked happy to see her as she drew near the stables outside of Yspleash. His wife Zashi accompanied him today, and their son was visible in the distance, running through the dunes chasing a friend. Enjoying their free time before returning to school the following day.

"Only one night then, eh?" said Lorrne with a grin.

Kali nodded, clutching her knapsack at her side. "Yep. Got everything done that needed doing. How was my boy this time around?"

"A true gentleman, like always," the man said. "Let me go grab him." He disappeared into the stables while Zashi stepped forward to give Kali a hug.

Her white hair was much longer than her husband's, trailing down to her belly. Kali didn't understand how the woman could stand it in this heat. They embraced, and Zashi gave her a friendly pat on the back.

"Sorry I missed you yesterday," she said as she pulled away. "Busy day. Seems like every day is busy, though. It just doesn't stop."

"I can agree with that," Kali said.

If she wasn't selling, she was traveling. And if she wasn't traveling, she was gathering products to sell. The cycle never ceased, though part of her enjoyed always being occupied with something to do. She often yearned for time to relax at home, lounging in bed reading, but whenever she took a day or two off she couldn't help but feel restless and guilty. Like precious time was being wasted.

Lorrne soon returned with Bango plodding alongside him. The ayote was thrilled to see Kali, and she was sure to give him ample ear and chin scratches.

If she could get her hands on that exotic ranneth—what Vonoshreb had called *noxspring*—maybe she could afford to buy her own ayote. Maybe even Bango. Make sure he lived the best, most comfortable life possible.

But first, she would need to reach Atlua, where she could sell all of her Herrilockian goods and pick up Atluan fare to sell back home.

But it won't be cheap.

She had looked into tickets for passage to Atlua during a previous trip to Restick, so she knew it was far out of her price

range. Continuing to sell ranneth and duragas to people like
Bryieshk wouldn't cut it.

Striking a deal with a fellow merchant would be more cost-
effective than buying a ticket on a passenger ship, but it would
still be costly. Her best bet might be to track down the merchant
Zara. The woman could be her ticket to Atlua.

Bango yipped happily as Lorrne saddled him up for her.

Zashi asked, "Where to next? Any other stops on your
route?" They knew she sometimes traveled from Yspleash to
the Repository to visit her sister, but that was not the case this
time.

"Just home," Kali replied, watching Bango stamp his feet
in the sand. He was ready to get moving. She handed her bag
over to Lorrne and he hitched it to the saddle. The ayote yowled
with giddy impatience.

With the task finished, Kali then purchased a sack of dried
beetles to feed Bango on their journey back to Seroo's Eye. It
would take a few days to reach their destination, and she was
running low from the first leg of the trip.

It was mid-day and the sun was at its peak. Not the ideal
time to venture forth into the desert for most, but faifs had few
issues living in the desert climate, which made travel a lot less
strenuous for her than some of her colleagues. Kali also knew
that if she set off now, she would reach the first outpost by
nightfall, giving her plenty of time to settle in.

She hopped up onto Bango's back, positioning herself in
the saddle, and tied her bright red hair in a high ponytail to keep
it off her neck and stave off some of the heat. Her skin was
strong against the sun and would not burn, so there was no
worry about leaving her neck exposed.

"Know when we'll be seein' you again?" Lorrne asked with his hands on his hips. Zashi wrapped an arm around him and they both smiled up at Kali on the ayote's banded shell.

Kali gave the question serious thought for a few moments, then answered, "I'm not sure." She hoped to find some way to make it to Restick soon, and then from there, Atlua.

After a few minutes' travel, a good distance away from the city at her back, Kali tore off her facemask and crumpled it in her hand. She breathed in the fresh, hot desert air and reached forward to rub her hand on Bango's neck. Already she knew she would be spending the next few days silently reflecting on how to raise enough money to buy passage on Zara's ship.

"Let's get goin'," she said, and gave Bango a flick on his right ear.

He took off, spraying sand beneath his feet.

- -

Rather than seeking out any sort of enlightenment, Puk did what he did best: got drunk.

His favorite tavern in Seroo's Eye was a joint called the Tilted Tailbone, which was meant to be a reference to the fact that the city was housed inside a skeleton, but nevermind the fact that the bones of Seroo's tail were located all the way in Restick.

Puk sat at the bar (after a struggle to pull himself up onto the, in his opinion, very tall stool) with a glass of neat whiskey in his hand. In his other hand he held his head, propped up with his elbow on the dark wood.

The bartender was an old, rough-looking rocyan with knotted gray fur and a single fang protruding at the end of his long snout. The heat had to be killer, having a body covered in thick fur.

Puk swirled his nearly-empty glass and the gruff rocyan poured another shot of whiskey into it. Puk nodded in appreciation.

It was now hour three in the pub, which was quite a feat, given that it was only now approaching dinnertime. The first hour had been spent with Puk feeling angry and sorry for himself; the second trying to figure out a new plan for his life given that he was no longer a member of a troupe; and now the third would likely be spent wallowing again.

He did not want to know the amount of crescents he'd racked up on his tab so far.

It was going to totally drain his funds. That realization had come during hour two while trying to figure out a plan, and there had been a mild panic when he realized—not for the first time—that he would have no money left, and so the futility of his situation led him to the decision to spend it all on booze. He might as well.

That drink turned out to be his last, as the bartender cut him off afterwards.

Puk grumbled and paid his tab, which left him with only sixteen crescents to his name. Not even enough for one night at an inn, let alone a ticket back to Atlua.

He was stuck.

He needed to do something to make money. Any amount of money would help, really. But the more the merrier. He grumbled to the bartender, who returned with a scowl.

"Don't bother asking for more," the man said in a low growl. "You've had enough. Go home."

"I don't *have* a home, thank you very much," Puk slurred matter-of-factly. "So I will not be going there. And I am not thirsty," he said, which was an outright lie. "D'you know any..."

His drunken mind sought the correct word. The first one it found was "parlor," which was not right, and not particularly close to what he meant. Next it stumbled upon "grocer," which was even farther. Finally, it landed on what it was looking for.

"...games?" Puk mumbled.

The rocyan stared dead-eyed at him. "Games?" the man repeated blankly.

"Yes!" exclaimed Puk. "D'you know any games goin' on in town? Perhaps in this bar? Somewhere a guy like me could, as you might say, gamble and win some damn crescents?"

The rocyan huffed and dipped his head down, indicating for Puk to turn around. "There's a game right there," he said, somewhat bemused.

Puk rotated one of his eyestalks, keeping the other on the bartender.

Behind himself, he saw a collection of ruffians gathered around a table playing cards with a sizeable pile of crescents at its center. They were hollering and slamming hands down on the table, making quite a bit of racket, and Puk considered that perhaps he was more inebriated than he realized, given that he had not noticed the noise at all.

"I thank you," said Puk as his stalk languidly turned back around and he pushed himself off the stool. His ass ached from sitting on the hard, uncomfortable wood for so many hours.

Puk ambled toward the gang, attempting to decipher which game they were playing to determine if he had any chance of winning some money off them. He could not figure out what the game was, which was not a good sign, and it was a sign that he ignored.

His opening move was to clap the nearest person on the back and say, "Hello there, brethren," which was a phrase he would have never uttered if sober.

The person he had touched was a rail-thin man with long, greasy red hair draped over his shoulders and down his back. His face was clean-shaven and surprisingly smooth, though his chipped teeth left a lot to be desired.

"What?" the man muttered.

"I'm lookin' to join your game," Puk said, hoping that none of his words had morphed together into an incomprehensible mess.

The man sputtered a laugh. "Buy-in's ten crescents."

"Fuck," Puk accidentally said aloud. But the group ignored his outburst and he produced the money, which he tossed into the center of the table.

"Pull a chair up," said the red-haired man. "What's your name, brethren?"

"Puk," he answered, grabbing a chair from a nearby empty table and dragging it noisily along the ground to slot it between the man and an amused jeorn that he realized was a woman. From a distance, and in his current state of mind, the group had been an amorphous blob.

"I'm Randolph," said the red-haired man. "This is Virra," he said, nodding toward the jeornish woman, then continued around the table: "That's Baku, Carl, and Paya."

Baku was a hulking brute with a bushy beard dyed purple and a tattered hat covering his head. Carl was a scraggly faif with a scar etched across the front of his neck, and he smiled at Puk as Randolph introduced him. Paya was a woman who looked remarkably similar to Randolph, and if Puk hadn't been nearly blackout drunk, he likely would have put together that they were related.

He was distantly aware of the fact that none of these names would be even the slightest blip in his mind the next day. Possibly even the next hour.

"Greetings, all," said Puk. "I need some money, so I am going to play this game to win some money."

The group guffawed at his declaration, and they set to playing their game, finishing up the round that Puk had interrupted before folding him into the proceedings.

Hunt was the name of the game, which was unfortunate for Puk because he had never played it. It originated in his home country of Atlua, and he had certainly heard of the game before, but never played. It involved each player being dealt a hand of six cards, delineating weapons and various hunting supplies, while random monster cards were flipped over in the center of the table and players had to compete to slay the monsters. Each player started the game with thirty health points, and if their points were fully depleted, they were out for the remaining rounds. It seemed that in the version this group was playing, the person with the most kills racked up at the end of three rounds got to keep the pot.

Puk squinted his eyes at the cards in his hand. He held two potions, a "bad bow and arrow" as described by the card, dry bait, "smelly bait," and, ironically, a halberd. He grimaced at the last card, but then saw how good its stats were, and hoped the halberd would come to his aid in the end.

Baku flipped the first monster card over, revealing an intricately-illustrated lamatka. Lamatkas were large, stupid animals that lived on the western edge of the country, in the savannahs that led into Gillus. They walked on six wide legs and had a thick, red hide that was impossible to pierce without the sharpest weapons or most powerful magic.

The bad bow and arrow was not going to cut it.

At the sight of the lamatka card, Randolph let out a soft chuckle. Puk found the man's arrogance grating.

I will annihilate the lamatka, he thought to himself. *I will win the money. I will have the money.*

Puk more closely inspected the monster card and read over its attacks. It could pierce players with one of the three horns on its head for ten damage, stomp on them for five, or go to sleep to restore its own health. It also had a resistance to "piercing damage," a category which both of Puk's weapons fell under. It was not the best starting card to go against.

"Fuck," he said again, and everyone laughed.

Baku won the previous game, so he got to go first. Each player was able to make two moves per turn: attack with a weapon and use a supply. They could opt to only do one of the two, but Baku went all-in.

He laid down a weapon card—a dagger—and a modifying card that granted him some resistance to whatever attack the monster used on him. He brought the lamatka's health down from 50 to 45. He then rolled a die to determine which move the lamatka would use; a one or two would be the horns, three or four the stomp, five the rest, and six nothing. He rolled a three and sighed with relief, avoiding the devastating horn attack. He then drew two hunting cards to replenish his hand.

Next up was Carl, and then Paya (who held no weapons and irrelevant supplies so she skipped her turn but was hit by the lamatka for ten damage), and then it came to the confident Randolph.

As it turned out, he had reason to be confident, as everyone discovered when he laid down a broadsword card, which through reasons drunken Puk could not understand did extra damage to the lamatka, and on top of that a dry bait card, which described "lulling the monster into a false sense of security," adding even more damage to the player's attack. He knocked the monster's health down to 30, and then rolled a six. Randolph cheered for himself and then looked to Puk for his turn.

Puk inhaled deeply and glared at the six cards he held. His weary brain struggled to concoct a sound strategy, but it came up short. He was too tired and hungry for this. He yearned to take back the ten crescents he had tossed carelessly into the pot, and he also yearned to slap Randolph in the face for even allowing him to enter the game in the first place. Why had he not been less friendly? If he'd told Puk to fuck off, all of this could have been avoided.

But alas, he was playing Hunt, and he needed to make a move.

Now that he knew what a dry bait card did (the text written on the card had been too tiny for his blurry vision to make out), he deemed it a worthy card to lay down, so he did. Then, given it was his best card, he set the halberd card with its bent corner on the table and waited for someone to tell him what he had done.

Once they realized why he was sitting in silence, someone informed him that he had done ten points of damage to the lamatka, which was not half bad.

Randolph handed over the die, which was cool in Puk's cupped hand as he shook it around before throwing it onto the table with a clatter.

It was a five, and the lamatka restored all of its health. Everyone swore.

"For fuck's sake! I was about to kill it," said Virra. Puk did not respond.

Instead, he drew his two cards from the hunting pile, and read them over. One was simply called "Trip," while the other was yet another potion.

He moved an eyestalk closer to the "Trip" card to read its description and, upon doing so, let out another swear. He laid the card down on the table as Virra prepared for her turn. Again, everyone laughed at him.

In Hunt, tripping was a card the player laid down immediately upon drawing it. It dealt ten points of damage to the player, as well as made them vulnerable on their next turn. It was not an ideal position to be in.

The sixty crescents in the middle of the table felt farther and farther from his tiny grasp.

By the time the game circled back around to Puk, the lamatka was down to five health points.

Completely attainable. It was a miracle.

Puk read over the "bad bow and arrow" and saw that normally it would do five points of damage, but given the monster's resistance to piercing, that number was reduced to three.

But with his smelly bait...

He laid down the bait and bow cards with a triumphant grin.

"I will annihilate the lamatka!" he declared, pumping a fist in the air.

Randolph burst out laughing. "Well, no," he said, pointing at the smelly bait. "Look at the icon. It doesn't match the lamatka's. You use this card on something like a cordol or baiar or somethin'. It has no effect on lamatkas, so all you did was three damage."

Puk's fist hung in the air as he absorbed this staggering news. The lamatka wasn't dead. He had to roll the die.

His hand slowly descended and grabbed the carved cube, only shaking it two or three times before letting it loose on the table.

It tumbled over his poorly-chosen cards before coming to a stop on a single dot.

"Fuck," he said for the third time.

Randolph couldn't contain his laughter. When he regained control of himself, he said, "So that's ten points of damage. But since you tripped and are vulnerable, it's doubled, so that's twenty. And you already took ten from tripping, so…"

The math, simple as it was, proved to be too complex for Puk at the moment.

"…so you shoulda used a potion, brethren," Baku finished for him. "You're outta the game."

Puk's heart sunk. Eliminated already, after merely two rounds. And with only six crescents to his name now.

He felt nauseous.

"You got a buy-in for the next game?" Randolph asked.

Puk shook his head and got up from the table, sullenly striding toward the door.

The sun was only just beginning to set when he stumbled out of the Tilted Tailbone. The city was already fairly dim and streetlamps were lighting up, with the diminished sunlight having to filter through the long-dead aeon's skull. Little light shone through the eyehole at this time of day, though many still gathered around the Gaze. Soon a hint of moonlight would shine down and grant the pool a mesmerizing sparkle.

What he craved was a dark, quiet place away from everyone else where he could ingest some fire-spit. That would really hit the spot. A pleasant pairing with the whiskey that was weighing him down, and a reprieve from the thoughts of the game he'd just blundered.

Each step was sluggish. It was like walking through quicksand, though his feet only sunk half an inch or so into the white sand. He had done his best to resist while concentrating on the game, but now he leaned hard into the stupor of inebriation.

Double-vision plagued his sight, and he moved out of the way of people who weren't actually there, only to knock into others who shouted at him to watch where he was going.

"I am," he mumbled at them, his eyestalks drooping.

Lethargy gripped him tight as he stepped forward, dragging his meager bag of belongings behind him, and held onto the skinny metallic body of a streetlamp for support.

Puk slid down the length of the pole onto the ground, relishing in the warmth of the sand. His eyelids fluttered and his body was heavy as an anchor.

"Are you okay?"

The voice was distant. Hardly an echo. But Puk opened his eyes and saw that it belonged to a chubby jeornish man who was kneeling before him, not so distant after all.

The man cocked an eyebrow, staring down at the pathetic qarm, and asked, "Can you hear me? Are you alright? Let me help you."

He reached for Puk, but he shooed away the man's hand.

"Mmfine," he said, not even convincing himself.

"Please," said the man, "let me help. I own an inn, and we have vacancies tonight. You can stay there."

"Nuhmunny," said Puk.

The man smiled, revealing dimples in his puffy cheeks. "You don't need to pay," he said. "Just come rest. It'll do you a world of good."

Puk blinked away the man's double and let out a sigh so hefty he thought it would turn his body inside-out.

"Fine," he relented, allowing the man to help him to his feet.

They walked together down the street, past the Gaze, and turned down an alley that Puk couldn't catch the name of in his drunken state. The two came to a wide, three-story building with a sign that read SHIAR'S SLUMBER.

The name barely made sense, but Puk wasn't sure if that was completely true or if he was simply too drunk to comprehend it.

He followed the kindhearted man inside and was blinded by the lights hanging from the ceiling. He shielded his eyes and let out a gurgled moan, which elicited laughter from the man as well as a woman who stood behind a nearby counter.

It was an excruciating walk up to the available room—all the way on the second floor—but the relief Puk felt as he collapsed onto the bed was immense. The sheets were ten times as soft given how drunk he was and how uncomfortable the church cot had been the night before.

Sleep was closing in fast, but the man stood at the bedside and said, "My name is Botro. I'll be downstairs if you need anything, though I reckon you're about to be out cold for the night." He chuckled. "I'll see you in the morning."

"Thanks," Puk said, hardly getting the word out.

He closed his eyes and welcomed the dark. He could hear the door quietly shut as Botro made his exit, but moments later, all else fell away.

CHAPTER III

SWALLOWED BY THE SANDS

Sunlight was hell. Movement was hell. Noise was hell. Everything about the morning was hell.

Puk groaned (which was hell) and rubbed at his eyestalks as he shifted in bed, his legs tangled in the sheets, which were still incredibly soft even though he was now sober. A headache pounded within his tiny skull and he pledged to simply lay there and die in that bed.

But an hour later a knock came at the door, and he grumbled for the intruder to come in. The jeornish man from the night before—*Botro?* Puk tried to recall—pushed the door open slowly with an agonizing creak and peeked his head inside.

"How're you feeling?" the man inquired.

"Bad," was Puk's answer. He tried to tone down the irascibility in his voice.

Botro chuckled. "I figured as much. You were far beyond what I'd charitably call *out of sorts* when I found you last night. If you're feeling up to it, please come downstairs and partake in some breakfast."

Puk sighed, then reminded the man, "I don't have any money." Every syllable he spoke was like a shot to the head.

"I know," said Botro. "That's alright. We'll fill you up with some eggs anyway. Come on down whenever you'd like." And with that, he disappeared back into the hallway, careful to shut the door as quietly as possible.

Despite his insistence on dying in bed, a free breakfast did sound pretty alluring, so Puk forced himself to sit up and crawl out from under the sheets. He examined himself in a full-length mirror propped up by the window and frowned at the unfortunate visage that was frowning back at him.

His general appearance left a lot to be desired. His stalks were droopy and his posture was slouched; his shirt was covered in a dried brown liquid that he hoped was some sort of alcohol as opposed to vomit or, somehow, shit; and he would swear his gut was paunchier than usual. He burped.

With trepidation, he stepped out into the hallway and looked in either direction. He spotted an open door several feet away to his left, across the hall, and figured it must be the communal bathroom. He trundled that way and locked the door behind him, stripping off his shirt and tossing it into the sink, running warm water over it.

Puk slumped down on the floor, leaning against the door, while the water soaked into his dirtied shirt. He knew he should probably be scrubbing it already, but resting his eyes felt good. He momentarily dozed off but was awoken by a ginger knock on the door, to which he replied he'd be done in a minute.

After he finished scrubbing out as much of the stain as he could manage (which was not a lot, given that he had no actual cleaning supplies), Puk realized that he also had no way of drying off the shirt, which was now sopping wet after soaking for close to ten minutes.

There came another knock at the door, and Puk said, "Yeah, just a second!"

"I'm 'bout ready to burst out here!" a man barked on the other side, pounding on the door again to accentuate the *burst*.

"Fuck me," Puk mumbled to himself, holding up his wet shirt, which would be even worse to wear amongst company than if it was just dirty. He felt like an absolute buffoon.

But probably worse than going downstairs for breakfast in a dirty or wet shirt would be going half nude, so Puk reluctantly pulled the shirt over his head. He struggled to slide his arms through the sleeves and push his head out through the hole. The wet fabric refused to cooperate with his naturally sticky skin.

"What in the hell you doin' in there?" the man in the hall demanded to know. "You shittin' all your innards out?"

"No!" Puk shouted from within the confines of his shirt. "I'm trying to put my fucking wet shirt back on!" He finally poked his head and one arm through, which he used to help the other arm along.

The man mumbled to himself, "Wet shirt...?"

Puk flung the door open, smacking it against the man's body as he stumbled backward out of the way. He gaped at the qarm standing before him with his shirt dripping onto the floor.

"Yeah, a wet shirt," said Puk.

"Why's your shirt wet? What happened in there?"

Puk shoved past the man and told him, "Go piss." He marched toward the staircase in a sour mood.

The stairs led down to the lobby, where a receptionist had his elbows propped up on the counter and was holding his head in his hands. He glanced over at Puk with a befuddled look.

"Are…you alright, sir?" he asked, not bothering to sit up. "Do you need me to…" He trailed off, not sure what service he could offer.

Botro appeared in the wide doorway to the adjoining room on Puk's right, which led into the dining area. Behind the man, Puk spotted a long table furnished with steaming plates of fresh food waiting to be devoured.

As more water dripped onto the floor, Botro cocked an eyebrow and said, "Let's get you some dry clothes."

Puk appreciated him not asking what had happened. "I don't think you've got anything in my size," he said.

But Botro assured him, "Of course we do. We have something for everyone here. Could you please fetch our guest here a new shirt?" he asked the young man behind the nearby desk. "Perhaps a pair of pants, as well."

The receptionist hopped up and scurried into a back room behind the counter to obtain the clothes.

Given the general lack of qarmish travelers in the desert, the inn's preparedness surprised Puk. "Thank you," he said to Botro. "Sorry I got your floor wet."

"That's alright," Botro said, displaying what Puk considered an extraordinary amount of patience in spite of how much trouble he had already put this man through. "It's just water. Easily wiped away."

The receptionist returned a minute later with the requested clothing, and Botro showed Puk to the downstairs bathroom, where he promptly changed out of his wet attire and handed it over to the innkeeper for a proper wash.

The clothes he now wore were all white, with the flourish of a red S embroidered on the left breast. Puk knew eating in white clothes would be a dangerous game given his proclivity to spill, but after Botro Shiar's seemingly endless generosity, he was going to make a concerted effort to be careful.

Shiar's Slumber had an impressive Herrilockian breakfast spread. Puk wondered if this was a daily occurrence or something for a special occasion, but he had no idea what day of the week it even was, so he had no way of knowing if there was a special occasion to celebrate.

The main attraction was a large skillet filled with eggs poached in a mixture of tomatoes, onion, peppers, and various spices. It was a classic regional breakfast to give a person a kick of heat on their tastebuds before heading out into the desert, which seemed unwise to Puk, but he knew the dish was delicious so he was all in.

He scooped a pile of eggs onto his plate, as well as a few thin strips of fried hollion meat and a slice of toast with a lavish heaping of butter. That would do for round one.

The meat was crispy and flavorful, pairing well with the creamy richness of the eggs and tomatoes (which, due to being a hotel spread trying to accommodate the widest swathe of people possible, were not particularly spicy).

Puk sat alone at a circular table that could easily seat four, which was the smallest accommodation in the room. He breathed deep through his nostrils as he shoveled food into his mouth, which helped settle his roiling stomach.

While he ate, he pondered what the day would bring.

Deep down, he felt like he needed to repay Botro in some way, but he had very little money and even fewer possessions, and therefore couldn't think of anything that would make up for how the man had taken care of him.

Surely there's something in a pawn shop you could buy, he told himself. *Or you could just spend that money on fire-spit.*

He immediately chastised himself. There was no way he was going to blow his last six crescents on drugs.

That wouldn't even get me much of it, if any at all. Not in any good quality, anyway.

Puk shook the thought and tried to think of any shops he could browse for a gift.

Beyond that, with his troupe abandoning him, he needed to get back home to Atlua, which meant purchasing a ticket on a ship in a coastal city such as Restick or Toralas.

But given that Seroo's Eye was in the middle of the desert, the voyage to the coast would be long. And hot. Even if he traveled along the Ribroad, he doubted it would offer enough protection from the climate for him to survive walking all the way there. He'd have to buy passage on a carriage.

So that was what he'd do: search for a gift and buy a ticket to Restick. Although the ticket would probably require all of his current funds, if not more. Maybe he could steal a gift instead.

But before that, round two. He was shocked to discover his plate was already empty.

- -

The first day of travel had been uneventful and mercifully less exhausting than Kali had feared, both for herself and for Bango. The animal plodded along without a care in the world, reaching the first travelers' outpost between Yspleash and home well before sundown.

They were now bounding across the Gogol Desert once more, Bango filled with energy after a long night of rest and a hearty breakfast of dried beetles and raw cactus. Kali did not eat anything; after the knaff in Yspleash, combined with the sunlight crashing down on her, she would be perfectly fine for several days.

Day two was shaping up to be just as boring. It was a trip Kali had undertaken countless times, and surely one that she would undertake countless more if she failed to work out a deal with Zara.

The ride gave her plenty of time to reflect on how she would approach the conversation with the merchant. There was a bit of excitement in planning the interaction, but also a great deal of stress. It felt like her only opportunity to make this work. If she blew it, then what?

She was nearly thirty years old, yet still felt like a kid. She still felt as if her parents were "adults" but she wasn't, and yet at this point in their lives her parents had already gotten married and had their first kid.

Not to mention Lissia, who was the same age as her but far more accomplished. It was a prestigious position, becoming a scholar at the Repository, especially for a non-centript. But her sister had worked hard and achieved her dream.

She knew it was stupid to compare her life to theirs, and that she shouldn't try to adhere to some imaginary roadmap for how a life was meant to play out. Still, she felt like she was running out of time to make her mark. To feel fulfilled.

And so she was stressed about talking to Zara.

A typical trip to Atlua would cost someone around six hundred crescents, if they wanted to book passage on a ship that was not halfway falling apart and crewed by miscreants. It was closer to eight hundred if they wanted to fly on an airship instead, which were all-around nicer than seafaring ships. She would not be on an airship any time soon.

Kali had roughly six hundred crescents to her name, including all of her savings. The profit margins on the products she sold were not spectacular, and she was endlessly grateful for still being able to live with her parents. But leeching off them was yet another reason why she needed to make this work, to get over to Atlua and truly strike out on her own.

Bango came to an abrupt stop, thrusting Kali from her pitiful thoughts and nearly literally thrusting her over the ayote's head. He let out a low, threatening growl.

She swiveled her head side to side, but could not make out anything in the vast expanse of glittering white sand. It sparkled like gemstones in the unrelenting sun. They were utterly alone, not a thing in sight apart from the towering spire a few miles away to indicate that they were still on the correct path to the next outpost.

"What's wrong with you?" she muttered, rubbing Bango behind the ears. He stared straight ahead while she soothed him.

And then she saw it. It was subtle, and she guessed the ayote had been able to smell or hear the animals. An ayote's sense of sight was best in the dark, so if she could barely see it then Bango surely couldn't. When she really concentrated, she could see the shifting of sand about half a mile ahead of them, moving across her field of vision from left to right.

It had to be a cordol migration. This pack was heading north, in the direction of the gulf coast. The creatures would bury under the sand and travel across the desert in packs, though Kali did not personally know the reason for the behavior.

Lissia would probably know. Her sister knew everything that she didn't. Perhaps Lissia had left behind some sort of bestiary at home that Kali could consult.

Generally, cordols left people alone, but if they felt threatened they could quickly turn vicious. Bango had been smart to halt and allow them to pass rather than incite any fury by running above their pack.

"Good boy," Kali cooed, patting the ayote on his head. His reaction was to let out another low growl and continue staring at the pack of cordols as they made their way north.

Once the cordols were out of sight, Bango deemed it safe to continue their journey. His demeanor changed immediately and he was back to being the spunky, excitable guy that Kali knew him to be.

She smiled, but her expression soon changed as she returned to swirling thoughts of how to approach Zara or raise enough money to buy a ticket to Atlua.

The sun beat down on them as they traveled in near silence. The only sounds were of Bango's feet plodding along the sand and Kali's knapsack slapping against the side of his shell. She absentmindedly ran a hand along the banded shell, her fingertips rubbing against the granular bumps.

She sighed.

- -

After eating a second, and third, and fourth round of food, Puk thanked Botro profusely and sauntered out of Shiar's Slumber with a full, swinging belly and his sights set on Restick.

He had been wandering through the streets for close to twenty minutes before realizing he should have asked the receptionist at the inn for directions to the carriage station. He cursed his own incompetence and then cursed the young man as well for good measure. With a clear head and satisfied appetite, he was feeling reenergized, and cursing people felt good.

Seroo's Eye was one of the largest, densest cities in the country, and Puk had been incapacitated the previous night when he'd made his way from the pub to Botro's inn, so his sense of direction was entirely shot and he hadn't the faintest clue where he was. He had not spent enough time in the city for anything to look particularly familiar. At least he wasn't roving aimlessly in a wet shirt.

Part of him felt like he should be more stressed about the situation he had landed in. He was stuck in a foreign country with almost no money, he had been kicked out of his qarmish troupe, and he had a severe hankering for some fire-spit. None of these things were good on their own, and combined they were downright terrible.

Yet he strolled down the streets, peering through shop windows as he passed and smiling to other denizens as they smiled at him.

Despite it all, he was cheery.

Though it might have been that he was simply still a bit drunk and the reality of it all had not yet seeped in. For the time being, he decided to enjoy his stint in the massive dead animal's skull while he could.

It was then he noticed a sign on a shop door that promised CHEAP BUT GOOD. If that didn't describe Puk, he didn't know what did. He didn't even take the time to glance at the shop's name before sliding through the front door with the tinny ring of a bell overhead.

The place was small and dingy, as he had anticipated given its advertisement. The only word he could think to describe its odor was "old." Its floor was a cheap, faded wood dusted with sand kicked in by customers from outside. Shelves towered from the floor to the ceiling, several feet higher than Puk would ever dream to reach, and were set up like a labyrinth from the front of the store presumably all the way to the back. There was not an employee (or anyone at all) in sight as Puk ventured further into the store.

"Hullo, there!" came a disembodied voice from somewhere in the stacks. It was light and jolly, leading Puk to picture an exceptionally tall, skinny man with rosy cheeks and a smile from ear to ear. A real creepy guy.

"…hi!" Puk yelled back with a touch of confusion.

"Welcome!" said the jolly creep.

"Okay!"

Puk hoped that would be the end of the exchange and that someone else would be handling his payment. He was not confident he could deal with that level of cheeriness from someone who worked in a shop such as this every day of his or her life. It was hard for him to imagine extracting any joy whatsoever from any job, let alone one as seemingly drab as this.

He scanned the lofty shelves for anything at his eye-level that he might give to Botro.

It was starting to dawn on him that they'd only shared a handful of interactions, and one hundred percent of them had involved Botro aiding him in some way, so he knew nothing about the man's interests or hobbies. An unfortunate realization to have while shopping for a gift.

"What the hell do innkeepers like…?" Puk muttered absently under his breath.

"What was that?"

"The hell?" Puk sputtered before shouting back, "Nothing! Just talking to myself!"

"Feel free to talk to me!"

"Okay!"

Puk made a note to keep his thoughts internal so as to not draw the attention of the jolly creep with supernatural hearing. Was the guy a rocyan? Puk had never heard such a happy rocyan.

Nothing was catching his eye. He slowly snaked his way through several rows of shelves and figured he must be in the middle of the shop by now, nearing its proprietor. His eyestalks drooped with disappointment, but he continued the search. He owed Botro that much.

Ahead of him, on a shelf that he could probably reach if he stood on his toes, was a dusty yet pretty tea set. Or part of one, anyhow. There was one cup with a chipped saucer, a pot without a lid, and a two-tier pastry tray that was in surprisingly good condition. There was no sugar bowl, but Puk knew nothing about tea or tea sets, so he wasn't totally sure whether they came with sugar bowls or not.

But inns served tea. It might make a good gift, despite its smattering of imperfections. The ceramic was white, with delicate purple and blue lines painted all over the surfaces, depicting scenes of the ancient Ustrel battles against the Asrani.

The set must have been crafted by the jeornish, and Botro was jeornish. It was all coming together.

There was no price listed near the set, however. Puk sighed and called out, "How much for this jeornish tea set?"

"The good one or the shitty one?"

"I guess the shitty one?"

"Three crescents!"

Puk decided it wouldn't hurt to ask. "How about the good one?"

"Twenty crescents!"

"I'll take the shitty one, then."

"Excellent! Bring it to the back and we'll get you sorted!"

It took more stretching than he originally estimated, but Puk managed to grab each piece of the set off the tilted shelf and wind his way through the rest of the maze to the back of the shop, where he was greeted by the exact image he had conjured in his mind.

The jolly creep grinned widely and remarked, "That's quite an armful you've got there, friend!"

"Yes," Puk huffed, carefully piling the goods onto the countertop before the lumbering shopkeeper.

The man's smile faltered for a split second and he asked, "Where's the sugar bowl?"

"There was no sugar bowl with the set. Maybe that's only with the good one."

"No, no, I'm positive there was a sugar bowl with the shitty set as well."

"Well, it ain't there."

"Hmm. That's unfortunate. A good tea set really should have an accompanying sugar bowl."

"Too true, but this is a *shitty* tea set. If there's a missing sugar bowl, how's about you knock a crescent off the price for me?"

The man shook his head and tsk-tsk-tsked. "I'm afraid I can't do that, sorry."

He paid the man the three crescents and waited while he stuffed all the pieces of the set into a cloth bag and tied it up tight.

He handed the bag over to Puk and said, "Be sure not to rattle it too much. You might chip some of the pieces!"

"More than they're already chipped, you mean?" said Puk dryly.

"Precisely."

"Alright. Well, thanks," said Puk, and he turned to navigate the maze again to find his way out of the shop. Once he was halfway back to the front, he shouted to the jolly creep, "Hey, where's the carriage station?"

"There's one at each entrance to the city!"

"Well, no shit, but how do I get there? Where's the Gaze?" If he could at least make his way to the Gaze, he could easily navigate to one of the stations. Luckily, the man was able to provide directions for him, and they were fairly simple.

Outside, the contents of his bag clattered together with every step, and he prayed he wouldn't be handing Botro a bag of ceramic chunks by the time he made it back to the inn.

It took another solid fifteen minutes of walking before he found his way to the Gaze. From there, it was an easy trek to the carriage station at the Mandible Gate. Puk wondered whether he would ever find his way back to Shiar's Slumber.

He stopped for a moment to gaze at the unending desert outside the city. The Mandible Gate opened up to the eastern

Herrilock desert, the Cascades. Seroo's Eye was, in essence, the dividing point between the Cascades and the Gogol.

At the edge of the Cascades was a beautiful, serene savannah, which bled into Gillus, an all-around much less hot and more green country than the one in which Puk currently found himself stuck.

He looked at Seroo's teeth on the gate to his right, all of which were much bigger than his entire body. The teeth lined the beast's skull all along the ceiling, curving up from the sand the skull sunk into all the way back into the station that was carved into the side of the upper jaw.

Puk ducked inside and bee-lined for the ticket queue. After a few minutes, he was attended to.

"Hi there. I'm looking to see how much it is for a ticket to Restick," he said.

"Restick wagons depart from the Spine Gate," said the woman with a dazed look in her eye. "You'll need to go there to get to Restick."

Puk nodded. "Okay, yeah, that's fine, but I'm not looking to depart *right now*. Can you just give me a price?"

The woman groaned and consulted a pricing chart sitting in front of her, out of customers' reach. Her eyes flickered over the list, and finally she said, "The current price for a ticket to Restick is thirty crescents for a public wagon or eighty for luxury."

"What's in a luxury wagon?" Puk asked, his interest piqued.

"Are you interested in booking a luxury wagon to Restick?"

"Interested? Yes. Able to? No."

The woman huffed. "Luxury wagons are for our most valuable patrons. They offer a higher class of seating, more space, and complimentary food and beverage on the journey."

"Sounds nice."

"It is luxurious."

"I'm sure," said Puk. "Thanks for your help."

It was a simple task, and it was complete. He left the station and sought an unoccupied bench on which to rest and contemplate the new information.

Thirty crescents was a lot of crescents to a man who only had three crescents.

"Dammit," he whispered, half-expecting the jolly creep to shout a reply he somehow heard from his horrifically-constructed shop. He never did catch the name of it.

It couldn't be helped. He found himself thinking, *How much fire-spit could three crescents snag me?*

He sighed and hopped up off the bench, in search of a darkened alley somewhere deep in the skull of Seroo.

- -

The second outpost was farther along the trail than she remembered. It always was.

Kali and Bango arrived just before the sun disappeared completely behind the distant dunes, igniting the sky in an orange and purple blaze that engulfed the Gogol.

The best thing about travelers' outposts was that they were owned and operated by the Herrilockian government, so all amenities were free. Herrilock was mostly desert, which could be a cruel, unforgiving place no matter the time of day, so the officials had wanted to establish safe havens for travelers throughout the country.

Which meant that Bango was now stabled free of charge, and Kali was on her way inside the modest building for a bit of relaxation in the lounge.

Most outposts comprised of a dining area, a lobby, and five to ten rooms. This one, however, was one of the bigger establishments, given its central location in regards to several popular destinations such as Seroo's Eye, the Repository, and Marrowlash. Due to the increased traffic, it contained a handful more rooms and a bar lounge area where guests could unwind. It was nothing fancy, as to be expected since it was government-subsidized, but it was appreciated.

First things first, Kali checked in to a room and headed upstairs to unload her possessions. The room wasn't any bigger than her bedroom back at home, which for some reason felt cramped when she was there but gave her a sense of familiar coziness at the outpost.

There was a window by the bed, which overlooked nothing of note. She gazed outside and watched the last minute or two of sunset as wind kicked up flurries of sand.

Her sister Lissia had always been deathly afraid of sandstorms. They were no laughing matter, and of course Kali would rather *not* be in one if given the option, but even the prospect of them threatened to send Lissia into a panic attack. One of the things she was most excited about when getting a job at the Repository was that the entire staff had living arrangements inside the massive building. Everything was there for her: her home, food, her work. She never had to venture out into the dunes if she didn't want to. It was a chore getting her to come visit the family nowadays.

With the sun swallowed by the sands and a dark cool settling over the Gogol, Kali left her room to make way for the
lounge.

There were more people roaming about than she thought
the outpost could house. Perhaps it had recently expanded without her realizing? Regardless, twenty or so people were
gathered at the bar, sitting around tables, or chatting in shadowy
corners.

Three centripts, who she suspected were brothers, stood at
the bar chittering away in Carsuak and laughing heartily at each
other. Their anatomy made sitting in chairs an unwieldy task.
The biggest of the three had glittering multicolored gems en-
crusted on almost all of his segments. Kali shuddered at the
thought of catching the sunlight bouncing off his back.

In the farthest, darkest corner of the lounge was a man discussing what appeared to be gravely serious business with an
ujath. Kali swiftly averted her eyes from the scene, not wanting
to cause any trouble or become wrapped up in anything unsavory.

At least half of the tables were occupied by groups of people long lost to their drinks, having settled in for the night and
gladly indulging in free alcohol while they could.

Kali wasn't much of a drinker, but she had stayed there
enough times to know the bar closed early, only an hour or two
after sundown. It was meant to be a measure to stop people
from getting too drunk (and bankrupting Herrilock), but all it
truly resulted in was travelers arriving as early in the day as
possible to get started on drinking before the bartender cut everyone off. It was not the smartest system, so everyone wanted
to take advantage before new rules were inevitably imple-
mented.

She took a seat at an empty two-person table near the bar and let out an exhausted sigh. The long day of travel left her exhausted, and there was one more ahead of her. By the next night, she should be home in her own bed. The speed of ayotes was a marvel.

A young man stopped by her table and asked if there was anything he could get her. In her fatigue, it took her a moment to realize he was an employee and not someone trying to hit on her.

"Just a water, thanks," she said.

The boy smiled and hurried away to fetch her order. He returned only a minute later with a nearly-overflowing glass of ice cold water. She downed half the glass at once then set it back down on the table, still gripping it in her hand, letting it cool her vibrant, colorful skin. She hadn't realized how parched she was; she instantly felt perkier.

It was then a man sidled up to the table and plopped himself down in the seat opposite hers. He had bloodshot eyes and olive jeornish skin that was caked in a layer of grit. His long, white hair was greasy and knotted. On top of his head sat a brown hat with a wide, bent brim. When he smiled crookedly at her, Kali was genuinely shocked that he still had all of his teeth, though they were yellowed.

"Hey there, pretty lady," he said. Kali forced herself not to groan. "Always love meetin' a pretty faif like yourself. Your skin's the prettiest I did ever seen, you know that? Blue and pink *and* purple? How often's a faif got *three* colors in there, huh?"

"Is this meant to be charming?" Kali asked him.

The man's smile faltered, but he recovered quickly. "Name's Jeth," he said, reaching for her hand to shake it. She retracted, not wanting to give him even the smallest opportunity to touch the skin he was evidently so fond of. He pulled back and asked, "What's yours?"

"You don't need to know," she said. "You can leave, though."

Jeth frowned at this. "I'm just tryin' to be friendly. Ain't that a good thing? Bein' friendly?"

It was the hardest thing she ever had to do, but Kali refrained from rolling her eyes. She didn't want to set the guy off. There was no telling what he might do.

"Alright, well, you've been friendly, and now I'd like to be left alone," she said. "If you'd so *kindly* leave me to my water."

The bedraggled man's eyes flicked toward her half-empty glass. "I can fill that up for you," he offered. "Or I can get you something a little stronger. Something to make you feel good."

"I feel fine."

"You sure about that?"

"Quite sure."

Her patience was growing thin, as was Jeth's. The smile had completely evaporated from his face, and his eyes narrowed to slits.

"You travelin' alone, ma'am?" he asked her.

Kali remained silent, glaring at him.

He continued anyway. "Desert's a rough place for a pretty, delicate thing like you to be wanderin' through all alone. I'm just tryin' to look out for your best interests, is all."

He pushed himself up out of the chair and tipped his hat to her. He then stalked away into the back corner of the room and struck up a conversation with the ujath and man who were standing there. Kali was unsurprised that they were all getting along.

The young waiter suddenly reappeared and asked her, "Are you alright, ma'am? Do you need our staff to intervene?"

A bit late to act valiant, Kali thought, but she said, "No, I'm fine. He's gone now."

"Very well. Please let me know if there's anything we can do for you. Would you like a refill of your water?" She nodded and he took her glass to fill up.

While she awaited his return, a woman at the table next to hers leaned over and asked, "Are you *actually* okay?"

Kali smiled. "Yeah, I'm fine."

"Let me know if you need help dealing with him," the woman said. Her face was stern. She was a bit older, probably older even than Kali's father, but she was in great shape and looked to be a formidable opponent in a fight. She could crumple Jeth like a piece of paper.

"Thanks," said Kali. "I appreciate that."

"No worries. I used to be an Atluan Guard before I retired, so I've dealt with plenty of assholes like him in my time," she said. "Looks to me like he's a bit buzzed on fire-spit. I heard him say earlier that he's goin' down south, and I hear the supply there is good right now. But that's none of my concern anymore, unless he starts some shit."

Kali was familiar with the drug, but had never partaken in any. The only illicit substance she had been involved with was getting into her father's alcohol stash in her early teens. He was angrier about the lost revenue than the fact she had gotten disgustingly sick.

"I saw a group of cordols moving north today, actually," she said. Where there were cordols, there was ample fire-spit.

The woman nodded. "Yeah, they've been roaming around the south for a while now and I guess it's the time of year they head north. I'm sure suppliers up there are just giddy with anticipation." Her voice was tinged with bitterness.

"I was actually wondering about that today when I saw them. Do you know why they migrate?"

The woman shrugged. "There's a lot I don't know about. I know how to swing a sword and shoot a gun. Don't know why animals do what they do, especially some of the crazy shit y'all got here in the desert." And with that, she leaned away to rejoin the conversation with her own companions.

The waiter brought her glass of water back to the table, some of it sloshing over the rim and splashing onto the wood as he set it down.

"Anything else I can grab for you, ma'am?" he asked.

Kali glanced over the guy's shoulder and watched Jeth chatting with his newfound friends in the corner. His back was turned to her, yet she still felt like he was acutely aware of her presence.

"No, thanks," she told the young man. "Just the water is fine."

- -

Three crescents did not buy any fire-spit, but it bought Puk some pity, which bought him some fire-spit.

He snorted a line with the dealer he'd found, a short, ratty-looking guy with ugly orange overalls, a mushroom cap, and an unbelievable stench. Their names were not exchanged, but the guy thought it was funny and pathetic that Puk had so little money ("Even my kid's got more money than that!") and so he shared a line.

A while later, he had made his way back to Shiar's Slumber with more than a bit of drowsiness in his gait. He certainly wouldn't say no to a nap.

As he entered the inn, the first thing he noticed was that a young woman had replaced the previous receptionist behind the front counter. "Good afternoon, sir," she greeted him with an air of politeness he did not feel he deserved. "What can I help you with?"

Puk grinned stupidly and held up his noisy cloth bag full of ceramics then said, "I'm lookin' for Botro."

The woman wore a puzzled expression but, still smiling, asked, "Is that a delivery for Mr. Shiar?"

"It's a gift."

"Oh!" she perked up again. "You're a friend of Mr. Shiar's, then?"

"More like a charity case, but would you find him for me?"

The woman was again confused by his words, but she nodded and disappeared to locate her boss.

Puk thrust himself into a nearby couch with plush green cushions and nestled in while he waited. His eyes fluttered shut and his stalks drooped forward, nearly descending into his gaping mouth.

His nap did not last long, as a pat on the shoulder from Botro suddenly snapped him to attention.

"Welcome back," the man said in his unwaveringly friendly demeanor. "Did you have a good day?"

"It was decent," said Puk, raising the bag and presenting it to Botro. "Got you a little something for all the trouble I put you through. Sorry again. If I already apologized, anyway, I don't remember. If not, then just sorry."

Botro chuckled and accepted the bag. He pulled it open and reached inside to extract the saucer. He flipped it over, examining the detailed painting.

"It came like that," Puk said as Botro eyed the chipped edge.

The man laughed again and thanked him. "It's a lovely set," he said after looking through the rest of the bag. "I very much appreciate it."

"There's no sugar bowl, but not everyone likes sugar anyways, so..." Puk trailed off.

"That's very true. I was just about to have some tea myself, with no sugar. Would you like a cup?"

"Sure, but with sugar."

"Excellent. Let's go sit. I'll have someone give these pieces a thorough washing so we can use them next time we want some tea."

Puk followed him into the dining area and took a seat while Botro slunk into the kitchen and returned a few moments later with a tray of steaming hot tea, a couple pastries, and plenty of sugar.

They prepared their respective cups in silence. Puk's spoon clinked against the side of his teacup, which was a pastel pink with yellow trim.

Botro then said, "Please don't take offense to this, but you seem to me a bit...out of it. Are you okay?"

"Out of it right now or out of it in general?" asked Puk, still calmed by the effects of the fire-spit. He had no idea if Botro could tell he was high. It was a struggle to keep his eyes open, but he thought he was doing an admirable job.

"Both, I suppose."

"I'm alright," Puk shrugged.

Botro nodded and considered his answer. "You kept saying to me that you have no money. Is that true? Or was it an exaggeration?"

"It's true."

"Is the tea set stolen?" It was the first time Botro looked more serious than jovial.

"Nah, I bought it," said Puk, taking a sip of the tea. It soothed his throat but still wasn't sweet enough. He added more sugar. "I've now got three crescents to my name."

"How is it you only have three crescents?" Botro asked with genuine concern and bemusement.

Puk grunted. "I was part of a traveling qarmish troupe, but they kicked me out after our show the other night. I'm from Atlua, but they were my ticket back home, where all my shit is. I've got nothin' in Herrilock."

Botro frowned. "Why did they kick you out?" He immediately caught himself and added, "You don't have to answer that if it's too personal."

He appreciated all that Botro had done for him, but the man did not need to know about his affinity for fire-spit. "It's a long story," was all that he offered.

"Fair enough." Botro contemplated this for a moment, pausing to drink his tea. He then asked, "What did you do for the troupe?"

Puk sighed. He hated talking about his performance. "I was a singer."

"Were you kicked out because you're a bad singer?"

"No," Puk laughed.

"You're good?"

"I'm not bad."

"'Not bad' is just another way of saying 'good.' Here's the thing: I take it you want to return to Atlua, right?"

Puk nodded.

"Which requires getting on a ship in Restick or Toralas or I guess even Rus Rahl, but I take it any ship harboring in Rus Rahl is significantly out of your price range. And then even before that, you need to get to one of those cities."

Puk nodded again.

"I think we can arrange something mutually beneficial here. I've been searching for some talent to perform at the inn a couple nights a week, like singers or musicians. I admit, I've already signed a contract with someone, but she isn't able to start for another few weeks after she takes care of some family affairs in Gillus. If you'd like, you can work here at the inn singing for the guests, and I'll pay you for it. Just until my other singer is available, of course. But by then I think you'd have enough to at least get yourself to the coast. And, of course, I can arrange for you to sleep and eat here for free. How does all of that sound?"

Realistically, there was nothing to consider. Puk would be a fool not to accept the incredibly generous offer from the absurdly generous man, but a nagging part in the back of his mind wanted to just find some more fire-spit and waste the day away. Singing was the very last item on his list of things to do.

"That sounds good to me," he finally said, conceding to good sense. "That's a very kind offer, Mr. Shiar."

Botro laughed. "Even if I'm your boss, you can still call me Botro," he said. "No need for formalities. But I'm glad to hear that. And I am excited to hear your voice! My father would take me to see qarmish troupes as a boy, and I always loved them. Qarmish music is so great."

Puk smiled. Getting back into singing after the few rough days he'd had might not be the worst thing for him.

"When do you want me to start?" he asked.

The man looked him up and down once more and said, "I can tell you're tired today, so how about tomorrow night? That'll give you time to enjoy your tea, maybe get some dinner, and relax in your room to prepare whatever you'd like to sing."

Puk nodded in agreement, and with that, Botro stood and returned to his duties managing the inn, leaving Puk alone to finish the pot of tea still steaming on the table beside him.

He poured himself a bit more, being sure to scoop in a sufficient amount of sugar, and sighed contentedly, pleased with how everything was working out.

He'd be able to afford more fire-spit soon.

- -

The night was heavy but her sleep was not. Kali's eyes flashed open with the tittering of her door's lock.

She was in bed, facing the window. A black square sprinkled with starlight.

For a moment, she wondered if she'd hallucinated, or perhaps was hearing a noise from elsewhere in the outpost, but then the sound came again. Someone was trying to break into her room.

It was not hard to predict who it might be.

Lucky for her, he was incompetent and making a racket with the lock. Kali soundlessly leapt from the bed and rummaged through her knapsack on the floor, fumbling for the antique dagger she had bought from Vonoshreb. She grinned as she wrapped a sweaty hand around the weapon's cold hilt.

Jeth was still tinkering with the door when she slid back into bed underneath her sheets. She faced the window again, feigning sleep. Ready for him.

It took almost two full minutes, but finally the door creaked open and Jeth's unsteady footsteps followed. Kali clasped her eyelids shut tight and tried to keep her breathing regular, inconspicuous.

"I know you're awake," came Jeth's raspy drawl. "Heard you doin' somethin'."

So neither she nor Jeth had been as sneaky as they'd planned. Kali swore internally but kept her eyes shut for the moment. Maybe he would fall for it. Doubt himself.

"Don't make a sound," Jeth warned her. "Make a sound, I'll have to do somethin' less than favorable. I ain't here to hurt you. I don't wanna hurt you. Just here for your shit."

She then heard a rustling and opened her eyes to spy him crouched low to the ground, going through her bag with his free hand. In the other, he held a pistol with a long barrel. It was currently half-cocked, and she wondered if it was loaded or simply for show.

Jeth looked up and saw her observing him. He grinned.

"If you scream, so does my gun," he said, nodding toward the firearm. "And I think I know which of you is louder."

Kali slowly swung her legs over the side of the bed and stood, not bothering to conceal the dagger. There wasn't much in the sack, but she didn't have much in life. What was there was a lot to her. She wasn't going to let this person take it from her.

At the sight of her dagger, Jeth chuckled and stopped his search. He grabbed the handle of the bag and stood up straight, holding his pistol farther out, fully cocking it.

"Don't need to get closer," he said. "Might be easier if I just take this whole thing, don't you think?"

"No, I do not think."

"What a shame," said Jeth. "With such a pretty face, I'd hope there's a big brain to match. But you can't win 'em all, I s'pose." He turned to leave.

She had to act fast. On instinct, she threw the dagger at the man's back.

There was a gross miscalculation and the dagger's hilt smacked into the back of Jeth's head rather than the blade stabbing into his back, but regardless of her intentions, it bought her some time.

Jeth stumbled forward, dropping the knapsack to clutch his aching head, which caused him to trip over the knapsack he had dropped and slam the front of his face into the side of the door, sending it swinging shut with a thunderous *thwump*!

Kali raced around the bed and snatched the dagger up off the ground. In front of her, Jeth was lethargically rolling from his belly onto his back, the pistol still gripped in his hand.

She swiftly stabbed the arm that held the gun, and Jeth instantly dropped it while letting out a high-pitched shriek.

In dropping the gun, his finger had squeezed the trigger and the flintlock fired, but no bullet came out. It hadn't been loaded after all.

Dipshit.

Jeth clutched at his arm, which was bleeding profusely. Globs of red gushed between his fingers and ran down his uninjured arm as well.

"You *bitch*!" he yelled.

"Yeah, yeah," she muttered, giving him a hearty whack on the chest with the dagger's hilt. He huffed out a pained moan.

The door was shoved open, hitting Jeth in the head as he lay there on the floor, and the retired Atluan Guard that Kali had spoken to earlier in the evening stood there. She absorbed the scene for a moment before barking out a hoarse laugh.

"You really laid this fucker out!" she beamed.

Kali had to laugh as well. "I guess I did," she said.

"Fuck you both!" Jeth chimed in.

The woman was still holding onto the doorknob, so she took the opportunity to swing the door into his head again. He wailed but kept his comments to himself.

After a few moments, a mustachioed man bearing an outpost uniform appeared in the doorway behind the woman and looked aghast at the mayhem before him.

"What in the world happened here?" he demanded to know.

The retiree took it upon herself to explain for Kali. "It seems this unpleasant fellow was forcing himself into the lady's room and so she laid the fucker out. Is that about right?"

Kali nodded.

Jeth decided to speak up. "Can you help me with the bleeding here?" he wheezed desperately to the employee. He got the door slammed into his head again.

"Ma'am, please, that's quite enough," said the mustachioed man, who was clearly trying to wrap his head around how to tackle this bizarre situation. He ducked into the room and helped Jeth to his feet, leading the injured man out into the hallway and down the stairs, leaving a trail of blood behind him.

"Hell of a job, kid," said the woman. The smile had not yet left her face. "The name's Beatrix." She held out her hand.

Kali took it. "Kallia," she introduced herself. "I go by Kali, usually."

"Nice to meet you, Kali," said Beatrix, retracting her hand. "I always enjoy meeting someone who can handle themselves. It fills me with glee, I must say."

Kali laughed and thanked the woman. "It was just necessity."

Beatrix nodded, her expression turning severe. "He didn't...?"

She knew what Beatrix was getting at. "No, no, thankfully not," she said. It gave her chills thinking about Jeth's flesh touching hers, even for an instant. "He was only trying to rob me."

"'Only,'" Beatrix chortled. "What a guy." She crouched down to pick up the man's gun that he had left behind. She tossed it over in her hands, inspecting it at each angle. "Not a bad gun," she said. "Back in my day, these things were a lot worse and a lot less common. But I guess someone's going to keep working on improvements so we can keep killing shit easier." She grabbed it by the barrel and held the grip out toward Kali.

She shook her head adamantly. "Oh, no, I don't want that."

"That shithead certainly doesn't need it, and I don't want him to have it," said Beatrix. "Might come in handy for you."

Kali continued to shake her head. "No, thank you. You can keep it," she insisted.

Beatrix nodded and shrugged. "Works for me. Could use it in my line of work."

"I thought you were retired," said Kali.

"Yeah, well, you know. Retirement doesn't always suit everyone." She took a step back out into the hallway and said, "I'll go fetch someone to come clean up in here so you can get back to sleep soon."

Kali thanked her again and watched as she shuffled down the stairs in search of an employee.

She was suddenly aware of how frantically her heart pounded in her chest. Its rhythm finally began to slow as she took long, steady breaths. She knelt down on the ground, avoiding the intruder's blood, and looked through her bag to ensure every item and crescent was accounted for.

Satisfied that Jeth had not made a getaway with anything, she latched the knapsack again and slid it underneath her bed. She stood back up and sat herself down to await the arrival of an outpost employee to clean up the mess for her.

Her hand still firmly gripped the dagger. She needed to wipe the blood off its blade.

CHAPTER IV

SWEET SHERI

"Look at this boy! Look how beautiful! You treat him like a prince, I can tell just by looking at him."

The stablemaster was a muscular old man by the name of Gregori, whom Kali's father had grown up with, remaining friends throughout the years. Gregori was a bit older than her father, but their childhood homes had been on the same street and they had ended up running in the same circles.

He stood watching with his hands on his hips as Kali and Bango approached. A goofy, proud grin was plastered across his wrinkled, weathered face.

Bango squeaked happily at the sight of his owner and wagged his tail wildly behind him, whacking Kali in the back and putting some pep in her step. She hurried ahead of the ayote and greeted Gregori, who wrapped her in a hug.

"Was he alright this time around?" the man asked, already knowing the answer. It was always the same.

"Of course he was," Kali smiled. "Bango is always a consummate gentleman. Aren't you, boy?" The animal had caught up and she scratched him behind his ears. His tail continued whipping around like a crazed snake.

Gregori attached the blue-dyed lead rope to Bango and began guiding him back to the stable. Kali followed, as she did every time, wanting to give Bango a proper farewell once he was housed.

Plus, Gregori usually had the best gossip waiting for her when she returned from her trips.

"So," the man started, unprompted, "have you heard the latest?"

"The latest about what?" she giggled.

"Word has it they mighta found the bones of a new aeon!" He gasped for effect, despite already knowing the news he was relaying to her. "One out in the ocean somewhere, between here and Vareda."

Kali was intrigued. And Gregori knew she was, but he never divulged the full story at once. He had to bait her, make her ask questions. It was the thrill of the gossip for him.

"How did they manage to find that? Why would someone have been at the bottom of the sea?"

"Terrible business," Gregori muttered. "A Gillusian airship was flying over the ocean—wasn't on any official trade or governmental business or anything, just a sightseeing cruise, you know how those fancy Gillusians are—and some Varedan ship shot it down."

"Pirates?"

Gregori shrugged. He pulled open the stable door and led them down the long row of stabled ayotes. Each side of the building was able to hold fifteen of the animals, and a little less than half were currently occupied. The stable's residents yipped at the arrival of Gregori.

He went on, "The ship was sporting the official military flag. That's all I've heard. Pirates are no strangers to waving false flags to trick other sailors, but things have been tense between Gillus and Vareda for a while now..."

"True," said Kali, "but attacking a ship full of socialites seems like a pretty low tactic." Her face scrunched up at the smell of dung as they passed by excited ayotes on their way to Bango's stable.

"I agree," said Gregori. "It makes a lot of sense for pirates to go after the wealthy. That's what pirates want, right? Wealth. But the thing is they shot it down and the ship crashed into the ocean, as an airship does when it's in the air, and the Varedan ship just left. Like it didn't give a dang about what it'd done."

They came to a halt at Bango's freshly-cleaned stable. The ayote gleefully waddled inside, his shell just barely slipping through the entryway. He was still growing.

Gregori unhooked the lead and Bango turned around once inside to face the stable to his left, which housed his best friend there, a female named Letty. The two yipped and yowled ecstatically at their reunion. Kali grinned, warmed to see him so happy.

But the old man wasn't done telling his story. He had a habit of being somewhat long-winded. "Anyway, regardless of whether Vareda's starting a war or not, the Gillusians managed to get the word out and contracted some people in Lyukashi to go search the wreckage for 'em. The official word was to 'seek out any survivors,' but we all know the dang Gillusians just wanted to recover whatever valuables woulda been lost on that ship."

Kali had never been to Lyukashi, and she was impressed that Gillus had been able to send a message to its residents with such haste. It was primarily a centript hive on the other side of Vanap's Peaks, opposite Yspleash, and it was fairly isolated from outsiders. But it was very close to the eastern coast and probably closest to where the ship went down, if it had gone down between Herrilock and Vareda, which lay east across the sea. Centripts' respiratory systems made them exceptionally skilled divers, able to submerge for up to three hours at a time without issue.

She had a guess as to how the rest of the story went. "So the divers swam down to find the shipwreck, and while they were down there they found the bones?"

"Exactly!" Gregori beamed. By his feet was a pail of dead, dried bugs; he snatched a handful and tossed them into Bango's stable, but the animal was too distracted by his pal to bother eating yet. "I'm not sure if they even ever found the ship. But they certainly found bones. No skull, though. Always a disappointment to not find a skull."

"Sure."

"You know what I think?" Gregori then asked.

The sun was only just starting to set, so it wasn't too late in the evening. She wanted to get home, but she could indulge her father's friend a while longer.

"No, what?"

"I think there's an aeon living under the sea still!"

Kali tried not to laugh. "Oh yeah?" she grinned. "What makes you think that?"

"Just a hunch," he shrugged. "This is only the second time we've found hard evidence of one. It seems silly to assume there aren't any alive at all in the world, right?"

"But if there were, wouldn't they have made themselves known at some point?"

"Not necessarily!" Gregori objected. "One might just be swimming along far beneath the surface, minding its own business. Having the time of its life down there, blissfully unaware of all the nonsense we're getting ourselves into up here, like some ill-conceived war with Vareda."

"If that happens, you think we'd be wrapped up in it?" Kali asked him with a frown. She hadn't really considered that prospect.

Gregori nodded. "Surely," he said. "We've been staunch allies with Gillus for years and years. Atlua, too. Any sour affair one of us gets into, the others follow, for better or worse."

"Well, let's hope it was only pirates, then," Kali sighed.

"Let's hope, my dear."

"Any other sensational or dreadful news?" she inquired.

"I've got one that fits both: I might be jumping back into the dating pool."

Kali laughed. "You say that every time I see you," she pointed out.

"Well, it's true this time!"

"You always say that, too."

"Well," Gregori chuckled, "whatever you say. I'll leave you to your goodbyes. Come back soon! The little guy misses you when you're not around. I can tell."

"Thank you, Gregori." As the old man marched away, his boots pounding imprints into the sand with each slow step, she turned to face Bango and said to him, "You don't seem so little to me."

Bango managed to tear himself away from Letty for a moment to say goodbye to Kali. She stroked his scaly head, running her hand past his beady black eyes all the way down his long, curved snout. He huffed in appreciation.

Kali found herself occupied with thoughts of war as she strolled through Seroo's Eye. She was sure it had simply been a pirate attack; there was no reason for the Varedan military to sink a civilian ship, and besides that, Gregori was an old man who'd seen a lot in his day and he was more interested in the sea bones than any impending war. It must be fine.

The city was oddly quiet. Not that it was usually raucous except during the Direlight Festival, but it seemed especially subdued. Perhaps it was just her dour mood casting a haze over the world.

She already had enough to worry about with her plans to book a ticket on a ship to Atlua without throwing pirates on top of it. They were always a concern in the back of her mind, but it had been so long since she'd heard of an attack—such a fatal one, anyway—it had felt like a distant, fantastical concern. Not anything real. She decided she would ask her father about the events once she saw him. He had always been a wise, worldly man.

In the lower half of the city, it was possible to see through the oval eyehole from anywhere you stood. As Kali navigated the streets, her feet sinking into the familiar sands of home, she occasionally glanced up and peered at the bright moon against the black canvas of the sky. It was a rare sight for the moon to be completely visible within the scope of the hole, and it felt somehow like a good omen. She had come back home to dive head-first into her journey to Atlua, and hopefully it would be a promising start in spite of Gregori's grim tale.

Home was a pretty substantial walk from the Gaze, tucked away in the streets on the southeastern edge of the skull, not too far from the bone wall that caged the city.

Her family had originally lived on the north side of town, near the Spine Gate, but moved here when she and Lissia were eight years old, roughly twenty years prior. Her father had since claimed many a time that he would die there. He and their mother were settled in for good.

When they first moved, Kali had been fascinated by the bookstore down the street. She and Lissia spent countless hours inside, leaning against walls, reading whatever they could get their hands on. At first, they had been scared of getting kicked out by the owner for reading the books without buying them, but the first time they got caught the woman laughed and assured them it was fine.

So they continued to visit every day after school, reading book after book—Kali loved reading novels, trying to find new ones with more advanced prose after each completed volume, while Lissia opted for textbooks. Whenever one of them discovered a book they were truly passionate about, their father usually bought it for them so they could read it as much as they wanted at home.

Eventually, Kali's fire dimmed, though she still enjoyed reading a good book every so often. Lissia never let up, though, and it clearly steered her in the direction of her current career as a scholar.

Maybe Lissia has some books about aeons at the Repository...

The thought was swept away as she entered her home, immediately trudging upstairs, clutching the knapsack to her side.

"Dad?" she called as she marched up the steps, growing farther from the dining room chatter. She was thankful her appetite had not yet returned. It sounded like a madhouse in there.

As she came to the top of the staircase, she nearly collided with an older woman who whipped around the corner. The woman let out a small yelp before realizing who stood before her.

"Kali!" she smiled, wrapping her arms around the girl. "Welcome home!"

"Hi, Mom," she said, squeezing tight. "Is Dad around?" She couldn't imagine anything that would've taken him away from the inn at this time of day.

Knyla Shiar pulled away from her daughter and said, "He's in Double-Six, talking to our new performer."

Kali was taken aback. She was under the impression the singer they'd hired wouldn't be arriving for another few weeks at least. "She's here already?"

"Oh, no," said Knyla, shaking her head. "Your father found someone passed out on the streets and took them in. Naturally. As it turns out, the young man is a singer, so your father offered him a temporary job to earn a little money."

"Ah."

It certainly sounded like something her father would do. Botro Shiar was the most kind, generous man she had ever met. Literally the first interaction between them was, technically, him providing her with help. He and Knyla had adopted Kali when she was two years old, abandoned by her birth parents. Since then, they had never stopped showering her with love and generosity.

On cue, over her mother's shoulder she spied her father exiting Room VI-VI (a numbering system her father had devised, which seemed convoluted to her, but it apparently worked for her parents). He slowly pulled the door closed behind him, and his eyes lit up when he realized who his wife was talking to, which only took about half a second. The swirling pastel colors of Kali's skin were impossible to mistake.

She approached him and they trapped each other in a hug. "You're back earlier than I expected," he said once they separated. "Business not too booming?"

He was a perceptive man. "Not too booming," she echoed. "That's actually something I kinda want to talk to you two about, but it can wait until tomorrow."

Botro frowned for a moment, but then put on a smile for his daughter. "I hope your trip was pleasant, at least?"

There was no reason to worry him with what had happened at the outpost, so she simply said, "Pleasant as can be."

He smiled and scratched at his protruding belly. "Very glad to hear it. Hey, our new singer is about to perform. Come downstairs and watch with us."

The three meandered down into the inn's bar, which was a relatively new addition, only built three or four years earlier. It proved to be a wise investment, as guests loved gathering there at night to drink and chat after being served dinner.

They stood off to the side of the diminutive clay stage, leaving the various tables open for their patrons. As they waited for the mystery singer to make an appearance, Kali leaned over and whispered, "Have you heard about this Gillusian airship that went down recently?"

Her father nodded. "Sunk by Vareda?"

"Yep. Gregori was telling me about it."

"Nasty business. Close to a hundred people killed, is the statistic I heard. So senseless."

"Do you think it's gonna start a war?"

Her father pondered this for a moment. Kali and her mother both watched him mull it over with anticipation.

"I'm not sure," he finally said. "I don't see any good reason why officials would attack the ship, but then again, I don't know who was on it. Perhaps someone important."

Kali's heart sank. "So you think it's possible." She did not know whether it was better or worse than a pirate attack; at least the Varedan government wouldn't have any real reason to target a ship she happened to be on.

Botro shrugged. "I think it's unlikely, but it's not outside the realm of possibility."

It reassured her, but only slightly. She tried to put it out of her mind. With her position in the world, there was no use worrying over something like that unless it actually came to fruition.

A stout fellow then entered the bar. He was a qarm, dressed in a smart suit a shade of pink that popped against his blue skin. From the expression he sported, Kali guessed he was unaccustomed to wearing such clothing and wasn't much of a fan. His eyestalks rotated wildly, taking in every detail and angle of the room.

The man ambled up onto the stage and faced the audience with his hands on his stomach. After a couple seconds, he removed them and clasped them together behind his back, leaving behind faint wet markings on the front of his suit.

"Hello," he croaked for the audience of ten or so people who had already migrated over after dinner. "My name's Puk. I'm gonna sing a couple songs for you tonight, I suppose. If that's alright with y'all."

There was a smattering of approval from the crowd.

"Well, alright," Puk muttered. Kali chuckled. "This first one's called 'Sweet Sheri.'"

The qarm cleared his throat and once again placed a sticky hand on his belly. He inhaled deeply, and then the words spilled out of him in a beautiful, surprising tenor.

"I saw her underneath the sway
Of branches twisted a hundred ways
She smiled and the leaves, they fell
And I saw her close her eyes, I pray
Sweet, sweet Sheri, sweet, sweet Sheri,
It's hard to believe, what I can see
The shade of the tree
Left me in peace, somehow."

Evidently many in the audience were familiar with the tune, because once Puk glided into the second verse, some began to sing along with him. It didn't quite seem like a pub song for others to join in on, but Puk was undeterred and even appeared to crack a smile that Kali almost missed.

There were a few more songs in his repertoire, none of which Kali had ever heard before. She wasn't sure if they were traditional qarmish songs or Puk originals, but no matter the case there was no way she would have recognized them. "Sweet Sheri" had been a solid opener, but her favorite ended up being a fast-paced tune titled "Hop Along."

When he finished, Puk thanked the audience (which had since doubled in size) for being so kind and inviting, then hopped down off the stage and approached the Shiars.

"Thank you, Botro," he said, genuine gratitude evident in his voice. "The last time I got on stage, things…well, they didn't go as well as that, let's just put it that way. It felt really good. Thanks for giving me a shot."

"You're quite welcome," said Botro. He then placed a hand on Kali's back and said, "This is my daughter, Kallia. No relation," he grinned. It was a joke he'd trotted out relentlessly over the past twenty years that somehow never grew stale to him.

"Nice to meet you, Kallia," said Puk, extending a hand.

She took it and said, "I go by Kali. I really enjoyed your performance!"

"That's very kind of you. I fucked up a few times, but I still had fun up there. It's all about fun, I guess."

"The crowd seemed to have a good time as well," Botro observed. "Would you like to sing again tomorrow night? Or wait a day?"

"Tomorrow's good, I think," said Puk. "Let's do tomorrow."

"Same time, same place," Botro grinned.

"You got it. I'm gonna go grab a drink, if that's alright. Y'all have a good night, now." The qarm nodded a farewell and ambled over to the bar, pulling himself up onto a stool.

Knyla muttered, "He sure is eager for a drink, given how little money he has…"

Kali was not surprised by her mother's pettiness. Botro said, "I told him he was allowed one free drink each night he performs, but yes, he would have to pay for any additional ones."

"Did you tell David that as well, or will he try to swindle our bartender out of extra free drinks?" Clearly her mother was not as big of a supporter as her father. Kali wondered in what state he had found the man to garner such ire.

"David is well aware," Botro assured his wife.

Knyla huffed and took her leave.

Botro then addressed Kali. "I take it you're beat after a few days of traveling. You haven't even been up to your room yet, have you?"

"Nah, but I'm feeling okay. Tired, but okay. I think I'll grab something to drink before I head upstairs for the night."

Her father hugged her and wished her a good night, then departed to carry out the various tasks required of an innkeeper.

Puk was already nursing a beer when Kali sat on the stool beside him. He turned his right eyestalk toward her, then turned it back facing forward. The bottle parted from his lips and he said, "Hello again."

"Hi. Interesting choice for a free drink. I would've thought liquor would be the best value."

"You'd be right, and perfectly in line with my tastes as well. But alas, your dad placed some limitations on my options."

"That doesn't sound like him," said Kali. The bartender, David, then asked her what she wanted, and she requested a water.

"Yeah, well, maybe he saw somethin' special in me," Puk mumbled. "I can't complain about a free beer and a paycheck, though. Not for something as simple as singing."

"Is it really that simple?" she asked him, smiling at David as he handed her a cold glass of water. She took a sip, then said, "You're very talented. I'm sure it took a lot of training."

The qarm shrugged. "I've had my fair share. There are plenty of good places to learn in Atlua."

She perked up. "You're from Atlua?"

He scoffed. "I sure as shit ain't from the desert."

Of course. Stupid question.

"Right," she mumbled, embarrassed. "I've always wanted to visit Atlua. I'm working on saving up some money to get there right now, actually."

"Me too," said Puk. "Fallen on a bit of hard times."

"Me too," Kali echoed. "Ranneth doesn't sell like it used to down here."

"What?" Puk asked before glugging more of his beer. His head faced forward, but his eyestalks were looking at her.

"Nothing," she said. "Doesn't matter." She drank from her glass and noticed that Puk had nearly finished his drink. She asked, "Where did you learn those songs you sang tonight?"

"Which one?"

"All of them, I guess."

He paused a moment to recollect. Then he said, "The first one I sang I picked up from a rocyan in a huge city called Din's Keep. You ever heard of Din's Keep?" Kali shook her head. "It's a real shithole, if you ask me, so I wouldn't recommend goin' there. But anyway, I'm what you'd call a 'heavy drinker,' so I frequented a tavern there and learned it from a fellow heavy drinker."

As if to illustrate his point, he chugged the remainder of his beer and slammed the empty bottle on the counter with a belch.

"Sorry," he apologized. "The second one—"

"'Hop Along,'" she interrupted.

"—yeah, 'Hop Along,' that one, uh…I think my dad taught me that one. When I was a kid. It's a drinking song, but ol' Doro was a heavy drinker too."

"I didn't notice it was a drinking song," Kali admitted.

Puk grinned. "It's not too obvious. There ain't anything in the lyrics about it, but yeah, it's sung by teenagers as a sort of drinking game a lot of the time. It's stupid. It'll come as no

surprise to you that I, uh…sang it a lot in my youth. Long before your time."

"I'm sure that's not true," Kali said. "I'm nearly thirty myself. Hardly a blossoming flower these days."

"I'm sixty-six."

Kali almost blurted out something rude at this revelation.
The qarm was so spritely and youthful, she would have wagered he was in his twenties, maybe early thirties. But he was
even older than her father.

"I, uh…" she stammered. "Sorry. My mom described you
as a 'young man' earlier."

Puk couldn't keep himself from laughing. "Not met too
many qarms, have y'all?" She shook her head. It wasn't often
they had qarmish visitors out in the desert. He told her, "Sixty-
six is basically middle-aged for us. So I guess I'm no blossoming flower over here neither. Just an old, busted frog."

"You look good for your age," she grinned. "You've got
my father beat, and I'm sure you've noticed the wrinkles on
him. And that bald head is not a fashion choice, by the way."

Puk rotated on his stool and promptly slapped his belly
three times, emitting three loud, wet slaps. "I'd say we're
evenly matched on paunches, though." He scooted off the rickety wooden stool and landed with a thud.

"Leaving already?"

"Yeah," he said. "A free drink is all I can afford until your
daddy pays me for my songs."

She wasn't quite ready to go to bed yet, and she was enjoying the strange qarm's company. Naturally, the inn had several
Atluan guests on any given day, but with her interest in the
country recently renewed, she was feeling giddy with the opportunity to chat with someone from there. She wanted to hear

everything she could about the place. Its geography, its food, its weather, its sights…

"I'll trade you drinks for stories about Atlua," she offered. "If it's a really good one, I'll even pony up for some liquor."

The pudgy qarm pondered her offer for only a moment before agreeing. "That sounds like a reasonable trade," he said, ambling back up onto the stool.

Kali smiled and told him, "Trades are my specialty. What'll you have?" She motioned for David to come over again.

"Just another beer," Puk said. "I don't have any really good stories about Atlua."

CHAPTER V

PAY-OUT

The next morning was a quiet one in Shiar's Slumber. Kali ate alone downstairs in the dining area, mindlessly gazing into the lobby, watching as guests checked in or out. She had finally worked up a little bit of an appetite, but still her meal was light: some mixed-fruit jam spread across thin bread. It was a typical faif breakfast, much sweeter and lighter than what many other Herrilockians preferred, her father included.

She did not spot Puk among the morning diners, and she wondered if he was nursing a hangover in his room. The two had haunted the bar for a couple hours, with Kali soaking up any tale he would provide while he soaked up any beer she would buy.

Her favorite was a story from his youth, back in a marshy village called Trillowan, wherein he and his friends had sought an abandoned house a mile or so out from town, nestled away in the woods somewhere. Rumors circulating amongst Trillowan's children indicated that the house was, of course, occupied by some type of ghoul. So Puk and his friends dared each other to enter the decrepit building and suss out the truth for themselves.

Puk, being a self-described coward, never ventured inside, but he told her that most of his friends did. One who had explored on his own ran outside screaming, claiming that he found the ghoul in an upstairs closet, withering away with its skin hanging sallow from its bones, asking the young boy for his flesh.

Such stories had never been a part of Kali's childhood. The sparse deserts of her home country gave way to other mythical terrors, like city-devouring leviathans living beneath the sands, as opposed to abandoned haunted houses on the outskirts of towns. The only buildings outside of cities in Herrilock were travelers' outposts.

"Did you believe he saw a ghoul?" Kali had asked Puk, fascinated by the town's urban myth. She couldn't recall any at all about her own hometown.

Puk nodded. "At the time, yeah, of course," he said. "But now? I dunno. I mean, I've never seen no ghoul, so maybe they exist or maybe they don't. But even if they do, that kid was always full of shit, always trying to be the most interesting one. I always talked shit about him for being an attention-seeker. And then I became a musician, so who am I to talk?"

While she consumed her petite breakfast, Kali wracked her brain for any sort of folktale about Seroo's Eye that she might regale Puk with later that night.

All that came to mind was a story she'd once heard of a giant that roamed the Gogol, towering as tall as Seroo's skull, dragging a club on the ground behind him fashioned from the trunk of a mighty oak tree. Where the giant would have found an oak tree in the desert, she had no idea. Legend had it that if you came upon the giant, who was named Daradossa, he would ask you a question (was it a riddle, or a trivia question, or your opinion on something? Kali never had clarification), and if you answered correctly, Daradossa would kneel down to the ground and extend his massive jaw, allowing you to step inside and choose a piece of treasure that he bafflingly carried around in his mouth. If you answered wrong, then naturally he would smash you with his tree trunk.

It was an absurd story, not rooted in any kind of reality or logic, but it was all she had. She was disappointed. Why did no ghouls want to haunt the myriad streets of Seroo's Eye?

Even if her childhood folktales were a disappointment, her breakfast was not. She finished eating and returned upstairs, heading down the hallway toward the back of the inn, where her family's cluster of rooms was located. Reminiscing about a fantastical desert creature reminded her that she wanted to do some minor cordol research.

During the inn's construction, three rooms had been specifically cordoned off for the Shiar family: a master bedroom for her parents, and a room each for her and her sister. The master bedroom had its own private bathroom, while Kali and Lissia's rooms were connected by one that they shared.

Having moved out years ago, the door to Lissia's room was locked so that guests could not enter, but Kali could easily access it from their shared bathroom. She slipped into her own room, which was a horrific mess, with clothes and objects scattered across the floor and on her bed and misaligned on her shelves. Wishing to further ignore all of those problems, she entered the bathroom and marched through the doorway to her sister's long-abandoned room.

Lissia had surely visited home sometime in the past year, but Kali could not recall exactly when that was. Hardly any work in the Repository was urgent, yet she liked to pretend that it was and insisted she had to spend a majority of her time there. It suited Kali just fine. She appreciated her sister's company, but it was best delivered in small doses.

If Kali's room reflected her own current mental state, then Lissia's reflected hers as well. Kali's disaster had been left behind before she shot off to Yspleash, while Lissia would never dream of leaving her room in disarray, no matter how long she was planning to be away from it.

Her bed was perfectly made, her desk was neatly organized and spotless aside from some dust that had settled in her absence, and her bookshelves—of which there were many—were all completely filled, with each book in its proper place, organized by author. It was a system that had never appealed to Kali; the comparatively few books she owned were arranged by spine color, when she bothered to arrange them.

Kali groaned at the sight of her sister's immaculate room, then approached the row of bookshelves that lined the far wall. They nudged up against the bed, positioned by the window that filtered a minimal amount of light into the room. Lamps and candles were a necessity indoors in Seroo's Eye with the small amount of sunlight that shone through the city's off-white dome.

She started with the middle bookshelf for no particular reason, scanning the rows of titles in search of the bestiary she knew Lissia owned. There was no way she had ever been aware of the volume's author, and even if she somehow had been, the knowledge had long since departed, so the shelves' organization was lost on her.

The middle shelf yielded no results, so she backtracked to the shelf at the end of the wall, closest to the locked entry door. Her eyes glazed over plain spines with unexciting titles such as a powder blue book by Avon Brahne titled *Your Canary*, which was the most dreadfully boring name she had ever heard.

She finally found what she was looking for on the bottom row of books, a volume entitled *The Desert's Wonders* by Artur S. Burosh.

It was a thick book, full of highly-detailed illustrations done by Mr. Burosh himself, which had enraptured her and her sister when they were children. Neither of them had been especially interested in the animals' descriptions or behaviors, but they loved flipping through the drawings and attempting to recreate them on their own. Glancing through the index, Kali noted that there was not an entry for giants, nor for Daradossa.

But the book *did* contain plenty of information on cordols. Kali turned to the appropriate page and first absorbed the beautiful illustration on the left-hand side.

In Burosh's illustration, the cordol was bursting out from the ground, spraying sand everywhere. Its body was wide and cylindrical, with no arms or legs, and a huge, round mouth at the front end. Rows of rounded teeth filled its mouth, more fit for grinding down cactus than rending flesh. They had two tiny eyes on either side of their mouths, which had a translucent protective eyelid covering them so that the animal could see while it burrowed through sand. The illustration was not colored, but she knew that its skin was red and leathery, with rough bristles of hair that Burosh had painstakingly detailed.

She remembered staring at the drawing endlessly as a young girl, her imagination running wild with thoughts of her riding on the back of the creature as it swam through the desert sands, diving in and out of the dunes.

Kali tore her attention away from the illustration and began to read the information on the right-side page. Some entries were more detailed than others, depending on the rarity of the creature, but cordols were relatively common, so there was a decent amount written about them.

She ran her finger down the page's text, skimming through looking for information about their migration. She found her mind once again fluttering away with childlike daydreams of riding a cordol north through the desert.

She skipped past their habitat (solely the Gogol Desert), their diet (primarily cactus, sometimes bugs), and their mating rituals (she did not want to know), then finally came to a section on their behavior.

According to the author, cordols were mostly docile animals unless they felt threatened by a predator. Most other desert animals left them well enough alone, but they were easy prey for a desert tantalus, should they unfortunately stumble upon one. The paragraph was mainly dedicated to describing their demeanor, how they raised their young, and other such things, with a sole sentence about their migration:

> At the height of the summer season, cordols gather in packs and migrate to the northern end of the Gogol, in an effort to avoid being trampled by the lamatka herds that are traveling from the mountains back to the savannah after mating season; during this time, cordols congregate between the coast and the Ribroad, where plant life is more common and predators are scarce.

So that solved that mystery.

Kali didn't know what she had been expecting, but still the answer was mildly underwhelming. They were just moving to get out of the way of something else. Going through the motions, doing it out of necessity. Nothing special pulling them to the coast.

Before putting the book away, she flipped through the pages, smiling at all the pictures she and Lissia used to obsess over. Even when Kali had begun to drift away from reading while her sister delved deeper into the literary world, *The Desert's Wonders* had been the one tome they continued to bond over.

As she slid the book back into its rightful place on the shelf, after a brief dalliance with the mischievous thought of switching it with another book, Kali inhaled deeply and considered how she would approach telling her parents she was being pulled to the coast.

She traipsed past her mess of a room again and exited back into the hallway, approaching her parents' door. Her knuckles were inches from the dark wood when it suddenly swung open and her mother stood there, wide-eyed, staring at what appeared to be her daughter readying to punch her face.

"Good morning," Knyla greeted her.

"Hi," said Kali, lowering her arm. "Are you and Dad busy?"

Her mother shook her head and then said, "Your hair looks awful."

"Okay. Well, do you have a minute to talk?"

Knyla's face scrunched up in concern. Her daughter never just wanted to talk. She could sense it was something important. She moved aside to grant Kali entry to the room.

Her parents' room was easily twice the size of her own. A perk of designing your own building was being able to determine precisely how big you wanted your living quarters to be.

The place was sparsely furnished, with no more than the bare necessities: a bed, some dressers, a single desk where they could do paperwork. A large painting hung by the window, an abstracted depiction of the moss-covered peaks of the western mountain range. It was an incredibly "Botro Shiar" piece of artwork to display. The man loved landscapes.

And the man also loved to shave. Kali could hear him in the adjoining bathroom, running the water and shaving the stubble he'd grown overnight. He used to enjoy sporting a modest beard, but lately he had taken to shaving every morning. Personally, Kali was of the opinion that a luscious beard would pair well with her father's gleaming bald head, so she often teased him for doing his damnedest to look like a baby.

"Dear! Kallia wants a word," Knyla called to him. He popped into the doorway with a patch of white foam still lathered on his left cheek.

"Good morning!" he greeted his daughter. "I'll be done in a second." He then whisked himself away again.

Knyla sat in the chair at their desk and motioned for Kali to make herself comfortable on the bed. She obliged, sitting at the foot of it, sinking down into the soft mattress and white sheets.

Her father emerged less than a minute later, his cheeks smooth and tan, and he smiled at the two women. "So, what are we all gathered here to discuss?" he asked jovially. Much less suspicious than his wife.

"Well…" she began. She couldn't place what was making her nervous about the conversation. It wasn't as if she was planning to permanently move to Atlua. She simply wanted to start traveling there for work, and perhaps in doing so finally earn enough money to strike out on her own. That was a reasonable desire for somebody to possess. Surely her parents were eager for her to finally move out of the inn and quit mooching off their hospitality.

She sighed. It would be fine. She just had to start.

"I'm wanting to travel to Atlua for a while," she finally said. "I want to try trading over there. It'll cost a bit of money, but I think I could really turn a nice profit. Don't you think they'd be interested in some of our goods? Stuff that they don't have over there, like duragas?" Her parents were perking up, nodding and smiling along to her explanation. "I could spend a few weeks or a month or two over there, and then I could come back with a bunch of Atluan stuff to sell over here. Just go back and forth, you know? I'm making okay money now, but…it really could be so much more. I could maybe finally get out of your hair."

"Oh, you're not in our hair," said Botro reassuringly.

"Your father's right. He doesn't even have any hair to be in," Knyla teased. He shot her a smirk.

Kali nodded. "I know, I know, but I feel like I am. I *want* my own place. I *want* to be more successful. I'm not quite sure yet how I'm gonna raise the money to get a ticket over there, but I'm working on it."

Her father opened his mouth to speak, and she immediately knew what he was going to say. "We'd be happy to pay for a ticket over there," he said.

"No way," she refused, shaking her head. "I appreciate it, but I really should do this on my own."

"It's really fine," said Botro. "Think of it as a loan. You can repay us when you get back."

But she shook her head again. "I'd prefer paying my own way. Thank you, though, really."

"Okay," Botro conceded. He then asked, "When are you planning on embarking on this voyage?"

"I'm not sure," she shrugged. "Like I said, I need the money first."

Botro smiled and told her, "Well, until then, we're happy to see you home."

She smiled back.

With their talk out of the way, the Shiars got to work while Kali headed downstairs and out the door. She walked through the city, smiling at others as she passed them by on their way to work, to visit friends or family, to shop, to get a bite to eat. Seroo's Eye was one of the oldest cities in Herrilock, and its population was fairly diverse, though most centripts stayed closer to the mountains or coastline and there weren't a ton of faifs, either. The skull's shielding was ideal for every other race, protecting them from the harsh sun's rays and heat, but faifs thrived on that. They quite literally needed it to live.

So while she was home, each day she'd take a walk outside the city limits to absorb some sun and relax in the peaceful quiet on the other side of Seroo's skull. This time, she exited through the Spine Gate on the northern end of the city, which was directly connected to the Ribroad that snaked through the desert all the way to Restick. The aeon's bones curved up and out of the sands, providing a good amount of shade on their own, with the spaces in between each bone covered by a leather awning stretched taut across them.

Kali stepped out from between two of the wide-set, towering bones to escape the shade and take in the invigorating sunlight. It was a particularly bright and hot day in the Gogol, and the sun was refreshing on her skin. She closed her eyes and breathed in deep. The smell of the sand was subtle, but it soothed her.

She sat down in the sand, leaning her back against the massive skull, and stretched her bare legs out in front of her to take in as much sunlight as possible. It helped fend off hunger, so combined with her breakfast, she was feeling pretty full and satisfied. She basked in the warmth.

It was nowhere near visible, but she gazed in the direction of Restick. From where she sat, the most she could see was the Ribroad bending toward the coast and disappearing into the wavering distance.

She imagined what was at the end of that road. A bustling coastal city, with its crowded docks and busy markets and the glimmering sea lapping up on the shore. Part of her had always daydreamed about living on the coast, and perhaps there was no better time than now to move there, to help facilitate her new lifestyle traveling back and forth between countries.

It had been a while since she'd last visited the sea. She shut her eyes again and dug her fingers into the hot sand, pretending she was on the beach. She inhaled again, trying to smell the saltwater tickling her feet. Waves crashing in the distance. She took another deep breath.

\- -

His first night on the job had been a piece of cake. Barely any crowd, and the people present were drunk, so they hardly gave a shit what he did up on that stage. A perfect scenario, and one that he expected would repeat each night he performed.

But his performance *after* the performance had been even better. Telling stories in exchange for free beer was probably the easiest thing Puk ever agreed to, though he might've loaded up on more than his small body could handle. He knew his limits, and he had completely ignored them.

When he awoke the next morning, well past breakfast hours, he discovered an envelope slipped underneath his door with his first payment and a short note from Botro tucked away inside explaining that he didn't want to disturb him. An explanation Puk did not particularly care about, so the note was hastily tossed in the trash and the crescents stuffed into a pocket.

He knew precisely what he wanted to spend them on.

Before he left his room, he did pause for the thought that he should set aside a bit of the money to start saving up for his trip back to Atlua, but mere seconds later he eschewed said thought and decided he could start saving with the next payment. But he was proud of himself for having the thought in the first place, and gave himself credit for that much.

After patting himself on the back, Puk puttered out of the inn with his head pounding and praised whatever gods there were for placing him in a city that blocked out the sun, because even the small amount that filtered through the bone was enough to make him dizzy. Waking up in Seroo's Eye with a hangover was becoming a habit. His father Doro would be proud.

With the Shiar's Slumber kitchens temporarily closed between breakfast and lunch hours, the first place Puk found himself was a street cart near the Gaze he and his troupe had eaten at the night they rolled into town. It was a simple joint, run by one sweaty man, which served a dish called a *fajik*, derived from the Carsuak word for "morning," *fajikiis*, which was one of perhaps three (if he was being generous) Carsuak words Puk knew.

Fajik consisted of a bread pocket stuffed with fried cactus, hard-boiled eggs, fresh peppers and onions, and a healthy drizzle of sweet and spicy red sauce he did not know the origin of, but loved. He ordered his with extra sauce and found a nearby step to sit on while he ate.

With lunch consumed, he set out to complete the next and only other task on his to-do list, another thing that would have filled the late Doro with pride: buying some fire-spit.

He sought out the orange-overalled rat-faced man from a couple days prior, but he was not in the same spot as before. Puk asked around in a few of the more run-down taverns, eventually learning the man's name was Damian, and was told where he could be found that day.

Lucky for Puk, his source was already planning on making a purchase from Damian, so he led the way. Puk followed him through twisting, unlit alleyways back toward the northwestern edge of the city. They were walking along the curve of the bone wall on a mostly-deserted street when his escort came to a stop outside of an unmarked, faded green door.

The man rapped his knuckles on the wood in a staccato pattern that Puk mentally noted, and a moment later the door creaked open. A sniveling face filled the crack.

"Hey, Markus," the man indoors said in a rasp, opening the door up all the way. His eyes then trailed down to Markus's side and narrowed to a glare at Puk. "Who's this, then?"

"A new friend," replied Markus. "He's alright. Damian'll vouch for him."

The gatekeeper remained unconvinced. "I'll let Damian do that, then," he said, closing the door again. The metallic click of a lock sounded from inside.

"I'm flattered he thinks I'm a threat," Puk joked. Markus remained silent. "The only thing I'm a threat to is a buffet line." Still nothing.

While the two stewed in his failed attempts at humor, Puk spared a glance at their surroundings. They were on the opposite side of the city from his lodgings, which filled him with relief. The last thing he wanted was Botro or any member of his family stumbling upon him here.

Based on Markus's mumblings in the pub, Puk knew they were in a district called Farrowheart. It was mostly devoted to slaughterhouses and meat production, and the scent wafting on the air certainly corroborated that fact. The entire district smelled heavily of shit and blood, which he had to admit was a solid cover-up for drug production, to mask the associated scents. Puk couldn't fathom anything cutting through what he was currently smelling.

Puk was on the cusp of foolishly asking Markus what his least favorite smell was when the greasy man swung the door open again. He shot another glare toward the qarm, then told Markus, "Damian says he's alright."

"Told you."

With that, they were allowed entry.

The den smelled better than the outdoors, but only by an inch. The air was musty, like everything was caked in sweat or grime. Puk heard the licking of a flame somewhere around a corner but couldn't detect if it was food or drugs being cooked. If it was food, it was rancid. The smell of shit was pervasive in the building as well.

The gatekeeper led Markus and Puk down the hall to a room at the back of the building with shuttered windows and bright lamps set up in each of the four corners, illuminating the pitiful proceedings.

Men and women lined the walls, slouched over with dazed looks in their eyes, if they weren't already unconscious. Most of those who were passed out had needle marks tattooing their arms, which made Puk queasy. He knew a straight injection was much more potent, but he had never been able to handle needles. He would stick to the powder, thank you very much.

Others were clearly not on fire-spit at all, and were instead rubbing a pitch-black powder on their gums. Puk had tried ash a few times but despite his affinity for powdery substances, he always found it to be either too intense or he would experience not even the tiniest buzz. Always one of two extremes, and never satisfying either way.

Words and phrases were carved into the walls around dark smears of unknown substances, the blathering of paranoid drug addicts. Insane thoughts like "The Asrani still rule" and "Seroo isn't dead" and "The jeornish are eradicating us." Utter nonsense, all of it. Puk chuckled at an etching that only said, in nearly unintelligible lettering, "Mama and Papa."

Damian, wearing his orange overalls once again (or at least Puk hoped it was "again" rather than "still"), was sat in the back of the room next to one of the lamps, leeching off its residual heat. Looking in his eyes, he appeared to be relatively clear-headed at the moment. Puk and his escort approached the man, who grinned at the sight of Markus.

"Hey there, old pal," Damian greeted the tall man. "Come for the usual?"

"Come for the usual," Markus nodded.

The dealer reached into a surprisingly clean bag propped up beside him, but didn't remove his gaze from Puk. "Way he described you was familiar," he muttered, squinting his eyes in thought. "What was it you bought, again?"

"I bought some spit off you a few days ago. Well, actually, shit—I didn't buy it, we shared some," Puk corrected.

"Ah, that's right!" said Damian. His eyes widened in faint recognition. He finally found what he was looking for in his bag and extracted a considerable pouch of ash, which he tossed to Markus.

The man inspected the goods for a brief moment and then, deeming the product worthy, handed over a large amount of crescents that Puk couldn't count before Damian stuffed them into his bag, not bothering to count them either.

"Pleasure," Markus nodded, stuffing the pouch into the inside pocket of the vest he wore.

"See you next week," Damian smiled, exposing a gap in his bottom row of teeth. While dazed on fire-spit the other day, he had told Puk about the brawl he'd gotten in a month ago that resulted in him losing the teeth. He advised not getting on a rocyan's bad side, especially taking Puk's small stature into account. As Markus departed, Damian turned his attention back toward Puk. "What can I help you with, then, new pal?"

"Same old, same old," Puk told him. "I can pay this time, though."

"That's what I like to hear."

The grubby man submerged his hands deep into his bag, shuffling trinkets and bottles and pouches around in search of Puk's fire-spit. The qarm swayed back and forth, his eyestalks rotating around to observe the others in the room, growing antsier by the second.

Damian asked him, "Can I interest you in some ash or oporist?" He held up a small jar of the orange slime, and Puk realized a lot of what was smeared on the walls was likely oporist.

"No, thanks," he shook his head. "Just the spit."

He didn't trust ingesting a substance that had to be crafted by black mages. It was perhaps the only drug he hadn't tried. Seeing that the man dealt oporist, Puk realized the rancid odor floating through the building was black mages creating it in another room.

Damian shrugged and placed the jar back in his sack, then pulled out a large container full of powdered fire-spit. "This is the kind you like, yeah?" Puk nodded, and he popped open the container. "How much you lookin' for today?"

Puk wasn't entirely sure of the man's prices, so he said, "However much twenty-five crescents can get me." Botro had paid him twenty-five for his services the night before, and he'd spent the three he'd already had on the fajik. The money was burning a hole in his pocket.

It took a minute for Damian to dole out the correct amount, which he then handed over to Puk in exchange for the twenty-five crescents. Awake for barely over two hours and he had already spent all the money he had.

"You're in for a treat," Damian grinned. Puk could see the pink flesh of his tongue in the gap of his teeth. "We just got that from our guy up in Toralas. Way better than the shit you and I were on the other day."

Puk smiled politely and said, "Great. Always glad to hear that."

He was about to make for the exit when Damian said, "You wanna hang here a while?"

In truth, the answer was no, he absolutely did not want to hang there a while. Powdered spit was a much lighter, more recreational sort of drug than its liquid form, and both were far less severe than ash or oporist. So Puk was wildly uncomfortable indulging while surrounded by the junkies propped against the walls like life-sized dolls.

But another side of the truth was that he realistically had nowhere else to go. The risk of getting caught on the street was unappealing, and he wanted to avoid getting high at the inn if at all possible so that Botro didn't throw him out.

So he said, "Sure."

The dealer was thrilled and pulled out the diminutive jar of oporist he'd offered only a minute prior. "You sure I can't tempt you?" When Puk again refused, Damian shrugged and uncorked the bottle. He dipped a finger into the viscous slime, swirling it around like he was digging in his nose, and scooped out a hefty chunk which he then began to rub across his upper lip. Most of the slime was rubbed into his skin, though some globules were caught in his wiry mustache. The oporist left behind a dull sheen on his lip, and he breathed in deep, inhaling the vapors.

Meanwhile, Puk had taken a seat on the floor beside Damian. There was no seating of any kind in the room—everybody was either sitting or lying on the floor. He was careful to avoid leaning his head or stalks on any wall stains. He lined up a bit of powder on the back of his sticky blue hand and sniffed it up with a grunt before letting out a tiny yelp. The batch really did have a bit of a kick to it.

He felt invigorated.

"Good shit, right?" Damian laughed.

For now, he couldn't form any words. He just nodded.

Damian laughed at him again.

Puk's vision doubled as he stared ahead blankly, reading words on the walls before they grew too fuzzy to make out anymore.

A jeornish woman to his left grinned at him and mumbled something that he couldn't understand, but he assumed that she was asking if she could have a hit as well, so he obliged. She gleefully took a bit of powder from him, placing it along her index finger. Puk noticed fresh Ustrel symbols etched into her arms and wondered if she was one of oporist-producing mages or merely a fellow customer.

His body tingled as he leaned back against the wall, no longer caring what nastiness his skin touched. It didn't matter anymore. Colors swirled before him and remained in his vision even when he closed his eyes, drooping his stalks downward.

He could faintly hear other voices in the room, Damian's and the jeornish woman's among them, but the syllables morphed and twisted together into white noise. Even the smell of shit and burning chemicals and blood from the slaughterhouses was beginning to fade away.

It didn't matter anymore. He breathed out, the tension in his muscles relaxing. He was at ease.

- -

The qarm's second performance was considerably livelier than the first, much to Kali and her parents' enjoyment. She supposed he was settling into the groove of things, becoming more comfortable with this type of audience.

Once again, he sang "Hop Along," encouraging those in the crowd to raise their glasses and bellow the tune with him. He wrangled many enthusiastic, tipsy participants.

Other songs on his setlist included a catchy melody about two quarreling qarmish brothers, another drinking song that one particular table was deeply invested in, and a somber tune with lyrics about watching the light through swaying tree branches and a lost love and other depressing things that brought the room down. Thankfully, he had ended on a high note—both figuratively and literally—with "Hail to the Sea," which he described as an Atluan folk song traditionally sung at the commencement of the west's spring hunt.

Afterwards, Kali congratulated Puk on another successful show and invited him to join her at the bar.

"I'd be a fool to turn that down," he said, ambling over to the same stool. She took her place as well.

He ordered his free beer and Kali asked for a glass of water.

She took a sip of hers. It was cold and refreshing on her throat. "I've been trying to think of a good story to tell you, to make up for the ones you told me."

"Have you?"

"Yep, been wracking my brain all day."

"No, I mean have you thought of one?"

She mulled it over for a second. "I thought of a few, but none are all that great. Nothing like your haunted house."

Puk gulped down a mouthful of beer and said, "You sayin' nothing interesting happens in this big, empty desert? I'm shocked."

Kali grinned and said, "The desert is actually the source of the single decent one I can think of, about a giant that travels across the dunes—"

Before she could even properly begin telling the tale, Puk interrupted her by asking, "If a giant is walking around outside, how come no one can see it? Wouldn't it be visible from, like, everywhere?" He took another swig.

"You have a point," she said. "Not much about it adds up at all. It involves answering a question the thing asks, and if you get it right, it lets you step into its mouth to take a treasure home."

"Well, see, now I'm even more confused," said Puk. "If this fucker has a gourd big enough for people to step inside, then he's gotta be *huge*, right? Let's go outside, right now. We should be able to see that giant stumbling around like a drunk in the dark, I assume."

She laughed at the image. "I think we'd both be disappointed if we went out there. Most of all, it's cold as hell right now."

"True," Puk said, then dipped his eyestalks slightly as a sort of strange nod while he drank. He swallowed, licked his lips, and said, "I'm perfectly content right here, in that case. Don't you have any stories about the city? Ain't this one of the oldest cities in the whole country?"

"Yup."

"Old as shit city and you're trying to tell me it has *no* good urban legends about it? Or even some true, nasty stuff that went down here? I gotta say, I was in the meat district earlier, and I'll be damned if someone hasn't been murdered in there and probably mixed into some sausage. Believe you me."

Kali cackled. "I really hope not," she said. "Let people be murdered, sure, but leave the sausage alone. Although, I don't eat sausage anyway, so on second thought, do what you want with your murdered bodies."

"I wonder if I've ever eaten someone while eating a sausage," said Puk, scratching his chin thoughtfully. "I've had some truly bad sausage in my day, so I bet it's possible. I'd almost call it certain."

"Well, if so, I suppose it can't be too bad for you," Kali shrugged. "You seem to be doing alright, anyway. Oh! There *is* something horrific that happened in the city, I just remembered!"

"Oh, do tell!"

"I was three or four years old when it happened, I think. So I don't actually remember it, but my dad told me about it at some point. Apparently one day, everyone woke up and found a severed head in the Gaze."

Puk nearly choked on his beer laughing. "Fuck," he sputtered. "I was not expecting that. A whole head, eh?"

"Not quite whole. It was missing its tongue and teeth."

"Damn."

"Mhmm. I'm not sure if you know how important the Gaze is to the culture of the city, but this was a *huge* scandal, even beyond the fact that someone had been murdered. Finding the killer was the guards' number one priority."

Puk's eyestalks were bobbing up and down with curiosity. He said, "Let me guess the motivation: some kind of crazy religious bullshit? Sacrificing a person to some stupid god, blah blah, ascend, all that?"

Kali shrugged, then waited for his reaction.

He waited a second. "Is that it?" he demanded. "How can a shrug be your response?"

"We don't know the motivation. The guards never found the person who did it."

His eyes widened and he removed the beer bottle from his lips. "Never?"

"Nope. It was an active case for over a year, but they never solved it. Eventually they just gave up. Called it a wash."

Puk laughed. "Wow," he said, taking a drink before he continued. "That's pretty wild. I can't imagine something like that happening in Trillowan. If someone's head showed up in the middle of town with his stalks cut off or something, no one would rest until the killer was found. Though that would partially be because half the town would be staying awake into the wee hours trying to craft the perfect song to encapsulate the tragedy and be the first to perform their masterpiece."

Kali laughed and asked, "Are people from your town really that vain?"

"Oh, yeah, most of them are," the qarm said with a smirk. "My dad Nork wasn't a singer, but he was a painter, and he was the exact same way. Always neglecting everything else in search of 'inspiration,' always saying that anyone else not 'nursing their creative energies' was wasting their life. I mean, I enjoy singing and playin' music, but he drove me fucking nuts with all that."

"I thought you said the other night your dad's name was Doro," Kali pointed out, confused.

"Yeah. Yeah, I've got four dads and a mom." Kali didn't want to be rude or prod any further, but evidently her expression betrayed her. Puk laughed and explained, "Qarms need four males and one female to reproduce, and then all five raise the kids together as a unit. My unit's a mess, honestly."

"I see," Kali said. Her knowledge gap about qarmish culture was larger than she'd realized.

"Anyway," Puk went on, "Nork was a pretentious idiot. None of my other parents liked him."

"Not even your mother?"

"Nah. He and Doro were both just necessary to the process."

"So I take it you did not inherit his endless creative drive." Only as the words escaped her mouth did she realize how insulting they might sound.

But Puk didn't seem to notice. That, or he didn't mind. "Not at all," he replied bluntly.

"Have you ever written your own music?" she asked, unsure whether anything he had sung on stage was an original.

He shook his head in reply. "Nah. I mean, yeah, a little bit, but not in a really long time. Too much work," he chuckled. "Singing songs is fun, but writing them? C'mon. That's so much time and effort that can be spent on other shit. I'll pass. I don't need that weight on me." He took one last swig of his beer and placed the empty bottle on the countertop.

"I'm sort of feeling that weight right now," Kali confessed.

"Writing a song? Don't bother. I'll teach you some easy ones," Puk teased.

Kali smiled. "I appreciate that," she said. "But no, just...I'm a merchant. Or at least trying to be one. I've had *some* success trading back and forth between cities here, but not enough to really branch out on my own. As you can surely tell, given that I live in my parents' inn."

"What's the weight on you, then?"

She sighed, then gulped down some water. "Well," she started, "it's actually sorta simple, which is part of why it annoys me that I'm so stressed out about it. But I'm trying to save up enough money to book a boat out of Restick and travel to

Atlua, to sell some foreign goods there and then buy some to bring back and sell here."

The qarm's eyestalks appeared to perk up at the mention of Restick and Atlua.

"You and I are in similar figurative boats," he said.

"Oh, yeah?"

"Yep. And maybe the same literal boat, eventually," he said. "I took this job so that I could save up enough for the same exact thing: get to Restick, then get to Atlua. I'm ready to be home. Fuck this desert."

"I love this desert, but right now I'm kinda right there with you: fuck it," she grinned.

Puk rolled the base of the bottle along the counter. She hadn't offered to buy him more drinks, and didn't want to spend what money she had left on doing so anyway. It seemed he didn't have crescents to spare to buy himself another.

"So, how do you plan on earnin' your boat ticket?" he finally asked her, setting the bottle down flat on the bar.

She shrugged. "Nothing specific planned. Just by trading, I guess." She downed the remainder of her water. Then she asked him, "How are you earning yours?"

He shrugged as well. "Oh, you know," he said. "Just singin', I guess."

Kali began rolling the base of her glass along the counter-top too. David was bartending again, but he was currently preoccupied with another patron. She could tell the conversation was probably winding down anyway.

She asked Puk, "Do you think we'll be able to pull it off with just that?"

He peered into the long neck of his bottle, watching the amber remnants of liquid slosh back and forth. Kali could tell he was giving her question some serious thought. She had meant for it to be somewhat lighthearted.

"You know," he said, "based on my experience, I'm not especially hopeful."

- -

The stash of fire-spit Puk purchased was already depleted, so he found himself once again trudging through Farrowheart District in search of the faded green door.

Without Markus as a guide, it took him a bit longer than he anticipated, but finally he located it and gave the door the same rhythmic knock he'd memorized Markus doing.

The greasy gatekeeper pried open the door a sliver to see who had come knocking. Recognizing Puk—possibly the only qarm who had ever entered this building before—he pulled the door open all the way and welcomed him.

Inside, the scene was much the same as it had been a couple days earlier. The atrocious stench still stifled the air, threatening to choke him. He could hear murmurs from the back room and mages cooking oporist in the side rooms.

Puk walked down the hall toward the den, where he was surprised to find that it was less of a shit-show than before. Junkies were no longer lining the walls like cheap furniture, and in fact there were no junkies at all to be found.

A table had been set up in the center of the room, and some form of gambling was taking place. The men were playing cards, but Puk didn't recognize the game. It definitely wasn't Hunt, but regardless of the game, he was smart enough to not get involved this time around.

What he did recognize, though, was one of the players: it was the red-haired man he had played Hunt with, Randolph.

The man looked up from his hand to see who had entered the room, and he grinned at the sight of the qarm. "Look who it is!" he roared, placing his cards face-down on the table. "If it ain't my brethren Puk!"

He waved meekly at the man, then tried shuffling over to the side of the room where Damian was sat cross-legged with his drug bag in his lap, but Randolph insisted he join them for a moment.

Puk approached the group of burly men and muttered, "I really can't play. I appreciate the offer, but I'm sure I can't afford the buy-in, and I don't even know what this is."

Randolph guffawed. "As much as I'd love to take your money again, I'm in no mood to teach you another game." He picked his cards up and read them over again as he said, "If I'm honest, I'm a bit shocked to see you're still alive and kickin'. You looked proper fucked when you left the Tilted Tailbone."

"I was," said Puk. "I'm here looking to get proper fucked again. Though not by you, this time."

The quip earned another hearty holler from Randolph. The man was larger than life, his voice carrying throughout the whole building. Having thoroughly assessed his cards, he pushed twenty crescents into the pot piled up in the center of the table. Puk wished he had money to throw around like that.

"Well, it's good seeing you, brethren," Randolph said, motioning for the man to his left to play. "If you ever feel up to hunting again, find me in the Tailbone. I'm there most nights."

"You've got it," Puk nodded, intending never to return to the Tilted Tailbone or play Hunt ever again in his life.

With that awkward reunion out of the way, he walked over to Damian, who sat waiting patiently for him.

"Welcome back."

"Thanks," Puk mumbled. He felt like he was being watched now, even though Randolph had already slipped back into loud conversation with his fellow gamblers.

"How much this time?" Damian asked. "That last pouch didn't seem to last you long, eh?"

"It did not," Puk admitted. He'd gone through a lot of it during late nights after talking to Kali at the Slumber's bar. Despite those late nights, he'd been diligent about waking up early enough to feast on the inn's breakfast spread so that he wouldn't have to spend his own money out buying food. He had also begun saving up for his trip, though he could admit to himself that he wasn't doing as good a job in that department as he should. "Twenty crescents worth will do me this time, I think."

Damian nodded and reached into his trusty bag.

While he did so, Puk tried to make light conversation. "Pretty empty in here. Had a full house the other day, huh?"

Damian grunted in the affirmative.

"What's the deal today?" Puk asked. "Some special event goin' on?" He jutted a thumb over his shoulder at the group playing cards.

"They meet here once a month for their game," Damian replied, pulling his big container of fire-spit from the bag. "Couple of bigshots from all around. Think a few are black market dealers, one's a mercenary, one's a banker—not sure about the rest." He measured out the appropriate amount of spit and poured it into a smaller pouch for Puk.

He took the pouch and thanked Damian, but hesitated leaving. The dealer knew what was on his mind.

"Not in this room. Go back in the hall, first door on your left. That's where I'm headed in a minute anyway. You caught me packing my bag back up after getting these fellas situated."

Puk nodded and thanked him again, then ducked out of the room before Randolph could holler anything else at him. He entered through the doorway Damian had indicated, and inside he discovered the scene he had been expecting, though on a smaller scale. Only a few users were milling about, one or two ashers and a guy who had rubbed so much oporist on his lip it had barely absorbed into his skin and was dribbling down his face as if he were a drooling baby.

Slumped down near the doorway, Puk could still hear Randolph's voice booming through the hall. He hadn't been paying attention to the start of the conversation while he held his own with Damian, but whatever it was the men were discussing, it had intrigued them.

"It seems like a waste of fuckin' time to me," Randolph said.

"How is it a waste? Do you need to be reminded of the pay-out?" asked an incredulous second voice.

A third chimed in with, "Ten thousand crescents is nothing special. I see that type of money thrown around every day." Probably the banker, if Damian's intelligence was to be trusted.

"Ten thousand is great, before you count all the expenses!" Randolph shouted. "First, getting into Myrisih to accept the contract if you can even figure out their stupid-ass schedule, then hiring a crew for the job, then traveling to fuck-knows-where for it, then traveling all the way back. The pay-out's gotta be a bit more than that to make a job worthwhile for me these days. Expenses aside, I'm sick of traveling! If I'm hauling my lazy ass outta the Eye, it's gotta be worth a lot."

The second voice said, "Well, you might have a point. But ain't you a *little* curious 'bout that book? What kind of book is worth ten thousand crescents?"

"Probably a thick one that I'd have to lug across the desert after I found it," Randolph snorted. "All the more reason not to take the job!"

The gruff men soon changed the subject, having all agreed that the pay-out was not worth the hassle and costs, but Puk's mind was racing with possibilities.

The line of powder on his hand had gotten wet from the moisture of his skin. Ruined. He wiped it away and thought about what the men had said, and then he recalled his conversation with Kali Shiar the night before.

Ten thousand crescents was a mighty appealing pay-out, even split two ways. Myrisih wasn't exactly easy to get into, but Puk had been there a few times and knew somebody in Restick who could take them there. If he and Kali both needed to get to Restick anyway...

The bounty wasn't a particularly huge amount to split amongst a regular crew, so it was entirely possible that not many would take up the job. He had just spent the past few minutes listening to several arguments for why it was a shitty job to take.

It might be the perfect opportunity for him and Kali.

From the sounds of it, all they'd have to do is find some book, then bring it back to Myrisih, get paid, and be on their way back to Atlua with five thousand crescents each.

A worthy sum. Plenty of money for Kali to start a new life with, and plenty for him to do with as he pleased.

It seemed easy enough. Even if the book was super thick and heavy.

Surprising himself, he hopped up off the ground without snorting a new line and darted out the door to find Kali.

- -

Kali had spent the past half hour reading Lissia's textbook on Carsuak in a meager attempt to reacquaint herself with the language. No part of her believed she would ever be as fluent as her sister, but she felt some motivation to gain a better understanding.

It was a small yet thick book, as if it were originally intended as a guidebook for one to easily carry around on their travels and refer to, but the author got carried away and went too in-depth. It was entirely impractical. But it was evidently a useful teaching tool, seeing as Lissia was required by her job to converse with elder centripts who only spoke the language.

The book was proving to be a good refresher on what she previously knew, though she was stumbling a bit. She was reading the section on verb conjugation and getting an increasingly worse headache when a knock at the bedroom door interrupted her concentration.

Kali stood from her desk littered with scrawled notes, an empty cup, and the textbook, which flipped shut with a *thwump* the moment she removed her hand from it. She took a second to make sure she was wearing something presentable, then scurried over to the door.

On the other side was Puk. The qarm was probably somewhere near the bottom of a list of individuals she would have expected to find standing in her doorway.

"Oh, hey," she said.

"You busy?"

"Not especially. Just studying Carsuak."

"Why?"

"So that I know how to speak it."

"Why?"

"To communicate with other people."

"Why?"

"Do you need something?" she asked him, cutting off the inane line of questioning.

He nodded, then asked, "Can I come in?"

She stepped aside and the short man waddled in, twisting his eyestalks in every direction to absorb the room.

"Wow," he muttered. "Your room is as messy as mine. Which is a bad thing."

She rolled her eyes but had no rebuttal. Closing the door, she asked him, "What do you need?" She didn't know what time it was, but she knew there were still a few hours until his performance.

Puk pulled the chair out farther from her desk and hoisted himself up onto it. His stubby legs dangled a few inches from the ground.

"I've got a business proposition for you," he said. His mouth stretched to a toothy grin.

Her interest was piqued. "What kind of proposition?" Given his defeatist attitude over the course of the week, she was surprised he had any sort of financial prospects at all beyond what her father was paying him.

"The kind of proposition that'll net us each five thousand crescents. Does that sound good?"

Her heart leapt.

Five thousand was a big number. Big enough to get her to Atlua. Hell, it was big enough to get her all the way to Vareda if she felt so inclined. The possibilities for her life seemed endless with that kind of money.

But how was this broke, alcoholic lounge singer kicking his feet in front of her planning to get his hands on money like that?

"That's a lot of crescents," she said with some apprehension.

"It is."

"Honestly, it sounds like an illegal amount of crescents."

The smile on his face curled into a grimace. His stalks curved backward then shot straight back up. "Well, it's probably not strictly *legal*, but it's probably not especially *illegal*, either."

Her heart sank.

And yet…it was a lot of money. She could accomplish a lot with it. Finally kick things off in her life.

"What is it?" she asked, betraying the sinking feeling in her gut.

The qarm's rapscallion grin returned. "Have you ever heard of Myrisih?"

She nodded, though it only felt like a half-truth. Being a merchant, she had heard plenty of stories about a black market city in the gulf called Myrisih. Rumors claimed that it was hidden somewhere in the Loranos Gulf, a city-sized marketplace solely for trading illegal goods, exotic animals, hiring assassins, and other illicit activities. Some stated that there were officials who knew where to find the city, but due to it being in the gulf, it was in nobody's jurisdiction so it was left alone. It all sounded too absurd to be believable.

"Well, there's a job in Myrisih that I think you and I would be perfect for."

The statement was outrageous.

"Why would you think I'm perfect for some illegal, shady job? And how are you even sure Myrisih is real?"

Puk blinked. His expression read as if her question was asinine.

"I've been to Myrisih," he said. "So I'm pretty sure it's real."

It was her turn to blink incredulously. "How in the world have you been to Myrisih?"

"I'm not friends with good people!" he barked. "Look, you're missing the point. The point is I heard about a job in Myrisih and it sounds like an easy one. So easy, it's putting off the bigger crews 'cause the pay isn't big enough for 'em all to split—but I'd bet some smaller groups will be sniffin' around, so we probably wanna get there quick as we can."

Kali cocked an eyebrow, still taken aback by the whole thing. Puk was not the most convincing orator.

"How'd you happen to hear about it?"

He grew visibly uncomfortable at the question and shifted in his seat. "Like I said, I'm not friends with good people."

That answer would have to suffice. "Fine. So what's the job, then?"

Once again, he seemed more at ease. He explained, "Apparently there's some book that somebody in Myrisih wants to get their hands on, and they're willing to pay a shitload for it."

"What book is it? My sister has a ton of bookshelves in her room, all totally filled."

Puk laughed, a wet, throaty sound, and said, "I don't know what book it is, but I'd wager this buyer isn't shellin' out ten thousand crescents for something he could find in the local marketplace."

"Fair enough," she said, feeling foolish for having even suggested it. Then, "What would be your plan, then? Assuming I agree to this?"

"Simple. We gotta get to Myrisih as fast as we can to accept the job. I dunno if they're gonna be taking on multiple crews and then paying whoever succeeds or if they're just gonna hire one, which is why we should try to get there before anyone else. Hopefully no one who's already there is showing any interest in it. I've got a friend in Restick who can get us to Myrisih. I'm not sure who the contractor is, but I know a guy there named Voya who's well-connected and can maybe arrange a meeting for us." He paused a second, then added, "There *is* one hitch, though."

"And what is that?"

Puk sighed. "This buddy of mine—Voya—we didn't exactly part on the best of terms the last time we saw each other."

Kali's interest was piqued yet again. She grinned and nodded for him to continue on.

"We were both on a boat. I hadn't seen him in a while and had no idea he was gonna be there. I still owed him money for—uh, stuff that I had bought from him, and he wanted me to pay."

"Of course," Kali said. Why would a merchant not want to be paid for their products? Though she had to briefly wonder what Puk would have been buying from a black market trader, but she decided to let that question slide for now.

"Right. Totally reasonable. But I did not have sufficient funds at the time, and so, uh…well, the guy's an ujath, so he's pretty top-heavy. I sorta just panicked and pushed him over the side of the boat."

"What the fuck?" she blurted out.

"I know! I know! It was not my best moment, I admit that. I feel terrible about it. Well, maybe not terrible, the guy is kind of an ass—but the point is I did not pay him what I owed, I pushed him out of a boat, and given the bulky satchel he was carrying, I'm pretty sure he had a bunch of shit in there that I ruined by submerging it in the ocean."

She could not comprehend how the innocent-looking qarm before her seemed to continually get himself into such ridiculous situations. She asked, "Was this a long time ago? Do you think maybe he's cooled off about the whole thing?"

"This was a couple weeks ago when I was coming to Herrilock."

"Well—"

"Yeah. Not great. But I have an idea about how to pay him back! It'll be a little tricky, but worth it to get those ten thousand crescents."

She waited to hear him out.

"I know the type of shit Voya's into. If we can snatch some cordol eggs and bring them to him before they hatch, I'm sure all will be forgiven. He traffics in a lot of fire-spit, so having his own cordols to gather the spit from would cut down on a lot of costs for him. He'd be thrilled. I assume."

Everything Puk had told her was already a bit shaky, and now aiding a drug dealer on top of it all was pushing Kali nearer to the edge. She was uneasy.

"So, let me lay this all out there: your plan is for us to find cordol eggs, bring them to your friend—which seems to be a very loose term in this context—in exchange for more information about this job. And then we'll take the info, go find the book wherever the hell it is, and get paid?"

"Exactly," said Puk. "Told you it was simple."

Aside from tracking down cordol eggs, it honestly did not sound like an overly complicated plan, though she still didn't feel totally right about stealing the eggs.

But five thousand crescents...

"If it's so simple, why do you need me to help?" she asked him.

"Well, that's simple too," he said. "I'm just a dumb little qarm. I am not equipped to handle the desert, not like you. Even aside from being a faif, you've just got more skills and experience. I would probably dehydrate and die halfway down the Ribroad on my own. Plus, you've got more money than me."

"So you need my money."

"I mean, yeah, for some stuff. Food, travel, whatever. It'd be an investment. A beautiful investment opportunity with a return of five thousand crescents. Can't beat that."

Another fair point. In the scheme of things, the amount she would have to cough up to feed Puk and get them where they needed to go would pale in comparison to the payment they'd receive for locating the mysterious book.

She said, "I don't feel great about the egg part of this plan."

"I don't feel great about anything most of the time."

"That's not reassuring."

"It is what it is."

Over Puk's shoulder, she glimpsed the Carsuak textbook she'd taken from her sister's book collection. She said, "The other day I actually read about where cordols migrate during

the summer. I saw a pack when I was coming back from Yspleash, so I guess they're there by now."

"Great!" Puk beamed. "It's all comin' together. I told you
we were the perfect team for this job."

She smiled weakly, still unsure deep down.

But she wanted that money.

"When do you think we should leave?" she asked.

"Tomorrow," Puk answered. "That should give you enough
time to gather up any funds we'd need and we can buy some
supplies in the morning. And I can also sing tonight so I can
grab another twenty-five crescents from your daddy before we
go."

"Okay. How much money will you be able to contribute,
then?"

"About thirty-five crescents."

She laughed, thinking for a moment that maybe she was a
complete fool for agreeing to this scheme. But the reward was
so enticing, and this crazy qarm was so confident in the plan.

"Alright," she said. "Let's do it."

CHAPTER VI

WARMTH

An important part of Puk's plan hinged on the assumption that his old friend Voya had managed to swim ashore and then make it back to his home in Myrisih, rather than drowning in the Loranos Gulf.

They had only embarked an hour prior before he knocked him overboard, right? Surely they were close enough to the coast for him to make it back and get on another ship?

He would know soon enough whether Voya had made it home or not.

They had not stayed up at the bar drinking and sharing stories after his energetic performance the night before. Hatching the plan with Kali before he went on stage had filled him with a sort of excited anxiousness, and he had practically bounced around the red clay stage while he sang.

Afterwards, he had to break the news to Botro that he would be cutting his residency at Shiar's Slumber short. He told the man he truly appreciated all his generosity, but it was time for him to hit the road. Botro, as always, completely understood and happily handed over his final payment.

In the morning (after a deep, restful fire-spit sleep), Puk met Kali in the lobby to commence their shopping trip before departing later that afternoon.

She was already waiting for him as he descended the staircase, and for a second he wondered if he was late, which admittedly was more likely than not. She wore a thin, white sleeveless shirt and baggy white pants cuffed around her ankles. Her hair was pulled up in a high ponytail, which swatted at invisible flies as she swung her head to face him.

"Got your shopping list ready?" she asked him with a smirk as he trundled down the stairs.

"No," he answered dryly. "You will come to learn that I am an idiot, and I do not know what we need." The only thing on his mental list was some more fire-spit, but he would fetch that on his own when Kali went to procure their travel funds.

"You'll come to learn that faifs have vastly different needs in the desert than qarms, so I don't know what you need either. Might wanna think on it while we walk."

"Noted."

Their first stop was what Kali described as a "one-stop shop for travelers," a modest-sized adobe storefront situated in the market square surrounding the Gaze. It was a squat building, its neighbors looming high above it on either side, and there were some visible but minor cracks in its façade. The place was obviously old, surely a staple of the marketplace.

Its owner, an ancient, hunched faif woman with dark yellow skin streaked with blue, greeted them as they walked through the front door. There were several others browsing the shelves, preparing for their own journeys out of the city.

"Am I wrong in assuming you need a lot of water?" Kali asked him, immediately navigating around the corner, her destination locked in.

"Nope," said Puk, shuddering at the memory of his dehydrated, drug-fueled performance that got him kicked out of The Rusty Halberd.

"Me too. I get by with just water and sunlight."

She led him to a shelf lined with waterskins of various sizes, shapes, and colors. A majority were tan and shaped like the animal bladder from which they were crafted, but a few had been dyed flashy colors such as purple or red, acting more as accessories than survival tools.

Kali scanned the shelf for a moment, then held up a large, brown waterskin the size of Puk's head. It had been made from a hollion bladder and looked like it could keep his thirst quenched for a long while.

"This is the one I use," she said, tossing him the limp container. He fumbled but caught it, its surface smooth and satisfying to the touch. She went on, "It can hold a lot of water. Usually enough to last me an entire day of travel, then I can fill up again at an outpost. Think it'll work for you?"

He nodded and replied, "It looks like it can hold my weight in water, so it should be fine." He slung the waterskin over his narrow shoulder, where it clung to his sticky skin.

Next on the list were some boots for Puk. He had sandals, which kept his feet cool in the heat and were fine for wagon travel, but if they were hiking, he'd need something more durable that would also protect the soles of his feet from the hot sand.

While they browsed footwear, Puk asked why they weren't riding in a wagon or renting ayotes. When Kali then asked if he knew how to properly ride an ayote, he said no, so that idea was promptly shut down. Then she told him that generally wagon trips were booked from city to city, but their destination wasn't actually Restick yet, and that they'd be venturing out from the Ribroad's shade and into the open desert. It would be less of a hassle in the end to make the trek on foot rather than going all the way to Restick and backtracking.

So Puk chose a mundane pair of boots, the cheapest available that were still good enough quality for Kali's approval, and resigned himself to the terrible reality of hiking down the Ribroad on foot. It would take days to reach Restick at the end of the road. He sometimes grew winded mounting two flights of stairs.

They then came to the food section. Everything in the store was specially suited for travel, and the food section was no different. Nothing was substantial or appealing to Puk on any shelf. There was an assortment of dried fruits, unsalted nuts, and—the last thing Puk noticed, which actually did sound appetizing to him—dried meat marinated in a sticky, sweet sauce.

But Kali caught him eyeing the latter and said, "Stick to the fruits and nuts."

"Those ain't gonna do it for me," Puk complained. "That meat will, though."

"The meat is for faifs," Kali explained, just as patient as her father. "The marinade contains a lot of sugar, which we need. Sugar that I'd recommend you avoid out there. The nuts and fruit will keep you energized without weighing you down or making you thirstier than you'll already be. You can have full meals at the outposts; these are just to get you through the day." She grabbed a small pack of the meat for herself. "I'll need some in a few days. Stock up on what you want."

He sighed. The meat looked delicious, and hearing that the sauce was filled with sugar made him want it even more, but he would acquiesce to Kali's experience and advice. Though he would try his hardest to convince her to share some on the road.

Puk stuffed the sealed pouches of nuts and dried fruits into the boots and followed Kali to yet another section of the store. Despite her earlier snarky retort about not knowing what supplies he needed, she sure seemed to have everything in mind.

As they slid past other shoppers, Kali asked, "You have a bag, right? Or a backpack?"

"Yeah."

"Good." She veered to the left, and he followed.

They came to a stop in front of a mass of white clothing hanging from racks. Kali frowned and placed her hands on her hips.

"I'm…not sure they'll have anything in your size, actually."

Puk was used to places in Herrilock not being especially accommodating for his kind. He didn't take it personally at all; he didn't blame his fellow qarms for not frequenting the desert. He wanted to get the hell out of there as soon as possible anyway.

He said, "The clothes I've got should be fine." Just to be sure, he closely looked over the types of clothing the store offered, and deemed them unnecessary for him. "We can adapt well in the hot and cold. I need a lot of water, and I personally really don't care for the heat, but it won't ruin me."

"Your skin doesn't burn in the sun?"

Puk shook his head. "I've got long-sleeved shirts anyways. And yes, before you ask, the material's thin. I won't overheat."

Kali nodded, satisfied with his response. Granted, he had only ever traveled by wagon in Herrilock, so he hoped he wasn't overestimating his own capabilities. He'd let her know later that if he passed out and died, she shouldn't feel guilty leaving his body to rot.

With the clothing eschewed, Kali said, "I think that's all we need here," and proceeded to pay the elderly faif, who smiled crookedly as they approached her counter.

The whole haul was kindly paid for by Kali, and they stepped back outside into the bustling market square with their arms full.

"What's next on the docket?" Puk asked, blissfully ignorant about any preparations they needed. He was along for the ride.

"There's a food stall nearby that I think we should visit to grab you a few more things, but then we'll probably be good after that. I can go get the rest of the money we'll need while you finish packing up at the inn."

It was a short walk to the stall Kali had in mind, where they bought a greater variety of unsalted nuts ("You'll be thankful to have options," she told him), as well as a selection of fresh fruits that she insisted would help keep him hydrated and offer some natural sugars. She also advised he eat them relatively early in the journey before they spoiled in the extreme heat.

They agreed to meet back at Shiar's Slumber in an hour, which did not give Puk a huge window to get to Farrowheart District and back while still packing his belongings in time. He kicked himself for not being proactive and getting everything ready the night before, but that was never really his style. The thought hadn't even occurred to him.

Once Kali was out of sight, he raced toward the western side of the city, his newly-obtained possessions bouncing wildly in the small, poorly-made complimentary sack the old faif woman had given him to carry everything in.

By now Puk had memorized the fastest route to Damian's den, and he was at the green door in no time at all, giving the secret knock which might have just been how Markus normally knocked and did not hold any sort of secret meaning at all.

Whichever the case, the gatekeeper let him inside, but Damian had unfortunate news for him.

"I'm out right now," he told Puk with an apathetic shrug. "Got plenty of other shit you'd like, though." He was wearing his signature orange overalls and smelled mustier than ever.

The two stood in the hallway while they talked. Out of the corner of his eye, Puk could see black mages in adjoining rooms casting Fire and Bio spells, crafting more oporist. There had to be a large swath of people in the city using it to justify how much they were cranking out all week.

Puk's eyestalks dipped. "I don't want any ope," he sighed. He also declined Damian's offer of ash, even though the discount he added on was slightly tempting. Puk left the den empty-handed, frustrated, and wondering if he had time to find a dealer on the street with any supply left. The spit he had back in his room would last another day or two, but definitely not long enough to make it all the way to Restick.

Do dealers stay at travelers' outposts?

He pondered the notion as he wallowed through the streets of the slaughterhouse district, the acrid stench of raw meat assaulting his nostrils. On his left was a row of shops including butchers, taxidermists, and at the end of the street, a hunting supply store.

The sight of the store sparked a thought in him, causing him to recall the game of Hunt he'd played with Randolph when he'd lost all of his money.

The bait card he'd tried to play was ineffective on lamatkas, which led to him losing said money, but Randolph had mentioned off-handedly it would've worked if their target was a cordol.

Well, his target was a cordol now.

Puk ducked into the empty store and headed for the bait section, trying to appear as if he knew what he was searching for despite never having gone on a hunt of any kind in all his life.

The shopkeeper, a centript man with a few carapace segments missing, easily noticed how lost he was.

"What needed?" he asked.

"Uh…" Puk desperately searched for real terminology, but had to rely on the Hunt card. "I need 'smelly bait,'" he said, embarrassed.

Clearly Carsuak was the man's first language, and Puk watched as he tried to wrap his mind around what was meant by "smelly bait." Pondering the phrase for a moment, the centript then scuttled over to where Puk stood and snatched up a tightly-sealed pouch with the words "Bor Sludge" embroidered on its front.

"Import from Gillus. Very bad smell," said the centript.

"Will this help catch a cordol?" Puk asked.

"Very bad smell," the shopkeeper nodded.

Puk wasn't sure if he totally understood, but he had to rely on the man's expertise, and handed over the crescents for the pouch of dried sludge.

Once back on the street, Puk pulled the opening of the pouch loose and a rancid smell escaped, sending him into a hacking cough. Spittle soaked into the pouch as he tightened it back up, double-knotting the string keeping it closed.

"Fuck me," he gurgled, heading back toward the inn.

He was definitely feeling more confident in the quality of his smelly bait.

- -

The bank clerk gave Kali an unsure look when she requested to withdraw more than half her entire savings, and if she was being honest, she felt somewhat unsure herself.

She still wasn't totally okay with helping a drug dealer, and now with the knowledge that Puk had dealings with the man in the past, she was less trusting in her companion. Though he had been amiable and good-natured in the week she'd known him; perhaps all that behavior was in his past. He had turned over a new leaf.

Plus, there was a part of her that was intrigued by the prospect of seeing Myrisih in person. She wanted nothing to do with any of its back-channel trades—after she completed this book job, anyway—but she was fascinated by the hidden city's existence, and there was no telling if she would ever get another opportunity to see it.

Counting the slips of paper and engraved metal coins, three hundred crescents in total, Kali considered how foolish it was investing so much of her own funds into the trip. The return would be vast if they successfully collected the bounty on the book, and Puk exuded confidence in their abilities, but still doubt danced on the edges of her mind.

The amount was correct, so she stored the crescents in an inner pocket of her knapsack and started back toward the inn.

Much to her surprise, the receptionist at the front desk informed her that Puk had already returned and was upstairs preparing to leave. She had taken the time to pack her things the night before, so she took these last few minutes to find her parents and say her goodbyes.

It was mid-morning, so she knew her father would be in the master bedroom drinking a cup of coffee and either reading over various workplace documents or his current novel. He had been a voracious reader in his youth, just like his daughters, but ever since founding the inn, he'd had less time to indulge and snuck in a few minutes of reading whenever he could spare.

As expected, Kali found him hunched over his desk, with her mother standing nearby. They were examining an expense sheet she had written up, discussing the quantities of meat and vegetables they should order from the grocer the following day.

She was greeted with warm smiles as she entered the room. Knyla said, "Heading out now, I suppose."

Kali nodded. "You suppose right."

Her parents tabled their discussion and stood to wrap Kali in a tight embrace. She squirmed and struggled to free her arms from underneath their bodies to reciprocate the hug.

After they split apart, Knyla's face turned serious. "You'll be careful, right?"

"I wasn't planning on it, but if you want me to be careful, then sure," Kali joked.

It usually wasn't such a big deal when she left on her frequent trips across the country. The only thing different about this one was the length of time she'd be gone. She had made sure to tidy up her room before departing.

Of course she had not mentioned any of the side-journeys she and Puk were taking: no cordol hunt, no Myrisih, no scavenger hunt. But traveling to another country for the first time in her life was a big enough deal for them to express a smothering amount of parental concern.

When detailing her trip, she had told them she would be traveling with Puk, which caused a great deal of confusion. Ultimately it had given her mother some small comfort, knowing her daughter's companion was an Atluan who had made the journey before, despite her previous reservations about him.

It was her father's turn to be serious. He looked her in the eye and said, "Remember that you can always come back here when you need to." His eyes implied *if you can't make it to Atlua, just come back.*

She hoped it wouldn't come to that.

If she blew all of her money and didn't end up in Atlua, then her dreams would be well and truly dead.

"I know, Dad," she smiled, pushing the thought of failure from her mind. Dwelling on it would be of no help.

They spoke for a few minutes more about the route she was taking (the Ribroad, of course); which Atluan town she'd sail to (whichever had the cheapest tickets in Restick, of course); and if she needed any extra money (she could handle herself, of course). Soon, her parents needed to get back to work, and it was time for Kali to meet Puk downstairs.

Her heart swelled with one last hug from her parents. She had already been planning on living away from them, on spending most of her days traveling, but only now was the reality of it setting in. She was going to miss them.

"Thank you," she told them. She hoped they knew the two words encompassed a lifetime of gratitude, for everything they'd done. Every kindness they'd granted her. Every bit of aid, every opportunity. For her room just a few feet away that she knew would always be waiting for her when she came back, the key tucked away safely in her bag.

Botro and Knyla each planted a kiss on her cheeks and told Kali they loved her and would miss her.

"I'll be back before you know it," she promised them. "You won't even have time to miss me. Not *too* much, anyway." She grinned.

They then returned to the drudgery of ordering ingredients, and she grabbed her knapsack from her bedroom and locked the door behind her.

Downstairs, Puk leaned against a wall waiting for her. He was wearing his new, clean boots, which provided him with an extra half-inch or so. His backpack, which was sized to strap to the back of a short qarmish body, looked positively stuffed after their morning shopping trip.

"How'd you fit everything in there?" she asked, pointing at the stained bag. It was obvious the bag had seen many adventures.

"With great effort and trouble," was his reply. "I almost ate one of the apples just so I wouldn't have to pack it, but then I managed to squeeze it in somehow. Though I might've crushed an orange in the process. We shall see if it soaks through the bottom and leaves a trail of juice behind us. It'll be fun."

"You know citrus attracts sandmites, right?" she asked, her voice low, grave.

Puk's stalks perked up in alarm. "For real?" he whispered.

He set his backpack down and was about to unclasp it to see if his joke was actually a joke or not when Kali chuckled.

"I'm kidding," she said.

"Oh," Puk said, relieved. He heaved the pack onto his back again, straining with the weight of it. "I've never heard of sandmites before, but you had me worried."

"Sandmites are real," she said, "but they aren't attracted to citrus. Not as far as I'm aware, anyway."

That hint of uncertainty appeared to disquiet Puk, which amused Kali.

Seeing him pull the bag up onto his back, though, did concern her. Puk was a small man, and weighing himself down with a heavy backpack would make for a deeply unpleasant journey, not only for himself but for her as well. If he was struggling with every tiny step, it could easily double their days out in the desert.

"Here, let me take some of that," she said, removing the backpack and opening it up.

Lucky for Puk, he had not obliterated an orange with his absurd packing method, but the backpack's innards were still a horrific sight to behold. Clothes were wadded up and smushed down as far as possible, with his dirty sandals placed on top to further flatten the fabrics, imparting plenty of stains in the process. The fresh fruit was stuffed into whatever available crevices the bag contained, and Kali could already see several bruises on one of the apples. Not to mention all the pouches and other extraneous items he'd already owned and needed to make room for. It was the worst rush job she'd ever laid eyes on.

Puk leaned a solitary stalk over the backpack, peering at its contents. It then curved upward to look at her. "Yeah, I know," he said, addressing the horrified scowl on her face.

"This is insane," she said.

"I already said I know!"

She started unpacking the bag in the middle of the lobby floor, tossing aside light pouches she knew were filled with dried fruit and unsalted nuts, though there were a couple more than she remembered buying earlier.

Puk noticed her eyeing the pouches and blurted out, "Oh! I bought some more stuff. For the thing, I mean. The trip. I bought some smelly bait to attract a cordol."

"Smelly bait?"

"Yes. And trust me, it stinks worse than shit, so, uh…don't open those two pouches." He pointed at two in particular, and she nodded her understanding.

Kali re-packed the qarm's bag for him, carefully choosing which items would be okay traveling with her instead. She decided he should keep his pouches of snacks, so that he could eat them whenever he needed to without asking her, but she thought it'd be alright if she carried the bait.

This garnered fervent protests from Puk, who insisted he carry the bait—"Trust me, it smells horrible and is gonna make all my stuff smell horrible too, you don't want that"—and so she found room for his sandals and some of his clothes instead, as well as a few other personal items he wouldn't need at-hand on the road.

With his pack lightened and neatly organized, Puk had less trouble hiking it up onto his back and profusely thanked her. Even with his few belongings loaded into her own bag, her load was relatively light.

The last thing they did before leaving the inn was filling up their respective waterskins in the kitchen.

Outside, they made their way to the northern district of the city where the Spine Gate was located. They were able to get their errands completed in a timely fashion, and therefore Kali knew they'd be able to reach the first outpost along the Ribroad long before sundown. It would be the next day, halfway to the second outpost, when they would veer off the designated path into the open desert to seek out the cordols. She typically left the city from its other gate, traveling that open pathway east toward the mountains, but she was familiar enough with the Ribroad and northern geography to feel confident in their travels.

They were only just passing through the Spine Gate and exiting the city when Puk said, "Would it be bad to admit I'm already sick of walking?"

"Yes," she laughed. "I'm gonna pretend that's a joke."

"Probably a wise choice for most complaints I'll inevitably make."

The bones of the Ribroad towered high above them, and Kali could feel the heat of the sun bearing down even through the tarp stretched across the curved white bones. A few minutes into their journey, beads of sweat were already rolling down Puk's forehead.

The Ribroad served as the primary route connecting Seroo's Eye with Restick on the country's coast. It was wide enough to allow wagons, ayote riders, and those like Kali and Puk who unfortunately had to travel on foot. Construction was underway in the north to connect the two cities with a railway, allowing travelers to ride a steam-powered locomotive with engines similar to those used in airships, though the rails currently only spanned half the distance. Originally the plan had been to convert the Ribroad itself into the railway, but that was quickly abandoned in favor of giving those who couldn't afford a train ticket the option of still traveling underneath the road's shade. Instead, the railway was being built adjacent to the Ribroad, curving along the same trajectory. In Kali's opinion, the rails should have been built decades ago, but it took a long time to get construction started in the desert.

"I've never gone down the Ribroad," Puk said, his eye-stalks curved backward to gaze upon the bones and leather high above. "It's pretty spectacular."

"It is," Kali agreed.

Growing up in Seroo's Eye, she often caught herself taking for granted how unique and magnificent the city she lived in was, with all of its adobe buildings clustered inside the skull of an extraordinarily massive beast. Every once in a while, she took a step back and looked at it from an outsider's perspective. Trying not to let the gigantic bones bursting from the earth seem like an everyday occurrence.

"There's nothing at all like this in Atlua, is there?" she asked.

"Nope," said Puk, his stalks still focused on the leather ceiling. "Not even close. Pretty much all of eastern Atlua is a forest, except for where some cities are built, of course. It's a little sparser in the west and southwest, where the land starts to curve and become Gillus, but still there's a ton of green. Not like here, where there's just nothing for miles and miles and then suddenly a fucking skull that's bigger than any building I've ever seen back home."

"Do you think any aeons ever lived up there?"

"I mean, probably, right?" he said. "You'd have to assume. Seroo couldn't have been the only one. Or maybe it was the one true god, who knows? My guess is that there's one still alive in the ocean over in the west. Or it's dead and idiots are still sacrificing to it every spring for no reason. That's probably more likely."

Kali imagined a great beast breaking the surface of the water, waves cascading off its glimmering wet flesh as it devoured poor sacrifices pushed over cliff edges.

Whether there was a living creature there or not (perhaps a relative of the dead aeon Gregori claimed had been found at the bottom of the sea?), she was glad Herrilock wasn't forced to contend with any threats of that size. It was a good thing Seroo had been dead for centuries, otherwise it could stomp out all life merely by traipsing around without even realizing it was doing any harm.

"You gonna miss anything from home?" Puk then asked.

The question caught her off guard. She pondered it for a moment, not wanting to sound either too sentimental or uncaring.

She answered, "The warmth."

"You ain't gonna be hard-pressed for warmth out here," Puk told her, wiping moisture from his face.

"I mean the comfort of being home," she clarified. "I'm sure you know how it is being home. Everything feels safer, your troubles seem less urgent and terrible. Sometimes it feels like all your responsibilities wash away and you can just *relax*. Just be happy."

Puk grunted. "Not sure I can relate," he said. "My parents were fine, but, uh…I would call 'home' a stressful environment for sure."

His confession saddened her. She couldn't comprehend going back to the inn and not being enveloped in its comforts. Even though she constantly kept herself busy with her work, being home put her more at ease.

"And besides, if home is the only place you're happy, then I'll give you some advice: it might not be a faif thing to do, but you should really give alcohol a shot."

Kali wondered if that bit of advice might have originated with his father Doro.

"Is there *anything* you miss about your home?" she asked him.

He didn't need to take a moment to consider his answer. "Nope," he said. "I miss Atlua, sure, but not home. I'm glad to be outta there."

They pressed on in silence. Kali trailed a few steps behind Puk despite his shorter stride.

She reached her hand into the knapsack slung over her shoulder, sliding it into the inner pocket where she kept her money and the key to her bedroom back at the inn. She grasped the key, the coolness of the metal coursing through her fingertips, and she thought of the warmth of her home.

- -

Puk's devotion to the Waranex Church had forever wavered.

It was never something he had been interested in himself, purely something forced upon him by his parents. His mother Mip and his fathers Grut and Brek, in particular. It was no wonder that Doro had no ties to the church, and Nork was largely indifferent to both the church and Puk.

Mip, Grut, and Brek surely wished that Doro was similarly indifferent toward Puk, but alas, the man's influence had seeped in. He had been considered no more than a necessity in mating for Mip and the others, but Doro had always been eager to have a child.

Puk dutifully attended sermons with his three devout parents, as well as the myriad community functions the church organized each month. Those were always his favorite part of being ingratiated into the church, as he loved filling up on the free food prepared by the Anures and other churchgoers.

Their faith believed in the Ustrels' creation of the world's living species, just as the jeornish believed, though in a more abstract sense. They did not believe in the ancient Ustrel war against the Asrani (a subject Puk knew little about), and actually did not believe the Ustrels were physical beings at all.

Waranex Anures preached that Ustrels were metaphysical beings that existed in the aether, flitting between the fabric of the world, breathing life into all that existed in Ustlia: its peoples, its animals, its plants. They therefore believed that when jeornish mages casted magic, they were not drawing on ancient powers bestowed on them by their ancestors; they were harnessing the Ustrels themselves, which were manifesting in reality as different forms of magic. That was why magic was capable of such varied and tremendous powers. It was the Ustrels being channeled into their world.

It was important for followers of the faith to take time each week to thank the Ustrels for all they shared with the world, and to grant some of their power back to them in return.

That was what Puk always found silly about the whole thing. His young mind kept poking holes in the practice every time his parents made him enter the local church's Spiral.

If the Ustrels granted him life, why would they want or need it back?

If they were sapping life from him, was he slowly dying each time he entered a Spiral?

If the Ustrels were giving him life, and he was giving it back, and then they were giving it back again, what was the point of the whole thing?

There were never any satisfactory answers from any Anures he inquired about this. Only vague replies and recited scriptures that by now he had long forgotten. Empty justifications that left his head no sooner than they had entered.

But he had entered the Spiral anyway, to appease his mother, and always came out feeling refreshed, if not mildly annoyed.

Puk and Kali had been walking down the Ribroad, with nothing but blazing sands stretching out endlessly on either side of them, for close to an hour. In the distance, Puk spied a large stone jutting out from the earth outside the bone structure encasing them. It was one of the Spirals that Anure Rahk had mentioned lining the Ribroad.

The structure was built exactly like the one in Trillowan and the others scattered all over his homeland. It was one huge piece of stone, only wide enough to fit one person inside, but reaching into the sky four or five times the height of a typical qarm. It was a largely unremarkable piece of stone, with no fancy adornments of any sort aside from the Ustrel symbol for "Rest" carved above the archway that allowed entry into the stone tomb.

Custom dictated that traveling qarms stop in every Spiral they found. Releasing one's self to the Ustrels was meant to show gratitude and humility and invite good luck and safety on their journey.

It had been a long while since Puk last entered a Spiral. He definitely hadn't seen one since arriving in Herrilock, and there had been a few he ignored in Atlua, which had caused a pang of guilt with each instance.

Well...

He was heading toward a reunion with a fiery man who he'd capsized, and he was also running low on his precious fire-spit, so Puk thought that maybe making a quick offer to the Ustrels wouldn't hurt.

"Do you mind if we stop there?" he asked, pointing ahead at the Spiral growing steadily closer.

Kali seemed surprised by the request, but she said they were making great time and it shouldn't be a problem.

It took another ten hot minutes to reach the structure, and when they did, Kali positioned herself on the ground with her back against one of the road's colossal bones.

The azure curtain covering the Spiral's entryway was drawn, indicating that it was unoccupied. Puk slipped into the stone and yanked the curtain closed, cutting himself off from the outside world.

He instantly began to feel the stone's cooling effect that Anure Rahk boasted about back in the city. It emanated off the rock, and when Puk pressed his palms to the blank stone in front of him, he moaned in relief.

The desert heat was bad enough under the Ribroad's shade, so he didn't know how he would fare in the open desert the following day. He wanted a black mage present to conjure a mass of water to drop on his head every ten minutes.

With his palms still pressed to the stone, Puk retracted his stalks and closed his eyes, bringing them closer to his head. He exhaled loudly, the air blasting through his nostrils and re-sounding through the small chamber.

Even as a child, when he had been more well-versed in the church's teachings, he never knew what to say or think in the Spirals. It was an awkward experience, going in for ten minutes while his parents waited outside. Now he had Kali waiting on him in their stead.

Help me get through this, he thought, feeling foolish. There was no one around to witness what he was doing, no way for anyone to read his thoughts, and yet he was embarrassed by them.

He continued.

Let my small, shitty body not shut down while I try to cross this fucking desert. I want to get back across the sea.

Puk caught himself making one appeal after another, which he was fully aware was not the purpose of a Spiral. He couldn't stop himself from internally vocalizing these wishes. It had been a long time since he had felt good or safe or whole, and he wanted to be encased in the Spiral's cool embrace and never let go.

Thank you for cooling me down, he thought stupidly. *Thank you for providing me with an opportunity to go back home. Thank you for the fire-spit in my bag.*

The last one had slipped in by accident, but it was truly something he was thankful for.

He tried to recall the proper recitation for ending one's time in a Spiral. No doubt he fumbled a lot of the correct terms and phrases, but he thought it was a noble attempt:

"Thank you for all, for you are all; all you are has let us prosper. I offer what I can back to you, to share with others."

And then he added, *Oh, and let Voya be alive.*

Puk extended his eyestalks as his eyes fluttered open. He took one last deep breath and released it, then left the comforting cool of the Spiral.

Kali was going to town on an itch on her knee when he emerged. She looked up at him and said, "Oh, I thought that would take longer."

"Nah," he said, lifting his backpack up off the ground. "You ready to go?" She nodded and gathered her things.

As they continued down the road, perspiration already building on Puk's watery-blue skin, he couldn't help but chuckle at what he'd said back in the Spiral.

'Thank you for all, for you are all.' Who comes up with this shit?

He stopped walking for a second to reach into his bag and extract a pouch of nuts, which he merrily munched while he jogged to catch up to his new friend.

CHAPTER VII

A TRADE

Kali wanted to swear, and so she swore.

Half an hour earlier, they had arrived at the first travelers' outpost along the Ribroad. She was sitting at a table in the dining area while Puk was still settling into their room upstairs. The place was lively, as it always was. The two Ribroad outposts were consistently the most occupied, since it was one of the most well-traveled roads in the country.

Kali wanted to swear because as she sat at the uneven table, nursing her cloudy cup of water, she realized that she had royally screwed up in the planning stage of their journey.

It was going to take them, at minimum, half a day's travel to reach the area where her sister's bestiary claimed the cordols would be. Once they reached that location, they would then have to spend time searching for the animals, however long that took, plus however much time it took acquiring the eggs.

There was no way they could realistically get back to the outpost before nightfall, and trudging through the dunes in the severe cold would not be a great situation for either of them.

Why the hell did I not think of this sooner? she berated herself, taking another sip of the water, which tasted slightly off. But it was good enough after a long, hot day.

She wracked her brain for a solution.

Leaving earlier in the morning would yield the same result of walking in the bitter cold for several hours, which would likely wear them out by the time they reached their destination, so that was out.

The closest town she could think of was Toralas, on a small peninsula jutting out from the coast. It was a notoriously rundown city, one that tourists and travelers tended to specifically avoid if at all possible, but that meant one advantage would be cheap rates at the local inn.

She tried to conjure her most accurate mental map of Herrilock, attempting to determine whether Toralas was a shorter distance than simply returning to the outpost. She wasn't sure. If it was closer, it was by a negligible amount, which would not be felt in the cold.

Perhaps it was a sign.

She'd had doubts about the entire operation right from the start, not only ethically speaking but from a purely logistical standpoint. Now here was another bump in the road in need of a speedy solution.

Maybe the answer was to call it quits and return home, explain to her parents that the opportunity just wasn't right after all. She'd have to eat the cost of the supplies she had bought Puk, since he obviously could not pay her back, so that was unfortunate. But not the end of the world.

With a sigh, Kali looked up from her near-empty glass and saw a clean-cut jeornish man sitting at the bar, watching her. For a split second, she thought it was Jeth, but it was definitely a different man, though his features were strikingly similar. He smiled at her, nodding a hello.

She returned a weak smile, not wanting to anger or offend. Her gaze was then drawn back to her glass.

Kali wondered if her sister ever wrestled with doubts about the lengths she went through to achieve her goals. Becoming a scholar at the Repository was no easy feat. It was the largest library not only in Herrilock, but on the entire continent. Possibly even in all of Ustlia, though Kali had no way of being sure.

It was originally built by a colony of centripts, and therefore a majority of the current librarians were still centripts; only the best of the best were folded in, and it was even harder for others to integrate themselves into the tower's stacks.

The Repository was a bastion of knowledge at the center of the desert, which Kali always saw as a less-than-ideal location due to how remote it was, necessitating many long, hot days of travel. But centripts never were concerned with the heat and in fact welcomed it; the lack of moisture was great for preservation of the books and other documents. It was a tower twenty stories high, with three underground levels consisting of living quarters for its scholars, outfitted with small apartments, a dining hall, and other commodities.

Scholars in its employ were expected to be on-hand at all hours of the day, on rotating shifts, in order to assist visitors with any questions they had about any topic imaginable, or help them locate a book within the endless rows of shelves the tower held.

When they weren't at visitors' beck and call, many of the tower's scholars were pursuing their own research, either individually or within groups. Once again, the research topics were wide-ranging and varied, though Kali did know that her sister was on a team dedicated to finding a permanent cure for the mold and perhaps a way for afflicted centripts to re-grow carapace segments that had fallen off.

In order to join the Repository's esteemed ranks, one had to demonstrate an encyclopedic knowledge of a range of subjects so widespread Kali couldn't even perform the simple task of remembering what all the subjects were.

She remembered Lissia studying multiple bestiaries (mostly Herrilock-specific, but some that covered both Gillus and Atlua as well), histories of the region, spellbooks (given that she was jeornish, Kali often wondered why her sister did not pursue attendance at a mage academy; that was what she would've done, if she could master magic), and a ton more. Potential scholars also had to be at least mostly fluent in Carsuak, which was possibly the most difficult aspect of the training.

Earning the title of a Repository Scholar was a high honor and extraordinary achievement. Those who lived in the tower were highly regarded by everyone in the country.

Lissia had sacrificed hours of time up in her room studying countless textbooks rather than hanging out with Kali and their friends. She missed out on jovial dinners, parties with varying degrees of wildness, and building relationships with people in Seroo's Eye. Kali knew of a few specific friends that stopped bothering to invite Lissia out because they figured she'd decline, as well as one or two guys who were interested in her but were pushed away in lieu of furthering her studies.

It all seemed incredibly isolating to Kali, and she wondered many times if her sister felt lonely locked away in her room with nothing but worn leather covers and musty pages, or if she was truly happy in there, expanding her knowledge and growing closer and closer to her dream every day.

Either way, she had a lot more to show for all her efforts than Kali did. She felt like she had worked equally hard in her own pursuits with so much less gained.

And now here she was, attempting one big move that would be generous to describe as a longshot and was probably blatantly illegal if not simply morally dubious, with a man who was barely more than a stranger.

She suspected she might be met with more regrets at the end of her life than her sister would.

- -

It was a sweet relief when the two of them finally arrived at the travelers' outpost. Puk had never felt so exhausted. The first thing he did was chug a massive glass of water in the bar area, then he followed Kali upstairs to their shared room.

Now she was downstairs, and he was still tucked away in the room regaining his strength.

Part of that entailed sprawling across the tiny bed set up in the far corner of the room, cut in half by a window granting a view of the bustling stables below.

While he lay motionless in bed, Puk lifted one eyestalk up to peer out the window, observing the horses and ayotes that were currently being stabled. There were only two horses, as ayotes were the preferred method of transportation in the desert. The horses' coats were a beautiful roan, despite the thin layer of sand dusted on them.

The horses reminded Puk of home. They were much more plentiful in Atlua. He had never learned how to ride one, but he'd ridden on the back of a few with other people, and it had always been an exhilarating experience.

Puk laid his stalk back down on the bed and clamped his eyes shut. His entire body ached. The greatest soreness was in his tiny webbed feet, and it coursed up through his stumpy legs, through his heaving belly, and up to his head, culminating in a remarkable headache. For a brief moment, he wondered if this whole mess was even going to be worthwhile.

But he quickly banished those thoughts and sat up to commence the second part of his recuperation: snorting some spit.

It had been nagging at him the entire length of the Ribroad. At one point, he had almost attempted sneaking some, but in the end didn't want to risk being caught by Kali and have her abandon the plan. He needed her help. Her money.

He snatched up the small baggy of powder out of his pack and felt its lightness in his palm. He stretched the opening and looked inside to confirm what he already knew, which was that his supply was running distressingly low.

There would be an abundance of dealers in Myrisih, and probably plenty of them in Restick as well, but he wasn't confident his stash would last even that long.

Shoulda bought more before we left. Idiot. It wouldn't have taken too long to find another dealer...

There then came a pang of self-awareness about how pathetic he sounded.

And that pang was just as swiftly dismissed.

He carefully poured a line of gray powder onto his outstretched finger, then set the pouch down on the bed and raised the finger to his nose. He inhaled deeply, running his nostril down the line, and flung himself backward onto the mattress.

The comfort of the drug flooded his senses immediately. His headache dulled, and he felt the euphoric warmth traveling down his body to his aching toes. It was like his entire body was pissing itself, a thought which disturbed him, but only for a brief moment.

Puk knew he couldn't reasonably stall for much longer. When Kali was heading downstairs, he told her he was going to get things situated then join her. Soon she would surely wonder what the hold-up was and come check that everything was okay with the room.

For now, though, he wanted to bask in this glow.

He reached his eyestalks up to once again look out the window at the horses. They were stabled next to each other, and he could guess that the people they belonged to were traveling together. It seemed an unlikely coincidence that there would be two separate travelers on horseback.

One of the oldest memories he had of his father Brek was riding with him from Trillowan to Padstow as a child.

While his fathers Grut and Doro were constant presences in his life and Nork practically pretended he didn't exist, Brek tended to strike a middle ground. He was always glad to see Puk whenever he did, but it was never much of a priority in his life.

Brek was a trumpeter in a troupe called The Bards of Pluto, and had been since before Puk was born. They were planning to embark on a new tour and had never been to Padstow before, so the other members tasked him with the job of scoping out the town's scene and finding out if there was anywhere good for them to perform there.

He asked Mip if Puk could come along with him, show the boy some new parts of the world, and she had reluctantly agreed. Her trepidation was young Puk's first indication that his mother possessed no real affinity for any of his fathers aside from Grut. At that point in time, Doro had not yet drawn her deep disdain—that Puk had noticed, anyway.

But Puk, around ten years old then, was thrilled to leave his hometown for the first time. He thanked his mother profusely and met Brek at his home a few days later, where he was saddling up a horse he had rented.

The animal stood easily three times as tall as Puk, who by all accounts was still a mere tadpole, and it intimidated him. But Brek (whose stalk tips still only reached barely past the horse's belly) patted it on the back—or as close to it as his arm could stretch—and showed his son that there was nothing to be afraid of. It was a gentle beast.

Once everything was packed up and hitched to the saddle, Brek used a stepstool to help Puk up onto the horse's back then hopped on himself. As they trotted away from the stool, left behind in front of Brek's home, Puk asked how they would climb back onto the horse again. His father assured him anywhere they went would be able to accommodate their needs, and so his fears were assuaged once more.

He wrapped his arms around Brek's stomach and held tight. The horse picked up its pace once they were out of the marsh, increasing from a trot to a gallop as they came to firmer ground. Puk hadn't the faintest idea where his father learned to ride, and he was impressed with the control he exerted over the animal.

The ride had been the most memorable part of the trip. Padstow turned out to be a bit of a dud; it was to the west, a small town without much going on. Plenty of houses, a few shops, a run-down pub without a stage or anything. There was a town square that Brek suspected the troupe might be able to perform in, but he guessed that the townsfolk wouldn't feel overly generous with their crescents, so he decided they should travel elsewhere.

But to this day, Puk held fond memories of riding that horse with his father. Laying there in his stiff bed, doped out and watching two horses stand around doing nothing, he yearned to one day learn how to ride by himself.

His eyestalks came to rest on the mattress and he inhaled deeply. He held his breath for as long as he could, about thirty seconds, then pushed the air out of his mouth with a *pop!*

The warmth had since left him, but his body still felt relaxed. Unhurt.

He was ready for a drink. Or two.

Puk lifted himself up off the bed with great effort and absentmindedly stuffed the fire-spit pouch into his pocket before leaving the room.

The staircase was embarrassingly difficult to navigate, requiring him to concentrate on every step he took. But once he found himself on flat ground again, he felt more confident in his gait. He entered the dining area, where he knew Kali would be, and spotted her at a table in the middle of the room.

He gave her a friendly wave, which she reciprocated, then made his way to the bar, running through the various drink options in his head in an attempt to decide what he was in the mood for. A whiskey? A simple beer? Something with a lot of vodka in it?

There was an empty barstool in between two people, so Puk slipped in. To his right was a rugged, clean-shaven jeornish man who sat with his arms folded back as if imitating a bird, his elbows resting on the countertop as he faced out toward the rest of the room. On Puk's left was an elderly faif woman, the swirling yellows and oranges of her skin dulling in her old age. She seemed to be keeping to herself, morosely staring down at the wooden bar as the bartender slid her a layered cocktail that intrigued Puk.

He asked the man behind the counter, "What's that?" and pointed at the woman's drink.

The bartender simply responded with his own point of the finger, gesturing toward a hand-scrawled sign on the bar that described two drink specials the outpost was running for the week.

The first drink had to be what the woman had ordered. It was a three-layered drink called "Triple Rings." The bottom layer was coffee liqueur, the middle was a whiskey cream liqueur, and the top was cherry brandy. Puk had never been one for brandy, so he ignored that option.

The second specialty cocktail was much stranger and piqued his interest. Dubbed the "Kick in the Mud," it was essentially a combination of spiced rum, chocolate syrup, and hot pepper powder.

He had never had a chocolate cocktail before, but he sure as hell loved chocolate, so that was what he requested.

The man on his right laughed at Puk's order as the bartender got to work.

"Yes, it's quite funny," said Puk.

The man turned around in his stool to sit properly and began to fiddle with the hat he'd placed on the countertop. "Sorry," he said, "didn't mean to mock. Just didn't figure you for a sweet-tooth when I saw you."

"I'm a man of many facets," Puk said absently, staring straight ahead. "A true gem."

184 · travis m. riddle

The man laughed at this too. He held out a hand and said, "Name's Gael."

Puk accepted the handshake and introduced himself. It was impossible not to notice that Gael was wearing riding gloves.

"Nice gloves," said Puk. "Is one of those horses out there yours?"

"Unfortunately not." Gael shook his head. "I've just got a crummy ayote."

Damn. For a second he hoped he had found the horses' owner and could persuade him to let Puk go out and meet them.

"Crummy? Don't get me wrong, I love a good horse, but ain't pretty much every ayote better at desert travel than a horse?"

Gael shrugged. "That's true, sure. But there's no denying a horse is so much more majestic. And smarter too, I bet. But ayotes are way cheaper out here."

"Ah," Puk nodded. "You're on a financial expedition." He paused a moment, fearing he had slurred the last two words. Maybe he'd be written off as drunk, despite only just showing up at the bar. "As am I. Where you goin'?" He kept one eye on Gael, but twisted the other stalk to check the bartender's progress on his drink.

"East," Gael replied. "An airship sunk in the ocean, and I intend to do some treasure hunting."

The bartender brought over Puk's drink, which was poured in a tall, thin-stemmed glass. He felt fancy.

He intended to join Kali once he'd gotten his drink, but Gael's quest interested him. "How you gonna do that?" he asked. Centripts were naturally equipped for deep dives in the sea, but jeorns certainly were not.

Gael grinned, obviously pleased that the question had been asked. Puk could tell the man was a bit of a show-off. He was fairly keyed-in to that type of arrogance, having surrounded himself with performers for so much of his adult life.

"I'm a black mage," Gael explained. "I concocted myself a pretty useful spell. Not sure if anyone else has experimented with something like this, but I felt pretty damn clever when I thought it up. I call it an Aero Helmet."

He held his gloved hands out in front of himself, palms facing Puk, who was too entranced to taste his drink yet. The mage then closed all of his fingers except his pinkies and swiftly swooped his hands inward toward himself, his pinkies coming together to point in the middle of his chest. He then unraveled his fingers but joined them together while pushing his palms up toward his face, and a miniscule gust of wind blew his hair.

His hands then fell to his side and he grinned with smug satisfaction.

Nothing appeared any different to Puk.

He was about to point this out when he caught the slightest distortion ripple in the air on either side of Gael's face.

Then the man spoke, his voice muffled and wavering, as if he was speaking to Puk from underwater. "I know it's hard to see, but it's pretty fantastic, right?" He made another fast series of gestures with his hands, then the distortion was gone and his normal voice was restored. "It's similar to a normal Aero spell, but I figured out a way to shape it to encase my head and create an air bubble I can breathe in while underwater. Tested it out a bunch back at home, and it worked great. I can only get it to last around three hours at a time, though, so I'll have to work in shifts."

Puk was genuinely impressed by the display.

"Seems like that treasure's all yours," he said.

Gael grinned toothily. "Yep," he said. "It was actually a buddy of mine's idea to check out the wreckage. I hadn't even heard of the ship going down. But he couldn't figure out a way we'd get down there to it." He laughed before saying, "I came up with the Aero Helmet on my own, then uh…told him I was going to visit some family in Restick. What he don't know won't hurt him." He shot Puk a conspiratorial wink.

"Sounds like you're kind of a dickhead," said Puk. One of the many effects of the fire-spit was that he often lost any sort of social filter.

Gael laughed at the jab. People like him always knew they were assholes, and they liked it.

"Well," Puk grunted, pushing himself off the stool with his drink in hand, "good luck on your future endeavors."

"And you as well," said Gael.

Puk sauntered over to the table where Kali sat waiting for him with a curious expression.

"Make a new friend?" she asked.

"Not really," said Puk. "Bit of a fuck, in my opinion."

She chuckled. "He's been staring at me for most of the time I've been down here. Real creep."

"Sounds about right," said Puk.

Kali then took a good look at the dark brown drink he'd placed on the table. "Got yourself a cup of shit?"

"Woulda been faster, but no," he answered. "It's got chocolate and rum and spice."

She scrunched her face up at the description. "Is it any good?"

"I don't know yet. I keep getting distracted, because I am easily distractible."

Even he could tell the words had come out more like *"eas-istractable,"* and it was apparent on Kali's face. She cocked an eyebrow again. No way of fooling her into thinking he was already drunk, especially not after openly admitting he hadn't tried his drink yet.

He pushed past the moment in hopes that it'd be soon forgotten. He brought the red powder-rimmed glass to his lips and gulped down some of the thick liquid. The spiciness of the pepper powder danced around the sweetness of the chocolate and warmth of the rum in an unexpectedly pleasant way, with no one flavor profile overpowering another. With another swig, he had already downed half the drink.

"Good?" Kali asked.

"Great."

"What an odd drink." She gulped down some water before continuing on. "So, we've run into a problem," she said.

"Problems is bad," Puk sputtered stupidly. "What's the problem?"

She cast him another suspicious look. He needed to get his act together before she started asking questions.

But she let it slide for now.

She went on to explain the situation to him, which was that with their current plan, they'd find themselves stranded in the extreme cold of the desert's night air after acquiring their cordol eggs the next day.

"That's bad," he said when she was finished, contributing nothing of value to the conversation.

Kali nodded. "Yes," she said. "It is bad."

Puk's mind immediately jumped to the horses in the stable.

"The problem's just that walking is too slow, right?"

"Yeah," Kali said. "But at this point, we can't rent an ayote anywhere, and we didn't want to sink any funds into that anyway."

Puk shrugged and gulped down more of his Kick in the Mud before offering a suggestion. "Let's ask my new fuck friend," he said.

Kali smirked at the implication of the phrase, which had eluded him in his high and inebriated state. She said, "What makes you think the creep can help?"

"He's heading all the way to the east coast, so he's got an ayote. Says it's a crummy one, but a crummy one's faster than we are."

She pondered it for a moment, taking another drink of water. Even in his current state of mind, Puk knew she was weighing whether it was worth interacting with the guy who'd been gazing at her all evening. He felt guilty for putting her into that position, but it was the only idea he had.

"Fine," she said.

Puk turned around in his chair and saw that Gael was already looking their way, obviously intrigued by his new acquaintance having taken a seat with the pretty faif woman.

"Gael!" Puk called. "Come take a seat!"

The man sported his signature grin while he carried his hat with him over to the table. *Probably thinks I was talking him up to Kali,* Puk thought as the man sat.

"Hello there. I'm Gael," he said, extending his hand toward Kali. She took it and meekly introduced herself. "Beautiful name," he said, withdrawing his hand. "Perfect for such a beautiful woman."

Kali rolled her eyes as she downed the last of her water.

Dumbass, Puk thought and nearly said aloud. So his filter was not entirely broken.

"Let me get you a refill," said Gael, either not noticing her contempt or simply not caring. He snatched Kali's glass from the table before she could respond and marched back over to the bar with a swagger in his step.

Kali immediately said, "This is a bad idea."

"Yeah, he's a bit of a dickhead," Puk conceded. "Let's just try to get the ayote from him and be done with it. We're using him, that's all."

Kali sighed, clearly displeased. But she said, "Alright. Let's just get to the point fast."

Puk nodded.

Gael returned to the table with a tall glass of water, which Kali eyed suspiciously. Puk would be surprised if he caught her taking even one sip of it.

He pressed on with their business. "Look," he said, drawing Gael's attention away from Kali. "I called you over 'cause we wanna ask you somethin'."

"Yeah?" He winked at Kali. The man truly had no shame.

"*I* wanna ask you somethin'," Puk then emphasized. Gael looked less intrigued by this notion. "I was hoping we could borrow your ayote tomorrow. Head out early in the morning, then we'd have it back by nightfall. Nice and fast."

Gael let out a low whistle. "I dunno..." he muttered, making a real show out of it. "I'm on a pretty tight timetable here. I've gotta get to the Peaks and cross those to get to Lyukashi..."

Now Puk wanted to roll his eyes.

Instead he said, "That shipwreck ain't goin' nowhere. You've got plenty of time to cross the mountains and find your treasure."

The man smiled, knowing how much leverage he held. He wanted to milk this for all he could. He said, "I'm not so sure about that. Lots of treasure hunters are surely converging on the wreckage, and if I get there too late…"

Puk couldn't stop himself from groaning. "The only other people who're gonna be down there are centripts from Lyukashi, and I doubt there are many of them who care enough about whatever was on that ship." He added, "Plus, getting across Vanap's Peaks ain't an easy task. Might do you good to have one more day of rest."

Gael put a hand to his chin in theatrical thought. He considered Puk's words, but they were evidently not enough to convince him.

"It'll be a huge dent in my profits," he said. "Of that I am sure."

Kali kept her mouth shut. She had her arms crossed over her chest and was ignoring the glass of water in front of her. She stared daggers at the man to her right.

Gael continued, "I could propose a trade, however."

"What kind of trade? We ain't got much," said Puk.

"Oh, you have what I'd like," Gael said, sliminess dripping from every word he spoke. He turned his gaze from Puk over to Kali and grinned wide. He then reached a hand underneath the table and placed it on her leg, saying, "If you—"

She shot up from the table before he could finish the sentence. "Fuck off," she told him, and retreated upstairs.

Somehow, Gael appeared genuinely shocked by what had transpired.

"She's got a lot of spirit," he said once she had totally disappeared from view. "I like fiery women. Don't you?

Especially on a faif. There's nothing I love more than a rambunctious faif woman, with their colorful skin, their flat chests, their silky hair..."

Puk was appalled by the man's gall to do and say all of this to him, a complete stranger. He was opening his mouth to echo Kali's sentiment and storm off himself before he realized that he could use the type of man Gael was to his own benefit.

"Yes, love those flat-chested faifs," Puk said, which was probably the biggest lie he'd ever uttered, given qarms' asexual nature. "Tits sure are great, big or small."

"I hear that," Gael nodded, kicking back some of the beer he held in his hand. Puk did likewise with the last of his chocolate delight.

"Know what else I love? Aside from great tits?" Puk asked, nearly retching from the vocabulary he was using.

Gael perked up, awaiting the reveal.

"Fire-spit."

The man's wide grin returned, though it had hardly faltered even when Kali declined his gentlemanly offer of the ayote in exchange for sex. Puk wondered what in the world it would take to deter him.

"I hear *that!*" Gael beamed. "You got any on you, friend?"

"I do," said Puk. He extracted the pouch he had unconsciously slipped into his pocket earlier and plopped it onto the table.

Gael gawked at the pouch with longing.

"To be honest," Puk said, mumbling all three words as one, "I don't need it. I'd be willing to give it up if you let us use your ayote tomorrow."

Gael tore his eyes away from the baggy and leaned back in his chair. "I don't know," he said, still trying to drive a bargain. "Maybe your friend would reconsider..."

"She ain't gonna reconsider," Puk said definitively. "You can get that outta your head now. This is the trade." He edged the pouch closer to Gael.

The man considered the offer, his eyes darting back and forth between Puk and the drugs. He then reached forward and plucked the bag off the table, securing it in the breast pocket of the tight vest he wore.

"Glad we came to an agreement," Puk said, trying his best to smile at the vile man.

"Yeah, yeah, whatever," Gael grumbled. "Just have the dumb animal back tomorrow night. And let your friend know my offer still stands, if she changes her mind."

Puk refrained from saying anything to spoil the deal and got the stable number from Gael, as well as a written note stating he was allowing them to borrow the ayote to present to the stablemaster.

"Pleasure doin' business with you," Puk lied, getting up from the table with the slip of paper in his pocket.

His stomach sank at the prospect of giving away his entire stash of spit, but it was for the good of the mission. He hoped Kali wouldn't hold a grudge against him for dealing with Gael, who had turned out to be even worse than he anticipated.

Back in their room, he found Kali already changed into nightwear and tucking herself into bed.

He knew she didn't need to eat dinner, but he was going to grab something from the kitchen soon. He wanted to tell her the news first.

"I got us the ayote," he said.

Kali turned to him with disgust in her face. "*His* ayote?"

Puk nodded.

"How'd you manage that? Are *you* gonna fuck him?"

"No."

"Hmm. I'm not sure what else he could want." Her tone was understandably sour.

Puk sighed. "I'm sorry," he said, doing his best to enunciate. "I knew he was a fuck, but I didn't know he was *that* big of a fuck. I wouldn'ta suggested him if I did. Trust me, I didn't like him any more than you did."

"Still made a deal with him though, it sounds like."

"Well, yeah," Puk said, and he did feel grimy about the whole thing. "But we need a ride, or else we're screwed, according to you. And you're the expert. So I convinced him."

"Yeah? How?"

By giving him the rest of my drugs. His filter caught the sentence before it escaped his lips.

"Guy is just a dumbass, and he's drunk too, so I talked him into it. Got a note right here for the stablemaster saying we can take the ayote tomorrow."

Kali shook her head. "I don't want anything to do with him. We can figure something else out. There has to be someone else down there who'll let us borrow their ride. Talk to people when you go down there for dinner. You're good at talking, apparently. Well, *sometimes*."

Puk knew the last bit was a barb at how much he'd been slurring his words. He ignored it and said, "Yeah, maybe someone else will let us borrow an ayote, but there's no one else down there I wanna fuck over."

There was a pause before Kali asked, "What do you mean?"

Puk grinned. "Like I said, the guy's a fuck, so let's fuck him. After we get the eggs, we're goin' to Restick. So let's just go to Restick and forget returning the animal to him. All he does is talk about how 'crummy' it is anyway."

"What'll we do with it? If—"

He cut her off. "Who cares! We can keep it or let it go free in the desert, where it's from. Or better yet, we can sell it to someone in Restick. Let Gael deal with not having a ride to the coast *and* having to pay more money for another mount. Win-win for us, lose-lose for him. I don't give a shit about double-crossing someone who's obviously an asshole. Do you?"

"No," she replied without thinking about it.

"So it's settled then," said Puk. "We'll borrow his ayote and then forget to return it."

Kali considered it for a few seconds, then nodded. A sneer snuck its way onto her face. "Okay."

"Perfect!" Puk smiled. "The plan is back on track."

CHAPTER VIII

THE EGG HEIST

The next morning, they woke up bright and early to head down to the stables to get a head start on their arduous day, and to ensure they got to Gael's ayote before he rescinded the deal.

Kali had been fuming as she pounded her way up the stairs after the man's insane suggestion that she sleep with him in exchange for a favor. It was hardly past dark, but she changed into her pajamas and threw herself into bed, too angry to interact with anyone else. She wished she'd had room to pack a book to read. Even *Your Canary* would have been better than nothing.

After Puk barged in with his news then left again to eat dinner, it took her a while to fall asleep in spite of how tired she was from their long walk.

A piece of her was still irritated with Puk for forging ahead with Gael, but a larger piece was undeniably excited to screw him over.

Kali felt refreshed after a good night's sleep, putting the dining room's events behind her. Unfortunately, her companion could not count himself so lucky. It took several attempts at waking him before he finally stirred, and he was lethargic in gathering his few belongings and trudging down the stairs, complaining about a headache the entire way.

At the foot of the stairs, she double-checked that he still had the note from Gael. Once confirmed, they stepped outside.

The stablemaster was a kind, elderly faif man. His skin was a faded green with streaks of blue and red like multicolored lightning strikes. He wore a loose-hanging thin green shirt that was frayed at its edges and perpetually dirtied by his work. He gave the two of them a warm smile and a hello as they approached. Two horses, a surprising sight to Kali, whinnied behind him.

"Good morning!" he said to them, setting down a large sack of dried bugs at his feet. "What can I do for y'all? Just getting in?" He leaned to look behind them, though if they had an animal to stable it would've been clearly visible regardless. The old man was puzzled.

"The opposite, actually," Kali smiled back. "We're getting an early start today."

The stablemaster frowned and said, "My apologies, but we don't rent here, unfortunately. All these beauties are already accounted for."

"We know," said Puk, stepping forward. He pulled the crumpled note from his pocket and unfolded it before handing it over to the man, who took it with a quizzical expression.

Puk stepped back to stand beside Kali, and they waited as he slowly read the note.

"I must say, this is peculiar," the stablemaster muttered, more to himself than to them. He looked up from the wrinkled paper and said, "I should check the signature against my sign-in records, to make sure it's legitimate. I'm sure you understand."

"Of course," Kali said before Puk could say anything snippy. The qarm rubbed at the space on his head between his two eyestalks, obviously still grouchy from being awoken so early.

The stablemaster shuffled into a makeshift office, a small rectangular wooden structure with a door emblazoned with a symbol of a crescent moon and a star in its curve. A misshapen square sign hung on the door under the carving with the word IN painted blue in a messy scrawl.

He emerged a minute later with the note still in hand. "It matches!" he declared, still confused but coming to accept the situation. "It looks like Mr. Berei's ayote is in the fourth stall."

They followed him to the correct stall, where Gael's ayote was standing awake and perky, munching on a pile of dried bugs and slices of cactus scattered on the ground.

The animal looked far from crummy to Kali, with a healthy sheen to its shell and a long, curved snout. It looked like it could give Bango a run for his money.

"Do you know its name?" she asked.

The stablemaster nodded. "Her name's Bella."

It was a pretty name. Kali smiled and cooed, "Hey, Bella!"

The ayote's ears perked up and she momentarily ceased munching on her breakfast to look up at the person calling her name. Her tail wagged slowly, sweeping up sand in the back of the stall.

The stablemaster swung open the stall door and led Bella out to greet her new riders. She immediately took to Kali, but was more dubious about Puk. After a few minutes, though, she began warming up to him.

They continued getting to know Bella while the old man hitched up her saddle and attached some extra bags on either side, explaining that it was all equipment Gael had included when checking in to the stable. One bag was empty, but the other contained a packet of dried bugs, three slices of cactus, and two tall, thin glass jars that were filled with water.

"Gael paid for all of this already," he told them with a smile. Kali wanted to laugh out loud, but she refrained.

With everything taken care of, the friendly stablemaster asked if there was anything else he could do for them. Kali gave it a moment's thought, but nothing came to mind, so she told him they were fine.

She helped Puk up onto the ayote's back, much to his annoyance, but given his stature he had to concede that some assistance was necessary. Kali then pulled herself up into the saddle and thanked the stablemaster again.

"No problem at all!" he said. "Have a pleasant day. See you tonight!"

Kali again resisted the urge to laugh. Puk did laugh.

And with that, they were off.

She directed Bella around the corner of the outpost, heading in the opposite direction of the shaded Ribroad, which surely was causing the aged stablemaster further confusion. Nothing about their entire interaction was ordinary.

They were headed north in the open desert, in the direction of the Loranos Gulf. There were no towns in the sands between the outpost and the coast, where the disreputable city of Toralas was situated on a small peninsula jutting out into the sea.

Somewhere in the sands should be the pack of cordols she'd spotted migrating. The beasts were fast under the dunes and should have had no trouble reaching their destination by now.

As Kali mapped out the geography in her head, she suspected they might be pushing it trying to reach Restick before the desert grew too cold, but they would certainly be able to reach the Ribroad's second outpost.

It was a bumpy start to their journey as Bella raced through the sands with excitement. Kali could tell the ayote was young and somewhat inexperienced with riders, showing little consideration for the people she was jostling on her back. She did her best to slow the animal down, but Bella was too energetic after being cooped up in a stall all night. She wanted to run.

Kali feared the ayote's voracious appetite for speed would buck Puk off her backside, and it seemed the qarm shared her concerns.

Up to this point, he had been grasping the sides of the saddle as best he could, but he leaned forward to ask, "Is it okay if I hold on to you?"

She nodded and then felt his stubby arms wrap around her waist, clutching at the fabric of her shirt for support. She looked down at the chunky blue fingers holding on to her and giggled.

They bounded through the desert for close to an hour before the sun started showing its face over the horizon. It crept up slowly, its yellow ink spilling across the sand ahead of them, which glittered in the light.

"It looks pretty," Puk half-shouted over the wind whipping at their faces and the enthusiastic huffs of their mount. "I don't think I've ever seen the sunrise in the desert before."

Kali was glad to hear his mood was improving. A nice sunrise could help anyone in that respect, she figured.

"It's really pretty," she agreed as they raced onward.

For a few joyful minutes, watching the sunrise as she bounced up and down on this delighted creature's back, Kali was able to forget the questionable nature of everything she had agreed to do.

She simply enjoyed the ride.

- -

Riding on an ayote was not nearly as majestic as riding horseback in his childhood. Puk considered that perhaps he was romanticizing the memory, and back then it had been just as bumpy and uncomfortable and he had been a dumb kid who didn't care.

As the heat bore down on them, Puk was thankful for swindling a ride out of the asshole mage. Another full day of walking would have proven to be quite a chore for him. In fact, he thought it might kill him.

His feet were still sore as they slapped against the hard shell of the ayote. Quality of ride disregarded, there was no denying the horses back at the stable were much more majestic than an ayote. To Puk, it was like a giant rat poking out of a rounded shell. He was in constant fear of its whip-like tail lashing him from behind.

He tightened his grip around Kali's waist, not wanting to be thrown off and lost forever in the unending dunes. She intermittently barked orders at Bella, but they didn't do much good. Bella was an unruly animal.

Eventually, after the buzz of an early morning run wore off, Bella began to slow her pace to a mere jog rather than a full-on sprint. Puk found this much more palatable, and he was able to remove his arms from Kali's waist and hold onto the saddle.

"See 'em?" Kali asked after around half an hour of their new speed. She squinted into the distance.

Puk did the same, including stretching his stalks forward to get a slightly closer look, but all he could see was the horizon wavering in the heat.

"No," he answered. "Unless you mean the sun. Because yes, I see the sun."

"Not the sun," Kali laughed. Puk breathed a sigh of relief that her attitude toward him had improved since the night before. He worried all throughout dinner that he had soured their relationship. She went on, "I can see the cordols."

He strained harder to spot the animals in the far distance, but still came up short. Her eyesight was staggering.

Kali described what she saw to him. "It's a pack of six. They're all fairly spread out. I read that they travel in packs, but tend to like their own space once they've settled down. They're pretty solitary creatures."

"Are there any mommies in the group?" Puk asked.

"Not sure," she replied. "If there are any eggs, I can't see them from here."

They continued to ride at a steady pace, and after a few minutes Puk was finally able to make out vaguely cordol-shaped and -colored things against the backdrop of sand and sky. The animals were all a couple hundred feet apart from each other, forming a circle with nothing at its center.

Three of the cordols were sticking straight up out of the ground like red stone pillars. They were completely motionless, and Puk was baffled as to what they were doing. One other was slithering around on the ground, while another leapt dramatically into the air before coming back down to burrow into the sand. The last lay in the sand, curled around a collection of four eggs.

Puk didn't have to say anything; Kali had spotted the eggs too, likely before he did. She pulled on Bella's reins, and the ayote veered to the left toward their mark. At least she heeded that instruction.

He braced himself as the ayote's speed increased, sensing a newfound purpose in their journey. Kali had to yank on the reins again to urge her to slow down, which she ignored. So much for obedience.

They circled around the pack of cordols, and Kali managed to bring Bella to a stop in front of their curled-up target, far enough away to hopefully not raise any suspicion.

"So what's the plan?" Puk asked, sliding off the ayote's banded shell. He landed with a thud as his feet sunk into the sand.

Kali unmounted much more gracefully and asked, "What do you mean? This was all your idea! You don't have a plan already?"

He blurted out something to alleviate her annoyance. "No, I totally have an idea, but I wanted to see if you had anything in mind."

"Well, I don't," she said. It was evident in her tone that she hadn't bought the lie.

He didn't blame her.

Bella stood nearby, shifting around impatiently. She wanted to run some more. Standing was boring. She still had energy to unleash.

They stood in silence for almost half a minute before Kali said, "Well?"

"Oh," Puk sputtered. "Right. Okay. Well…" He tried to concoct a decent plan in his head. But first, he asked, "What are those three doing?"

She knew he meant the three stiffly pointing up into the air. "They're asleep," she said. "At night they burrow under the sand, but during the day they sleep like that to absorb warmth."

"Weird," said Puk. "Okay. Well, I think we don't need to worry about those three then." He looked around for any sign of the one that had jumped into the air, but it was gone.

Maybe it went out for a bite to eat, he thought.

Their target was flanked by two sleeping cordols, and the remaining one that was awake was on the opposite side of the animals' huge circle. Far out of view, if its eyesight was as bad as Puk's. He inquired about the subject, and Kali told him that their eyes were indeed not the best.

"So we only gotta worry about ours and two sleepyheads," he determined. "I'm pretty sure we can grab the eggs without waking up those two. I ain't *that* big of a loudmouth."

"I think that's still undecided," Kali interjected.

"Fair. But anyway, here's what we'll do: I'll circle around that way a bit, and then open up the smelly bait. That shit is *pungent*, believe me—it'll have no problem catchin' a whiff. It'll slither over to the bait, and then you'll run up and grab the eggs."

"If the smell is that strong, don't you think it'll wake up the two that're sleeping?"

Puk hadn't considered that. Scheming was not his strong suit, which he would never admit to Kali after roping her into this grand idea of his.

"I think it'll be alright," he said, having no real basis for the statement. "If not, we'll deal with that as it comes."

"That's not reassuring."

"Well, life ain't reassuring."

Kali shrugged off his cynicism and said, "There are four eggs. How many do we need?"

"All of 'em, if you can carry 'em all," Puk said.

She adamantly shook her head. "I don't wanna take them all. Let's leave at least one."

"Whatever, that's fine," Puk said. It didn't make a huge difference to him, as long as they got one or two. The rest would just be nice bonuses. "You ready to do this?"

A frown graced Kali's face, and Puk once again felt guilty about dragging her into this mess. He tried to tell himself that she had willingly agreed to it, there were no surprises about anything they were doing and it had all been laid out from the start, but it did little to alleviate the knot in his stomach.

With more poise than he expected, she said, "Let's go."

Puk snatched the packet of dried bor sludge from his knapsack and darted across the sands, putting a good amount of distance between their base of operations and the spot where he would be attempting to attract the cordol.

He came to a halt when he felt there was sufficient space between himself and three other creatures—Bella, the mother cordol, and the closest sleeping cordol—and knelt down to the ground.

The sand mildly warmed his leg through his pants, and when he touched it with his fingers, he was surprised by how hot it actually was. He scooped out a small divot in the sand, for reasons unbeknownst even to himself, and then opened up the bag of bait.

Predictably, the smell was horrendous.

Puk gagged as the scent wafted up from the bag into his innocent nostrils. He was going to vomit. He knew it. He could feel his dinner rising up his throat. He had to choke it down.

Keep it down. It was so hot. The sand was hot, the vomit was hot.

Fuck, here it comes—

Before unburdening himself, he shot a glance at the mother cordol and saw that it had poked its head up. Investigating the new, tantalizing scent on the air.

With one eyestalk on the mother, he turned the other to observe their slumbering friend. It remained unmoved, thankfully. For now.

Puk succeeded in keeping his food down and bolted back in the direction of Bella.

For a second, he feared that the cordol might spy him running, assume he was the smell, and come chasing after him, but thankfully, it had keenly picked up on the scent and began to slither toward its source.

With the mother cordol on the move and its sleeping neighbor still undisturbed, Puk saw Kali take off toward the eggs, her blazing red ponytail smacking rudely against her back.

- -

The cordol was quite literally taking the bait.

Now was her chance. Kali's heart and lungs heaved in her chest as she dashed toward the pile of pale orange eggs, huddled together and nestled snugly into the sand.

She didn't bother to look over her shoulder to find out what Puk was doing. She needed to concentrate, to act as quickly as possible.

Kali came to a sliding stop before the eggs and saw that their mother hadn't yet reached the bait.

Plenty of time.

206 · travis m. riddle

She gathered two of the eggs in her arms and held them close to her chest. Two should be enough to satisfy Puk's acquaintance in Myrisih. It was a more than generous offer, she thought.

Kali turned on her heel and started toward Bella. Puk had not made it back yet with his unimpressive stride, but he wasn't far off.

To her left, she saw the cordol had arrived at the bait and was busy devouring the miniscule amount of food. It would only be a handful of moments before it curved around and returned to its eggs. She urged her legs to move faster.

Puk was leaning one arm against Bella's side and panting heavily when Kali made it to them.

"Two?" he wheezed.

"Two," she said.

He shrugged.

She unclasped the empty sack that had come with Bella. The added space was incredibly useful, granting them an entirely empty bag to house the eggs without fear of them smashing against their other belongings. As she closed it tight, Puk uttered a swear.

"What?" Kali turned around and saw what had elicited his alarm.

Somehow, the cordol had already made a speedy return to its den and discovered two of its eggs missing. It reared up and began to sniff the air for its stolen offspring.

There was no time to waste.

Without warning, Kali reached over and grabbed Puk under the armpits then hoisted him up onto Bella's back. The qarm yelped in surprise and righted himself.

They had to move faster. The cordol had spotted them.

Shit.

It slithered toward them with ferocious speed. Bella let out a soft whine.

Kali and the cordol moved in tandem.

She leapt up onto the saddle at the same moment the cordol propelled itself into the air. As Kali kicked at the ayote's sides to take off, the cordol slammed into the ground and burrowed into the sand.

Shit, Kali thought again.

Maybe she hadn't memorized the bestiary front to back like her sister, but she knew enough about cordols and ayotes to be fully aware that there was no chance they could outrun the beast.

But she had to try.

Better that than give up or resort to violence.

It was a good thing Bella was so young and hated being cooped up. Those factors combined with her fear of the approaching cordol injected her with an absurd amount of energy.

Kali had never seen an ayote run so fast. They were a blur.

Puk's arms found their way around her waist again, and Kali had to lean forward to avoid being knocked back by the intense wind.

Their mount instinctively weaved side to side, charting a semi-unpredictable path, but it wasn't enough to outsmart the cordol. It burst from the ground directly in front of Bella, who skidded to a halt, causing Kali and Puk to tumble forward over her head.

Kali crashed head-first into the sand, her legs accidentally whacking Bella on the face. The ayote yipped in shock, but seemed otherwise unharmed.

Puk had absorbed most of the momentum and was flung right into the cordol, knocking the huge, thick worm onto its back.

He scrambled to stand up, but the cordol was faster.

It whipped its lower half into his torso and sent him flying again, screaming *"Fuck!"* as he careened through the air.

If the stakes weren't so high, Kali would have laughed at the ludicrous sight. But as it were, she pushed herself up off the ground and swiftly backed up to her knapsack which hung from the saddle beside the bag carrying the eggs.

"Shit," she muttered aloud this time, distraught that it had come to this.

She extracted her antique dagger from the bag and gripped its hilt.

Just in time, too, as the cordol slid past Bella and rammed into Kali. She braced herself and held on to either side of the beast's head, stabbing the blade into what amounted for its neck.

It gnashed its rounded teeth and roared with fury, rolling away from her and Bella. As it rolled onto its left side, it pushed the dagger in deeper.

Unfortunately, the beast was undeterred by the weapon sticking out of its body. Once righted on its stomach, it reared up again and charged toward Bella, who held the bag that contained its babies. The scent was probably all over her.

Puk was still many feet away, struggling to rise and rejoin the fray.

Kali needed to do something.

But the cordol was fast. Faster than she could have imagined. It smashed its head into Bella's side, sending the ayote crashing down.

The egg bag slammed against Bella's side as she landed, but mercifully it was the bags on her other side that had been crushed by her weight. Hopefully Puk wasn't carrying anything too valuable.

A line of blood trailed from where the cordol had rolled over to where it now slithered around Bella's frantically kicking body. It might be more concerned about retrieving its eggs than the dagger in its head, but apparently, the weapon was causing some damage.

That was good.

Kali tried to leap forward but slipped on the shifting ground, once again slamming her face into hot sand.

She looked up, spitting sand out of her mouth and blowing it from her nose, to see Puk running past her toward the fight.

"Hey!" he called in a feeble attempt to wrangle the cordol's attention. "Look at me! Look at me, I'm a big fat idiot!"

His self-inflicted insults naturally did not register with the cordol aside from earning a passing glance. It quickly turned back to the bag where the smell of its eggs was strongest. Blood streamed from the wound in its head.

Puk stopped running.

Curiously, he reached down and began to undo his boot.

Kali got to her feet and rushed past him as he continued to mess with his shoe. With more preparedness, she jumped forward and grabbed hold of the egg bag.

The cordol roared at her as she tried in vain to pull it free from the saddle. The stablemaster had done too good of a job securing it.

Suddenly Puk's boot zoomed through the air and lodged itself in the cordol's throat while it was preoccupied with another intimidating roar.

The beast began to choke and sputter, which was Bella's cue to get the hell out of there. She scrambled to her feet and took off straight ahead, dragging Kali along behind her as she held on to the egg bag. Bella's wiry tail whipped her face twice before Kali decided to let go.

She rolled a few times before coming to an awkward stop. Up ahead, Bella continued to run for several feet, but soon came to a halt and looked back at her companions.

Good girl.

Kali spun herself around in the sand and witnessed what was possibly the stupidest death ever orchestrated.

Puk too stood motionless, stunned by his own handiwork.

The cordol was still choking on the boot he'd thrown. It thrashed about wildly, kicking up its own tiny sandstorm as it tried to dislodge the sturdy footwear.

Finally, the animal's body slowed, and it lay down in the sand before coming to a complete stop. Kali watched its body bob up and down in a handful of halting, beleaguered breaths before it ceased.

Puk was astonished.

He was standing on one foot to protect the naked one from the heat, and he hopped to face Kali.

"I killed it!" he yelled, relief and amusement in his voice. "Killed it with a shoe! Dumbass!"

She didn't know if he meant himself or the cordol.

Kali exhaled deeply then threw her head back and let herself be lost in the soft sands.

- -

Against all odds, they had pulled off the egg heist.

Puk was still incredulous, even as they inspected the eggs for any signs of damage from the fight. There was a sliver of a crack in one of them, but it seemed cosmetic rather than anything serious. They counted themselves incredibly lucky.

He and Kali both drank from their extra jars of water that Gael had graciously—and unknowingly—bought them. It was crisp and delicious and washed down the lingering taste of vomit.

They stood by Bella, who was making sure to keep her distance from the cordol, dead or not.

With the eggs in fine shape, they were just about ready to depart. There was just one more thing.

"I need to get my dagger," said Kali. It was still lodged in the side of the corpse.

She was about to plod off toward the body when an idea occurred to Puk. Likely a monumentally stupid one, but an idea that he wanted to pursue nonetheless.

"I'll get it!" he offered with enthusiasm. "I gotta get my damn boot outta there anyway." It was not viable for him to hop on one foot all day every day.

Kali laughed softly. "Good point. And I sure as hell don't wanna reach in there."

When they first regrouped next to Bella, Puk had thought Kali would be pissed about killing the cordol, but her mood was lighter than he anticipated. Perhaps she was still high on the adrenaline of the fight and it hadn't fully hit her yet. Or maybe his method of killing had been too stupid and comical for her to even be mad about it.

Whatever the case, he ran to the cordol's corpse. The sand burned his bare foot with every touch.

The cordol had died on its stomach, so it was easy enough to yank the dagger out of its head. In one hand he held the dagger, and in the other was his near-empty glass vial of water.

Puk kneeled down by the cordol's mouth, setting the dagger aside in the sand. After casting a surreptitious glance at Kali, who was busy re-fastening their belongings to Bella, he poured out the remainder of his water on the other side of the cordol's head, out of Kali's view if she so happened to look his way.

He then held open the animal's mouth with one hand and reached the bottle in with the other. He dragged the lip of the bottle across the enormous pink tongue, and across the gums, and everywhere else he could, gathering as much saliva in the vial as he could muster.

All the while, he kept one eyestalk focused on Kali. Her back was still turned to him, so he removed the jar from the cordol's mouth and grinned at the clear liquid sloshing around inside.

It had worked.

After giving Gael all of his fire-spit, he wasn't sure what he'd do, but now he had his own supply of cordol saliva. He didn't have the first clue as to how the saliva was usually distilled and turned into powder, but that was neither here nor there.

Surely it'd still be good if he drank it straight.

That was an experiment for later. He corked the vial and set it next to the dagger, then reached back inside the animal, searching blindly for his damned boot.

It took some amount of effort to reach far enough and find it, then even more to tug it free, but finally the boot was back in his possession. He wiped it along the red worm's leathery skin to dry it off, then slipped his foot back into it with some apprehension.

With the dagger and bottle of saliva in hand, looking no different than the water previously stored inside, he wandered back over to the ladies, who appeared ready to depart.

Puk handed Kali the dagger, and she took it with thanks. After storing it, she helped him up onto Bella then mounted the ayote herself.

"Where to?" he asked her.

She looked up at the sun, judging its position in the sky.

"Y'know, I think we can make it," she said.

"To Restick?"

"To Restick."

CHAPTER IX

SURELY AN EXTREMELY BAD IDEA

It was not often that Puk had a reason to visit Restick. His trips to Herrilock were infrequent enough, and when he did make the voyage across the gulf he always ported in Rus Rahl, to the west, after departing from the southwestern coast of Atlua near his hometown.

Still, he was somewhat familiar with the city. Its layout was just as varied and eclectic as its denizens were. People from all over called Restick their home. It was the largest port city in the country as well as a popular tourist destination, and there were countless cases of individuals coming to visit only to uproot their entire lives and make a new home there. Humans, centripts, faifs, jeorns—even some rocyans and qarms, in spite of their general distaste for the climate. The only underrepresented race were the ujaths, but they tended to stick to themselves anyway, opting to remain in the darker corners of the world.

Kali and Puk arrived at the city arches as the sun was beginning to set. Bella was finally running out of energy, panting gleefully as Kali slowed her near the Ribroad's end.

The path led to two final, gigantic bones piercing the sky, curving toward each other with a gleaming white sign carved of bone that read RESTICK hanging between them. On either side of the two bones were long stretches of white wall standing around one story high. Seroo's bones had initially stretched all the way to the coast, but long ago centript builders had deconstructed them into bricks with which to fashion a perimeter wall to enclose the city.

Along the western wall was a stable. Puk asked, after removing his arms from Kali's waist, "We gonna check Bella in?"

She sounded unsure in her answer. "I guess so," she said. "I really wanted to avoid the cost of a mount, but I suppose stabling is much cheaper than renting *and* stabling. We have no idea yet where this little job is gonna require us to go next, right?"

"Right."

"So we might need her again if we wanna be quick about it. I screwed up before estimating our travel times, and we have no idea where we're headed next, so…it's possible we could get stuck out in the cold if we walk. The added expense is probably worthwhile. We can let her go when we're finished."

Puk chortled. "Why's that? Why not keep her? The way I see it, you lucked into a free ayote."

"We didn't 'luck into it,' we stole her," Kali corrected him. "And besides, Bella here is a great girl, but I've got my eye on an ayote already, and he's back in Seroo's Eye."

Puk rolled his eyes behind her back. He never understood others' affinity for their mounts. A pet dog, sure. Or even a cat, though their fur did not exactly agree with his perpetually slimy skin. But horses and ayotes seemed more utilitarian to him, not really animals to forge an emotional connection to. One ayote was the same as any other.

They rode Bella over to the stable, where a gruff, obese man with a ragged beard huffed a greeting to them. He stared at them expectantly as they slid off the ayote's back and stepped forward.

Both Kali and Puk remained silent, waiting for the interaction to begin.

Eventually, the man grunted, "Yeah?"

Kali wasn't sure how to react. Neither was Puk, so he let her take the lead.

"We…want to stable our ayote?" she ventured, as if that might not be the correct answer.

The man huffed again, losing more patience with them. "Yeah," he said again, though this time with an inflection that said *no shit* in between the lines. "How many nights?"

That was a question neither of them actually knew the answer to. Kali looked to Puk for help, but he shrugged. He had no idea how long they would be stuck in Myrisih. Of course he hoped the errand wouldn't take long, but the city's docking schedule was highly irregular, and it might result in them being stuck there for an extra day or two after concluding their business.

So Kali answered, "Indefinitely."

The man grinned at this. An answer he liked to hear. He could probably already hear the crescents jangling in his pockets.

Kali completed the sign-in process while Puk waited by the entry arches, kicking up sand onto the Ribroad. He could visualize the person they were there to see, an associate of Pillbug's, but he was having trouble remembering the man's name.

The guy was a centript who Puk had only met one other time, but they had hit it off pretty well. It was a long night of boozing and ingesting substances. A typical night out with Pillbug in the flashy city of Rus Rahl.

Part of the reason his memory was so hazy (aside from how drunk he'd been that night) was due to a painful craving he felt for some fire-spit.

The drug didn't contain any addictive properties, but he knew a good hit of it would relax him right about now, and it was driving him insane knowing that he possessed some that he couldn't ingest. His mind refused to be separated from the bottle knocking around in the backpack strapped over his shoulders. Hopefully the centript he was looking for knew someone with the expertise to refine it.

With Bella stabled, Kali returned to Puk's side and asked, "Where to next? Where does your friend hang out?"

He had to shrug. "Can't remember the damn guy's name. He's a centript, though, so I'd think to look in Nyek Hollow."

In his few trips to the city, Puk had never entered Nyek Hollow. It was an exclusively centript neighborhood on the eastern side of town, with rows of buildings constructed of adobe, the way they preferred their hives. Everywhere else in the city was mostly built of wood and stone, which was a rarity in Herrilock, so the Hollow clearly stood out.

She raised her eyebrows. "I thought you knew someone here," she said accusatorily. "I only agreed to this because—"

"Look, I know someone," he cut her off. "It's just been a while since I've seen him and I don't remember his name. That's all. Don't you forget people's names?"

"Not people I claim to be friends with, no."

"Did I say he was a friend?"

"Yes."

"Well, shit."

Kali sighed. "So you think he's in the Hollow?"

Puk shrugged again. "That's my best guess. That's where all the centripts here live, ain't it?"

She nodded. "It's a labyrinth, though. I don't know how you expect to find him in there, especially without a name. It's not like we can go door-to-door asking centripts 'Hey, have you seen a centript?'"

It was a valid point. He had no rebuttal.

He wracked his brain for the damn centript's name. Pillbug had introduced the two of them, explaining that they'd met years earlier when Pillbug was traveling back home to Rus Rahl. The guy stopped Pillbug on the road to rob him, but did a terrible job of it, and they ended up becoming thieving buddies and made a career of robbing people on the road from Toralas to Rus Rahl for a year. Not the most savory introduction to somebody.

Suddenly it came to him.

"Zenib!" he blurted out. "Guy's name is Zenib. He works for some crew that steals from the warehouses by the docks. Or at least he did when I met him." As he said it, an idea came to mind. "How about you search the Hollow, and I'll check out the docks? Sun's goin' down soon, so he might be setting up down there to steal a barrel of pickles or whatever the hell people steal these days."

"No," Kali said.

"Okay, not pickles. What do people steal?"

"I meant no to your suggestion."

"Fine, I'll take the Hollow and you can go see the ocean."
If he could slip away for just a little while, he might be able to
procure some powdered spit before they had to regroup.

"Nah," she said again.

This was troubling.

She went on, "I wanna meet this friend of yours. Scope him
out for myself."

Puk knew he couldn't really argue with that, so he dropped
the subject and suggested they try searching the Hollow first.

They passed underneath the white bone arches and entered
the city proper. It was bustling, as always. There was never any
downtime in Restick.

There were always ships docking at the city's numerous
ports, tourists coming to visit the beach or arts district, merchants in the market square or hobbling down back alleys
peddling their wares. Puk was hard-pressed to imagine anybody finding a second to relax here.

Directly ahead of the entryway was the main market
square, enclosed on all sides by lines of shops selling mostly
inessential items. Restick's market was another of its famous
qualities and attractions for visitors. The items sold there were
mostly all high quality, and were shipped in from various regions around the world that Puk couldn't even dream of visiting
in his lifetime. Naturally there were goods from Atlua and Gillus, but also countries on other continents such as Vareda and
Mayazai.

The two of them veered right, ignoring the infamous market, heading down a cobbled street lined with brick houses on one side and one of the city's two schools on the other.

The eastern side of the city contained fewer homes and establishments than the west end, which was largely considered the affluent side of town. Instead, most of the east end was home to Nyek Hollow, with its towering adobe buildings and confusing, intricate streets interweaving together. When the city was first established, its inhabitants wanted to do away with the massive bones that were cutting through the middle of their land. They hired the help of centripts, who were adept builders and could easily cut through the bone with their incisors. The centripts that migrated to the newly-founded city made camp in the area and began the long, arduous process of cutting down all the bones and crafting them into the walls that now protected the city. Their campground grew as the centripts settled in and it eventually became Nyek Hollow, which was now the home of those workers' descendants.

They passed by a carved wooden sign welcoming them to Nyek Hollow in both Commonspeak and Carsuak, and then they were entombed in the clay labyrinth.

Puk tried to recall if Zenib had mentioned anything about where he lived on the single night they hung out, but nothing came to mind. All he remembered about the man was that he could drink gin as if it was water and absolutely adored stealing things from hapless individuals.

Maybe I don't keep the best company, Puk considered, following Kali down an alleyway darkened by looming buildings on either side.

A little ways ahead there was a centript attached to the side of the lefthand building, latching on to the adobe structure with the many legs (arms?) of her lower half while her upper body curved outward and worked on hanging a sign above a window.

"Hello!" Kali called to the woman.

Her crimson head whipped around to peer at them from above. She grumbled something in Carsuak that Puk couldn't understand, then asked, "What want?" The words came out laboriously and in a heavy accent. She probably kept to the Hollow most of the time and had no use for other language.

Puk was about to answer until he saw Kali start to formulate a response. He could tell she was working through something in her head before she spoke.

"Qumatsk Zenib?" she asked with trepidation. Unsure of her words.

The woman on the side of the building appeared just as surprised as Puk that Kali had crafted a sentence in Carsuak. She replied, *"Blots, kumatsk ceu. Hihtsh."* She then returned to hammering her sign into the building, and Kali resumed walking down the alley.

Puk didn't know much, but he knew that "blots" meant "no." He hurried up alongside Kali and said, "I didn't know you could speak Carsuak that well." He recalled barging in on her studying a book on the subject, but still, he was impressed. Even knowing only a few words of the complicated language was possibly a bigger achievement than anything he'd done with his life.

"I only know a little, and I'm rusty," said Kali. "My sister's way better at it."

"Who cares about her?" Puk scoffed. "Being able to speak it at all is a hell of an accomplishment."

The hint of a smile graced her face. "Thanks," she said.

They turned the corner and something Zenib had said suddenly struck him. It wasn't much of a clue, but it was something to go off.

"Zenib lives near the docks," he told Kali. He remembered the man bragging about how one of the docks was only a couple minutes' walk from his home, which made his job a lot easier. The city had three major docks, along with a few smaller piers, but there was only one that could be considered close to the Hollow.

Armed with this minor knowledge, they turned left down the next street to head toward the northern edge of the Hollow. The neighborhood didn't extend all the way to the docks, but it was likely that Zenib lived somewhere on one of the outermost streets.

"I know I said this mockingly before, but do we need to just…go knocking on doors asking about him until we find him?" Kali asked now that they had at least narrowed down the street.

Puk shrugged. It was as good an idea as any.

She took the initiative again, given that she had a rudimentary understanding of the residents' language. They had no luck with the first few houses, and it was much to their surprise that the fifth house they tried belonged to a rocyan.

"Hello?" said the man timidly, only opening his door a crack. He wore thick-rimmed glasses atop his long, furry canine snout. "Is something the matter?"

"No, everything's fine," Kali assured the nervous man. "We're just looking for someone. Do you know if a man named Zenib lives on this street?"

The rocyan raised his eyebrows and glanced back and forth between Kali and Puk. From the look on his face, he clearly had run-ins with Zenib in the past, and he was trying to work out why this innocent-looking faif woman and tiny qarm were involved with the scoundrel.

Finally, he said, "Yes, I know of Zenib. Why? What's the matter? I thought we were square." He looked as if he were about to slam the door in their face, anxiously clacking his claws on the wood.

"Nothing's wrong!" Kali said again. "Honest. We've just got some business to handle with him but we're not sure where he is. Do you know?"

The man was still apprehensive about the two people standing on his doorstep. But he said, "He lives three houses down. You're not going to mention my name, are you?"

"We don't know your name," Puk chimed in.

The man shut his door without another word.

Kali turned around with a brightened look on her face. She followed Puk to the door three houses down, where he took a deep breath before knocking.

They waited. Behind them, the sun had nearly disappeared behind the sea. They heard a rustling inside the home, and after another few moments, the splintered door swung open.

Zenib stood before them, looking far different than Puk remembered from a few years prior. The centript was now much skinnier, and he was missing two pieces of his carapace near the middle of his body. He had caught the mold. Three of his many arms were also missing, but that was surely job-related.

The man let out a harsh hiss that Puk interpreted as amusement.

"Look who it is!" Zenib said in his raspy voice. "How the fuck'd you come to be on my doorstep, Puk?"

He was genuinely shocked that the man even remembered who he was, let alone his name. "I was in town and thought I'd look you up after the fun times we had," he said.

Zenib laughed at this. "No one else could do you a favor in all of Restick?"

"Not the kind of favor I need, I don't think," said Puk.

Zenib did not need to extend his body to see over Puk's head. He asked, "Who's the lady?"

"My name's Kali," she answered for herself. Based on the little she knew about their disreputable new comrade, Puk had expected her to provide an alias.

The centript clacked his pincers together, a gesture with an unknown meaning to Puk. "Come inside," he then said, welcoming them into his home.

Puk shuffled in with Kali close behind. Zenib's home was as run-down as he would expect. The space was small and cramped with items of varying degrees of uselessness. Over by the window was a table, but there were no chairs for them to sit in, so they stood around it. His shoulders were aching from their journey, even after Kali's lightening of his burden back at Shiar's Slumber, so Puk slid his pack down onto the ground while they all spoke.

Puk wasn't sure what to say to the man. He awkwardly blew air from his mouth, puttering his lips stupidly, and said, "You look well."

The centript guffawed. Or at least made the closest noise possible to a guffaw that a centript's mouth could make, which was akin to a ceramic plate shattering. He said, "No I don't. I lost another shell just last week. Bet my fuckin' head's next. I can feel it pulsing."

Puk wasn't sure if Zenib was being serious or if his words were an attempt at gallows humor, but either way, it made him uncomfortable. He didn't know many centripts back home, and had little experience with the infected here in Herrilock.

"Have you tried that new potion?" Kali piped up. "It's called noxspring. It's supposed to be more effective than ranneth. I've heard it can reverse some of the effects."

Zenib shook his head. "Heard of it, but it ain't too easy to come by yet," he said. "Trust me, I've been searching the warehouses every couple nights, but I haven't found any shipments. It's bein' sold as soon as it's comin' in."

"Why don't you buy some, then?"

The centript gestured around his decrepit home. "Look at where I live," he hissed. "This is the shittiest shithole in a whole hive of shitholes. You think I can afford to buy as many bottles as I'd need?"

"When did you get it?" Puk asked, not knowing if it was rude to ask.

Zenib did not seem to mind. "Only three months ago," he replied. Puk heard Kali gasp behind him. The centript chittered then said, "Yeah, it's workin' fast on me. Probably some sort of god punishing me for all the shit I've done in my life, eh?"

Neither Puk nor Kali responded. Again, Puk wasn't sure if Zenib was speaking in earnest or jest.

"So, what's this favor?" Zenib asked, moving on. He did not offer them anything to drink, which was not unexpected. Puk had not assumed the man would be a spectacular host. "I don't have anything for sale at the moment, I'm sorry to say."

Puk was grateful Zenib spoke vaguely, however unintentional, keeping Kali in the dark. But the two men knew what he'd been referring to.

226 · travis m. riddle

"Not looking to buy," Puk said, hoping Kali assumed that Zenib had simply meant stolen goods—which, to be fair, had probably been lumped in with the drugs. "We're trying to get to Myrisih, and I know you've got a connection."

Zenib laughed again at the prospect. "I do," he nodded, "but what do two fine folk like yourselves have going on in a place like Myrisih?"

Puk glanced at Kali, whose gaze had not shifted from Zenib. He wondered what she was thinking.

He explained that they intended to pick up a job there and would probably need help getting back as well once said job was completed. This piqued the centript's curiosity.

"What kind of job?" he asked.

"Item retrieval."

"That's ambiguous," said Zenib. "Also sounds like a fancier way of saying 'stealing.' I know all about stealing, friend. I also know all the ways to dress it up to make it sound nice."

"Whatever you wanna call it."

Kali remained silent, watching the two interact.

"I wanna get in on it," Zenib then said.

Dammit.

Before Puk could respond, Kali said, "We're not looking for a third. Sorry."

This elicited another plate-shattering laugh from the man. He said, "I don't want to *be* a third. I just want a percentage of the take. In exchange for fast, safe passage to and from Myrisih."

"What do you think your services are worth?"

"A thousand crescents," Zenib answered without missing a beat.

Kali laughed now. "And why would they be worth that much?"

Zenib scuttled around Puk to address Kali directly. "Have you ever been to Myrisih, girl?" She shook her head. "Thought so. It's not easy to get in, I can assure you. The process of gaining a passbook to enter can sometimes take over a year, but I know the guy who doles 'em out."

"I'm sure we'd have no trouble finding someone else in town with a passbook."

"Probably not," Zenib agreed, "but they'd price you same as me. Maybe even more. I'm being generous because Puk is a friend."

Did I really call him my friend before? Are we friends?

"Still, a thousand crescents sounds steep," Kali said. Puk admired her stubbornness.

"You'll need me to bring you there and back, then again when you *retrieve your item*, right? That's gonna take time. Myrisih only opens its port every few days, to ensure they can properly screen everyone coming in and out. Which means once we get there, we might have to stay for at least a couple days. This is all time that could be spent makin' money on other jobs."

"A thousand crescents to sit on your ass and wait sounds pretty nice."

"Don't it?" Zenib clicked.

The haggler in her was coming out. She countered with, "We'll give you five-hundred."

"I oughta ask you both to leave after an insult like that," said Zenib. "It'll cost you a thousand. If that don't seem fair, you're welcome to find someone else to ferry you."

"Look, let's make this work," Puk interjected. He didn't want to piss off Zenib, and Kali was about to blow the whole operation for them. He had no other connections in town. He wouldn't say he *entirely* trusted Zenib, but he definitely had no trust in anybody else they could potentially hire. A modicum of trust was better than none at all.

Kali shot him an irritable look for interrupting her negotiation.

"Seven hundred," she countered.

Zenib shook his head. He knew he had them on the hook, especially after Puk's outburst.

She sighed, realizing the futility of it. "Fine," she said. "A thousand."

"Excellent!" said Zenib. "We can head over there tonight, if you'll be ready. The port's open today. Otherwise we'll need to wait two days."

"Tonight is fine, then," Kali said, not looking to Puk for agreement, though he too did not want to waste any time in Restick. All it would do was cost them money and increase the chances of someone else snatching up the job before they arrived.

"Meet me at the bone dock half past midnight," Zenib told them. "From there, I'll bring you over to my boat and we'll depart. Sound like a plan?"

They both nodded, then said their farewells and left.

Outside, the sun had completely disappeared and stars sprinkled the sky. They had several hours to kill before they needed to meet up with Zenib.

Kali opened her mouth to speak, and Puk was not prepared for the verbal lashing he was set to receive.

But instead she said, "I have a friend who lives here, over on the west side. I don't know about you, but I could do with some food before we go out tonight, and I bet she'd be happy to have some guests."

Food did sound appealing. It had been a long day. He'd eaten some snacks while they rode throughout the afternoon, but he hadn't enjoyed a full meal all day due to their early departure from the outpost. He agreed to the idea.

Kali started toward her friend's home before Puk shouted out, "Shit, hold on!" He had forgotten his bag inside, and went back to Zenib's door while she awaited him outside.

With the door securely shut, Puk grabbed his backpack off the floor and asked Zenib, "I know you said you don't have any to sell, but do you know how to refine fire-spit?" He was positively itching to ingest the bottle of cordol saliva that rattled around in the bag slung over his shoulder.

Zenib shook his head. "Nope, that ain't my business. What the hell are you doing with raw spit?" he asked.

"Just came upon it," Puk said, not wanting to reveal the details of their earlier deed. "Please tell me you know someone who can turn it into powder."

The centript shook his head again. "Nope. Like I said, not my business."

Puk sighed. "Thanks anyway," he said, then left.

He and Kali walked together in silence through the city streets, across the still-busy market square, and into the west side.

- -

It was a miracle they made it to Restick without any significant hiccups. Kali still wasn't totally sure how they pulled it off. They were an unlikely duo, and not an especially effective one, but here they were.

Leg one of their journey complete.

She was annoyed with Puk for dashing her chances to talk Zenib's price down, but it was over and done with now. It would've been hard to make the centript budge, but she felt she could've done it if given more of a chance.

While they walked, she told Puk, "I think Zenib's fee should come out of your half." She had been mustering up the courage to say it for several minutes, and once she had, it was just as awkward as she imagined.

"Why's that?" he asked her.

"I could've knocked it down. I know I could. But then you jumped in and basically told him it was fine, don't worry. But I need every crescent we can squeeze out of this deal."

"So do I."

"Well, then don't you think it would've been smart to negotiate a bit?"

"Sure," Puk nodded, "but I know Zenib's type. He wasn't gonna back down. Not a chance. We needed to get the ball rollin'."

Kali still believed he would've reluctantly accepted her offer of seven-hundred crescents. "I'll pay half of what I offered him. The rest can come from your share." She hoped her voice wasn't shaky. She hated conflict. It was much easier hashing out an agreement in a business context than a personal dispute.

"Nah," said Puk bluntly. "That don't work for me. I'm sorry I stepped on your toes, but for better or worse, we're in this together now. We should be equal partners in this thing."

"But you—"

"I know, alright? I said I'm sorry. Maybe I shoulda let you keep workin' on him, but what's done is done. Can we agree to move past it?" After a few seconds of silence, he said, "In order for this job to go smoothly, we're gonna need to cooperate with each other, y'know?"

"That's my point," said Kali. "We need to be on the same page. We should've discussed this before meeting with Zenib."

"You're right. It was a mistake." Another brief pause, and then, "Whatever, I'll pay him. It's fine." They continued walking in silence.

Zenib had been irksome, as she imagined he would be with how cagey Puk described his relationship to the man. Though she couldn't help but feel slightly bad for him with his affliction. It wasn't common for the mold to affect someone so quickly and so powerfully. He was probably joking when he'd said he could feel a pulsing in his head, but she imagined he was not far from death, if the disease kept up its pace. Even with the simple ranneth that he could afford, he couldn't stave it off for long.

Something was off about Puk, but she couldn't quite put her finger on what it was. She wanted to keep an eye on him since he'd acted strangely at the outpost the night before, and she hadn't trusted him to venture out into the city on his own. She had some reservations about bringing him to the home of her friend, but they had a lot of time before meeting Zenib again, and they might as well try to get a free meal after the man's outrageous price for his assistance.

A childhood friend of hers and Lissia's named Eva had moved to Restick a decade earlier, marrying an art dealer who worked at the gallery on the western side of the city. Eva once worked as a white mage in the city's clinic, but was now a stay-at-home mother while her wife pulled in vast amounts of crescents from commissions on her dealings.

Kali led Puk through the wealthier neighborhood of the city, heading toward the homes at the edge of the arts district. Restick was renowned for its theater as well as its art gallery and wildlife museum. Kali had never been in the theater or museum, and had only checked out the gallery once, with Eva's invitation.

Eva and her wife Violet did not live in the richest part of the city (which consisted of a row of mansions along a private beach), but their house was mighty impressive on its own. Puk let out a low whistle as they came to the doorway.

The home was two stories tall and wide, easily spanning the length of two or three houses in the Hollow, possibly even four on some of the more crowded streets. It was painted a pleasant shade of light pink, and intricate, dizzying patterns were carved into the wood frame of the door. Similar details were sprinkled all over the architecture, appropriately turning the structure into its own piece of art. She was sure that Eva and Violet loved it, but it was a bit garish for Kali's tastes.

Her knock was answered quickly by Eva, whose eyes widened at the sight of her old friend.

"What are you doing here?!" she gasped, beaming. She had dyed her white jeornish hair a shade of pink that matched the outside of her house, which Kali found oddly disturbing.

"Just passing through," said Kali. "Wanted to stop by and say hello before we headed out. This is my friend Puk." He waved and muttered a quick greeting.

"Come in, come in!" Eva said, ushering them inside. "I was just finishing up dinner. Violet is out working, so it's just me and the boys."

The boys were Caleb and Fitz, twins that she and Violet had adopted a few years back. They had only been five or six years old when Kali last saw them, when she visited to check out the art gallery at Eva's behest, and they had to be close to ten now.

Whatever Eva was cooking smelled delicious even to Kali, who generally did not indulge in foods that weren't covered in sugar. The aroma floated through the hallway of her immaculately-decorated home. Colorful abstract art hung from the walls, small tabletops were adorned with beautifully painted vases filled with beautifully bloomed flowers, all of the furniture was arranged perfectly, and all the colors in the house matched—plus, not a speck of dust in sight. Just looking at the place exhausted Kali. She could not handle the upkeep of such a home. It would destroy her.

It had been several days since she'd eaten real food, and she was beginning to feel hungry again. While she usually opted for sweets, sometimes a savory meal really hit the spot, so thankfully Eva suggested that they join her and her family for dinner.

"Are you sure?" Kali asked. "We don't want to impose," she said, hopeful that her expression did not betray the fact that they had come over specifically to impose.

"Of course!" said Eva cheerfully. "I always make too much anyway, and on top of that, I wasn't expecting Violet to work late, so I have even more. The timing couldn't be more perfect, really!" She led them around the corner into the kitchen, where they could hear the sizzling of seasoned meat. "I hope you both like fish."

"Hell yeah," Puk blurted out, then apologized.

"That is quite alright," Eva chuckled, "but please refrain from coarse language when the boys come down. I accidentally said 'damn' around them one time and now they won't stop saying it. Everything is 'damn good' or 'damn bad' now. They keep asking us to get a 'damn dog.' It's driving Violet nuts."

"Got it," said Puk. He sniffed the air and asked, "Is that asparagus I smell too?"

Eva nodded. "You've got quite a nose," she said. "I just bought it fresh from the market today. It came in on a ship from Atlua."

Kali wasn't sure how well asparagus traveled, but she trusted Eva with her ingredients. The woman had always been as fine a chef as she was a white mage.

It was then a storm came rampaging through the house. Eva's boys thundered down the stairs and charged into the kitchen, declaring they were ready to eat, before stopping to observe the strange new visitors in their home.

Eva reintroduced them to Kali, who they had forgotten since their younger years, as well as Puk. "He looks goofy!" one of the boys said, earning a scolding from his mother. Puk didn't seem to care.

The boys washed up at their mother's request, and Kali and Puk did likewise. A day of sandy travel and combatting a cordol had left them both pretty dirtied. Kali could hear her companion's stomach gurgling as he washed and dried his hands.

Caleb and Fitz then took their customary seats around the table. Kali and Puk filled in, sitting opposite the boys, leaving the head of the table for Eva.

Ever the gracious host, she circled around the table filling everyone's water glasses, then placed huge steaming plates of food in the center of the table so that everyone could help themselves.

The main dish was piled high with small, whole grilled fishes that were common in the Loranos Gulf. They had been seasoned with dried lemon zest and pepper, a combination that was practically making Puk drool in his lap. On the side was the aforementioned asparagus, as well as freshly-baked bread rolls. Eva apologized for not having any dessert prepared, and Kali assured her that she was already being more than generous. Dessert was not necessary.

Eva made Caleb recite a short prayer before allowing them to dig into their dinner. Kali grabbed three of the tiny fishes and a few pieces of asparagus to start. She wouldn't bother with the bread; her palate could only tolerate baked goods that were sweet.

The first bite of fish burst with flavor in her mouth. The citrus added a surprising depth to the meat that she thoroughly enjoyed. Lemon icing had always been one of her favorites, after all. It only took a minute for her to devour the rest of the first fish.

Puk was enjoying himself as well. His plate held five of the fishes, an equal number of asparagus, and two rolls. Normally, Kali would've chastised him for taking so much food, but he hardly put a dent into what Eva had cooked. A truly absurd amount remained in the middle of the table, even after all five of them filled their plates.

"It's a shame Violet isn't here," said Eva. "She would've loved to see you. Maybe you can stop by the gallery before you head out?"

The house was on the edge of the arts district, so the gallery where Violet worked was only a couple blocks away, but Kali shook her head. "I don't think so, unfortunately. We're on a somewhat tight schedule."

Eva frowned and continued eating. Caleb and Fitz whispered conspiratorially to each other, casting sideways glances at Puk every so often.

"So, what brings you to two to town, then?" Eva asked, after Kali gushed about how delicious the food tasted.

"A business trip," Kali answered. Eva asked if she was still trading, and she nodded.

"That's wonderful," said Eva. "I always thought what you did was so cool. Traveling to different exotic places, seeing all the sights, meeting interesting people...where are you headed from here?"

"Atlua," Puk said around a mouthful of bread. Crumbs tumbled from his lips onto the lavender tablecloth. "Headed across the gulf."

"Wow," whispered Fitz in awe. "That's damn cool."

- -

When dinner concluded, Puk and Kali thanked their host profusely for allowing them to join in on the meal, and Kali offered to help clean up. Puk would have too, but the kitchen was not designed with qarms in mind. He wouldn't be much use washing dishes if he couldn't even reach the sink.

His thoughts were cluttered with other distractions anyway.

He excused himself upstairs to "sort through his things and prepare for their departure," as he put it to the two women. In other words, he wanted to get away from the gawking children and indulge in some spit.

Standing there in the locked washroom, corked vial of raw cordol spit in hand, Puk possessed a modicum of self-awareness. More than a modicum, really. He muttered aloud to himself, "This is fucking stupid."

There was no telling what drinking the spit would do to him. In all his years of carousing, he had not encountered anyone who'd done it, because why would they? It was perfectly easy to acquire the powder or distilled liquid. If he marched outside right now and sought a dealer, he probably wouldn't have any problem doing so.

But there was no possible way to slip past Kali, especially with the extra scrutiny she seemed to be giving him. She had steadfastly refused to split up earlier in the evening, and he doubted she would be okay with him running out into the night on his own.

Now that they possessed the eggs and made it to Restick, maybe she was worried about him abandoning her. Hopping over to Myrisih on his own to collect the bounty after using her and her money to get here.

If only he could explain to her that wasn't the case.

I just wanna get high, for shit's sake.

Puk stared at the bottle of spit in his hand, wondering whether drinking it would send him into a drug-induced death spiral or perhaps have no effect at all.

More than ever, he regretted giving that asshole Gael the last of his fire-spit.

Puk's body ached. It'd been aching all day. It was impossible to tell whether it was due to all the physical exertion or because it was craving the high.

He uncorked the bottle. The stopper tottered to the floor.

This is surely an extremely bad idea, he told himself. Then he said aloud, "This is not smart."

His mind raced with reasons not to do it:

It could kill him, maybe. Who knew? He could recall no tales of people drinking raw cordol spit. There was no telling what effects it might have on his body.

He was a guest in some kind woman's home. She would not appreciate what he was doing upstairs.

He needed to be sharp for their boat ride in a couple hours.

Kali would be pissed.

Any one of the reasons was enough to not follow through with his terrible idea, never mind combining them all.

But he really wanted it.

He brought the bottle's opening to his nose and took a tentative sniff. The liquid smelled sour and he nearly retched. Another item to add to the list.

But I really want it.

Puk had done many stupid things in his lifetime. He knew that. He was not an intelligent man. Sixty-six years was a lot of time to engage in stupidity. If he were lucky, he would have sixty-six more.

Or this bottle of animal saliva would kill him.

It was probably not worth the risk. Refined spit was totally harmless, but drinking it raw…

Alas, he really wanted that high.

He held his breath and kicked it back.

It came out like sludge, coating his throat as it traveled down. The taste was awful, an acrid sweetness like rotten fruit. He forced himself to swallow, and once he did, he came close to vomiting.

He let out a hacking cough, spittle spraying onto the countertop before him. He corked the near-empty bottle and stuffed it back in his pocket. There were still one or two spoonfuls sloshing around inside, though he truly did not want to experience that flavor ever again.

The effects were extreme and immediate. He could no longer form a coherent thought, and his entire body was going numb. It was inconclusive whether this was better or worse than the aches. Puk took a hesitant step backward, and there were tiny pinpricks on the bottom of his foot.

"Fow," Puk said, which was not a word.

What he tried to do next was take a step toward the door, to—for some reason—leave the room and go downstairs, but this seemingly simple task proved troublesome.

When he took the step, his foot lethargically came down on top of the other. He attempted taking another step, tripping himself, sending his foot shooting backward and causing Puk to slam face-down onto the floor, scraping his stalks against the door. He uttered more muffled gibberish into the floor.

Without getting up, he reached his hand toward the doorknob. His arms were stubby, though, so he could not reach it, and ended up only rubbing his fingertips up and down on the smooth wood. The numbness sent a tingle through his hand that he found mostly unpleasant.

Aside from his hand, which now seemed to be stuck in a never-ending loop, Puk found he could not move his body at all.

This had gone worse than he'd anticipated, and he had anticipated dying.

It was to his great despair that he heard the door swing open. His hand continued to brush up and down against nothing but air.

With great effort, he succeeded in tilting his left eyestalk up and stretching open his eyelid to see Kali staring down at him, mouth agape.

"What the fuck is going on?" she demanded. "We heard you fall all the way in the kitchen."

Puk could not comprehend any of the words she said, though they sounded delightful. His head was spinning wildly and he was absolutely sure his stalk was still extending outward and would soon crash through the ceiling. Maybe his eye would extend to the skies and become a star.

Something in his brain recognized that, because he had been spoken to, it was appropriate for him to say something in reply. So what he landed on was, "Fogga ween mesh," which was nothing.

Kali rolled her eyes and muttered, "Fuck me." She lifted him up by the armpits and placed him on his unsteady feet.

His left eyestalk focused on her, but the right one began to drift into a sideways curve, so she grabbed it and straightened it out. After surviving the raw spit, the look on her face would kill him.

"What—the fuck—did you—do?" she asked, spacing the words out as if that would help with his comprehension. Her voice seethed with anger.

Puk babbled incoherently, thinking he was doing a swell job with this social interaction, but Kali ignored him and spied the dribbles of saliva on the countertop.

Her eyes narrowed to slits. She leaned forward slightly but did not need to give it a good whiff in order to catch its scent; it found her nostrils easily, and she gagged as she stepped away.

"What is that?" she asked him, then instantly groaned as he laughed at her.

Both of Puk's stalks then began to droop sideways, so the angle he saw of Kali arching her arm back was peculiar indeed.

And then she slapped him, though he only knew that because he saw her hand shoot toward his face. He did not actually feel the contact, though a slight warmth emanated from the spot where he assumed she had struck.

Kali swore and slapped him again. It accomplished nothing.

Puk straightened out his stalks (though the right one was still a bit wobbly) and gave his companion a stern look. She reciprocated, waiting to hear what he had to say for himself.

"Fung," he said matter-of-factly.

She slapped him.

- -

It took two full hours for Puk to regain any sense of normalcy. Kali had quarantined him in the washroom in case he threw up, and explained to Eva that he wasn't feeling well. She had to assure the woman that it was entirely unrelated to the fantastic meal she had cooked.

Now there was hardly more than an hour until they needed to meet Zenib at the docks. Kali ushered Puk into the guest bedroom to interrogate him.

At first, he tried to feign ignorance, suggesting he just felt sick from something he ate. She wasn't buying it.

"That wasn't someone who was *sick*," she whispered in harsh tones. She knew the boys were upstairs playing in their room and did not want them to overhear. "You were beyond fucked, and I want to know what's going on."

Puk sighed. "Look, I think I was just dehydrated from all the desert travel. I ain't equipped for it. Qarms are built to take in a bunch of water."

Kali shook her head at this explanation. "First of all, you had a shitload of water at dinner. Second, we had multiple water bottles on the trip. But whatever you spilled on that counter in there certainly doesn't seem like water."

Puk shifted nervously on the bed where he sat. Kali stood before him, chastising him like an angry schoolteacher.

She continued. "You were acting weird at the outpost the other night too, but I figured that maybe you're just a weird guy. Something's going on, though, and you need to tell me. Now. Or this whole deal is done. You can fuck off to Myrisih or Atlua or wherever you want, and I'm going home."

The guilty qarm rolled his eyes, and she resisted the urge to slap him again.

"I've been snorting fire-spit," he said. "I do it all the time. I've done it for years. It's not a big deal. I had some the other night at the outpost, alright? It's not somethin' to freak out about."

Of course Kali was familiar with fire-spit, as it was probably the most common drug in the country. But she had never really been around someone who was using it, and hadn't known the signs to look for. She felt like a fool.

But she wasn't a big enough fool to believe that what he was on tonight had been the same thing. Fire-spit was, all things considered, a pretty tame drug when used correctly. His reaction to it had been far too intense.

"What were you on tonight, then?"

He fumbled, but said, "It was spit. Just raw spit. From the cordol we killed today." His eyestalks dipped in shame.

"You...drank its spit?"

Puk nodded, averting his gaze.

Just imagining it made her want to hurl. Not to mention the lingering stench from the liquid. It must have tasted disgusting. No wonder he looked so ashamed.

"Why the hell would you do that?" she asked.

He groaned. "I just wanted it," he said bluntly. "I wanted some, and it was all I had. So I drank it, like an idiot."

"So you don't have any left?"

Puk hesitated a moment, then shook his head and said, "I drank every drop of this nasty shit, and I gave the last of my stash to that mage at the outpost in exchange for Bella."

That tracked. She should have pressed harder the other night when asking how he pulled off the deal, but she hadn't wanted to grace Gael with another thought.

"Well, good," she said.

He finally looked back up at her. "So are we fine now?"

"Not quite."

She was still furious with him, not only for doing what he did at all but because he had done it in her friend's house—how would Eva have reacted if he'd destroyed all of her family's beautiful, expensive possessions with his vomit or mania? Or what if he'd overdosed and the boys had stumbled upon a dead qarm in their washroom? It was wildly irresponsible.

"What do you want me to do, then?" Puk asked. "I can't un-drink it. I wish I could, 'cause I've still got the terrible

244 · travis m. riddle

fuckin' taste in my mouth. Do you think that's something a white mage could help me with?"

Kali ignored his quip.

"I want you to stop getting high," she said, awaiting the backlash.

As expected, Puk was not thrilled with the suggestion. "I've been fine until tonight," he countered. "How about I just don't drink straight spit from a cordol's mouth from now on?"

She had no patience for his flippant remarks. "No. Cut yourself off. Like you said earlier, we need to cooperate with each other and be on equal footing. I'm already incredibly un-comfortable with this whole situation as it is, and now I'm about to travel to a city I've never been to before—one that as recently as last week I wasn't even sure existed. If even *half* the stories I've heard about the place are true, then I'm not the type of person who will fit in there. You are. If I'm gonna go to Myrisih, then I need to trust that you're focused and alert. Not high on fire-spit with an addled mind."

Puk mulled her words over. She did not think there was anything to consider, though. It was a reasonable request.

"Alright," he finally said. "You're right. Totally right. Even if I was goin' to Myrisih alone, it'd probably be stupid to have my guard down."

Kali breathed a relieved sigh. She was still pissed at him, but at least they had come to an understanding. That was good enough until they got the job done, and then they could go their separate ways and he could snort all the fire-spit he could buy with his crescents.

He asked her how long it was until they were going to the docks, then said, "My head is killing me. Do you think Eva's got any coffee?"

"I would be surprised if you could think of anything in the world Eva *doesn't* have," said Kali, walking toward the door.

Together they headed downstairs to ask their host for one last favor while they waited to leave. While Eva prepared the coffee, she asked Puk if he was feeling better now.

"Yeah," he told her. "Just got a bit of a headache."

CHAPTER X

A LIE SOMEHOW

Gas-powered streetlamps illuminated the west end streets of Restick. Tall, thin, imposing things that loomed over Puk as his boots clomped on the cobblestone. The lamps glared down at him, casting light on his embarrassment and shame that he wished would recede into the darkness, tucked away and forgotten.

Tonight was the second time in as many weeks that he had, essentially, overdosed on fire-spit.

The first time had genuinely been due to dehydration, an excuse that held no water when he tried pawning it off on Kali, but it was tough to pin drinking a bottle of monster saliva on "being thirsty."

He didn't speak to Kali as they walked from her friend's house toward the port. It was late, and the west side of town was home to the city's most "respectable" of people, so they were all in bed, sleeping and dreaming in preparation for another day's work. Silence buffeted the two as they walked, the only sounds being the padding of their footsteps and the faint hum of the lamps.

A part of his conscience ate away at him. Gnawing at the back of his mind. Gnashing it up like a dog with raw steak.

He could feel the vial, still bouncing around in his pants pocket. It was a heavy burden, one that threatened to drag him to the ground, scraping along the path to the docks.

Just get rid of, he ordered himself. *When she's not looking, throw it in the ocean. You don't need it. It nearly killed you.*

And yet he couldn't. Because he wanted it.

The skinny bottle slapped against his leg with every beleaguered step, and with every reminder of its presence he chastised himself for lying to Kali about having some left. He tried valiantly to banish the foul jar of spit from his mind.

If he strained to listen, he could hear the rolling ocean in the distance, lapping against the shore of the beach not too far away. Near the arts district was a row of mansions with their own private beach, and close by was a public beach that ran up the coast to the docks. He imagined there were probably at least some men and women still toiling away into the night, unloading heavy crates from ships and carrying them off into the storage warehouses positioned on either end of the port.

The silence between the two of them started as they drank coffee in the kitchen while Eva put her boys to bed. It grew when Eva returned to the room, the two women engaging in friendly, nostalgic conversation while Puk stood idly by the counter, sipping from his steaming mug and waiting anxiously to leave.

All the while, he wracked his brain for something to say, some sort of rational explanation—words to smooth over everything between him and Kali. Beyond needing her help, he had grown to enjoy her company over the past few days, and he was angry with himself for jeopardizing everything.

But no words had come, and so they had said their farewells to Eva, each thanking her again for her hospitality (and she wishing Puk good health), then set off to meet Zenib.

He wanted to meet them at the "bone dock," which was formally known as Seroo's Tail, because that's precisely what it was: the bones of Seroo's tail. The ancient beast's skull housed the city of Seroo's Eye, which was connected to Restick by the Ribroad, and its body came to an end with the tail which extended out into the gulf, supported by posts. It was over a thousand feet long—Puk wasn't sure how long exactly—and its tip dipped into the water, the only part not propped up. There was plenty of space for ships to dock and unload, as well as multiple smaller slipways for personal boats.

There were two impressive ships docked at Seroo's Tail when they approached, but no sign of any workers or Zenib. They were alone.

Two additional docks were stationed a ways away on either side of Seroo's Tail, farther down the coast, and some workers milled about on each of those, so Puk was surprised by the lack of activity on the bone dock.

Kali walked out onto the bone, gleaming white in the moonlight. She sat down on its edge and kicked her feet above the gentle water.

"Guess we'll keep waiting," she said, her first words to him since his much-deserved chastisement in the guest bedroom.

Puk took this as an invitation and sat down beside her, dangling his own feet. He imagined pushing himself off into the cold water, sucked down into the depths.

He felt the silence sprouting up again, and he wanted to nip it before it grew too large. He said, "I'm sorry. Again."

For a second, he thought Kali wasn't going to say anything, but then she muttered, "It's fine."

But he wouldn't let himself off that easy. "Nah, it's not, really. You're right, I fucked up. I shouldn't have put you in the position I did. I know Myrisih ain't the most friendly of places, and I need to be aware of what's goin' on. Not babbling nonsense while I try to lick the floor."

She chuckled at that image, then said, "I'm not trying to dictate your life. If that's what you wanna do with it, then by all means, go for it. We can call this off and I can go home and figure something else out for myself." She sounded almost hurt. Something in him suspected this whole scheme was a last-ditch gambit on her part.

Puk fervently shook his head. "I'm gonna see this through," he said. "I'm done with spit." He didn't tack on *for now* to the end of the sentence; it would only elicit doubt. As he said it, though, it felt kind of true.

But it probably wasn't.

He decided to be fully honest with her. He had to regain her trust. Lay everything on the table.

He said, "The reason I was singing in your parents' inn is because I got kicked out of my troupe. I got kicked out for the same thing: I snorted some spit, and I genuinely was really dehydrated from traveling all day, and it fucked me up a lot more than it should've." He went on to describe, in excessive and probably unnecessary detail, how he had vomited on stage during his performance and drew the ire of all his friends.

Kali busted out laughing at his ordeal. "That's disgusting," she choked through laughter. "Did any get on the audience?"

"Fuck, I hope not," he sighed. "I hadn't even thought about that." He broke into a soft laugh too. He then said, "Anyway, my troupe was traveling across the country, performing shows, and then we were gonna go back to Atlua. Getting kicked out is why I needed to do this job. No shows, no money, no ticket back home."

She nodded, her laughter dying down, then asked, "Did you always get high before shows?"

"Most of the time, yeah. If I had anything on me."

"Why?"

He didn't really understand the question. "Because it feels good?" he offered.

Kali shrugged, looking down at the water. His eyestalks stayed trained on her as she spoke.

"I would just think that...well, I guess not everyone cares about their *job*, but wasn't singing something that you loved doing? Something fun and creative and fulfilling? Why would you want to dull that?"

It was a hard question to answer. But he tried.

"I don't think I've really put any effort into music in a long time," he said, the realization sending a pang through his chest. "We...the troupe was never particularly successful. We got by okay, I guess. People enjoyed our shows when they saw 'em, but there was never much of a turn-out. Not even here, where we thought a qarmish troupe would be a novelty that people would wanna check out. Seroo's Eye was the only place we got a big crowd. I dunno. We just never made any damn money, and it's hard staying motivated to do something when it's just...constantly failing." He curved his stalks down to look at the water as well. "No matter how 'fun' or 'fulfilling' it is, it's kinda demoralizing after a while. I just got tired of the futility."

He had put in the work. Had for years and years, with little to nothing to show for it.

So why work hard when he could have fun instead?

Silence. He turned one stalk to glance at Kali, and saw that she was still staring at the water.

"I get that," she said. "I've been wondering a lot lately if any of the shit I'm doing is worthwhile too. It's like you said: I enjoy doing it, but at a certain point, that's not enough." She turned to face him and said, "I haven't given up, though. I'm trying to do everything I can to make it work. Clearly, since this crazy adventure is way out of my comfort zone. But I have moments of self-doubt too."

Puk grinned. "Are you about to tell me not to give up on my dreams?"

"No," she replied. "I told you, I'm not trying to dictate your life. Do whatever you want. I'm just saying I know how you feel. I'm just also saying that I'm trying not to give in. But it *is* hard. No denying that."

Puk leaned back, placing his hands on the dock. He tapped the length of his fingers on it, enjoying the split second of suction from his sticky skin adhering to the bone.

"So you're tryin' to tell me you *enjoy* selling shit to people?"

She laughed. "Yes."

"Why?"

She shrugged. "It's kinda fun, honestly. Finding or making stuff to sell, striking bargains with other merchants, the thrill of a good haggle...plus, it's great traveling all over, seeing different towns and cultures. That's the part I like most."

"That's why you wanna go to Atlua?"

"Mhm. I think I could offer them a lot of stuff they maybe haven't seen much of before, especially in the smaller towns. I hear there are a lot more small-town places over there than here.

The desert makes for harsh living; most people congregate in the bigger cities."

Puk nodded. He had visited several of those tiny towns across Atlua. Gesh, Balam, Leeros—hell, even his hometown of Trillowan was relatively small.

"I bet there's a bunch of stuff over there that people here would love to get their hands on, too," Kali went on. "It's exciting thinking about all the different clothes and jewelry and medicines that I could bring over. What started this whole thing is that a white mage in Atlua invented a new potion for fighting off the mold."

He remembered she had mentioned something about that in Zenib's house. "Is that what noxspring is?" he asked, impressed with himself for not forgetting the name. She nodded. "Well, that's a noble cause. Zenib sure could use it. Guy looks like shit."

She chuckled, but whispered, "That's mean." Then she asked, "What got you into singing?"

That question was much easier to answer. There was nothing complex about his inspiration in that regard.

He told her about a traveling qarmish troupe that had visited Trillowan when he was still a child, only ten or eleven years old.

The group performed a play (a feat of organization and cooperation The Rusty Halberd never pulled off), complete with shifting sets on the small stage they brought with them. The production was set to music, played off-stage by two of the members who were performing double- and triple-duty with various instruments, and multiple songs were sprinkled throughout the story.

There was a duet sung near the start of the play that had enraptured a young Puk. Now, more than fifty years later, he'd be damned if he could remember the melody or lyrics, but back then it had captured his imagination.

Afterwards, he wanted to talk to the members of the troupe to find out the name of the song, but his father Brek insisted the entertainers were too busy to speak to a child.

So instead, Puk had gone home and started writing his own songs, emulating what he heard on that stage. As he grew older, he wrote less and less original music and instead learned pub songs, classical tales, and whatever else he thought might secure him a steady spot in a troupe.

It seemed like Kali was about to ask him something else when a shout came from the direction of Nyek Hollow.

"Sorry to keep y'all waitin'!" yelled Zenib, doing a terrible job of being discreet.

The two stood and approached the centript, who scuttled toward the dock on his countless clawed feet. An olive green cloak was draped over his back, covering up his missing carapace segments.

"You look in high spirits," Zenib observed, and when Puk looked to Kali, he was surprised that there was indeed a smile on her face. "That excited for the floating city, eh?"

"Floating city?"

"That's just what some people call it," Puk explained. "It don't really make sense, the city's not floating, but it takes up an entire small island on its own, so…" It was a name he personally found to be stupid and not entirely accurate, but many of the city's frequent visitors used the moniker.

Zenib clapped some of his hands together and said, "Shall we head to my boat?"

They nodded and followed the centript, who turned around and plodded off in the direction from which he had come. The group passed a warehouse on their left that Zenib surely frequented, then further on past another dock on their left and the Hollow on their right.

At the edge of the Hollow was a length of white bone wall, demarcating the city limits. The fence was obscured in shadows cast by clay buildings of the centript's neighbors. A knot tied itself in Puk's stomach as he gaped at Zenib climbing up the wall with ease then jumping down, no longer visible on the other side of the opaque wall.

"I can't do that," said Puk. It had nothing to do with believing in himself; his tiny body could not physically do it.

Kali hoisted herself up, her boots scraping noisily against the bone as she scrambled upward. Resting on top of the wall, she leaned over as far as she could and held out her hand.

Puk grabbed it and tried to assist with his ascent as much as possible, kicking his feet up the side of the wall like she had done to propel himself upward, and after a few strained moments he sat atop the bone wall with her. He offered his thanks, then they both hopped down into the sand where Zenib patiently waited.

They continued following the man for almost ten minutes, until the sand gave way to rock at the coastline, and soon they came upon a diminutive boat nestled away between two large, red rocks, only visible from the sea or if you came at it from a certain angle.

"Here she is," said Zenib with misplaced pride.

The boat could not fit more than four people, and Puk had his doubts that even just the three of them could squeeze in with their luggage in tow. It was painted a boring gray, likely to remain unseen in the night, but some of the paint was chipping away to reveal the brown wood underneath. Oars were propped up in the center of the vessel, though the paddle of one had a chunk bitten off.

But still, it was a boat, and they needed a boat.

"Does she have a name?" Puk asked sarcastically.

"Yep: the *Fiery Lass*."

"Incredibly bad name for a boat," said Puk. Kali giggled but nudged him to quieten.

"Watch your tongue, or you might find the *Lass* sending you overboard," Zenib growled. Puk apologized, eliciting more hushed laughter from Kali.

Zenib pushed the boat out from between the rocks and into the lapping waves. He held it in place while Puk and Kali piled in, pressing toward the front, then he slithered aboard himself. The centript's long, shelled body took up half the boat on its own.

He gripped the two oars and pushed off, sending them out into the sea.

Finally, they were off.

- -

The *Fiery Lass* did not handle waves well, so it was lucky for them that the Loranos Gulf was mostly calm that night.

Kali was sandwiched between the two men, with Zenib at the rear and Puk at the prow. The sound of wood scraping wood as Zenib oared made her skin crawl.

For a while, she couldn't even make out the horizon. The black of the sky and the dark of the water blended together, stars reflected on the surface, creating a massive dotted canvas that they sailed toward without any sense of progress or reality.

She decided to make small talk in an effort to dull the boredom. "So you said that Myrisih's port is only open every few days?" she asked Zenib. She craned her neck to look at the centript behind her.

He nodded and said, "On the third, fifth, and seventh days of the week. So strictly speaking it was yesterday they were open, but they won't close down for another couple hours. I don't think, anyway."

The uncertainty in his voice did not inspire confidence.

But she plodded on. "That's strange."

"Whole place is strange," said Zenib. "The entrance is smothered with an enchantment, too. The ujaths who first lived there struck some sort of deal with the jeornish that migrated to the desert from the north."

"What kind of enchantment?" she asked. She had never heard this aspect of the city's mythos.

Zenib said, after grunting with exhaustion from rowing, "I don't know how the spell works—that sorta thing is beyond me—but there's some spell within the entryway that makes the people who leave forget how they reached it in the first place. Just fades from their memory. The only way to find the city is to learn of an individual who's been trusted with its location and obtain a passbook from them, which informs you how to navigate there and is proof to the guards you can be trusted too."

It sounded ridiculously convoluted to Kali. "So that's what you were doing after we left your place? You had to go meet your contact in Restick who distributes passbooks?"

The centript nodded. At the front of the boat, Puk remained silent, watching the water lap up against their vessel. Kali couldn't tell whether he was uninterested in the topic or simply couldn't hear them.

She asked, "How many people actually know where to find Myrisih?"

"That info ain't for us to know," he said over the rolling waves. "The people in charge take security very seriously. That's how come it's stayed a secret for so long, and why no authorities anywhere have cracked down on it. It's in the middle of the gulf, too, so it ain't anyone in particular's problem, and the ones that somehow find it and try to get in don't make it too far."

"What happens to them?"

Zenib rolled his upper body a bit, the centript approximation of a shrug. "How'm I supposed to know?"

"Fair enough. How do they get found out in the first place?" she then asked. "How will they know I'm not an Atluan Guard or something?"

He shrugged again. "I ain't employed by 'em, so I don't know their methods. When you come into the port, you have to sign a records sheet with your full name and the vessel you came in on. How they use that info to weed out the authorities is beyond me. I ain't an authority, so it makes no difference to me."

Kali nearly groaned at the thought of having to write *Fiery Lass* beside her name. Taking into account her red hair, it was enough to make her puke.

"What if you provide a fake name?" she asked. Their boat rocked a bit, the waves getting a little rougher.

Puk chimed in for that one. "You don't wanna write a fake name."

"Why not?" she asked, turning to him. He was holding on to both sides of the boat, gripped by fear of falling overboard.

"You just don't," he said. "I've heard stories. Trying to lie or sneak your way into the city is just as bad as bein' an Atluan Guard or anything else like that. They're none too accepting."

The highly-secret black market city isn't accepting of deceit. Of course not.

"How would they even know?"

"I don't know," said Puk. Kali began to wonder if anyone knew how anything in Myrisih operated, or if any of this was actually true rather than rumor. "Maybe you can write a fake name and find out for yourself."

She hungered for concrete details about Myrisih, but it was becoming clear that they were as elusive as the city itself. Tucked away somewhere in the sea, shrouded in mystery.

Kali was lost in a trance for a long while, staring out at the sea, when suddenly she was shaken out of it by Puk's voice.

"Look," he said.

Both she and Zenib looked to their right and saw another ship floating along the waves. It was a schooner, quite a bit larger than the skiff they were confined to. In the dark, Kali couldn't make out the colors of their flag, but the markings were unmistakable. The ship was from Vareda.

"Are those pirates?" Kali asked, remembering the story stablemaster Gregori had told her back in Seroo's Eye. She wasn't well-versed enough to know whether the flag indicated they were military, or only that they were Varedan.

"Might be," Zenib replied. "Looks like they might be heading the same way we are."

"They're gonna raid us? Can they even see this tiny boat?"

Zenib laughed. "I don't mean they're comin' toward us. They're going to Myrisih, I think."

They kept their course steady, as did the Varedans, who kept their distance. Before too long, land peeked out over the horizon, illuminated by the moonlight.

"There it is," said Zenib with triumph.

As they sailed closer, Kali was able to make out that it was a set of five islands varying in size. The two islands that were the closest and the farthest away were the biggest, with two slightly smaller ones between those as well as one that could hardly hold more than handful of buildings if anyone tried to build atop it.

"Which island is it on?" Kali asked her two companions. She continued side-eyeing the Varedan ship, with intermingling thoughts of pirate raids and war cries.

"More accurate question would be which island is it *in*," Zenib corrected. "It's in the one closest to us."

"It's inside the island?" She had never heard this in all the myths and rumors she'd accumulated about the city over the years.

"The island belonged to an ujath colony. They dug out the insides of the island a long, long time ago before it became the place it is today. Ujaths been livin' there for years and years. Longer than any of us have been alive."

Ujaths were normally such a solitary race, Kali did not have much experience interacting with them. They kept to themselves in the darkest corners of the world, having originated in Vareda, and did not often venture out to countries like Herrilock or Atlua. She had no idea Myrisih was once one of the original ujath colonies.

Their centript captain steered them around the seemingly deserted island, topped with mountainous peaks, swaying grass, and looming trees. Nothing at all to indicate that an entire city with a dense population was nestled within the rock.

The Varedan ship pulled ahead, its sails granting them much more speed than Zenib's haggard rowing.

Kali watched with interest as the large ship navigated between the tiniest island and the one that housed their destination. The channel was incredibly narrow, and if the ship was any bigger at all, its sides would have scraped against the two islands. But it slipped through unscathed and veered into an inlet.

The *Fiery Lass* followed.

Once again, Kali watched with bated breath to see if the Varedan ship would make it through okay. Ahead was the entrance to a cave system, with stalactites hanging dangerously from the cragged ceiling. But the ship slid smoothly into the mouth of the cave, bypassing sharp tips above. The ship sailed with such confidence, its crew had to be regulars of the city.

The location of the cave entrance explained why fleets of military vessels didn't invade the island, granted they knew where it was; nothing substantial could fit, and surely there was some kind of defense set up that could effortlessly blow away any small boats that posed a threat. With only one way in and one way out, it was easy to keep an eye on the comings and goings.

On either side of them was smooth, shiny rock as they floated down the channel deeper into the island's center. They began to wind to the left, still trailing behind the Varedan pirate ship. Its wake rocked their measly boat more than the natural waves had on the rest of their journey.

"Are we gonna have to wait for all those bastards to be processed?" Puk asked.

"Usually, no," replied Zenib, "but with how late it is, I'm not sure how many people will be working."

Kali certainly did not want to be stuck rocking on Zenib's boat for an hour waiting to be processed. She hoped there were ample employees milling about, awaiting new visitors.

They soon came to a port outfitted with fewer ships than she expected, though it made sense given the limited amount of space. There were three other boats docked that were the same size as the incoming Varedan ship, and around twenty to thirty small vessels such as their own.

Glancing around, the space issue seemed more pressing than it had a moment before. "What if there's nowhere for us to dock?" she asked.

"Then we go back to Restick," said Zenib.

Their travel partner pulled into the last remaining space available for large ships, while the three of them scouted for anywhere else along the surprisingly sturdy dock they could sidle up next to.

The knot in Kali's stomach slowly untied itself as Zenib claimed a spot in between two ships named *Shadowstalker* and *The Cutting Blade*, both of which made her gag. She decided that there was no such thing as a solid ship name.

She also remained unconvinced that the spot Zenib had parked the boat in was meant for occupation, but theirs was small enough to fit, so he claimed it.

They helped each other tie the boat to the dock and stepped out onto it. Kali relished the feeling of being on solid ground again after so many hours out on the water. She hadn't quite felt seasick, but she was definitely more at ease now that her body was no longer in constant motion.

Zenib's claws thudded against the wood as he scuttled toward a rocyan who was fast approaching their position. Puk followed close behind, and Kali figured they were about to be processed. She was thankful they weren't waiting in line behind the Varedans.

"Welcome," said the rocyan, a much politer greeting than Kali would have wagered. She momentarily tried to push aside her assumptions and prejudices about this place, but then remembered it was a black market city full of thieves, mercenaries, and other ruffians.

"Hello," Zenib greeted the man. As they all addressed the rocyan, a crew of men sauntered past and began to inspect the *Fiery Lass*. There was not much to see or find.

The man requested Zenib's passbook, which he handed over with a chitter. They waited while the rocyan read over the first page of the tiny leather-bound notebook, then flipped to the next empty page and began to write in it himself.

He glanced up and confirmed, "These two are accompanying you? Or do you have passbooks of your own?"

"We're guests," Puk answered.

The rocyan nodded and resumed writing. Kali wanted to know what he was jotting down, what sort of security and records processes the people who worked here went through to validate their guests, but she didn't want to stir up trouble. No doubt it would look suspicious if someone came to the city for the first time and immediately started asking a bunch of questions about how it operated. Those in charge would not view that as innocent curiosity.

The rocyan, whose name Kali never learned, handed Zenib his passbook and had each of them sign a records sheet, just as her partners had said would happen.

She was the third to sign. The yellowed paper contained countless rows of names, both ship and person, scrawled in messy print. Near the middle of the page was the next available line for her to pledge her identity.

Lisa Meyers, Fireweaver

Zacharas Reis, Fireweaver

Tunu Re'ca, Shadowstalker

Zenib Mhaskarsk, The Fiery Lass

Puk, The Fiery Lass

She sighed and reluctantly put her name down.

Kallia Shiar, The Fiery Lass

It was her true, full name, and yet it felt like a lie somehow. This wasn't who she was. She wasn't some scoundrel, some miscreant scurrying through the streets of the black market island.

Except that it was. Because she was here, and that was exactly what she intended to do.

It was surreal.

She handed the sheet back to the rocyan. His snout was short and he had a wicked overbite, exposing a row of pointed fangs. His fur was gray and matted, damp from hours spent in the humid cave.

By this time, his crew was finishing up with their search of the ship. They returned to their leader and gave him curt nods.

Zenib seemed pleased with himself even before the rocyan spoke. Puk looked over at Kali and offered her a weak smile, which she returned in kind.

The rocyan said in a low growl, "Looks like everything's in order, Mr. Mhaskarsk, Mr. Puk, Ms. Shiar." He turned and headed down the dock, toward a smattering of cave openings leading to different areas of the city. He indicated for them to follow and said, "Welcome to Myrisih."

CHAPTER XI

OUTSIDE HIRE

They woke the next morning with aches in their joints. Myrisih's lodging options were not particularly robust, and the few nicer places in the inner caverns were too expensive for them to comfortably afford.

The city was exactly how Puk remembered it.

It was comprised of endless tunnels acting as streets, connecting several different cavernous areas within the island. These caverns hosted myriad establishments, including but not limited to black market trading posts, guilds of assassins and mercenaries (Puk could never tell the difference between the two), brothels, and exotic animal wranglers—if it could be put on a ship and its legality was dubious, it was here.

The tunnels were brightly lit with orbs of light strung along the ceiling like incandescent spiderwebs, trailing through the city to converge in a blinding web at the city's epicenter, in a cavern known as the Mass.

The Mass was their destination.

Or, more specifically, an unsuspecting building—more of a shack, really—on the outer edge of the Mass. The building had no sign to indicate what it was, and in fact it had no official name that could be put on a sign in the first place. This was where Puk's associate Voya lived and worked, selling stolen wares and, in the event he failed to supply a customer with something, connecting buyers with other sellers. For a small commission, of course.

The inn Puk and Kali had slept in was situated in one of the many smaller, nameless caverns throughout the city. The cave system was not lacking in caverns full of run-down, unmemorable places and people, not deemed worthy enough of a title like the Mass.

But despite how drab it all seemed to both Puk and Zenib (who found his own place to stay during the duration of their trip), Kali was titillated by everything she saw.

They stepped out of the inn into the dim cavern, unable to discern what time of day it actually was. They were forced to rely on rusty clocks hanging from the cracked walls of the inn, which Puk did not particularly trust.

He hadn't been able to get much sleep.

Typically, his use of fire-spit was intermittent. He indulged in it when he was in Herrilock and it was cheaper, then only every so often back in Atlua, where he primarily dabbled with marshweed. So some acute withdrawal symptoms were not uncommon to him, since he usually hit the spit pretty hard while in the desert; he usually had to deal with them at the tail-end of his trips here.

But this was worse than they'd ever been before, and it had only been about twelve hours since he'd last used. There was no doubt in his mind that it was due to the fact he'd ingested the spit raw.

He'd tossed and turned all night, had to get up multiple times to use the bathroom, and now his entire body ached. This was a constant feeling for him—not only in regards to with-drawals, but rather this whole journey he'd embarked on with Kali. He couldn't remember the last time he was so sore.

With her own exhaustion sloughed off, Kali was now able to absorb everything around them. Puk tried to look at it through her fresh eyes, but still he could not muster up the same naïve fascination. Their inn was located at the outer edge of the cavern, right up against the craggy rock wall, and stepping out the front door presented them with a view of similarly decrepit buildings.

One was a poison shop with a sign propped up against its wall, dripping with painted words advertising "Lowest Prices on Quillis & Barnas" and "New Concoction—Try Today!"

Another building had no advertising or signage; the only indication of what could be found inside was the silhouette of a woman painted on its door. Even at this early hour, men and women were filing in and out of the building. The brothel was the most active place in the cavern.

There was also a pen set up farther down the row of build-ings gaining some foot traffic with baby serokos and vissians mingling—which would surely end in a bloodbath—but aside from those two places, their chosen cavern was mostly de-serted.

Puk led them past the poison shop and ill-advised animal pen into one of the connecting tunnels. The pathway was better lit than the cavern, and up ahead he could see a group consisting of two centripts and a jeornish woman who were getting an early start to their day as well.

He wasn't terribly familiar with the city's geography, but he knew enough to at least get them to the Mass. This tunnel wound up in a dead-end, but it branched off into five other tunnels leading to various parts of the city. The group ahead of them veered off into one of the branches, the one that Puk was fairly sure led to the Mass, and so he followed.

"Are the eggs still okay?" Puk asked, prompted by nothing but his own wandering mind.

Kali had left their extra bags back with Bella at the Restick stable, and transferred the cordol eggs into her personal knapsack slung over her shoulder, acting as their protector. She opened it and peered inside, reaching in to turn the eggs over and inspect them fully.

"Perfectly fine," she confirmed. "Aside from that one crack."

Puk desperately hoped that his peace offering would assuage any anger Voya still felt toward him. There was a perfectly reasonable chance that this entire venture had been for naught if Voya was still too bitter to point them in the direction of the person hiring for the job.

While they walked, he recited an apology in his head.

Voya, I am sorry for throwing you overboard after cheating you out of a lot of money.

It sounded bad. Even in his head. There was not a good way to phrase what he had done. No smoothing its rough edges.

Voya, I am sorry for making you swim all the way home or whatever the hell it is you had to do.

Still not great.

Voya, I am sorry I fucked you over so bad.

Maybe vague and succinct was the best way to go about it.

Voya, I am sorry I fucked you over so bad. Here are some eggs.

That would work. He only hoped his fatigue and irritability didn't eke into conversation and ruin things with Voya.

They rounded a corner, finally coming to the mouth of the barren tunnel that opened up into the Mass. They entered.

The Mass was enormous, easily taking up half the island.

At its center was a spire that connected the floor to the jagged ceiling, a wide tower that was heavily guarded at all hours. The anonymous individuals who handled the city's operations lived there. Puk had once heard a rumor that they were two brothers, but that was the only identifying detail he'd ever gotten about them. They held an incredibly enviable position, and given the city's residents and clientele, no one would balk at committing a simple murder to attain the title for themselves. Anonymity was key to their survival.

The cavern's establishments were built in rings radiating out from the spire. Generally, there was some order to their placement. One ring was dedicated to weapon and armor shops, blacksmiths, places that sold accessories, and whatever other equipment-based goods a killer could dream of. Another ring sold animals, food, bait, harnesses, and so on. There was another for sex work, another for poisons and potions—the Mass contained so many rings, Puk didn't have the faintest clue what half of them were for, and he assumed there must be at least some repeats.

Kali's eyes were lit up as he explained all this to her. She told him she had never seen such a grandiose marketplace.

"How is *this* the biggest market in the world?" she wondered aloud. "Of all the great cities in Ustlia, how did this secret, illegal market end up as the biggest and most varied?"

Puk shrugged. He didn't know the first thing about trading. "No regulations, maybe?" he offered. "Anyone can come here and set up shop and sell whatever shit they have, no questions asked." It was the only explanation he could drum up.

The outermost and largest ring, the one that Voya's home and shop was a part of, was for the sale of "general goods," which meant any old stolen thing the merchants could get their grubby hands on. Clocks, silverware, drugs—anything that didn't fall into the more specific categories of the other rings.

He could tell Kali wanted to investigate further, venture into the different rings and check out how the shops functioned, but they had a job to do. They needed to track down whoever was offering the job before the port opened up again in two days so they could be on their way by then.

She followed dutifully behind him as he navigated around the outskirts of the Mass. They passed a huge number of shops, some of which he allowed Kali a few minutes to peek inside. She was particularly amazed by the low prices of most items, and Puk pointed out the high profit margins associated with stealing all your wares.

In the end, it took about twenty minutes to reach the front door of Voya's home. There was a large CLOSED sign hanging from it, which Puk blatantly ignored.

He reached up to knock, but stopped when Kali asked, "Is this gonna piss him off? Knocking when he's not wanting guests?"

"He's already gonna be pissed off when he sees me," Puk said·

"Exactly. Don't you wanna *not* piss him off more?"

"Pissed is pissed," Puk shrugged. He knocked.

There came a rumbling from inside. Angry thuds thundering through the building as its owner stomped to the front door, grumbling to himself, yelling to "read the sign and fuck off" and that "illiterates aren't welcome here."

But still the door swung open, and before them stood Voya, absolutely fuming.

His frown morphed into a vicious scowl as the tip of his gigantic tongue flicked in the air around Puk.

"Well," the ujath muttered in his deep, guttural voice, "look who the thuck it ith."

--

They stood at the threshold of Voya's home and, after seeing the look on the ujath's face as he stared down at Puk, Kali suddenly decided this was an awful idea.

"Twooth be told, I didn't think I would ever thee you again, *Puk*," said Voya. Venom dripped from the qarm's name.

"Well, truth be told, you've never really *seen* me, have you?" Puk joked. Prodding him.

In truth, Kali had never stood so close to an ujath before. Their torsos were saggy, fleshy orbs with no distinguishing facial features. Just rough, gray skin. Jutting out from each corner of their body were four long, spindly legs that rose into the air then sharply curved back down. Two limp arms hung from their torso as well, skinny and weak. There was an enormous opening for a mouth that took up most of an ujath's body. From there, their massive pink tongues hung out, trailing along the ground, too big to fit inside their bodies. Ujaths had no eyes, instead using scent sensors in their tongues to navigate the world.

"Tha's thunny. Thunny thucking guy over here," said Voya sourly, speaking around the huge, meaty appendage. It dragged along the ground, its tip pointing toward Kali now, leaving behind a trail of saliva. "Who'th thith?" he asked.

She decided to speak for herself before Puk could say something snarky to dig them a deeper hole. "My name's Kali," she answered. "It's nice to meet you."

"No it's not," Puk laughed. "Don't lie to the guy."

She shot him a sidelong glance, a silent urge to be civilized, but he laughed that off too.

"Look," Puk said, turning back to his old friend, "Voya, I'm sorry I fucked you over so bad. I brought you some eggs."

"You bwought me eggth? Why the thuck do you think I wan' eggth?"

"I haven't told you what *type* of eggs yet."

"I don't think there are any eggth that can make up thor what you did to me. Thuck off." He backed up on his four spidery legs, receding into his house. He was about to swing the door shut with one of his unnervingly humanoid arms before Puk leapt forward, blocking the action.

"They're cordol eggs!" he said. "We brought cordol eggs. I know you can make use of these, right? Hatching your own cordols to gather spit from? That'll surely cut your costs down by a lot, if you're your own manufacturer."

Voya's scowl turned into what Kali would describe as a look of contemplation, if such an expression were possible on an ujath's face.

"Come inthide," he said.

They followed him in, Kali closing the door behind them. Puk shot her an impish grin, but she offered him a scowl of her own.

They were truly an unlikely group. A spidery, fleshy ujath with his tongue sliding along the floor; a stocky, rubbery blue qarm; and a faif with fiery red hair and pastel-swirled skin. For the hundredth time, Kali pondered how she ended up where she was.

Voya's home was, astoundingly, in better condition than Zenib's back in Restick. It was a modest place, with stacks of boxes lining the walls, but at the very least it was neatly organized. There were multiple light fixtures on the walls, granting the room much more light than outside. Certainly more for his customers' benefit than his own.

The ujath turned to face them, his arms swinging with dead weight. His tongue waved back and forth across the floor between his two front legs.

"Tho," he started, "where are thethe eggth?"

"These eggs is here," Puk said, gesturing to Kali, and without hesitation she offered him the sack. He opened it up and placed the two pale orange eggs on a tabletop near Voya, who lifted his tongue into the air, hovering it above them. Kali wondered if he could somehow smell the slight crack in one of them. After a few more seconds of inspection, the tongue then fell with a wet *plop* back onto the ground.

"They thmell like cordol eggth."

"That's because they're cordol eggs. Why would I lie to you?"

"Why would you thwo me off a boat?"

"That's all in the past. Water under the bridge."

"Or under the boat."

"Now look who's the funny guy!"

Kali did not understand the relationship between these two at all. Every barb Puk threw at Voya made her flinch, thinking the ujath was moments away from charging them down.

274 · travis m. riddle

"Tho your githt to me is a bunth of eggth that will hath into animalth I have to take care of?"

Puk rolled his stalks back in exasperation. "You have to give the living creatures food and water, yes, and maybe pick up their shit and throw it away, but in exchange you get drugs. You love drugs, Voya, don't try to act like you don't. You once told me you'd morph into a bag of marshweed if you could. And also, we were both incredibly high when you said it. High on *drugs*."

Voya took a beat to consider the offering. It didn't take long.

"I'll take the eggth," he said, "but I don't thorgive you."

"That's fine," Puk conceded. "I was an asshole. *Am* an asshole. But I wanted to give you these eggs as a peace offering. And to, uh...ask a favor."

"Thor thuck's thake," Voya groaned. "You didn't even know if I made it home alive, and now you want a thavor?"

"I know, it's not ideal! And I already apologized!"

"Not a good apolothy."

"Alright, well, I'm sorry about that too."

Voya's limp arms reached up and began to massage the innumerable folds of skin on his body. It was done without any recognition from him whatsoever, causing Kali to wonder if it was an involuntary, subconscious action. Either way, it was not a pleasant sight.

The ujath asked, "Wha'th the thavor? Le'th get thith over with. I wan' you ou' of my houth."

Puk grinned. "I want me out of your house too."

Kali braced for an outburst, but instead Voya laughed at the jab.

She sighed with immense relief. Somehow, they had reeled him in. She caught herself almost laughing at the irony of the metaphor.

"We heard about a job someone's hiring for. Something about a book they want retrieved?"

"A book?"

"Don't play dumb," said Puk. "I heard about the shit all the way in Seroo's Eye, so there's no way you ain't caught wind of it here."

Voya nodded, moving his entire body. "I think I know wha' you're talking about. I think the job'th already thpoken thor, though."

Shit. We took too long.

Puk looked similarly irked. But he asked, "Do you know who the job's coming from anyway? Maybe we can work something out with them."

"I doubt it," said Voya, "but yeth, I know who to talk to. The guy'th name ith Hawa'i."

"What? What the fuck are you sayin'? Hawari?"

"Hawa'i."

"Not helpful. *Haratti?*"

"Yeth," Voya grunted.

"Is he a boss here, or just some underling? I wanna know if I gotta show this schmuck any respect."

"Underling," said Voya, "but tho rethpect anyway. I'm not thure who he'th working thor, ekthactly, but people aroun' here know not to thuck with Hawa'i."

Puk crossed his arms and muttered, "Fine, I'll behave myself. Do you know anything else about the guy? Something we should know going into a meeting?"

276 · travis m. riddle

Voya rotated his entire body like a shake of the head. His huge, wet tongue dragged across the hard floor, a sound like a knife cutting through fruit.

Another sigh from the qarm. Voya was definitely being useful, but he wasn't quite the fountain of information they'd hoped for.

Puk asked, "Well, you know where we can find him?"

"You know the Wabid Dog?" Voya asked.

Kali didn't know if the Rabid Dog referred to a person or a place, but Puk seemed to know what the ujath was talking about. He affirmed.

"Talk to a bartender there named Nithka. Tell her you're a dipthit thwend of Voya, and that you wanna thpeak to Hawa'i. Thee'll take you where you need to go."

"Do you want me to tell her I'm a dipshit because you think I'm a dipshit, or is that just the code you two worked out?" Puk asked.

Voya laughed, a disgusting, wet rumble. "Doethn't ma'er," he said. "You gotta thay it."

Puk rolled his eyestalks again. "Fine," he said. "Dipshit friend of Voya. Got it." He turned to leave, tossing Kali the empty knapsack. She caught it and slipped the strap over her shoulder as the qarm sidled past her.

"Thankth thor coming by!" said Voya, remaining stationary as they showed themselves out. His tongue still waggled slowly across the floor.

Kali did feel slightly awkward about only having said one sentence to the man, but she admitted to herself she was glad to be out of his company.

Puk stretched his short limbs as Kali pulled the door closed behind them. "Well, let's go to the Rabid Dog, I guess," Puk sighed. "Don't know if this woman's name is *Nithka* or *Niska*, but we'll find out soon enough, I guess."

"Is it close?" Kali asked.

"Kinda," he replied. "It's in this cavern, anyway. A few rings in."

Kali smiled. "Can—"

She didn't even have to finish her question. "Yes," Puk groaned, "we can stop in some stores on the way."

She was ecstatic.

- -

Allowing Kali to check out some of the shops on their way to the Rabid Dog gave Puk a chance to use the facilities' bathrooms. Since last night he'd had an unfortunate case of diarrhea, one of the more severe symptoms of a fire-spit withdrawal that he had mercifully not experienced in years past. He regretted drinking that damn spit all over again.

The generalized "hospitality" ring—home to establishments such as (nicer) inns, restaurants, and bars—was located in the middle of the rest, so as to be easily walkable from anywhere in the cavern. That was where they would find the Rabid Dog.

The Mass was much livelier, especially as the morning went on. There was the same hustle and bustle as any other city on the mainland, but it was a far cry from Seroo's Eye or Restick. Even Toralas. People walked the street with guns and swords strapped to their waists in plain sight, silently inviting others to mess with them; drug users lined the streets, stepping out of restaurants, giving a slight stretch and a yawn, then rubbed oporist on their upper lips; others hacked apart animals they had just bought, or otherwise trained them by having them attack their friends, in both cases spraying blood on the pathways.

Puk liked the exclusive and solitary nature of the city, as well as the ease of purchasing drugs and lack of judgmental stares, but hated basically every other aspect of it. His unwavering disdain for Myrisih gave him hope that perhaps he'd not totally fallen victim to this way of life yet. He was a dirtbag, to be sure, but he was no Voya.

After another bathroom visit and a gander around a potions shop, the two stepped outside and were only a few minutes' walk from the hospitality ring.

"I'm surprised they didn't have any noxspring," Kali commented as they walked. Puk had been shitting the entire time they'd been in the store, so he had no idea what she was shopping for.

"You said it's still kinda rare, right?" he asked. She nodded. "Maybe they just don't have any in stock."

"I asked the owner, and he said he's never heard of it."

"I dunno," Puk shrugged. He kept walking.

Kali was silent for a few moments, but then asked, "Do you think maybe Vonoshreb made it up?"

"Who?"

"Doesn't matter. I'm just wondering if...maybe noxspring is a lie? Either from Vonoshreb or the woman that sold him the bottles in the first place. It *did* sorta sound too good to be true..."

A potion that reversed the effects of the mold did indeed sound like a beautiful dream. In Puk's experience, beautiful dreams were just that: dreams.

"I ain't got a clue," he said.

Kali huffed. "It…noxspring was the whole reason I started this," she said. "Learning about it is what finally pushed me to get off my ass and get to Atlua."

She had stopped walking, so Puk stopped as well and turned, giving her another shrug. His stalks drooped empathetically. "I dunno if it's fake or not. You're basing this existential crisis on one asshole in one shop. He mighta just never heard of it. Or he mighta heard of it but didn't wanna tell you, for some reason. The reason probably being because he's an asshole."

This explanation didn't seem to put her at ease. She knitted her brows and her mouth slanted.

"You wanna get to Atlua regardless, right?"

She nodded.

"Good. Let's do this job, then."

"If Haratti even gives it to us," she pointed out.

Puk ignored that remark and resumed their trek to the specified bar.

Voya's comment about the job already being accepted by someone else worried him. Their detour to snatch the eggs might have cost them everything, though he hadn't seen any way around it. Myrisih was too big to go searching for a person whose name they hadn't known, and Voya was his sole point of contact here.

They turned onto the hospitality ring, passing by multiple restaurants with the scent of burnt food wafting from their open windows and doors. Just beyond a restaurant that had actual ink-black smoke drifting from its windows, there was a row of bars with their lights blacked out.

"It's just now occurring to me," Kali said, "that it's the morning. Isn't this place gonna be closed until tonight?" Puk saw her cast a concerned gaze at the bars they passed.

He chuckled and said, "The people who run these places are just lazy," he said, gesturing toward the shuttered taverns. "But I've been to the Rabid Dog plenty of times, and the people there ain't lazy, 'cause laziness ain't profitable."

"Bars are open this early here?"

"Bars don't close here. Unless, like I said, you're lazy."

"Wow."

"Are you genuinely surprised?" he asked her.

"I suppose not, now that you mention it."

The Rabid Dog wasn't too far down the ring. Its façade soon came into view, with a wooden sign carved in the shape of a snarling dog jutting out from the front of the building, its name painted in red script. It was one of the larger bars in the Mass, and therefore one of the biggest in the entire city. The bar was painted red to match the lettering on its sign, and the building itself was kept in better condition than most places in Myrisih. The place's proprietors had a reputation for being well-connected, so its patrons were plentiful and generous.

Inside, the walls were painted a creamy yellow color, with a mural banner at the top of every wall, depicting scenes of dogs tearing apart people and other animals. It was a strange theme to lean into, especially considering the bar's owner was a ro-cyan. Given the rocyans' history of being looked down upon as savages hundreds of years ago, Puk would've figured avoiding comparisons to rabid dogs would be preferable. But what did he know about cultural sensitivity?

The bar was well-populated, creating a din that would drown out anything they discussed, which was exactly what

Puk desired. Better to keep a low profile in a place like Myrisih. Paradoxically, it was both harder and easier for a qarm to remain invisible here. To some, he stood out like a sore thumb with his brightly-colored skin and short stature, while the latter characteristic was precisely why others took no notice of him.

He marched over to the bar and pulled himself up onto an unoccupied stool. The bartender almost laughed, which annoyed him, but he let it slide. Kali remained standing behind him, assuming they wouldn't be at the bar for long.

The man was clearly not who they were searching for, given that he was a man and not a woman. He had long, braided hair and rough stubble a few days old. "What can I get you?" he asked, his voice squeaky.

"Nithka," Puk replied. "Or Niska. Whichever one is the name of a woman who works here."

"Niska," the man clarified. "She's takin' a smoke break. Lemme tell ya, though, little man—I can make anything she can, and twice as good." He winked at Kali, and Puk almost threw up, not knowing if it was due to this guy's lame come-on or the spit withdrawal.

"We'll wait for Niska," Kali said, stone-faced.

The man tottered off, grumbling to himself. It made Puk chuckle.

He was indeed craving a drink, and he considered ordering one when Niska returned from her break. Something smooth but with a little bite, like a short glass of Jyukian rum. It probably wouldn't be a good look, though, to order something literally the day after assuring his partner he'd stay sober, especially while she stood beside him. He choked down the urge. Water would be better for him anyway.

A woman strolled behind the bar from a back door. She had the olive skin of a jeorn, but her platinum-white hair had been dyed green, and it had been chopped short and jutted up in spikes from her head. She wore piercing red lipstick on her lips, which she pursed.

"I heard you're looking for me." Her voice was low and husky.

"Yep. I'm a dipshit friend of Voya's. More specifically, we're looking for Haratti."

Niska looked from Puk to Kali, then back again. Obviously they were not the usual type of people who came to her with requests such as this, and she could tell just by looking at them.

"Okay. Follow me," she said, nodding her head toward the back door she'd emerged from less than a minute earlier. "I'm goin' on another break!" she called out to her co-worker.

The man groaned and spat, "Oh, come on!"

- -

Niska led, followed by Puk, and Kali brought up the rear.

The woman brought them through a back door into the depths of the Rabid Dog. They passed a couple storerooms and a break room, then stepped through another door into an alleyway that Kali did not remember seeing a way to access when they were wandering the Mass.

Their guide did not speak to them as they walked, and neither of them tried to initiate conversation. Niska led them down the alley and into an unmarked building that she possessed a key to. The door opened up to an unlit hallway, the only light provided by a meager amount that spilled from four rooms, two on each side.

Kali did not like the look or feel of this place.

But she continued following Niska and Puk to the far left room and they entered to find a man sitting at a desk, scribbling away in a notebook, his work lit by a bright lamp.

He glanced up from his records and peered at the trio. "Hello, Niska," he said. "Who are our guests?"

Haratti was an older man than Kali anticipated. His head was completely bald, sporting an impressive gleam from the lamplight. His forehead and cheeks were wrinkled, and his chin had a gray, neatly-trimmed goatee that came to a sharp point. He wore long, white sleeves that were cuffed tightly around his wrists.

Niska turned and gave them both a look, suggesting they introduce themselves.

"Name's Puk."

"Kallia." She had no idea what compelled her to give her full name. Haratti's presence was oddly authoritative, and she had lost herself to that for a moment. Puk shot her a curious glance.

Their host gestured toward a set of cushioned chairs in front of his desk and told them to take a seat, so they obliged.

He then asked, "What can I help you with?" Niska stood at the back of the room by the doorway, awaiting the conclusion of their exchange.

Puk dove right in, as he had with all of their interactions in Myrisih thus far. "We heard about a job you're offering, and we wanted to accept."

Haratti smiled, exposing crooked teeth yellowed by tobacco. "You want to accept without hearing any details? That seems unwise."

"Yeah, well," Puk shrugged.

"I have many open jobs," Haratti said, amused by the qarm sitting before him. "Which are you inquiring about?"

"The book job."

The old man frowned and set down his pen, leaning back in his chair. His notebook was left open. "I'm afraid someone else already accepted that one," he said.

"Well, fuck," Puk said in a sarcastically jovial tone.

"Indeed," Haratti nodded. He leaned forward, planting his elbows on the desk and resting his chin on his knuckles, deep in thought. After a few seconds of pondering, he said, "It might be your lucky day, though. Unless I can interest you in another job you'd like to blindly accept?" He shot a glance at Kali, sending a shiver down her spine.

"Why's it our lucky day?" asked Puk, ignoring the man's vague offer. She was thankful for him taking the lead.

Haratti explained. "The man I sent off to obtain the item should have returned by now. It is several days past when we expected his arrival. I suspect some ill fate has befallen him."

That really bodes well for us two chumps, then, Kali thought bitterly.

"We'll gladly pick up the slack," Puk told the man.

"I'm pleased to hear that," Haratti said with that same ugly smile. "Pardon my saying this, but you two do not seem like the usual sort I collaborate with. Are you sure you're well-equipped for the job?"

"Fetchin' a book? I think we can handle it," said Puk.

After hearing that something had happened to Haratti's man, Kali wasn't as confident as her companion, but she held her tongue.

"It's a bit more complex than that," Haratti said. "Which is something you would know if you had asked for the details.

The book is called *Malum*. Have you heard of it?" They both shook their heads, and he continued. "I wouldn't think so. It's an ancient text. It, along with a few other similar titles, was stolen from a library in Bral Han thirty-eight years ago. It is a text on the practices of red magic."

Red magic had been outlawed for years—since long before Kali had been born, and long before the books in question were apparently stolen. She only knew of it from history lessons, never from reports of anyone practicing it. It was also colloquially known as blood magic; it involved the user bending reality. Casting breathtakingly realistic illusions or literally reshaping reality itself. It was deemed too powerful and dangerous.

"All the texts on red magic were ordered to be destroyed twenty years ago," Kali blurted out. It was a factoid she'd learned from Lissia at some point during her Repository studies.

Haratti nodded. "Yes, twenty-three years ago, to be precise. In 1117. But this particular book was never found by the High Mages. The volumes that were already in their possession, as well as the other books stolen from the Bral Han library, were all destroyed. But not *Malum*. It has eluded them."

"The High Mages couldn't track it down, but you think *you* have?" Puk asked, incredulous.

Another nod. "We have."

"Where is it?" Kali asked, her interest piqued. She couldn't imagine how Lissia would react to this news. Her sister would be positively foaming at the mouth, knowing such ancient and forbidden knowledge had been recovered.

"Some associates of ours tracked the book's owner down to Pontequest."

It was another story Kali had learned from her sister. A mighty airship called the *Pontequest*, named after the man it was built for, Barnabus Ponte, was sailing over Herrilock when it experienced catastrophic engine failure and crashed into the desert, killing everyone on board. The wreckage remained out in the sands, there being too much of it and too far out of the way for anyone to care much about removing it. The stories told that some nomads had, at some point, decided to root themselves and built a small town in the skeleton of the ship. In that sense, it was kind of similar to Seroo's Eye.

"Pontequest isn't real, though," Kali piped up. Even Lissia thought it to be a tall tale.

"I assure you, my dear, it is a real place," said Haratti.

"The ship was real, sure, but it crashed and got buried in the desert. That's all. People *did* try to establish a town around it, but there was an accident or something that destroyed the ship. There were reports of it all over."

Haratti laughed lowly. "That is the public's general consensus, yes. But our associates have located the famed shipwreck and drawn up a map to it. They can confirm the township's existence. Pardon my pun."

Puk was skeptical. He asked, "If you guys know where it is already, why don't you go grab it yourselves? Why even hire someone just to grab a book?"

"My boss would like his involvement in this affair to remain out of the public eye. He is well-known in the community, and believes that if any of his usual associates were involved, it would be traced back to him and it would become public knowledge that he possesses the book. This is not something he wants, hence an outside hire."

It seemed like a flimsy excuse, but it wasn't totally unreasonable. Kali asked, "Who owns the book right now?"

"We know the persons who stole the books from the Bral Han library were two jeornish mages-in-training named Kleus Saix and Michio Loz. They each kept some of the texts, but Loz's were recovered by the mages. We believe Kleus Saix is living in Pontequest and still has *Malum* in his possession."

Puk's face brightened, his stalks extending slightly toward the ceiling. "The same guy's got the book still? If he stole it forty years ago, he's gotta be old as shit by now, right? This'll be easy!"

Haratti said nothing.

"Is the bounty still the same?" Kali asked, trying to keep the conversation professional. "Ten thousand crescents?"

"Yes," Haratti answered. His voice was like gravel.

She and Puk exchanged a look. Their eyes said to each other, *Okay.*

"We'll do it," Puk said, turning back to Haratti.

It was then Kali realized they had gotten slightly off-track. She said, "Wait. Why is this more complicated than just stealing a book?" Haratti had failed to elaborate before.

The man chuckled. "Have you been paying attention, dear? Red magic is the most dangerous form of magic in all of Ustlia, and every other text on the subject has been wiped out for two decades. Kleus Saix may very well be the last red mage alive, and he's been honing his skills for forty years. Theoretically, he could conjure up any number of illusions or simply rewrite the fabric of reality to separate your head from your shoulders."

He grinned devilishly, and another tingle traced down Kali's back. She began to bob her leg up and down nervously.

Haratti asked her, "What about that doesn't sound complicated to you?"

CHAPTER XII

CIVILIZED DISCUSSION

They accepted the job.

Haratti then produced a map that had been created by one of his nameless associates, showcasing the route from Restick all the way to Pontequest, secluded in the middle of the Gogol Desert. The old man told them to commit it to memory, as he would not allow them to take the map nor make a copy. Kali memorized a few different waypoints, including the travelers' outpost where she'd injured Jeth as well as an isolated town called Weynard.

Afterwards, when they had departed from Haratti's strangely secluded office and left the company of Niska, Kali asked Puk what he thought about everything, and his response was, "That 'Pontequest' is a really stupid name."

He wasn't wrong.

With their meeting concluded, they had no more business in Myrisih. Puk brought her to one of his favorite food joints in the city, a place that was no more than a stall crammed between two other establishments. The sign hanging from its roof bore no name, just the image of—well, Kali couldn't actually decipher what the image was.

Having eaten a full meal the day before, Kali normally would be nowhere near ready for more food, but the severe lack of sunlight was provoking her appetite. Plus, Puk promised she'd want to try this.

As it turned out, he was correct.

The stall's specialty was a dessert item originating from Vareda called a *churrystick*. It was a long, thin cylinder of fried dough coated in cinnamon and sugar.

She could never deny sweets.

The place sold churrysticks in two styles: either one single big stick, or a cup of several smaller ones. Kali opted for the latter, and bought each of them a cup.

They chowed down as they traipsed through the Mass back toward the unnamed cavern housing their inn. The dough was perfectly crispy on the outside and fluffy as a cloud on the inside, with a delightfully powerful sweetness from the sugar. She desperately craved more as soon as she crumpled the empty paper cup.

It helped to temporarily take her mind off their upcoming task, which was now filling her with anxiety.

It was idiotic of them to accept the job after hearing the risks involved. By all accounts, Kleus Saix was one of the most powerful mages in the world, and they were...*them*. A delicate little faif merchant and a toddler-sized alcoholic going through fire-spit withdrawals.

Who were they kidding? What chance did they have?

Yet the pay-out was too enticing. She couldn't find the words to speak up during the meeting and decline on their behalf. She had let Puk confirm their involvement because, deep down, she wanted to be involved.

The risk was worth the reward.

Maybe.

As they walked, a question crept in, and she asked Puk, "Do you think maybe this guy isn't as strong as Haratti thinks he is?"

"Who?"

Where the hell is your mind at? she wondered to herself, not for the first time while talking to the qarm. Aloud, she said, "This red mage we're looking for."

"I dunno, why?"

She tried to articulate her thought process. "It just seems a little odd to me that, if he really is all that powerful...why would he just hole away in some secluded village in the middle of the desert? Don't you think a power-hungry mage would, I dunno, seek out more power?"

"I dunno," Puk repeated. "Maybe he's got all the power he wants there. Maybe he's brainwashed everyone into bein' his sex slaves or something. Pontequest is just a giant orgy, all hours of the day. Fucks and fucks and fucks." He chomped down on the last of his churrysticks with glee, giggling at his own imagined scenario.

"Yes, maybe he's fucking in a massive, writhing orgy all day every day," Kali said, "but I'm wondering if maybe he's just not that strong after all. Maybe he never could master the magic, and he's just in hiding because he doesn't wanna be executed by the High Mages or whatever."

Truthfully, she had no idea what the punishment for the mage's actions would entail. The jeornish were the only people possessing the power to cast magic, so she did not know a great deal about their academies or the practices of their mages. No one in her adoptive family opted for the magical route in their lives.

Puk brightened at her suggestion. "You think so?" he squeaked, a coat of sugar dusting his blue lips. One eyestalk fixed on her while the other looked ahead where he was walking. "It'd be great if he was just some wrinkly old man sitting around with his book. That'd make the job just as easy as I assumed it was at the start."

"Yeah," said Kali. "I wish we'd known about the whole 'red mage' part of it before coming all the way here." She sighed.

"Cheer up," said Puk. "We'll be alright. We've come this far, right? There's nothin' we can't handle!"

"We haven't actually accomplished all that much," Kali pointed out. "We stole some eggs from an animal and got someone to give us a ride on their boat. That's about it."

"We also *killed* that animal—with a boot!—after stealing a different animal from someone. We're unstoppable!"

Kali laughed and further crinkled the paper cup in her hand. She tried to share in the qarm's optimism.

"You don't think we're in over our heads?" she asked him.

By now he had finished with his snack and balled up the flimsy cup. "Nah," he replied nonchalantly. "I think the job's the same as it ever was: steal a book. Easy."

It did sound easy. But anything sounded easy when put in simple, uncomplicated terms.

Kali tried to relax. There was no use getting worked up over it at this juncture. She simply had to adapt to the changing situation.

While they walked, Kali pored over Haratti's route to Pontequest in her mind. Luckily, given her years of constant travel, she could easily visualize a pretty clear, if not exact, image of the entire route even with only one look at the map. That gave them a leg up; perhaps finding the town was what had delayed Haratti's first recruit.

Like she always did before a voyage, Kali calculated how long each leg would take. With an early start, they could get from Restick to the travelers' outpost within one—admittedly long and tiring—day. She chuckled, thinking about whether Jeth's blood had stained the floor or been fully washed out, then banished the morbid thought.

From there, it would take another full day to reach Weynard. The town would be a little out of their way, but it was their best opportunity to get some rest in a real bed. The extra cost would be worthwhile. Not to mention, after two full, long days of travel, Bella would be exhausted.

Or maybe not. She's the most energetic ayote I've ever met.

Weynard to Pontequest would be the final stretch, and the riskiest. She estimated that it would take another full day, stretching into the night, to reach the elusive village. And that was assuming they found it at all. She couldn't be one-hundred percent positive it still existed, but...

Haratti claimed that it did. His "associates" did, anyway.

For now, that had to be good enough.

With Myrisih's port closed until the following day, they had plenty of time to meander around the city before bothering to figure out where Zenib had scuttled off to.

It was disconcerting how utterly *normal* the city felt in spite of all the illicit goings-on throughout its dark, damp streets and within its cavernous walls. Kali had to remind herself that the merchants and customers here were trading in drugs, illegal weaponry, stolen goods, maybe even other people (which she admittedly had not witnessed any evidence of, but she'd heard rumors)—yet on the surface, it seemed like any other city in Herrilock. People buying and selling in shops, restaurants hocking various styles of cuisine, inns with complimentary breakfasts.

At one point, Puk suggested she open up a shop here. Find a nook or cranny somewhere in the Mass and start selling.

She wrote the suggestion off as lunacy, but as the day wore on, she found herself wondering if there was a way to make it work. Though she quickly discarded the idea again after watching a man rub a healthy smear of oporist over his lip before strutting into a firearm shop.

They spent much of the day wandering the city. Puk showed her his favorite spots he could remember from his rare trips, which included a grotto over near the port that he claimed was a place for people to visit and flip coins into the water like a wishing well. It was outfitted with carved stone steps leading down into the clear water of the pool. The two meandered down to the point where the rock and water's edge met, and dipped their feet in while they sat and chatted. The water was icy cold and refreshing.

"Was there something you wanted to ask me?" Puk asked during a lull in their conversation.

It took her aback. "What do you mean?"

"It seemed like you were gonna ask me something in Restick," he said. "When we were talking about singing. Right before Zenib showed up at the dock."

"Oh." She tried to recall what she might've wanted to ask, replaying the conversation in her head, but nothing immediately came to mind. "I'm not sure," she shrugged.

Puk said nothing and stared down at the water's wavering reflection of himself. He then said, "I guess I'm done as a musician."

Kali was surprised by him leaning into this topic again. It must have been weighing on him ever since the incident in Eva's bathroom. Or probably since he got kicked out of his troupe. Maybe even for years before.

"Why's that?" she asked, granting him the opportunity to vent or talk things through.

"Like I was sayin' the other night, I'm just not getting anything out of it anymore. Might sound kinda cynical, but I'm not really making any money off it, and it's incredibly disheartening." He kicked at his reflected face. "If it's not succeeding and no one gives a shit, it's hard to give a shit yourself."

"What'll you do instead?" She didn't think resigning himself to spit or alcohol would be good, productive alternatives.

He stopped moving his feet and the water stilled. "I'm not sure yet. I have very few skills, as you can probably imagine," he laughed. "A childhood buddy of mine is an alchemist now. Am I too old to become an alchemist?" Another laugh. "I could picture myself being bored out of my mind all day, as long as the money's good."

"Somehow I can't really see you doing that," Kali chuckled. The prospect of Puk performing a "normal" job was impossible to grasp.

"What about a blacksmith? That's another hard-working, real person job. Something respectable."

"They make less money than you'd probably think, except for the really skilled ones."

"Well then I'd just be a really skilled one, obviously."

"Problem solved, then. There's a lot of heat involved, though, and you don't do too well with heat, in my experience."

"That's a good point. Probably why you don't see any qarmish blacksmiths anywhere, huh?"

"Probably," said Kali. "Is there anything else creative you've wanted to try out? You could become a writer. Maybe there's a good story in you somewhere."

"Fuck no, I'm not writing. I can barely speak coherently, let alone write a flowery sentence. Do writers even make money?"

"No idea," Kali confessed.

She was about to jokingly suggest he try his hand at teaching when an unfamiliar voice piped up behind them.

"Sorry to interrupt," the voice said. It was accompanied by a faint sizzle and crackling.

Kali turned to look over her shoulder and saw a jeornish man with short, shaggy hair and an unkempt beard standing at the top of the staircase, his hands engulfed in fireballs.

"Let's have a quick chat," the man said, descending a few steps.

"You wanna put those fireballs out first?" Puk asked him.

The man shook his head. "I don't think so, no."

\- -

The black mage stopped several steps above them, maintaining his higher ground. Puk nearly shit himself, though it was less out of fear and more due to the diarrhea he had been suffering all day.

Puk asked Kali, "You know this guy?"

"Why would I know anyone in this place?"

"I dunno, you're all over the damn country. Don't you know lots of people?"

The man spoke. "I don't know her, but it seems we have a mutual acquaintance. I couldn't help but notice the two of you leaving a meeting with Warren Haratti earlier today."

Suddenly Puk remembered spotting the man amongst the crowd at the Rabid Dog. The bar had been so full of people, he hadn't particularly stood out at the time. But now that he thought about it, Puk could place him.

"You're mistaken," said Kali. Simple. Leaving it at that.

The mage shook his head, unaccepting of her response. "Myrisih is my home. I know its ins and outs, the way it operates. The two of you spoke with Niska Cill at the bar and were escorted out the back. Which only means one thing: that you met with Haratti."

It was no use denying what the man had clearly seen. "Fine," said Puk. "Yes, we went and talked to our old friend Warren. He's hiring us to renovate his personal library. The shelves keep fallin' down. Can't hold any damn books!"

The fireballs flickering around the mage's hands grew slightly larger.

Kali groaned.

Well, I thought it was a solid lie.

"I'm no fool," said the man, "and you'll do well not to lie to me. I'm very good at picking out liars. My friend Jack is even better; I can introduce you both if you'd like. But I was rather hoping the three of us could be friends."

"Just you is fine," Puk muttered. "What's your name, again?"

The man smiled, though the fireballs did not decrease in size nor disappear completely. "Thom," he answered.

"What do you want?" Kali asked, cutting to the point.

Thom appreciated her candor. "My employer was recently made aware of the job Haratti is hiring for, and she is very interested in the book he's seeking. If you met with Haratti, then it had to be about the book."

"Sounds like a good book," said Puk. "I can see why everyone wants it."

"Indeed," Thom said in a low growl. Puk made a note to dial back on the sarcasm before he received a fireball to the face. "The issue my employer faces is that she is unsure of where to find the book. We've heard, however, that Haratti possesses such information."

"And I take it you can't schedule a meeting with him yourself," Kali said flatly.

"Correct. So, if you'd be so kind as to divulge the information Haratti passed on, I can be on my way." He raised his hands slightly higher, as if they could have somehow forgotten he was equipped with fireballs.

"We'll have to decline," Kali answered. Her voice was weak, unconfident.

Puk was impressed nonetheless.

"Yeah," he chimed in with his support. "We'll have to pass."

This was a disappointment to Thom. "If I may be perfectly blunt," he continued, "the information is going to come out one way or another. Either we can have a civilized discussion, or I can incapacitate you and introduce you to Jack. As I said before, he's very skilled at weeding out lies and learning what he wants to know."

"I think we passed the point of civilized discussion when you came to us already sporting fireballs," Kali pointed out.

"Yeah," Puk said again, contributing nothing but wanting Kali to know he was backing up her defiance. Though the idea of fighting this mage and then being tortured by his associate did not sound appealing in the least. The rumbling in his stomach did nothing to ease his reservations about combat.

Thom threw the fireballs.

Kali dove to the right, slamming her body into the cave wall and narrowly avoiding one of the flaming balls.

The other flew toward Puk, who instinctively leapt backwards, backslamming into the pool of water and sinking below its surface.

Both of the mage's fireballs impacted with the water and fizzled away. Puk remained underwater but poked one eyestalk out to assess the scene. What he saw shocked him.

Kali was rushing Thom.

He had the upper hand, being several steps above her, and he took advantage of the fact. His hands and fingers gestured in a blur and a blast of air shot from his palms, sending Kali flying backward and tumbling down the stone steps, her head smacking on the hard surface as she rolled down toward the pool.

Puk's eyesight wasn't good enough to see if any blood was spilled.

His stalk receded back into the water and his eyes shot open. There was a protective layer over his eyeballs allowing him to see underwater, and he desperately looked around for something to aid him.

The pool was empty, naturally, save for the expected flora and gravel at its bottom. The only other thing he could spot was a collection of old, forgotten coins.

There were a lot of them.

We should take some of these, Puk thought for a second before getting back on track.

But then he did take some of those.

He kicked his stubby legs down to the bottom of the pool, and while doing so heard a muffled splash behind him. He rotated one stalk and saw that Kali had completed her painful descent and ended up in the pool with him.

There was some murkiness in the water around her. Blood.

Puk told himself that Thom was not intending to kill them, he needed them alive to get the information he wanted—but then he realized only one of them needed to live.

He kicked his legs faster. The twisting in his tummy and the motion of his kicks increased the need to unload himself even more. He started to second-guess himself for a moment, wondering if he should turn back and help Kali instead.

His idea was inane anyway, it wasn't going to help.

But on the other hand, it was all he had, really.

It took a few more seconds to reach the pool's bottom, where Puk gathered up as many coins as his grubby hands could grab and shoveled them all into his mouth.

With his cheeks puffed out and a nasty metallic taste on his tongue, he made for Kali's location where she floated at the bottom of the stairs.

Above the water, Thom said something in a booming voice, but the words were unintelligible.

Puk reached Kali and grabbed her under the armpits, praying she hadn't swallowed too much water. Her eyes were closed and her head bled freely. They needed to get to a white mage, but he didn't know if there was one stationed in Myrisih.

Worry about that later, he told himself, *and worry about the black mage right now.*

He held on to Kali and popped one stalk out of the water again. Thom was still fairly far from the bottom of the steps, though he was methodically making his way down.

Puk popped the rest of his head above water, keeping Kali submerged for the time being, and spit one of the crescents from his mouth with as much force as he could muster.

The misshapen coin flew through the air and dinged the stone several steps down from where Thom currently stood.

Shit.

Thom laughed.

So Puk aimed higher.

This time, the coin hit its mark—kind of—and smacked Thom in the chest, falling to the steps in a noisy clatter. The mage laughed again and asked, "What the hell are you doing?"

Puk aimed slightly higher now and spit the remainder of the coins in rapid fire, most of them pelting Thom directly in his face.

Thom frantically threw his hands up to deflect the rest, which either clattered onto the steps or plopped back into the water.

With his ammunition now depleted, Puk ducked back underwater.

That was fucking stupid, he chastised himself, though he had known it would be. He was out of options, and Kali was heavy. Plus, she needed to breathe.

Puk repositioned himself to get a better grip on his companion in order to more easily extract her from the water. As he did, he noticed the clasp on her bag had been undone and the flap was floating freely, ruining the bag's contents. But he also spotted the reason she had been rushing the mage before being knocked back.

Inside the bag was her dagger.

Of course she wouldn't be walking around Myrisih without protection. How had he not realized it before?

An idea came to him in a flash.

He yanked Kali up out of the water and struggled to pull her back up onto the steps, bringing her to rest beside her own blood. More leaked out to form one large, crimson puddle.

"Gonna throw some more coins at me?" Thom asked, amused.

"She's dead!" Puk screamed, ignoring the well-deserved mocking. He gripped his friend by the collar of her shirt and tugged her face close to his. "You killed her!" he cried. His stomach gurgled.

He channeled what few acting skills Jit and Dern had imparted on him so many moons ago with their ill-conceived sketches and shitty scripts. Hopefully their expertise would be enough to help him power through this.

Thom seemed unfazed by the revelation that he had murdered a person. Fireballs engulfed his palms once again, and he continued down the steps toward the distraught qarm. "Let's go see Jack," he growled.

Puk placed his palm in the pool of blood by Kali's hand and then looked at it, caked in red. *"This is her blood!"* he screamed, recognizing even in the moment that he was laying it on a bit thick. He needed to tone it down.

"I'm sorry about your friend, but what's done is done," said Thom. He was now only a few steps away.

Puk surprised himself by crying real tears. "You..." he muttered. "She's..."

Thom dissipated his fireballs and walked the final few steps down to where Puk crouched beside Kali's unmoving body. He frowned, ever so slightly, at the sight of tears streaming down Puk's stalks in rivulets, dribbling onto his lips.

The mage stopped on the step above Kali's head-blood and crouched down. "Come on," he said softly. "Let's not make this any more difficult than it already is."

The man wasn't going to come down any farther. This would have to suffice.

Puk still propped Kali up, her cheek against his with one arm wrapped around her. The other had slipped into her bag.

Sorry, Kali.

He tossed her aside, yanking the dagger from the bag, and leapt forward. He jabbed first into Thom's ankle, then again into his calf.

Thom yelled in fury, falling backward onto his ass while blood gushed from his two wounds.

Meanwhile, Kali's head had slammed into the cavern wall again and her eyes fluttered open. She slid a short way down the wet steps, but caught herself and mumbled, "Huh?"

One stalk rotated to look at Kali while the other stayed locked on to Thom, who was preparing his fireballs again.

"Down!" Puk shouted.

Kali mindlessly obeyed and a fireball soared over her head, once again dissolving fruitlessly in the water beyond.

The second whizzed past Puk, who nimbly dodged to the left, slipping on Kali's blood and nearly careening over the edge back into the pool of water. But he retained his footing and propelled himself forward, stabbing the dagger into Thom's right leg a third time.

Thom yelped, and did not retain his footing as well as Puk had. He slipped in a streak of his own blood and crashed into the pool of water, sinking down to the coins below.

Wish I coulda got those coins.

Puk turned on his heels—nearly slipping again—and said to Kali, "We gotta get outta here right now."

Still disoriented, she nodded her head and ambled up the steps behind him.

They fled the grotto with haste, disappearing into the crowded maze of tunnels that comprised Myrisih, and Puk was thankful they had not led their pursuer to the inn earlier.

Kali clutched the wound on her head and Puk held the bloody dagger aloft as they slipped in between curious yet unconcerned individuals. Right now Puk was focused on getting them far from Thom and out of immediate danger; he would worry about tracking down a white mage shortly.

"What the hell just happened?" Kali asked, following dutifully with each twist and turn he took.

"We just beat a mage, I think," he answered with a grin. "And you thought we couldn't pull something like that off! *Ha!*"

"I have a gash in my head," Kali said. "I might die of blood loss."

"You won't die of blood loss," Puk assured her. "But even if you do, hey—we still beat a mage!"

"Ever the optimist."

They rounded a corner and tore through the Mass, circling around toward the tunnel system that would lead to their inn. Puk had been keeping one stalk trained behind them, watching the path for any sign of Thom, and so far they were still in the clear. The mage had fallen into the center of the grotto's pool, and with three gaping holes in one's leg it was assuredly an uneasy task swimming over to the steps. Puk believed they were safe.

There then came the familiar rumbling in his stomach, and he suddenly started to speculate whether finding a white mage or a bathroom was the higher priority.

He asked Kali, "Just how much does your head *really* hurt?"

CHAPTER XIII

IN A LOOP

Seven years earlier, when they were twenty-one years old, Kali and Lissia Shiar were at drastically different places in their lives, both figuratively and literally speaking.

Kali, much to her chagrin, still found herself living at home in her parents' inn. She was making small moves to get her own trade business up and running, but it was taking more time and energy than she anticipated. No matter how much she dedicated to the cause, it still wasn't enough, and so eventually she grew complacent.

For a long time, she was stagnant, and stagnation became comfortable. But soon Seroo's Eye buzzed all around her, and she was numbing to it. And that numbness slowly turned into an itch, exacerbated by her sister's departure.

Lissia had spent the last four years at home as well, devoting a majority of her free time to studying as many different linguistic, historical, biological, magical, and countless other -ical texts in preparation for her interview and exam to be anointed as a vaulted scholar of the Repository.

And she had succeeded.

When she returned from her trials, she was positively glowing, expressing to her family how titillating the tests had been and how well she believed she'd performed. A few weeks later, she received the letter informing her she was to be accepted into their ranks.

Hearing the news was like a punch in the gut to Kali.

In the back of her mind, she always knew her sister would be accepted. Over the years she'd seen how diligently Lissia was working toward her goal, and there was never any doubt she'd eventually succeed.

Still, the news came as a shock.

She shared in the pride her parents felt, and she loved her sister. She wanted Lissia to thrive and flourish no matter what. Yet she recognized that a part of her—a small part, barely there at all, yet still a part—was resentful.

Resentful of her for accomplishing her goals while Kali still floundered with her own.

Resentful of her for making a name for herself while Kali still felt like nothing.

Resentful of her for being happy while Kali—

She stopped herself. She wasn't unhappy, necessarily. Not really. Maybe "unfulfilled" was more appropriate.

And more palatable.

There was a seed inside Kali. A tiny, bitter seed. One that she strived to ignore, to let it wither away and die and be forgotten.

But when her sister began preparing in earnest for the trials, that seed was watered a little bit.

And when her sister learned her application to travel to the Repository for testing had been accepted, that seed was watered more.

And then when the news came that Lissia would be a scholar, the seed nearly drowned.

All the while, Kali wished for that seed to starve. Because really, she was happy for her sister—how could she not be?—but nonetheless, she was still stuck in the same routine, trying in vain to get her trade business up and running. To become the traveling merchant she always wanted to be.

Her jealousy watered the seed. Her failures watered it.

The only solace she found was that, in all honesty, she knew it wasn't Lissia she was angry with. It was herself.

Once Lissia had settled in and been comfortably living in the Repository's dormitories for three months, the family wanted to pay her a visit. The Shiars hired a wagon to take them from Seroo's Eye to the looming tower down south. Kali would've preferred taking a vacation to the oases in Nawa, but alas.

When they arrived, Kali had to concede that the place was impressive.

The Repository was a hulking tower looming high in the sky, blotting out the sun. Given its centript construction, it was built out of the typical adobe bricks then plastered over. Carved into the plaster, spiraling around the building starting from the bottom, was a history of Herrilock written in Carsuak. Kali couldn't tell if the tale reached the tip-top of the tower, her vision blinded by the sun, but if it did, she couldn't fathom the amount of planning that had gone into not only the construction but also writing out the painstakingly detailed story. What blew her mind even more was that the tower extended even further below ground, with several floors of dormitories and other amenities for the scholars who lived and worked there. She had never seen a man-made structure so enormous; the only thing comparable in size was Seroo's skull.

A greeter stood outside the front entrance, which Kali found peculiar. She was a centript woman with pink and green jewels affixed to her carapace, official colors of the Repository. She was laying curled up on the ground, a common practice among centripts since their bodies were not configured to sit in chairs, and she instantly shot up at the sight of approaching visitors. The woman rose and curved her long insectoid body into an S-shape.

"Hello! Welcome to the Repository," said the woman in perfectly-pronounced Commonspeak. "We have scholars ready to assist you on every level of the facility, as well as plentiful clear signage for self-guidance. But may I ask what knowledge you seek, so that I may direct you to the proper area?"

Botro explained they were Lissia Shiar's family and that they had come to see her.

The woman chittered in excitement. "Lissia is our freshest recruit, but she's an incredibly bright woman. I can see her going far here," the centript said. Botro and Knyla both beamed with pride for their daughter.

Hearing how well her sister was doing sent a pang through Kali's gut. The reaction startled her, and she was immediately uncomfortable with it.

The friendly centript woman told them they could find Lissia on the third floor, and Kali tried to swallow the unwanted and unwarranted resentment as she entered through the stone doors with her parents. It was a sharp lump in her throat.

Inside the Repository was just as impressive as out.

Upon stepping indoors, they were instantly surrounded by endless shelves of books towering from floor to ceiling. The shelves were constructed from the same material as the building itself and were actually a part of it, sprouting out of the floor like weeds and burrowing into the ceiling above. It reminded Kali of centript hive cities such as Yspleash and Lyukashi. Everything was interconnected and immovable. Designed with such clear, unwavering purpose.

She didn't see any other visitors. The only people she spotted as they twisted through the shelves to the staircase was another centript with the scholarly jewels and a man wearing loose-fitting robes of the same colors, pink with green accent stripes on the edges. More scholars, quietly tending to their affairs.

The family sauntered past the opening upward to the second floor and continued to the third. The staircase spiraled endlessly above them, dizzying Kali as she stared up at it. She nearly tripped over a step, mesmerized.

The third floor looked identical to the first, and it was no wonder why scholars were stationed on every level of the building. Finding the correct floor was a difficult enough proposition, let alone tracking down the exact tome one sought.

All the walls and shelves were the same dull tan color of the adobe, with no splashes of color anywhere aside from the scholars' clothing and jewels. The drabness suddenly weighed on Kali, and she imagined that being so utterly surrounded by a single dull color for hours on end every single day for their entire life must certainly take some sort of toll on a person's mental well-being.

But her sister was bright and cheery at the sight of her family. Lissia was wearing the expected pink-and-green robes, and her long, white hair trailed down in a braid over her left shoulder. She went down the line, hugging each of them in turn and planting a gentle kiss on their cheeks.

As she pulled away from Kali, she said, "It's so great to see you all! How was the trip here?"

"Boring," Kali answered with a wry smirk. "Too much sand."

"Yeah, you'll get that in a desert," her sister grinned.

"Oh, did you learn that here?"

Their parents insisted she tell them all about daily life in the Repository. Her new routines, how she was liking the place, who she had become friends with. Their father was especially interested in how the food tasted.

"C'mon, you can find out for yourself," Lissia told him. "They've got a fantastic cactus salad, actually."

Botro's face scrunched up at the suggestion of eating a salad for lunch, especially after a long journey.

Kali and Lissia both laughed at his expression, and Lissia said, "Don't worry, you can get grilled lamatka strips in it too."

"How about just a lamatka *steak*?" he asked, raising his eyebrows up and down devilishly.

"I'm sure that could be arranged. The menu is surprisingly extensive."

"Well, let's go!"

They followed Lissia back down the stairwell, beyond the first floor and underground to the scholars' quarters.

For lunch, Lissia ordered the aforementioned cactus salad (minus the lamatka meat), Botro had his steak with whipped potatoes and sautéed mushrooms, and Knyla ate a plate of various smaller dishes which included thick cubes of grilled cheese and a fresh salad of diced herbs and tomatoes tossed in oil. When it came time for Kali to order, she declined. She had a bite to eat before leaving home and the sunlight on the trip had further sustained her.

During lunch, the four continued their conversation about Lissia's new scholarly lifestyle. She admitted to them that visitors were few and far between—the Repository wasn't precisely meant to act as a typical library, with patrons coming and going frequently, but rather a collection of the world's knowledge on any and all topics imaginable.

Its scholars were there to not only aid the guests they did receive, but also further academic research both on subjects that they personally found interesting as well as ones requested by other professionals across the country. Lissia had been spending most of her three months holed up in the tower reading up on poisons and potion-making, something that had once fascinated her as a child when she thought she might want to become a white mage, before her interest dwindled.

"You know what's really fun?" Lissia asked. They all urged her to spill it. "One of the books I'm reading for my research is from a collection of forbidden books that we have here, locked away on one of the lowest floors. Not for public consumption."

"You guys have a bunch of books no one's allowed to read?" Kali said, amused.

Lissia nodded, her face split by an excited grin. "Texts written about the most dangerous topics are preserved for the sake of their knowledge, but outsiders aren't allowed to read them. That would ruin the purpose of them being forbidden. But scholars are able to access them. Let me tell you, some of the poisonous concoctions described in this book are truly vile."

She giggled just thinking about them. Relegated to laughing over poisons. It was evident how much she was enjoying her new life here at the Repository, where she could read and learn to her heart's content.

With the meal concluded, Lissia showed them her modest apartment, decorated sparsely but with a few mementos from Seroo's Eye, including a smaller recreation of the Shiar's Slumber sign that hung above the inn's entryway. Their father beamed with joy.

But as Lissia took them on a tour of the facility, that seed in Kali's gut began to fester and rot, no matter how desperately she wished it away.

Her sister's success was real, and tangible, and she was engulfed by it. It was inescapable.

She thought about her mild accomplishments, the biggest of which was probably making her first solo trip to the border cities along Vanap's Peaks. Pitiful, in comparison to all her sister had achieved in the same stretch of time.

That rot made her feel small, and useless, and ashamed.

Kali now sported a pounding headache to match the one Puk had been complaining about all day. They were quite the duo.

As it turned out, there was indeed a sizeable clinic in one of Myrisih's many offshoot caverns. Two impressively large domed structures connected by an enclosed hallway; one half was where patients were examined, and the other was a dormitory where the handful of busy white mages lived. A white mage's housing was always connected to the clinic where they worked in case of an off-hours emergency.

She once again found herself stunned by how *normal* Myrisih was in some respects, having a well-stocked and -employed mage clinic.

Upon arrival, it was clear to her why that was the case.

The clinic was packed with tons of unfortunate souls aggrieved by everything spanning from run-of-the-mill illnesses to more extreme cases such as severed limbs. The types of people who frequented Myrisih likely needed medical attention on a regular basis, in addition to the regular needs of those who lived in the city full-time and required medicine or other treatments.

In her mind, she told herself to stop being so surprised by everything here. There was clearly a lot in the world she didn't have the faintest clue about. The Repository was a monument to that fact.

She speculated over what her sister knew about Myrisih, if anything. Were there texts written about it at the Repository? Perhaps tucked away in the secret, forbidden section? Would Lissia have been similarly taken aback by the existence of a clinic here, which, in retrospect, seemed very obvious? Did she know the location of Myrisih, all its odd port rules, the layout of the Mass?

Was Kali just ignorant?

Why am I still always negatively comparing myself to her?

The stark self-awareness caught her off-guard and was swiftly dismissed. She had other, physical, things to worry about.

The clinic was one of two in Myrisih, as the front desk worker at their inn explained to them. Coincidentally, the other was located fairly close to the grotto where their brawl had occurred, and they both deemed it the more likely place for their assailant to end up. It would take a lot of time and dedication for Thom to walk all the way to this other clinic with three holes in his leg. They felt they were safe here for the time being, though getting out as soon as possible would be nice, on the off-chance Thom showed up in search of them.

Her case was deemed less urgent than others, as the wound in her head was thankfully not deep and the bleeding had slowed to a stop, so she and Puk sat in the waiting room.

Others amongst them included a mold-ridden centript, a battered man with rough bruising all over his face and neck, an ujath with what appeared to be intense burns on her left side, and many more who squirmed uncomfortably in their seats.

"It stinks like shit in here," Puk whispered conspiratorially.

"It's the general smell of sick combined with all the blood and pus and whatever else everyone is leaking, myself included."

"No, I think someone actually shit themselves. Look at that guy movin' around in his seat a bunch over there." He pointed at a particularly uncomfortable-looking rocyan whose torso had been wrapped in bandages while he waited for an available mage. "I think he shit himself."

Kali snorted, trying not to draw attention to herself, and said, "Or—and this is just a theory—or his side just hurts and he's uncomfortable. It looks like he got stabbed or shot."

"Nah, he's got a shitty diaper."

They both laughed at this and continued to wait. Puk told Kali about his coin ploy against Thom, which elicited barking laughter from her that made her head ache even more. He then went on to describe how he'd acted mournful to lull Thom into a false sense of security, and she was admittedly impressed. Only a little, though.

Several patients were seen to before her, including the rocyan that Puk had declared a pants-shitter, and she was finally called back nearly an hour after first checking in.

The white mage tending to her was a young jeornish man who had to be only a few years out of the academy. Kali couldn't help but wonder what unfortunate circumstances landed him here in Myrisih rather than a prestigious, legitimate clinic in one of the major cities.

Kali sat across from him while Puk hunkered down in a rickety chair set up in the corner. The mage introduced himself as Dahvi and promptly got to work examining the cut on her head, graciously given to her by the grotto's stone steps.

"An easy fix," he promised her with a charming smile. "The bleeding already stopped on its own, so that's good. Are you feeling light-headed at all?" His voice was smooth and surprisingly deep.

"No, but this headache is going to kill me," she replied.

Dahvi chuckled. "That's to be expected. A headache isn't great, but it doesn't appear you have a concussion, especially if you were passed out earlier. I think this injury *looks* worse than it actually was."

In his corner, Puk sighed with relief. It warmed Kali's heart a little to know that the qarm was so concerned about her, despite having thrown her limp body to the side to stab their attacker. Though that image nearly made her laugh in Dahvi's face.

"Let me just clear away the blood and patch you up, then you'll be good to go."

Dahvi set to gesturing with his hands, casting a spell to seal the minor wound in her head. Ancient Ustrel symbols sketched themselves into the tops of his hands as he cast his magic, signs that would slowly fade away over the course of a few hours. Ustrel symbols that were associated with other spells were still faintly visible on parts of his hands and forearms, acting as a physical record of the spells he'd used to treat patients that day which would dissipate in a few hours' time.

As the fresh symbols began glowing, the cut in Kali's head grew itchier. In her youth, she had gotten into some scuffles and landed herself in a mage's clinic a number of times, so she knew the wound was stitching itself back together at an accelerated pace. It didn't hurt, necessarily, but it wasn't a wholly pleasant feeling.

It was a relief when the itching finally stopped and Dahvi lowered his hands. The symbols no longer shone.

With the wound successfully healed, Dahvi wet a cloth and wiped away the blood that already dried to a crust against her scalp and in her hair. He made a lighthearted comment about how difficult it was to find the bits of dried blood camouflaged amongst her crimson-red locks.

They thanked Dahvi, and on their way out of the office Puk asked him, "Hey, did that rocyan earlier shit himself?"

Dahvi, to his credit, remained stone-faced. "Doctor-patient confidentiality," was his only response.

"Bastard," Puk muttered sourly as they paid for the mage's services back out in the lobby. They marched past the sordid souls awaiting treatment and Kali grumbled about the unexpected expense.

She still had roughly three hundred crescents in her bank savings, but that was back in Seroo's Eye. And that was not a considerable amount of money by anyone's measure. They had spent half the money she'd withdrawn on this voyage, a bit

318 · travis m. riddle

more than she had estimated, and they were now down to about one hundred and fifty crescents.

They weren't in any trouble quite yet, but now more than ever she needed those five thousand crescents from tracking down Kleus Saix and his much-wanted book.

They hastily scampered back to the inn. Kali's headache probably wouldn't recede for the rest of the day, but aside from that she felt fine. She was exhausted, though, in spite of it only being early afternoon.

Relaxing in their separate beds, Kali gingerly laid her head down on the pillow. It wasn't as soft as the ones her father sprung for, but it was comfier than it had any right to be. The puke-green paint coating the walls would've made her mother shudder.

She said to Puk, "We need to get out of here as soon as possible."

"Agreed," Puk nodded, fidgeting with his hands in his pockets. "I want that money."

"It's not just that," she said, though it was a hefty motivator. "Haratti said they already sent someone out looking for the book. They haven't come back yet, but it's possible they found it or are close, so we need to beat them to the punch. And not to mention fucking Thom."

"Thom sucks."

"Yes, I agree with that. That's my point: whoever Thom's working for is obviously well-connected here in town, just like Haratti's boss. And they're all dangerous. We need to get out of here before Thom's boss sends another crony after us. I know you're feeling cocky after dealing with him, but really we just got lucky."

"I think you're underestimating us," said Puk.

"I literally didn't even do anything in the fight. I got knocked down the stairs immediately and blacked out."

"Okay, well, then you're underestimating *me*," the qarm grinned.

Kali sneered. "Be that as it may, it's in our best interests to get out of Myrisih as soon as we can, and ideally undetected. I can't imagine Thom's crew knows where we're staying, but they're surely still looking for us. And I can promise you Thom is pissed after how you tore up his leg."

"The Mighty Puk strikes again."

"Mighty indeed. The ports open up again tonight, right?" Puk affirmed, and she went on. "Then let's find Zenib and get out of here as soon as they're open. Agreed?"

"Sure," said Puk. "Won't be for a few hours, though. We'll need some dinner beforehand. My tum's feelin' a bit glum, now that I think about it."

"I don't need anything," Kali said. She would eat something when they got to Weynard in a few days. She hoped the village had some high quality bakeries.

"Alright, you can stay here and get some rest. I'll go grab grub and Zenib. Hey, and he's kinda like a grub. Is that funny?" Kali confirmed that it was trite. Puk said, "Okay, well, we'll come get you when it's closer to the ports opening."

They agreed on the plan, but Kali said, "Be sure to keep a low profile, and be on the lookout for Thom. Not sure if he's the only one who knows what we look like, but he might've told others. Just…be careful."

"I will," said Puk, and then he disappeared out the door and onto the city streets.

It felt like her brain was slamming its fist against her skull as she lay in bed, but thankfully, the pain was not as unbearable as it had been before Dahvi's spell.

Puk's words about her underestimating them echoed in her head. It was true that she was incapacitated pretty quickly, but she proved her formidability when faced with Jeth's botched robbery at the travelers' outpost. And now Puk had shown that, while his methods were incredibly unorthodox, he could hold his own in a scrap as well.

Kali's doubt brought Lissia to mind again, and the self-imposed question of why she always compared her own accomplishments—or lack thereof—to her sister's. She had spent her entire life underestimating herself. Caught in a loop.

Maybe it was high time to break the cycle.

CHAPTER XIV

JUICE FIRST

Zenib had more than a few associates around the city who as-sisted the duo in making sure they reached the port undetected by Thom or anyone else from his crew. When Kali and Puk described the man who attacked them, Zenib immediately rec-ognized who they were talking about and the people he ran with.

"Nasty group," he told them. "Their boss is a woman called Brinn Natalja. You ever heard of Frederick Feiri?"

Kali shook her head, but Puk nodded and said, "The Flame."

The centript confirmed. "Well, the story goes that Brinn was sold to him as a young girl, and he was planning to sell her to some old Gillusian pervert or something, I don't remember. Point is, before it ever got to that, she murdered him. One of the most notorious gangsters on the continent, and some eleven-year-old girl cut off his prick and stabbed him in the neck. She's only gotten more ferocious with time."

Puk let out a low whistle.

"So long story short is that she's dangerous," said Kali.

"Yeah, I'd say so."

An hour later, they were loaded up onto the *Fiery Lass* with no trouble while Zenib talked to the portmaster. Puk was at the head of the ship, watching calm waves rock the tiny boat, while Kali stuffed her bag down by her feet. Soon Zenib scuttled into the vessel, sighing contentedly.

"Ready to push off?" he asked them. They nodded.

Kali noticed the centript wince as he used ones of the oars to push the boat away from the dock and began rowing. "Are you alright?" she asked him.

He shrugged it off. "Just the mold," he said, as if it were nothing to worry about at all. As if he hadn't already lost multiple pieces of his carapace and three arms. It seemed a fourth would be soon to follow.

She hesitated at first, but decided to ask, "What does it feel like when it starts to…" She searched for the right verb, something not overly inappropriate, but came up short. The affliction was so foreign to her, she couldn't comprehend the right words to describe it.

They slowly coursed through the canal, heading out to the sea. Their boat was one of perhaps half a dozen that had already disembarked. Everyone else was content to wait and leave in the morning.

Zenib answered, "It's an odd sensation. Not totally unpleasant at first. It's like…maybe the closest comparison is feeling your muscles relax. It's soothing. But then it turns into a light tingle, and then that turns into a burning sensation, which don't really stop. That's where I'm at right now, here." He pointed his head toward the body segment his rowing arms jutted out from. "It was only the tingle when we got here. The process seems to be speeding up."

Doesn't that worry you? she almost asked, but held her tongue. She didn't want to pry further or cause him to freak out.

"Near the end, it's like a pulsing. Basically the opposite of the muscle relaxing part. Your body part starts to feel like it's getting bigger and smaller and bigger and smaller like it's your heartbeat or somethin', until it finally just pops. Literally. Pus oozing out, the shell falling off, everything's discolored. It's a damn mess."

Kali had a basic understanding of the disease, but hearing Zenib describe it first-hand was horrifying. "That sounds so painful," she said, chilled.

Zenib laughed, a piercing clacking sound. "No shit it's painful," he then said.

She began, "How long until…"

"Until I'm a pussed-up mess?"

"I wasn't gonna put it that way, but yes," she said, surprised by his frankness. It genuinely did not seem like a big deal to him. Maybe after a few months living with the disease it was now, unfortunately, just an immutable fact of life.

He considered the question a moment, then replied, "Only a few days, I think. Especially if it's speeding up. Next time you two see me, I'll be a bit lighter, I suspect."

"You could stand to lose the weight," Puk chimed in from the front of the boat, not bothering to turn around. Zenib laughed at the jibe.

She found herself asking after all, "Doesn't that worry you? That the process is getting faster?"

"It's not great," Zenib said, "but I'll worry when it gets to my head. Until then, I've got money to make and money to spend."

324 · travis m. riddle

Kali shuddered. Her own head injury from earlier was bad enough; she could scarcely imagine her skull exploding into a wet, grotesque mess.

That effectively ended the conversation. She dipped her hand into the water as they glided through. It was ice cold, but soothed her spirit after a rough twenty-four hours. She was trying to be more confident in herself, in her abilities, in their capability of pulling off Haratti's job, but she was still shaken by the brawl with Thom.

Never before had she been so close to death, and for what? A few thousand crescents?

Eventually they came to the massive iron gate that blocked Myrisih off from the rest of the world. The guards were still mired in the process of raising it, and all six ships now bobbed in the water, waiting to be granted passage.

She watched the blackened metal rise, cold water dripping from its edges as it disappeared halfway into a thick carved-out slit in the cavern's ceiling, surrounded by stalactites. Kali was glad to be leaving the mysterious, shadowy city. It had been an exhilarating experience walking its streets and learning more about it, but she could not say that her time there was something she'd fondly revisit in her memories. She wished it wasn't necessary for them to return once they acquired the book, but alas.

The gate came to a creaking halt, and the first ship in line slowly inched forward, further into the tunnels. There were still a few twists and turns before they would reach the mouth of the cavern and the open seas.

The *Fiery Lass* followed, and Kali kept her hand trailing through the water while they were still within the safe, calm waters of the Myrisih tunnel system. She would retract it once they emerged into the Loranos Gulf.

A nap also sounded pretty good; she caught a little bit of sleep at the inn while Puk was out eating dinner and finding Zenib, but she was still pretty exhausted.

For now, though, she let the coolness flow from her fingertips up her arm, through her body, allowing her thoughts to get lost in it. Aimlessly swimming. She breathed in deep, cold air, and let it out slowly.

With her headache throbbing, she imagined her skull bursting.

- -

Zenib and Puk awkwardly clambered out of the boat, with Kali already on the shore ahead of them. It was obvious that she did not let herself relax until she had finally set foot on solid ground again. She was on edge for the entirety of their last hours spent in Myrisih, and Puk didn't want to admit to her that he'd felt the same way.

There were no boats on the horizon, nobody following them. They were safe.

For now.

He felt his muscles relax as he stumbled through the dirt. Zenib singlehandedly tugged the boat onto dry land and hid it away once more in his hiding spot between the shore's two large red boulders. A little obvious, in Puk's estimation, but he figured the centript knew how trafficked the beach was better than he did.

The rest of their short stay in Restick was unremarkable.

After they all scrambled over the perimeter wall again, their guide returned to his home in Nyek Hollow to await their triumphant return with *Malum* in hand. Puk and Kali reluctantly disturbed Eva late at night (they had wanted to stay in an inn, but after the mage clinic costs, decided they should save the money), but she was still awake and welcomed them inside. They chatted a bit—with the woman pressing Kali for details about her "work trip," questions that she had to dodge—before retiring for bed. The next day, they filled up their waterskins at the house and restocked on travel supplies before heading to the stables to fetch Bella.

The ayote was happy to see them both, which Puk had not expected. He'd never been great with animals and always defaulted to thinking they despised him. He giggled when Bella affectionately nuzzled her rat-like snout in between his eyestalks. Her skin was rough, almost scaly, and warmed by the sun. Her ears flicked with delight.

Leaving the city limits was a reminder of how much he hated the desert.

We better find that damned book good and quick.

The sun beat down on the two of them bouncing along on Bella's back. Despite the loose, thin fabric of his clothing, Puk was already sweating bullets, making his rubbery skin even more moist than usual. He felt disgusting.

When he acquired his money and lugged his ass back to Atlua, the first thing he wanted to do was find a natural spring and a lengthy massage. He was more than ready to exchange the endless expanse of sand for that of forest. Never did he think he would miss greenery so much, but now found himself oddly craving a salad.

They headed south out of Restick, at first following the Ribroad but soon veering off into the sea of sand. Kali appeared confident in where they were going, and he trusted her sense of direction.

While they rode, she explained to him the system travelers used to navigate the unchanging landscape. There were spires erected all throughout the Gogol Desert, each with their own different markings and colors to indicate which route they were on as well as the cardinal directions. The side of a spire painted lavender indicated south, so that was the color for which they kept a lookout.

He asked who originally built the constructs, and she confessed she wasn't sure; it was easy to assume centripts built them, as they had most of the architecture throughout the country, but they were also not known to be travelers and therefore wouldn't have a ton of use for them, so perhaps not.

It was a long day, and Puk had foolishly exhausted his supply of water with half the voyage ahead of them. When they mercifully arrived at the outpost, he burst through the door and practically affixed his eager mouth to the water spigot inside while Kali stabled the ayote.

"Anything else?" the bartender asked once Puk finished downing a second glass of water.

"Another fill-up, and a second glass," he said. He knew the drinks were free, but more water would really hit the spot for now.

With the glasses in hand, he found an empty table and hunkered down to wait for Kali. She sauntered in a few minutes later, brushing dust off her thin, white cotton clothing. Her boots thudded against the ground as she walked over to the table.

"Thanks," she said, taking the proffered glass. She had been more conservative with her own supply throughout the day, so he'd known she would be thirsty. She promptly gulped down a healthy portion.

328 · travis m. riddle

The two sat in silence for a couple minutes, worn out by their day of travel. While they hydrated themselves, Puk noticed the bartender speaking to another employee and pointing at their table. The employee scurried out of the room.

Wonder what that's about, he thought, suddenly paranoid about Brinn Natalja's influence and reach. Had they been found out already? After only a single day?

"Employees are chattin' about us," he whispered to Kali, keeping his cool.

"What?" she mumbled, her eyelids droopy.

He subtly pointed one eyestalk at the bar behind him. "Bartender just told someone we're here. They ran off to fetch someone or something."

"You're sure?"

"They were talking and pointing at us as soon as you sat down."

Kali furrowed her brow in thought, then asked, "What did they look like?"

"Skinny little guy, absurd mustache—"

Before he could go on, she smirked and said, "I think—"

"Ahem."

She was interrupted by the mustachioed man's return, who stood alongside a rocyan with a tuft of longer hair at the end of his snout, akin to a moustache. The two men were dressed in crisp, tan uniforms of the outpost and looked like bizarre, parallel versions of each other.

"Ma'am," the rocyan said, his voice high yet raspy.

There was a pause while Kali waited for him to continue, but he simply stood staring at her alongside his cohort, so she said, "Yes?"

"We gladly welcome you to our outpost, but we wanted to check in with you and ensure that there will not be any...*incidents* like your last visit."

"If no one tries to rob me this time, it should be an uneventful visit," Kali said with a sarcastically pleasant smile.

"Of course," the rocyan said with a curt bow. "Enjoy your stay." With that, he and the other man, who appeared much more irritated by her presence, shuffled away. The latter returned to the bar and resumed gossiping with the bartender.

Puk had trained one of his stalks on the mustachioed man and rotated it back to face Kali, letting out a soft laugh. "The hell was that about?" he asked. "It sounds like a juicy story. I like the juice. Give me the juice, I'm a thirsty boy." It was a relief that Natalja had in fact not tracked them down.

"I was here a little over a week ago," Kali explained. "Some asshole was talking to me, knew I was traveling alone, and I guess figured I was some helpless, defenseless girl. It's an assumption lots of people tend to have about me."

He could sort of understand why thugs would make that assumption. Every faif that Puk ever met was thin as a twig. He rested his hands on his paunch.

She went on. "Anyway, in the middle of the night he broke into my room to rob me. Honestly, if he'd been successful, he wouldn't have gotten much."

"But from the sound of it, he was *not* successful."

"Not quite. His arm got to meet that dagger of mine."

Puk laughed.

"It was a mess," she chuckled.

"That's *pretty* juicy, but not as juicy as I expected," Puk said. "Did you stab him in the dick, by chance?"

Kali shook her head. Unfortunate.

330 · travis m. riddle

"Oh well. The arm is a pretty good stabbing place as it is. At least now we've got solid proof that you *can* take someone in a fight."

Kali scoffed. "Was there any doubt before?" she asked, feigning offense.

Puk scoffed as well. "We've been in two fights together and you fucked up both! I had to deal with Thom myself while you were off bleedin' in a pool or whatever, and I had to kill the cordol, too!"

"Hey, I didn't want to hurt the cordol at all, I was holding back. But regardless, the cordol was a team effort."

"I distinctly remember it being *my* boot that choked it and subsequently caused it to stop being alive."

"Is that a story you're proud of? Is that one you plan on telling all the other hunters gathered around the bar late at night?"

"Yeah, it is!" he boasted. "They're out there killin' shit with their guns and their bows and their swords—bastard swords, probably, which are even bigger and cooler than a normal sword in spite of the dumb name—but how many of 'em can say they killed a vicious beast with nothing but footwear?"

"Probably very few," she conceded.

"'Few' implies more than zero," he said.

Kali slurped down some more water then asked, "Do you really think you're the first person in the world to kill a monster with a boot?"

"Yes."

"Wow. The arrogance." They laughed. "What would your old troupe members say if you told them of your recent accomplishments?"

He pondered the question for a moment. Everyone in The Rusty Halberd thought of him as a dunce, especially Hin, and with good reason. His greatest ally probably would've been Dern, but even he would struggle believing Puk's stories.

"Well, they all know I'm incompetent," he started.

"Hence the boot."

"Chucking the boot was a brilliant tactical maneuver," he said. Then, "They probably woulda all thought I was making shit up. I know Vick would find it hilarious. He would probably even try to write a skit around it and have me play myself. Or, rather, he'd have me play the cordol that chokes on a shoe, because he'd think the irony was funny even though no one in the audience would pick up on it."

"I would be amused seeing a boot thrown at your head," Kali teased. "I'll gladly buy a ticket to that."

"You ain't the only one, I'm sure."

She then asked, "So Vick was the writer of the group?"

"Mostly," Puk said before taking a sip of water. "He fancied himself a comedian, but I thought he was kind of a corny dingus. He usually did get some laughs, though, so what do I know?"

"Did he get you to act in skits often? I can't imagine you acting."

"Oh, yeah, he made all of us do it," Puk replied. "Me, Dern, Jit—even Hin, sometimes, when she could be convinced. And what the hell d'you mean you can't imagine me acting? I put on the performance of a lifetime back there with Thom!"

"Is that when I was unconscious?"

"Yeah, it was. Unfortunately for you. You would've been truly moved by it."

"I'll have to catch the next show, I guess. There were five of you in the group?"

Puk nodded. "Vick told his own jokes and wrote everyone skits to perform in between their solo acts. I sang. Jit was a juggler, and probably one of the best I've seen. I've watched my fair share of jugglers set their dumb asses on fire messing up a catch with flaming balls before. Hin was our leader. She organized all the shows, arranged the travel, all that fancy official shit the rest of us couldn't be bothered to handle, much to her annoyance. She and Dern were the musicians of the troupe. He was great with a flute, and she weren't bad pluckin' away at a lute."

"'Not bad'? Sounds like you think you could pluck your way through a lute better than her," Kali said with a glint in her eye. "Don't think I haven't noticed you refer to yourself as a 'musician' from time to time."

"Hey, I told you I was strictly a singer. But yeah, I'd say I was the better lutist. Is that what they're called? Lutists?"

"I doubt it," Kali said. "I wasn't *totally* sure you ever played, though."

"I haven't in a long time," he admitted. It had been years since he'd last strummed an instrument. Any skill he once had was surely diminished.

"So you don't write your own songs or play the lute anymore," she said. She arched her eyebrows over the rim of her glass as she downed the remainder of her water.

"That sounded like a barb," Puk said. "A rude barb."

"Is there any other kind?"

"The lute thing ain't my fault, at least. I used to play all the time, until mine got smashed up in Lors."

Kali grinned at this revelation. "Your turn now. Give me the juice."

"You need a refill first?" he asked, pointing at her empty glass.

"Juice first, then water."

So he dove into the tale.

"I was living in Lors at the time, probably…ten years ago? Somethin' like that. While back. I was playing at inns and pubs around town fairly often—usually songs that people already knew, but you would be pleased to know that a few of them were written by me. Puk originals! Anyways, one day—it was the middle of the day, sun's shining bright, everyone's out and about on the street—I was walking from my apartment to the market square, where they were throwin' a small annual shindig called The Honeycomb Festival or something like that, I dunno.

"I'd been hired to play a couple songs during the festivities, along with some other people who I thought were all way better than me, so I was pretty excited to be asked. Felt like an honor, kinda, to be put up alongside them. So I was walking with my lute strapped on my back. It wasn't nothin' special, just something I'd picked up at a secondhand shop a couple years before, but it was a good instrument. Sturdy, good tone. I had just strung some fresh strings, so I was feelin' fancy. Ahead, walking right towards me, was a guy who was infamous in the city. Everyone knew his name was Dallon, and everyone knew he was *not* blind like he claimed to be. Perfectly avoiding every obstacle and specifically commenting on people's appearance when he got mad at them were fairly good clues. He'd wander around, telling residents and tourists alike that he was blind and needed help, needed any crescents they could spare. The people who lived there knew it was a scam, but the tourists always fell for it and I'd bet he made a pretty good living off it. I dunno why he did it, if he was just an asshole tryin' to make a quick crescent or if he was mentally ill or somethin' and couldn't hold down a real job, but either way, he approached me.

"He gave me the usual spiel, that he was blind and couldn't work and needed some assistance in the form of crescents. No one ever confronted him or challenged his claim, and I wasn't gonna be the first, so I politely told him I didn't have any money on me. That pissed him off, as it always did when people denied him, so he started yelling at me, calling me a fat little worm, saying I was selfish, stuff like that. I ignored him and tried to slip past, but as I did he grabbed my lute and yanked it off my back, then smashed it on the ground. Over and over, until it was just shards of wood scattered all over the street, yelling about how if I'm not making any money with it then I didn't need it, right? I mean, he wasn't totally wrong. I wasn't makin' all that much money, but..."

Puk trailed off, eyestalks drooping, remembering the sight of his lute splintered into countless pieces on the dirty cobbled road. The people standing nearby, unmoving, not reacting to anything Dallon was saying or doing. All of them—Puk included—simply watching the man drop the narrow wooden neck of the instrument onto the ground with a light thud, then stomping away in search of a more susceptible mark.

Kali's face etched into a deep frown at the conclusion of his story. The juice was sour.

"Did anything happen to the guy?" she asked.

"Nah."

"But he destroyed your property." The concern in her eyes was genuine. "Shouldn't the authorities have done something?"

He shrugged.

Kali seemed unsatisfied with the response but moved on and asked, "So you haven't played since then?"

A shake of the head.

"Any instrument at all?"

Another shake.

"...why not?" Her voice was low.

Puk knew the question was coming. He didn't have an answer that would satisfy her. It lined up with the rest of his reasoning for how he'd decided to live his life, which he knew she did not find understandable.

But he laid it out for her regardless. "It was discouraging, y'know? It was like looking at my dreams smashed into pieces on the ground. I wouldn't be able to find another lute in time for the performance, not at a price I could afford, so the day was ruined already. I just went home. Didn't even attend the festival."

The explanation sounded even weaker aloud than it had internally.

In truth, the incident was somewhat of a relief, which at the time had flooded him with guilt. He hadn't quite been failing as a musician, but he was far from making a sustainable income off it, and he knew there was a lot of work that needed to be done for him to reach that point. A lot of effort.

But with his lute destroyed, it was out of his hands. He told himself that, hey, his instrument was gone, so he couldn't pursue that path anymore. He got to avoid funneling all that money into the endeavor. Got to avoid making that immense effort. And, as a result, he would avoid failing after throwing himself into it. This way, the failure wasn't his own fault.

Instead, he chose a path of frivolity. Drinks, drugs, whatever fun he could find.

Plenty of people throughout the world lived their lives without pursuing any creative avenue. It would be much less stressful to count himself among their number.

He didn't want to tell Kali that, though.

It was bad enough being a failure, let alone consciously deciding to take a shortcut to failure.

Thankfully, Kali dropped the subject after that. Maybe she sensed his innate discomfort. She seemed lost in thought herself as she rose a few moments later, asking if he wanted more water. He said sure, and asked for a short glass of Nawan rum if they had any. She smiled and obliged.

While Kali was at the counter, Puk's thoughts drifted to the near-empty jar of cordol spit nestled snugly in his backpack.

Reminiscing about his destitution in Lors naturally conjured hazy memories of tavern nights with friends that usually resulted in alleyway mornings. Entire nights lost to booze and drugs, whether that meant marshweed or fire-spit or whatever other illicit delights they could get their grubby hands on.

Now, though, his stomach churned at the prospect of such a night. At the idea of drinking that spit. Which he had absurdly found appealing only a few nights before. Puk wasn't sure if the effects of drinking it raw had put him off the substance entirely, or if it was something else.

When Kali returned to their table a minute later, she appeared to be in much brighter spirits than when she left. After his self-reflection in her absence, Puk was feeling lighter too.

"I wanna hear more stories about Atlua," she said, sliding a water as well as a stout glass of thick, dark liquid toward him.

Puk grasped the glass of rum and took a swig. It was spicy and sweet, dancing on his tongue and down his throat. He asked, "What kind of stories you wanna hear?"

"Anything," Kali said. "I wanna know everything that I can about the place. Maybe I'll finally know more about something than my sister."

She chuckled, but Puk frowned slightly.

He said, "I feel like that ain't the first time you've brought her up," he said.

Kali looked perplexed. "What do you mean? My sister? Sure, I've probably brought her up plenty of times."

"Yeah, but I mean like *that*—like you're some kind of dumbass and she's this mighty bastion of knowledge or something."

She shrugged and said, "Well, Lissia's a scholar at the Repository. She kind of *is* a bastion of knowledge. She's by far the most accomplished Shiar—way more than me, anyhow. She's up in that tower, wiling away the days working to research for the world, bring people knowledge, blah blah blah, and meanwhile I'm just puttering back and forth across the desert like an idiot..." She trailed off, her voice low and dark.

Puk shook his head. "See, that's stupid," he told her. She almost interjected, but he stopped her. "You're talkin' like your sister's the only person to ever do shit in the world, like you're nothin'. Which is stupid. You've accomplished a ton, I know you have. I've seen it. You've told me about it. You gotta stop acting like she's the measure of your success or whatever. The shit you've done is worthwhile too. Just gotta have a bit more confidence in yourself."

With those words pouring out of him, he felt corny, like he was Anure Rahk. He also knew the advice he gave was easier said than done; he knew it all too well, given that he rarely practiced it. But he felt it needed to be said anyway. His heart was beating fast and he anxiously awaited Kali's reaction.

She was quiet for a moment, looking down at the table, averting her eyes.

Finally, she glanced up at him and said quietly, "Thanks."

He smiled at her. "There's nothin' to thank me for," he said. "It's just the truth." He took another pull of his rum and said, "So, you still want some stories? I might have a few."

Kali cracked a grin as well, which warmed him. She said, "Yeah. I wanna paint a clearer picture in my head before we get over there."

He grinned wider. "That sentence seems more like a *when* than an *if*," he said. "Someone's feelin' more confident in our ability to find this damn book, I think!"

"How could I not be?" Kali chuckled. "My companion is the only person in the world to slay a mighty beast with his shoe."

- -

Weynard was a small village surrounded by miles and miles of desert. It was fairly secluded and modest, even compared to other desert towns. The population was small and self-sustaining, and its residents liked it that way. It was a close-knit community, far from the troubles of the world.

There was an oasis at the center of the village, a beautiful shimmering body of water lined with trees of dark green leaves and thick trunks. Buildings circled the water, red clay structures that were all connected to each other, acting like a perimeter wall enclosing the oasis. Various buildings were two to four stories high, home to different families or businesses, some establishments connected by rope bridges that swayed lightly in the wind. A lot of the architecture had sensibilities similar to centript hives, hence the connected buildings. There were even some that contained tunnels leading underground, then back up into buildings on the other side of town.

Kali and Puk had a bit of trouble locating the town's inn, which was a small, quaint establishment called The Restful Oasis that blended in with the other buildings. The place was smaller than any other inn Kali had seen before, and it took her a minute to realize it was actually someone's home; the village clearly did not anticipate many visitors. And with good reason, evidently, since the two of them seemed to be the only guests.

The homeowner, a kind elderly woman named Grace, welcomed them into her home with a gap-toothed smile. "I got three bedrooms available," she informed them, her voice shaky but cheerful. "The Ayote Room, the Mahnek Room, and the Wrenwing Room—*that's the honeymoon suite*," she added with a sly wink.

"The Wrenwing Room!" Puk said with a buffoonish grin.

"No, no," Kali interjected. "Whichever's cheapest is fine."

"The Ayote Room it is, then," Grace said. She hobbled over to a drawer and pulled out an old, black key. "This way!" She then began her distressingly slow ascent to the upper floor of the house.

Ever since their conversation at the outpost, though, there had been something Kali wanted to do once they arrived in Weynard.

She told Puk, "You go on ahead and get all our stuff settled in. I'll be back in a bit." She slung her knapsack onto the floor beside the qarm, who looked up at her quizzically.

One eyestalk turned to peer at the staircase before turning to address Kali. "At her rate, I'm only gonna be halfway up the stairs by the time you get back."

Kali chuckled and swooped through the doorway back outside.

The sun was nearly concealed by the horizon, but she still felt its warmth and nourishment soaking through her skin after so many hours basking in it. Between that and her plump water-skin, she wouldn't need a meal until they reached Pontequest, and maybe not even until they returned to Restick. Tracking down a delicious, sugary pastry might be on the docket, though.

The clay border of buildings practically opened right up to the oasis at the town's center. There was a pathway separating the various entryways and the line of trees and greenery, but it was no more than sand a few strides wide. There was no need for cobbled walkways here.

Kali strolled down the makeshift path, closely examining the entryways of each building she passed, trying to discern which were homes and which were shops. Very few had distinct markings to specify. Perhaps residents knew their way around, but Weynard was proving not to be an especially visitor-friendly town.

No luck. She would have to knock on every door if she wanted to find any answers here.

She glanced to her left, past the trees, and saw several people gathered at the shoreline of the oasis. There were kids running around, playing catch with a small ball painted a dull white, and many adults sprawled out in the sand taking pulls from beer bottles.

Might as well ask the locals, she decided.

She stepped through the treeline, appreciating the feel of leaves brushing against her skin after so long surrounded by nothing but sand and dry air. Down by the water, she approached two faif men who had made an impressive pile of empty bottles between the two of them and were guffawing over something they had said. Her footsteps were uneven in the shifting sand.

"Excuse me," she said, bringing their yaps to a stop. The two men turned to look at her over their shoulders and smiled amiably.

"Hey there, miss," the closer one said, nodding his head toward her in greeting. His skin was orange with bright stripes of green that culminated in delicate spirals.

The other did likewise and asked, "Some'in y'need help with?"

"I was wondering if either of you knew where I could buy a musical instrument?" she asked. "A music shop, or a secondhand store, or…"

"Ain't no music shops 'round here, f'sure," said the second man with an amused grunt. "Our musicians make their own stuff, don't need no shop to buy it from, eh?" His comrade nodded in concurrence.

Kali was slightly disheartened, but asked, "Do you know anyone who might have a classical lute? Or a duraga? I'd be happy to buy one from whoever might have them." Maybe a local player would be willing to part with one of their creations.

The men considered her question a moment, then the closer one piped up. "Jim plays, right? I bet he'd have some extras." He looked to his companion for confirmation, and received it. To Kali, he said, "Jim Reyn might have what you're lookin'

342 · travis m. riddle

for. He's the best duraga player either of us has ever seen, right?" More affirmation from the other man.

"That'd be great," Kali said excitedly. "Do you know where I can find him?"

Between the two of them, the men managed to cobble together directions to Jim Reyn's house, which was on the opposite side of the oasis.

It was a pleasant walk, though as the sun sunk into the distant dunes, Kali discovered there was no outdoor lighting of any kind set up in Weynard. She had to navigate solely by moonlight, which made things marginally more difficult.

But eventually she came to the nondescript door she believed belonged to Jim Reyn, and gave it a tentative knock. After waiting a full minute to no avail, she had to give it one more knock before someone finally answered.

"Yeah, yeah, hold on!" came a crabby voice from inside. Seconds later, the door swung open to reveal a hunched-over man whose skin was dark purple mottled with blue. He walked with a thin, crooked cane and wore a scowl on his wrinkled face.

"Jim Reyn?" Kali asked.

The man huffed and said, "Yep, yeah, what's it?"

She was rattled by his demeanor, and it took her a second to say, "My name's Kali. I was told you're a pretty skilled duraga player."

Jim waved away the compliment, still frowning. He said, "I's eatin' dinner."

"Oh, I'm terribly sorry," said Kali.

"Stew."

She blinked and said, "Okay." Then, "I can come back later, if you'd prefer." She certainly didn't want to intrude on the old man's meal.

"No, no, stew's hot and it'll only get colder. What's your need?"

Kali did not understand why that was a reason for her to stay, but she moved past it and said, "Well, I was wondering if you had a spare duraga you'd be willing to part with. For a price, of course." She pulled out her small cloth bag of crescents. The coins clinked together inside.

Jim's eyebrows raised and his scowl lessened at the sound of the coins. "I's a duraga player, mhm," he nodded. "Just made a new one last month. Good one. New one. Some old ones still knockin' around somewheres." He cocked his head back, indicating she could enter, and his neck audibly popped. But he ambled back into the house without another word, grumbling to himself. Something about his stew.

She followed him through his tiny home (filled with the spicy aroma of a meaty stew) and into his bedroom, where she smiled at the sight of six duragas leaning against the wall by a pillow and rumpled-up sheets on the floor.

While she inspected the instruments, Jim fetched the newest piece of the collection, of which he was wildly proud. He held it up for Kali to examine.

It was a beauty. Far prettier than any duraga she ever commissioned and sold. It was painted a gleaming white, a stark contrast against the six natural brown ones propped up along the wall. The end of the neck was painted black, which gradually faded to white as it got closer to the body. Lining the body and neck were dots of color, alternating green, blue, and pink.

344 · travis m. riddle

Around the sound hole there were words painted in the same colors, but Kali couldn't decipher what they said.

The man beamed as she looked it over, and she returned the smile. "It's gorgeous," she told him.

"I know," said Jim. "Thank ya. This the duraga I'm gonna die with. Hopes are that it'll be wrapped in m'hands when I go." He proceeded to tuck it away beside his pillow again.

Kali returned her attention to the older instruments, which looked drab now in comparison to the other. They were all the normal, natural brown color, with the rounded ayote shell backs pressing against the wall, causing the instruments to lazily roll to one side or the other. The bristles of hair had been retained on the shells, not sanded away like some more professional crafters tended to do. Jim was an amateur, but his passion was evident in the craftsmanship, and each successive duraga looked better than the last.

"Are there any you're open to selling?" she asked, trying to pinpoint the one in the bunch with the highest quality.

"Any o'em," said Jim with a grunt. "I's said I'm dyin' with th'other. Don't got no need for the rest."

Kali knelt down, having chosen the duraga she wanted. It was the fifth in the row, and appeared to be the newest one of the set. Its face was slightly less scratched, its neck free of chipping. It was plain, but well-made, and the strings looked relatively fresh.

She picked it up by the neck and asked, "How much would you like for it?"

Jim shrugged. It was obvious he'd never given any thought to selling his creations. In all likelihood they would have remained there, gathering dust while he plucked away on his shiny new white duraga. He didn't even bother to put forth an offer.

Kali had some experience selling duragas, so she knew what was fair. The ones she sold usually netted her anywhere between one hundred and one hundred and fifty crescents. These weren't the best she'd ever seen, and would typically garner a lower price, around twenty or twenty-five. But she wanted to help support the man. Especially after stealing him away from his stew for so long.

"How's thirty crescents sound?" she asked him. It was more than generous, though she doubted he knew that. Thirty would be a slight blow to their funds, but in her heart she knew it'd be worthwhile.

"Sure," he mumbled. Thirty was better than zero, which was the amount he would've previously ended the day with.

She gleefully handed over the money and walked back to the front door with the instrument in hand. She thanked Jim again, and he muttered something inaudible, probably about his stew.

The Weynard walkway was now more illuminated by the moonlight, and she raced back to the Restful Oasis. As she did so, she wondered if Puk made it to their room yet.

As it turned out, he had.

Grace greeted Kali as she reentered the tiny abode, and she bolted up the stairs to find a door with an ayote's silhouette painted on it. It had to be the Ayote Room. She gave it a light rap with her knuckles to warn Puk she was entering.

The qarm was outstretched in the middle of the floor, gazing dumbly at the ceiling. He had not yet looked her way and seen the duraga in her hands.

"What are you doing?" she asked.

"Laying."

"On the floor."

"Thought I'd let you get the bed. Didn't wanna get my sweat all over it. Not sure I can get up now. Too hungry and tired to move."

Kali laughed at him. Then she said, "Well, I've got something for you. Think you can move at least a stalk?"

"Maybe I can manage," he said, lifting his left eyestalk off the ground to look over at her, still standing in the doorway.

That one eye widened at the sight of the duraga. He pushed himself up off the floor, and his other eye widened to match. He opened his mouth to speak, but nothing came out.

"I'll be honest, it's not the best duraga I've ever seen," she said, "and I couldn't find a regular lute, but I assumed this was the next best thing." She walked over to him, still sitting on the ground, and handed him the instrument.

"Why'd...?" he muttered, examining the instrument. He shivered as the hairs on its back bristled against his skin. "I don't even play," he said.

She nodded. "That's why," she said. "I thought you might wanna get back into it. It's not your fault your last one got busted up, after all." She smiled. "Does it seem okay?"

"It seems great," he said. "A little morbid with the shell on the back, but really great. I should not show this to Bella," he chuckled. He flipped it back around and nestled the curve of the body on his leg. For a moment, it seemed he was about to play something, but he stopped himself.

"Go on," Kali urged him. She longed to hear him play a song.

But his eyestalks drooped.

"It's been so long..." His voice was a whisper.

"I'm sure you've still got the skills," she said cheerily.

"You don't know if I ever had the skills in the first place," he pointed out.

"I never said they were *good* skills, I'm just sayin' I bet you've still got the same skills you had before," she teased.

Puk looked back down at the duraga and sighed.

But then something within him changed. His eyes lit up, and he bolstered himself. He took a moment to readjust the positioning, then placed his fingertips on the strings, lightly grazing them along all ten thin strands.

"What should I play?" he asked.

The only song that immediately came to mind was "Sweet Sheri," but she'd heard him sing that plenty of times before. She yearned for something fresh. Something original.

"Play one of yours," she said.

That expression of worry returned to his round, blue face. But he did not contest.

"They ain't any good," he muttered, but readied his fingers. "You want a sad one, a happy one, or a horny one?"

The latter intrigued her. "I thought qarms were asexual. What inspired you to write 'a horny one'?"

"Money. People love horny ones. Sometimes you gotta write to the market to make any money," he grinned. "I've got one called 'The Cuckold in the Cannery,' if you're interested."

"Well, as intriguing as that sounds, let's go with happy this time," she said. "This is a happy occasion, isn't it?"

Puk nodded, thought for a moment, then said, "I never got to perform this one." He began to play.

The song started with him whistling a simple tune, accompanied by nimble, flighty plucks on the duraga.

"I've come to see the sea in spring
Ways the waves crash is tiring
You're why I'm stuck in this town
After the spring's come and it's gone
Waving goodbye, goodbye
You're why I'm sittin' here alone in the port
Watchin' the ships come and they go while I get high
Well, now
You're in my head, I've lost my mind
The salt of the sea engulfing me has froze to rime
My eyes are blurred, I've lost my sight
I'm sinkin' below, the dark has swallowed all the light
My ship has fallen to the sea
The waves are grasping, how they scream
I'm at the bottom of the sea
And I saw you
You watched me go, watched me go down."

He returned to the whistled melody, like a bird merrily chirping on the breeze. Kali listened and watched him with sad eyes. He whistled through the verse's melody, then sang the chorus again, ending softly with, *"You watched me go, watched me go down."*

Soon, the music stopped, and Puk simply stared down at his fingers as they ceased moving, as if in disbelief the sounds had been coming from him. He glanced up at Kali, who was at a loss for words.

Eventually, after several moments of shared silence, she said, "I thought you were gonna play a happy one."

Puk shrugged. "The music sounded happy, at least," he said. "Ain't all songs a little bit sad, anyways?"

She said, "I hope your horny ones aren't."

That quip made him crack a smile. She was glad to see his mood lightening.

Kali asked him, "Why didn't you ever play that one?"

His answer was simple. "I only wrote it a couple months ago," he said. "Never had the chance. Not 'til now." His stalks dipped down to look at his fingers again, before locking eyes with Kali. "Thanks," he told her.

To Kali's delight, Puk continued playing the duraga throughout the night, after they ducked out to grab him some dinner. He didn't sing anything else, but he did play a bit of music.

As they shut down for the night to go to sleep, Kali couldn't get the melody of his whistling out of her head.

CHAPTER XV

HUM

Bella sniffed curiously at Puk's duraga, eliciting laughter from the qarm, while Kali navigated the route in her head for the hundredth time.

She felt she retained a pretty clear picture of the map Haratti showed them in his office, but there was a pit in her stomach sinking lower and lower at the thought of riding out into the desert toward nothingness. They were still doing fine on supplies, but Puk's bag of dried fruit wasn't limitless.

"Should we ask the stablemaster?" Puk suggested, strapping his new duraga to the rest of the ayote's tack. Bella goofily craned her head around, trying in vain to catch another whiff.

"Not at all," Kali said, shaking her head. "It wouldn't be smart to let anyone in on where we're headed. If Thom or anyone else happens to be on our tail, we shouldn't leave behind any clues. It'd be as easy as them asking if the purple girl and tiny blue boy asked for directions somewhere. We're a strange pair, not easy to forget."

Puk nodded and said, "Makes sense."

"I thought you were a crime master," she smirked. "Shouldn't that have been lesson one?"

"Lesson one in crime school is actually an explanation for what crimes are," Puk retorted. "And no, I'm not a crime master! I don't do crimes!"

Kali shrugged. "Seems like you're a crime-y type of guy, given the people you run with. And you were awfully familiar with Myrisih…"

"I'm friends with scumbags, but I'm not quite that level of scumbag yet," said Puk. Kali laughed.

She took another minute to think through their route and how long it would take them based on her estimate of the fallen airship's crash site. She was slightly more confident in the plan now, and was pleased with herself. Maybe she wasn't quite her scholarly sister, but she knew a thing or two.

Kali ushered Puk onto Bella's back, playfully scolding him for intriguing and confusing the ayote with the duraga's scent. She lifted him up onto the animal.

He was about to take a sip from his recently-filled water-skin and she asked, "You sure you wanna do that already?"

"I'm thirsty."

"It's gonna be a thirsty trip."

He took a tiny sip.

She pulled herself up onto Bella's shell—nearly accidentally slamming her boot into Puk's face as she swung it over—and grasped the reins, gazing out into the empty tan expanse ahead of them.

And then they were off to Pontequest.

- -

The ride was like any other ride in the desert, which is to say that it made Puk miserable.

He felt overheated an hour into the trip. The temptation to chug his water was overwhelming, but he scrounged up the necessary willpower to resist. By now, he had mercifully gotten through the worst of his spit withdrawal symptoms, and was feeling considerably better than he had back in Myrisih. Needing frequent bathroom breaks while traversing the desert would not have been pleasant.

Though, if he really thought about it, the day's journey was not as soul-crushing as others had been. Sure, his underside was aching from multiple days of bouncing up and down on the ayote's rough shell, but his mood was surprisingly chipper, all things considered.

The instrument smacking against their mount had to be the reason.

Playing his song, finally bringing it to life, had unburdened him in a way he hadn't realized he needed. The song, and everything it represented, had been weighing him down for months. Possibly years. Letting it out of himself, bringing it into the world, vocalizing it, felt...

He searched for the perfect word. But sometimes, the simplest word worked best.

It felt *good.*

It felt good expressing those emotions through a song. Puk had never really been one for heartfelt conversation. Putting his feelings into some form of art felt more natural. More comfortable.

So he was gladdened by the fact Kali chose not to prod, not to question what the song was about. She surely knew it wasn't about a girl, or any real person.

Maybe she didn't ask because she already understood. Because it was about the same topic that had come up between the two multiple times over the course of their trip.

It always circled back to that. To the rut he was in. Had been in for years now.

Before, Puk had been perfectly content with his plan to collect the bounty on this stupid book that everyone wanted, bop his ass back to Atlua, and track down the nearest dealer he could find so he could get high and unwind. Probably sing in some bars to make a few crescents, maybe eventually find a new troupe to join, though maybe not. Too much work.

For years, he had been stuck in this rut, lending himself excuse after excuse not to yank himself out of it, starting with that man in Lors who smashed his lute to pieces.

Writing music was hard work. Expressing himself was hard work. Bringing something new into the world was hard work.

Getting high was easy. Playing Hunt or volleywag was easy. Doing *nothing* was easy.

Way easier than making music.

But that contentment had been paired with resentment. Everything he was doing was a waste. He had nothing to show for his life, nothing to be proud of. All he'd done for years and years was kill time.

Now, with the duraga slapping against her side as Bella bounded across the dunes, he wondered if that might have changed.

He smiled. His arms were wrapped tight around Kali's waist, fearful of letting go and flying off the ayote's back and careening into the sand. As he sat there, grinning like a fool, he was amused thinking about how the woman didn't have a clue to what extent she'd changed his life.

No more killing time, no more excuses. He needed to pull himself out of the rut. He had to break the cycle.

Inaudible to Kali over the splash of Bella's feet in the sand and the wind whipping at their faces, Puk began to hum a little tune to himself. The vibrations of his throat carried the melody up to him, and he began to craft something new.

After a while, Kali pulled back on the reins to slow Bella down. She wanted to give the ayote a bit of rest. It was only midday, and there was still plenty of blinding sand ahead of them. Bella cantered along at a brisk pace, squealing with pleasure. Her tail whipped back and forth behind them.

It had been a long while since Weynard disappeared at their backs, and nothing at all had taken its place on any side of them throughout the day. No other towns, no matter how far off in the distance. No oases. Not a single animal. Hardly any cacti. Not even a pleasant mirage to interrupt the boundless dunes.

Wherever it was they were going, it was remote. Even for the desert.

Puk still felt residually saucy after the prior night's performance, so even though the song he'd been working on throughout the day was far from polished, he was compelled to share. With their slower pace, a song could help break up the silence and monotony.

"I've been workin' on something new," he said.

"I could tell," said Kali. "I felt the vibrations of your humming."

He felt slightly awkward. "Oh," he sputtered. "Well—"

"Are you able to play it?" she asked. "Sitting up on Bella, I mean. Bouncing around."

"I think so," he said. "My arms are way too short to reach the duraga, though."

Kali assisted him in that regard. She reached down over Bella's side and unhooked the instrument, bringing it back up to place in Puk's hands. He smiled and thanked her.

"It's a little weird," he warned her. "It's not like last night's song. More like the stuff I wrote years and years ago. Kinda long and rambling, but hopefully with some good melodies. People didn't seem to care for 'em none, though."

"Hence writing to market," Kali chuckled. "So this isn't one of your horny songs, I take it."

"Not at all."

He cleared his throat, which was a senseless endeavor given how dry it was. There was a quick temptation to take a gulp of water before he began, but he resisted. He was trying his best to make his companion proud and—for once—not drink all of his water halfway through the day.

Then he dove into the song.

It began with simple chords strummed with the duraga's light strings. He believed keeping the music simplistic would enjoyably contrast and accentuate the more complex lyrical melodies. He began to sing.

"Each day they left before the sand could warm
Comfort lost, while the Ribroad pierced the sky
Each night of his far gone with spit and song
And hers a slog onward to the city sunk
Their paths aligned, the flower and the qarm."

He continued strumming, adding a few bright flourishes to the same chords. The music flitted through the wind, and Kali let out a soft giggle.

"So you're writing a song about us," she said.

"That was the plan, yep," he said. "It's still kinda sloppy, I admit. And I don't have much more than that and another half-verse. Got a lot of work to do, but it's a start, I s'pose."

He could feel his cheeks flushing with embarrassment. The lyrics were rough to begin with, and even so, he had stumbled over a few of them, thrown off by the ayote's gait. Plus, some of the chords did not entirely fit as well together as he'd imagined in his mind, so those would need minor tweaking as well.

"I like it," Kali then said.

Puk's shame diminished. He smiled.

"It's a little weird, though, that you use a metaphor to describe me but then yours is literal," she said. "Don't you think? 'The flower and the qarm' is sorta odd. I hope that's not too forward."

He said, "Nah. Good note, honestly."

Even in its rough stages, it had been fun writing the song. This journey had been the greatest—and, admittedly, probably the only—adventure he'd ever been on, and it only felt right that he dedicate a song to it.

That was what all the greats did, after all. An epic song for an epic tale.

"I'm not sure what 'the city sunk' is, though," she pointed out.

"That's supposed to mean Myrisih."

"I thought Zenib called it the floating city."

"Hey, I said it was a work-in-progress."

"What's the other part you have written?" Kali asked him. "The half-verse."

"Oh, it's in even shittier shape than what you just heard," he chuckled. "I'd be mortified to show you that part right now.

Not to mention, I think my throat is about to fall out of my neck."

"I'm not sure that makes any sense at all, and yet I know exactly what you mean."

"The mark of a gifted storyteller."

- -

"I'm gonna die," said Puk behind her. His stubby blue arms were wet and sticking to her shirt. "This is the end of me. My final day."

"You say that every day we travel," she pointed out.

"Well, this time it's true."

"You say that too."

Several more hours had passed since their break when the qarm had performed his new song, and Bella had been at a full run for most of it. Another long day. The ayote, at least, was finding immense joy in their travels. She loved dashing through the hot sands, zig-zagging back and forth with the wind whistling in her ears.

Given the frequency with which one of his arms had disappeared from her waist throughout the afternoon, Kali was sure that Puk exhausted his water supply long ago. She was gearing herself up to chastise him for the infraction when suddenly it crested the horizon.

Wood.

The frame of a ship, to be precise.

It was still difficult to fully make out at their distance, its image wavering in the desert heat, but Kali was confident they were looking at the fabled Pontequest.

"We're almost there," she shouted over the wind. "Look!"

She didn't feel his body shift, so Kali guessed that the qarm's eyestalks had slithered around either side of her body to peer ahead.

"That's it?" he yelped, his croaky voice barely carrying.

"I think so!"

From what she'd heard years ago, the glorious ship *Pontequest* had crashed headfirst into the desert, crushing its bow. The impact rippled through the hull, which stood nearly vertical, and the weight of its stern caused a crack to rupture the ship's center, leading the back half of the ship to break completely free. That back half had landed vertically as well, the pointed stern digging into the sands, before swiftly toppling over upside down. The front half sunk deeper into the sand, shifting slightly, ending up sticking out of the ground at a slight tilt with its broken center jutting out high in the air, piercing the sun.

What was currently visible over the horizon had to be that broken middle section of the ship, standing tall and proud.

So Haratti's crew was not mistaken.

The ship still existed.

There was no explosion that destroyed the remainder of the ship, hiding it away beneath the careless desert.

Which meant that perhaps there was indeed a town built around or within the airship. Kali had to imagine if so then by now, so long after the incident, the wreckage was no longer openly exposed to the air and had been built over. Granted, she had no idea how the makeshift town around the wreckage had been constructed.

"How easy you think it's gonna be to find our guy Kleus there?" Puk asked. Kali wondered if his beady eyestalks were still flanking her.

"Don't know," she answered, her voice bouncing with Bella's leaps.

"How easy you think it'll be to steal the book from him?"

From the secreted-away red mage who can supposedly use magic to warp reality itself?

"Don't know," she said aloud. Her stomach churned.

An hour later, they reached the village. The second mythical, unconfirmed town she had visited in a single week. This was quite the voyage. Definitely worthy of Puk's song.

Pontequest was not the magnificent sight she had pictured back when she'd first heard stories about the crash. In fact, it was a bit of a mess, as should have been expected from an insignificant town built around the wreckage of a crashed airship.

The opening in the hull had indeed been closed off, with differently colored wood boarded over the giant, misshapen hole. On that patch of lighter wood was a symbol painted in red, presumably a symbol of the village. It was a plain rectangle, with curved lines underneath like waves.

Scaffolding had been built connecting the two halves of the ship, with a vegetable-tanned leather tarp strapped atop, providing shade to the area below. It was not unlike the Ribroad.

Several doors had been built into the wall of the upside-down half of the ship. Kali was eager to explore the inside, which must be a surreal experience, walking around on the ceiling. There was a single opening allowing entry into the other half of the ship, which was located on the slant of its underside. Several feet above the entryway, jutting out from the ship and slipping through some of the scaffolding to dig into the sand, was a partially submerged mast that had seemingly been broken off the deck of the ship and planted into the ground.

In between the two ships, shaded by the tarp, was a collection of modestly sized dome tents, pitched around the sunken mast. Assuming that was where most of the town's population lived, there couldn't be more than thirty families there, so perhaps seventy to eighty people. It couldn't be too difficult a task tracking down Kleus Saix.

But if that were the case, it begged the question: why had no one else done so yet?

"Looks like a shitty place to live," said Puk.

"Don't be rude," Kali chided him, though internally she agreed.

There didn't appear to be a stable where they could safely house Bella. That could present a problem. The ayote stood by their side, panting gleefully after her hours-long run through the desert. Her energy was endless.

Additionally, there wasn't any place that obviously served as an inn. It should not have come as a surprise to her, given the town's existence was a guarded secret. No wonder they didn't have an establishment for housing visitors.

Only a few people were mingling outside in the tented area, and they stopped to peer out into the distance at the approaching visitors. It had to be an uncommon sight. Kali waved to them, but none reciprocated.

"I'm gettin' a weird vibe from this place," Puk said.

She almost told him again not to be rude, but she did not disagree with the assessment. The town and its residents seemed peculiar. She was not opposed to finding the book and getting out as quickly as possible.

"Hello!" she said with an inviting smile as they came to a stop in front of the few people who had gathered outside.

"Hi," said a woman with some apprehension. She was plump and wore a red bandana around her neck, the same color as the town's symbol looming above them. "Y'all lost? Need directions? We can get you outta here quick." She glanced down at Puk with untrusting eyes. If she had been born in Pontequest, it was entirely possible she had never seen a qarm in her life.

"Nope," Puk replied, and the woman nearly jumped. "We're right where we wanna be, thanks."

Kali moved right to the point. "Is there anywhere we can keep our ayote during our stay?" she asked.

"Stay?" a man piped up. Anger tinged his words. "What you plannin' to stay for?"

"To see the fuckin' sights," Puk blurted, clearly unable to contain his acerbic sarcasm.

Kali attempted to smooth things over, though these people's lack of even the most basic hospitality confused her. Granted, they undoubtedly valued their privacy and it had possibly been years since they had encountered a new face, but their entire village was founded by desert nomads who'd decided to settle down. Why were they so hostile toward fellow travelers?

"We just need a place to rest," Kali said, glossing over their true reason for visiting. "Only a day or two while we gather our bearings. Is that alright?"

The townsfolk mumbled to themselves, but nobody outright rejected them. More people began to emerge from their tents to catch a glimpse of the commotion.

So Kali asked again, "Is there a stable, or...?"

"No stable," said the woman, eyeing Bella with distaste.

Kali sighed. It was beyond obvious that Pontequest didn't want any visitors. But she pressed forward. "Well, is there anywhere we can lock her up to make sure she doesn't run off? This one certainly loves running. We can pay."

The woman remained silent, but the irritable man spoke up again. "I've got some extra storage that could fit her," he said. "I'll take your money."

Well, even if they didn't want visitors, at least they *did* want money. Some of them did, anyway. That was a start.

"That'd be great," Kali said, plastering a smile on her face, trying to show that she appreciated their time and efforts. Hoping it would help put the other, more distrusting, folk at ease.

"Gotta go clear it out," the man said before stumbling off toward the upturned stern of the ship. He swiftly slipped through one of the numerous doorways.

To the growing crowd, Kali said, "Thank you all. I'm also wondering, though, if there's a place we can sleep? An inn, perhaps?" She would even take a situation like Grace's house back in Weynard, though she would be truly shocked if anyone here gave enough of a damn to open their home to strangers. "We can pay for that as well," she added, in case they had already forgotten.

But the woman shook her head, and no one else corrected her. "Ain't no inn," she said bluntly. "Gonna have to find your own place to sleep. Hope you brought a tent."

They hadn't, and Kali knew all too well how cold the Gogol nights could get. Puk might fare okay with a thick blanket, but it would not be great for her.

Maybe we can find Kleus fast. Like...today, she thought optimistically, knowing it was delusional.

With their business seemingly concluded, many of the residents began returning to their tents. The chubby woman remained steadfast in her spot, arms on her hips, glaring at the two intruders.

"...we'll wait over here," Kali said, tugging on Bella's reins to lead her closer toward the stern and away from the unreasonably sour woman. Puk followed, kicking up sand with each step.

Once they were out of earshot, Puk asked, "The fuck's wrong with these people?"

"I don't know," Kali admitted. "Fair warning, we might be shacking up with Bella tonight. I'm not sure either of us could withstand the cold outside."

"That's fine with me. She don't kick in her sleep, though, does she?"

"Don't know," Kali chuckled. After saying the phrase so many times, she felt a lot less knowledgeable now than she had earlier that morning.

It was not yet night, but it was fast approaching. They could attempt to find some clues as to Kleus's whereabouts, but she wasn't confident they would sniff anything out.

Tomorrow, the hunt would begin in earnest.

CHAPTER XVI

SEEING THINGS

The storage room wasn't comfortable. Puk should not have expected it to be comfortable, and in truth he hadn't, but he was annoyed by the distinct lack of comfort all the same.

He was first to awaken the next morning, rustled to consciousness by his discomfort and a menacing rumble in his stomach. His body lay flat on the dusty wooden floor while he arched his eyestalks upward to more closely examine their surroundings.

It was a sizeable room inside the part of *Pontequest* that had separated from its front half in the unfortunate crash. The room's ceiling was only around seven feet high, considerably shorter than the full height of the ship. There might be a staircase leading up to more rooms somewhere, but Puk was damned if he knew where it was or what the second (and third? Fourth?) story held, if anything. With this portion of the ship being upended, the town's residents might have given up on making use of the rest of its space.

The room's gruff owner, whose name was Paul, had led the three of them into the stern of the *Pontequest* (which had been a tight fit for poor Bella). The entire bottom—or top, depending on how one viewed it—of the ship had been gutted, with the materials reused to build a layout more suited to the former nomads' means.

And that layout was completely utilitarian. There was a single walkway running down the center of the ship, and on either side of it, walls had been built up to the ceiling, creating a claustrophobic atmosphere that put Puk on edge. The walls were lined with a handful of doorways, which all led to similar storage rooms. Almost all the doors lining the outside of the ship led directly to individual work rooms, with only one at the front and back leading instead to the hallway. Puk did not understand why the storage rooms had inner doors and the work places had outer doors, but then again he did not understand anything at all about this village or its people, so he simply accepted it.

Based on the little evidence they had from their handful of hours in the town, Kali's best guess was that most residents of Pontequest worked as craftspeople; they created clothing, jewelry, and other valuables to transport to other nearby towns in order to trade for food and other necessities. Their location in the Gogol was not conducive to growing crops nor raising livestock.

"Sounds like a shitty life," Puk had said, which garnered no reply from Kali.

Bella was now curled up on her side, sleeping soundly with her shell pressed against the wall. Little snores escaped the ayote's snout, and one of her claws twitched, scraping against wood. Her body alone took up half their space in the cramped room.

Kali was similarly curled on the opposite side of the room from Puk. She had absorbed plenty of sunlight during their journey from Weynard, so he knew she was not in desperate need of sustenance like him.

He licked his lips, dreaming of the dish he'd eaten at Shiar's Slumber with eggs poached in the spicy tomato mixture. Given the villagers' approach to architecture, Puk ventured to guess that the most flavorful venture they embarked on was salting their meat. If even that.

He pushed himself up off the ground and groggily crept past their belongings piled in the middle of the room. As slowly and quietly as possible, he pushed the door open, and slipped out into the creepy barren hallway.

No one stalked the hall. He had no idea how early in the day it was, or to what sort of schedule any of these people adhered. Their demeanor had only grown colder toward the pair as the night wore on. Securing lodging had been dicey and uncomfortable; no one would show them where they could find dinner; everyone acted, simply put, hostile. It was obvious to Puk that the residents were doing everything in their power to make them leave, just short of physically shoving them out into the desert. A voice in his head told him to find the book as soon as possible and get the hell out of town. The place was deeply unsettling.

Puk shook off the shiver rattling down his spine and exited the bizarre warehouse, stepping out into the welcoming sun.

Never thought I'd be glad to get back out in the desert, he thought, amusing himself. Nonetheless, it was true.

His feet sunk into the sand, still cool from the night air. The sun was starting to appear over the horizon, casting a gentle warmth on the Gogol. The conditions were pleasant, for once. Puk nearly told himself he should wake up early more often, but then realized how crazy he sounded. Pontequest was already indoctrinating him. He shuddered at the terrible idea of becoming a habitual early riser.

Although, there *was* an appealing charm to the idea of playing his new duraga set against the sunrise. Plucking the taut strings, melodies dancing on the gentle air as dark melted into light. He *did* still need to workshop his "Flower and Qarm" tune...

Puk blinked himself out of the fantasy. Looking around, it appeared nobody else was awake yet. There was nobody walking about, and all the tent flaps were still closed. No activity.

He waddled around, taking in the town again, trying to pinpoint where he might acquire some grub once someone was actually awake to cook it for him, if he could somehow convince them to share. It would be a shame to have to eat jerky for breakfast, and after his pitiful dinner the night before, he was running low. Saving it for the trip back would be ideal. He was trying his best to avoid eating any more of the nasty dried cactus that had come stocked with Bella.

The stern of the ship held all the villagers' storage space and craft rooms, while between the two halves of the ship was the camp. They had not yet visited the ship's bow, and Puk wondered what it might hold. Surely not a high-class restaurant. But where did these people cook? What sort of food did they eat?

At the epicenter of all the tents, Puk noticed a slight dip in the sand surrounded by large stones. A place fit for a nightly bonfire. There was no wood visible anywhere, but a black mage could easily conjure a fire for the center of the pit. That had to be where they cooked all their food.

He could not fathom a life like this.

Living so far out, isolated from every major city. Cut off from major news or advancements or discoveries. Aside from how *tough* it'd be—their lack of resources was alarming, and it stressed him out thinking of relying solely on trade to survive—it also seemed incredibly *boring*.

He was a city boy, through and through. A man of the world. He needed to explore, needed to feel life all around him. The varied sights and sounds and smells of every city, their look and feel and culture uniquely different and setting them apart from all others. That was what brought him joy.

Pontequest, on the other hand, felt stagnant. Hollowed out. Dead.

But maybe that was too harsh. The residents probably loved it here, of course. Why else would they stay?

Kali's lifestyle, traveling from city to city to trade her goods, was hugely appealing and not too far off from what he had been doing as a troupe member. Going from place to place, trading his songs in exchange for money. And then money for drugs.

Puk gaped at the cooled, empty bonfire pit for a few moments more, imagining meat on a stick sizzling over a licking flame. Then he rebuked himself, mentally lowering his own expectations for breakfast. It would probably be jerky in the end.

His eyestalks gazed upward at the inane town logo, painted surprisingly neatly on the boarded-over half of the ship displayed proudly in the air. If the weight of the ship ever shifted, it would fall down and crush all the tents and people below. Perhaps there were additional reinforcements somewhere, aside from the relocated mast, keeping it aloft; or maybe the townspeople had never considered that fate. Either way, Puk decided, it was not his problem. Another item on the ever-growing list of reasons why he would resolutely never move to Pontequest.

As he was staring at the red paint, contemplating the demise of the whole township, he realized there actually was a single person awake and outside. Someone who had become enraptured by the sunrise, just as he had.

They were sitting at the top of the slanted bow, the spot where it had broken in two, just above the painted symbol. Their body was facing away from Puk, regarding the open sea of desert on the other side.

The outfit they wore was strange. From what Puk could make out, they were dressed in a puffy green coat with oversized tan cuffs and a collar that stood straight up, completely covering the back of their neck. Atop their head was a tall, pointy brown hat that bent and drooped over its side.

Suffice to say, the outfit was certainly a *choice*. Something flamboyant that was more suited for a stage production than everyday wear. It was not the type of outfit someone would only own one of in their wardrobe; if a person owned a piece of clothing such as that, undoubtedly it was their distinctive personal style. But Puk had not seen anyone so notably dressed among the welcoming party yesterday. They would've stood out and been hard to forget.

Suddenly the person rose and brushed themselves off. They were short, no taller than a child or a qarm. They walked no more than a dozen steps down the tilted deck of the ship before vanishing out of thin air.

That's probably noteworthy, thought Puk.

A person disappearing was not a typical happening. That seemed conspicuously like a red magic sort of thing.

There was a flutter in his chest, an excitement to report to Kali what he had witnessed.

Maybe they would accomplish getting out of Pontequest as quickly as they hoped to. Assuming they figured out some way to handle a red mage, anyway.

Waking up early had its advantages after all.

- -

After Puk told Kali his early morning tale, fighting through her yawns, she agreed that it sounded suspicious and likely had something to do with their elusive red mage Kleus.

They spent the remainder of the day milling about the drab town, holding short and mindless conversations with its denizens, who either responded to them with malice or mindlessness. If they didn't have a particular goal here in town, Kali would have long since departed.

She felt guilty leaving Bella alone in that cramped space, and promised the ayote she'd take her out for a run later in the evening. Paul, who was shockingly the most pleasant person they'd met in spite of his dour attitude, told them he'd changed his mind and the price to rent the room had increased. Kali was thankfully able to talk him down a bit, though they were still paying more than originally agreed. She had very little leverage, and the citizens of Pontequest were nearly impossible to appease.

After a while, the duo decided to check out the interior of the ship's other half. Secretly, they hoped to find the mysterious short figure ambling around somewhere inside. Puk assured her they wouldn't be able to miss them.

But that never came to pass. There was no sign of the person as they walked around the tilted floors of the crashed airship. Unlike the other half where they had slept, this half had seemingly been left alone and not undergone any sort of renovation. The *Pontequest*'s original layout was left fully intact.

The bottommost floor, where they entered, was home to a mess of machinery and engineering that was far beyond Kali's comprehension. They stumbled around in the dark for ten or fifteen minutes, but almost every door was locked. Puk tugged on each cold metal handle with force and sighed with defeat every time. Only one room remained unlocked, but nothing of note was inside. Just unopened metal crates that had shifted and tumbled in the crash.

Above the drab engineering deck was a floor dedicated to the workers' quarters and mess hall, and the floor above that held passengers' cabins, a once-fancy dining room, and a smoking lounge, with exits to the open upper deck.

Everything was covered in a thick layer of dust, long abandoned by the township. The air inside was stale and hot, drying out Kali's throat. She had to guess Puk was feeling even worse.

"Why'd they not come in here?" he asked, voicing her own question. "Why pitch a bunch of shitty tents outside when there's plenty of living space in here?"

It was a fair question. "Maybe it gets too overheated," she suggested, the only reasonable thing that came to mind.

They were inspecting one of the passenger cabins, having already combed through the employee barracks, and still found no signs of life beyond the ship's original passengers. Kali pulled open a drawer by the rumpled bedside and discovered a diary within.

She flipped through the pages, impressed by the owner's penmanship. She absentmindedly scanned the words, entries about a boy they had a crush on, the activities they were doing on the ship, other such things. Kali didn't want to further intrude on the person's privacy and returned the notebook to its place.

Thinking of the diary's presumably dead writer brought to mind another question.

"Where are the bodies?"

"Hmm?" Puk grunted from the other side of the cramped room. He was leaning on the doorframe, evidently waiting for her to conclude her pointless investigation.

"I just mean it looks like this ship hasn't been touched since it crashed, and yet there aren't any bodies anywhere. The place is spotless, aside from the dust and things being askew. Don't you find that odd?"

"Didn't really think about it," said Puk. "Maybe these weirdos came in, cleaned the place up, then decided they didn't like it after all and fucked off back to their tents."

Maybe.

She tried to dismiss the thought, but it still nagged at her. The two then stepped into the next cabin along the hall.

They carried out this process until all of the cabins had been closely examined. Every one yielded the same result: dust and abandoned objects. One room held a particularly attractive Gillusian jade necklace that had caught Kali's eye, but she did not feel right taking it. It was left where she discovered it, its silvery chain wrapped around the foot of an upturned bed.

Up on the deck, the sun was blazing with intensity. It was a welcome reprieve from the heat inside; at least the sunlight gave her sustenance. Puk, on the other hand, was quick to complain, with no shortness of vulgarity.

Standing was tricky, as it had been for their entire tour of the ship, but at least indoors they could steady themselves on the walls and other furniture. The tilt of the ship nearly toppled her when she first stepped foot on the unremarkable wooden deck.

She turned around and saw that everything the deck once housed—tables, chairs, umbrellas, drink carts, the list went on—had tumbled into a messy, destroyed pile at the front of the ship, now half-covered in sand. Some of the items lay scattered in the distance, nearly fully submerged, only hints of what they were poking out from the glistening sands. It had been years and years since the ship crashed, with a town full of people surrounding it, and yet no one had bothered to clean anything up.

"There's nothing up here," Puk said uselessly.

"You're right."

"I know I saw that person up here, though. I'm positive." His stalks swiveled on top of his head faster than his body could keep up with. Twirling around, looking for any sign of where his oddly-dressed morning companion had gone. Or at least an indication that they had been there at all.

Kali wasn't totally familiar with red magic and its capabilities, so she didn't know what this person was able to accomplish. Perhaps they'd made themselves invisible and walked all the way down the ship's deck, past the piled-up debris, hopping off into the sand and wandering into the horizon. Or maybe they'd popped out of existence and hid away in some netherworld. If netherworlds even existed. Maybe they had just been a mirage, brought on by the heat and a food-deprived brain.

Whatever the case, the deck was empty. That much was obvious.

As they made their way back down the stairwells toward the engineering deck, Puk posed yet another question.

"Where did they disappear to? They were gone in a blink, but I thought for sure they had to be in here somewhere."

Kali didn't have a satisfactory answer for him.

They soon exited the ship and found Paul standing a few feet away, gazing out at the dunes and smoking a cigarette. The man's dark face was leathery from a lifetime in the sun.

He eyed them quizzically and asked, "The hell were y'all doin' in there?"

"Just looking around," Kali answered innocently. She half-expected the man to suddenly charge them a fee for entering the abandoned ship. He was costing them too much money, but at least there was one person in Pontequest who could push past their coldness to lend a helping hand. For the right price.

Paul's eyes drifted upward to behold the broken ship, then looked back down at them, wearing an expression as if he was regarding two crazed individuals.

"Can't you see it well enough from here?" he asked.

Kali cocked an eyebrow, casting a glance at Puk. He rotated his eyestalks to look at the ship, its brown, worn hull warmed by the sun.

"No?" Kali murmured, unsure of what the man meant.

But all he did was laugh at them. He then said, "If you can't see what's in there through those giant cracks and holes, you might need to get your eyes checked." He took one last drag from his cigarette before tossing it carelessly in the sand and skulking off.

Kali turned around to give the ship one more good look before conferring with her companion.

"You don't see any holes in this ship, right?" she asked him.

"Nope," Puk answered.

Kali sighed. "Do you think we're seeing things, or is he?"

Puk laughed at the suggestion. "That dude's nuts," he said. "All these people are. We're well aware of that."

She shook her head. "It's not that," she said. "He—and I'm assuming the rest of the town—thinks this half of the ship is destroyed. That has to be why they haven't bothered going in there or doing anything with it. It'd be too much work to repair the hull. Why waste the effort and money?" She looked back up at the clearly-not-ruined ship while she spoke. "Remember how I mentioned it was widely reported that there was an accident here? People said there was some kind of explosion that destroyed the ship, which is why no one has bothered coming here in years. They think nothing's here. The people who settled here think that explosion happened too, and that the ship is beyond repair."

Kali stared down at Puk, and after a moment, he turned his eyestalks to face her. Finally the realization dawned on him.

"Oh!" he sputtered. "It's red magic, ain't it? Altering reality and shit?"

Kali nodded.

Riding Bella through the sandy outskirts of Pontequest was an effective way to clear her head. Kali felt refreshed as they came sauntering back to the township, leading the ayote back into their temporary living quarters.

She found Puk waiting for her in there, sitting on the floor with his back against the wall and duraga in hand. The qarm was strumming out a warm tune when she entered. It wasn't the song about their adventure, but it was good.

"Sounds nice," she told him.

"Thanks," he said. "It's some old song I learned way back in the day. Can't remember the name of it. Can't remember any of the words, neither."

"Do you remember what it's about?" Kali asked, wondering if she'd be able to recognize the song.

Puk pondered for a moment before answering. "I think it was an old jeornish folk song. Maybe about the Ustrels, or something? Or about some old dusty king of theirs. Not sure."

He continued playing the riff while Kali wracked her brain, trying to recall some of the classic jeornish songs her parents would sing in the inn. As girls, she and Lissia always enjoyed dancing around the guest rooms while their parents sang and cleaned up.

Just then, the melody started coming back to her. At first it was simply mumbled gibberish, but then actual words started to form on her lips. After a couple lines, she was fully singing along. Puk's face lit up and his plucking grew livelier, carried by her voice.

The song was called "King Fleurwyn's Recital," and it was a jaunty, goofy tune about an ancient jeornish king trying to pick out a new crop of musicians for his royal court. The lyrics detailed each of the potential artists' lives and personalities, culminating in the recital where each of them played in competition with each other to win the king's approval. In the end, the recital devolved into the three musicians engaging in a nasty fistfight (with some instruments broken overhead for good measure) and all of them being thrown in jail.

Puk let out a hearty laugh as Kali finished singing the final verse, strumming the song to a close.

With that, they fed Bella from her diminishing bag of dried bugs and then decided to find some food for Puk while hopefully gathering a bit more information. They wandered outside, quickly tracking down their unwilling host Paul and paying him to let them join him for dinner around the town's bonfire in the town's center, amongst its mass of tents.

There were very few people sitting at the fire with them, but Kali wanted to squeeze as much out of them as she could. She asked the group, "So what happened to that half of the ship?" She pointed her thumb over her shoulder.

"Been that way for years," said Paul gruffly. "Don't even remember a time when it weren't ruined."

"I do," said an old woman sitting across the fire. Kali had not seen her among the welcoming party. "When I first came here, it was still intact. Some men even boarded up the opening and painted our town crest on it. Such a shame to see it gone."

Kali noticed Puk glancing upward at the very-intact crest proudly displayed high above their heads.

"What happened to it?" Puk asked, returning his gaze to the woman. He took a reluctant bite of the cactus he'd been roasting over the fire, which Paul had requested ten crescents for. Pontequest certainly wasn't kind to tourists.

The old woman cackled. "A fool's what happened to it!" she declared in her raspy voice. Large hooped earrings swung from her drooping earlobes. "A young man, some mage. Moved into town shortly after the first of us, only a few months later. We had just finished boarding up that part of the ship after clearing out all the dead. It was long, hard work. He went in there one day, and before we knew it there was some magical explosion. Damn near blew apart the whole ship. All that work, wasted!" She clucked her tongue, shaking her head in disappointment. "He never came back out. No one ever found his body. Musta blowed himself to hell. Don't know what sorta spell he was doing, but the damage was too severe to fix it up."

"So you all just left that half of the ship alone after that," said Kali.

"Mhmm," the woman nodded. "We's perfectly happy here," she said. "Don't need much else. And I'm surely not gonna be the one to go start poundin' nails and choppin' wood."

"Me neither," Paul huffed. He popped a piece of meat into his mouth, which he had declined to sell Puk. The qarm was on a strictly vegetarian diet for the night.

Kali looked over her shoulder at the undamaged bow of the *Pontequest*. She felt sympathy for the old woman, who thought her town's crest had been destroyed and never recovered.

She was beginning to put the pieces together in her head. It was clear that the mage who'd come to town was Kleus Saix. The way she saw it, Kleus had learned about this new, totally isolated town and deemed it the perfect place to hide out from the authorities who'd been searching for him and his stolen book. So he made his way through the desert, entered the ship, and cast a red magic spell that made the entire township believe they'd witnessed the ship exploding. Maintaining that illusion every single day for years on end had to be taking a toll on the man, both mentally and physically. Kali shuddered at the thought of how deeply the Ustrel symbols must be scarring his flesh.

Back in their room, Puk complained about his rumbling half-empty stomach and Kali laid out her theory while scratching behind Bella's ears.

"Sounds plausible to me," Puk said once she finished. "So what's our plan, then?"

That was where she was running into trouble. Clearly Kleus's magic was not being imposed on them, meaning he might not know about their presence in the town yet. But they'd poked around his home for a good part of the day; it wasn't unreasonable to suspect they'd stumbled upon him but he had been concealing himself somehow. Still, there was a possibility they had the element of surprise to their advantage. Wouldn't he have already brainwashed them if he had realized they were in town, sniffing around?

She said, "I think we need to follow up on whoever you saw this morning. They have to be connected to Kleus somehow."

"D'you think it was Kleus I saw?"

"I don't know," she said with a shrug. "Maybe. Or maybe it's his kid or something, I'm not sure. Though I don't know how he'd conceive a child, being all alone in there for however many years."

"Maybe he made one with magic. Lopped his ear off and morphed it into a sweet little boy."

"Gross," Kali laughed. "Ear-Boy or not, we need to figure out where they disappeared to, because wherever it is, that's where we'll find Kleus. Although…"

"What?"

"I don't really know what to do after that," she confessed. "We're way out of our league, dealing with a red mage. We might be able to surprise him, but he'll probably still be able to get some terrible spells off on us."

Puk nodded and crossed his arms over his chest. "That's true," he said. "That's a later-problem, though. For now, let's just focus on where Ear-Boy's gallivantin' off to."

"Sounds good," Kali said.

As they lay down to sleep, Kali's stomach twisted. There was a sense of relief in having found Kleus's location fairly easily, but she worried about dealing with the mage head-on. She truly had no idea how they would acquire *Malum*.

But that was a later-problem.

Her now-problem was wrestling with her thoughts and churning stomach to ease them both into slumber. She tackled it with gusto.

CHAPTER XVII

A PLAN OF SORTS

Puk was tired.

Tired from lack of sleep, tired from countless days of desert travel, tired of not being home.

More than ever, he wanted to be rid of the Gogol Desert.

It was a bright and sunny morning when Puk and Kali dragged themselves out of bed in an effort to catch a glimpse of the *Pontequest*'s mysterious figure. Making sure to keep a low profile as they exited, he and Kali left Bella to snooze a bit longer and crept outside.

It only took a moment to spot their mark.

The person stood in the same spot as the previous day, wearing the same exact outfit. Oversized green coat, tall collar, absurd brown hat. Yesterday, Puk had thought to himself that this person must only own similarly flamboyant outfits; now he suspected it might be their *only* outfit.

Peculiar, to say the least.

"Wow," Kali muttered upon eyeing their subject. "Hell of a hat."

Giving it some more thought, Puk realized it was a pretty stereotypical "wizard's hat," like what mages wore in ancient fairytales. It was the type of hat that would undoubtedly draw attention to someone. Probably not a fashion choice that an undercover mage would wear to keep himself concealed.

Kali voiced his thought before he could. "No way Kleus would be wearing that," she whispered beside him, careful not to raise her voice too much.

Like the day before, the person was standing up on the tilted deck of the ship, looking out at the sands in the opposite direction. Totally oblivious to Puk and Kali's presence behind them.

And also like the previous day, after around ten minutes of admiring the sunrise, the green-clad figure turned, took a few steps, and disappeared.

Despite being told what to expect, Kali still let out a tiny shocked gasp. Puk laughed.

"So," he then said, "what's the plan?"

Kali replied, "I don't think barging into the ship again is wise. Somehow, Kleus isn't aware that we're here yet even with our intrusion yesterday, or else I'm sure our memories would be wiped or something and we'd be looking at a busted-up ship. We don't wanna push our luck."

"In other words, you just wanna wait."

For a moment, Kali didn't say anything, but then she nodded. "I guess so," she said. "It's not great. I wanna get out of here as quickly as you do, and Paul's fees aren't cheap. But I think it's the best move for now."

"Can we even afford to stay here much longer?"

The troubled look on her face was a sufficient answer.

Puk desperately wanted to be more proactive, but he was lacking any reasonable suggestions. So he conceded.

They returned to their dingy room to catch another hour or so of restless sleep, then proceeded with their morning. By that time, more of the town's citizens were awake and meandering about, not really doing much of anything. Once again, Puk was struck by how boring this sort of existence must be.

A few men and women were huddled together, all wearing light, long-sleeved shirts that covered their skin from the sun. They each wore a large pack on their back and had a waterskin slung over their shoulders. As the duo passed the group, they heard mumblings about Weynard and Nawa. Likely heading out to trade and gather supplies for the town.

Should probably grab some books and board games while they're out there. Give everyone shit to occupy their time with.

Given these people were traders, Puk took the opportunity to ask them a question. He had accepted the fact Paul's knowledge was going to be of no real use, and the man's limited hospitality was running short from the moment they'd arrived, so Puk wanted to obtain his own source of food. And hopefully at a cheaper, more reasonable cost.

"Hey there," he greeted the band. "I was wonderin' where a guy might buy some stuff around here." It was a silly question, but they had not seen any traditional marketplace in Pontequest; the town consisted of the tents, the storage facilities, work rooms, and the abandoned ship bow. The place didn't make any damn sense. He internally cursed it yet again.

Everyone in the group simultaneously cast him a suspicious look.

"Why do you want to buy something?" one of the faif women asked him.

"To have it," he answered.

Most did not find his response amusing or adequate, but one woman told him, "It depends on what you are looking for."

Prying simple, normal information out of this town was harder than getting Pillbug to come down on his spit prices.

"I want food," he said. "Just something to snack on. Get me through the day."

There was uncomfortable silence for a few moments as the group considered his inquiry.

What the fuck is wrong with these idiots? he wondered. Surely a set of people dedicated to the exchange of goods would want to sell a visitor stuff to make a few crescents.

Finally, the seemingly friendliest woman (which was still a stretch) said, "Nidra can sell you something. She lives in the tent closest to the bonfire on its north side."

Puk thanked the woman despite not having a clue which direction was north. Luckily, Kali was able to assist him with that minor detail.

While they walked, Puk said to her, "Everyone in this town's kind of lost their minds, don't you think? Those morons didn't wanna sell me anything, everyone was super hostile when we got here, they didn't want us to stay at all...hell, they don't even have an inn or a marketplace. What's goin' on here?" As he proceeded through his rant, Kali urged him to hush so that others wouldn't hear him and grow even more offended than they seemingly already were.

"My guess is the red magic," Kali said.

"Apparently everything can be blamed on the damn magic," Puk muttered dryly.

"Well, yeah. With red magic being able to change reality, it's kind of hard not to attribute weird stuff like that to it, right? One of the biggest reasons it was outlawed in the first place was because of mages' ability to shift people's perceptions. It's possible that Kleus has done something to everyone's minds here. Maybe in addition to deluding them to keep everyone out of his ship, he's also slightly altering their personalities so that they push outsiders away. He doesn't want anyone new here, anyone who might stumble upon him."

"How does he know if someone *does* come? Ain't he worried they'll go blab about the town existing?"

"Maybe that's what the Ear-Boy is for," Kali suggested. "Keeping an eye on the town, alerting Kleus of goings-on so that he can react accordingly."

"This guy's goin' through a lot of trouble just to stay hidden," Puk grumbled. "If I were him, I'da gotten rid of that stupid book a long time ago. Hell, he could sell it himself and make a nice profit. Buy himself a real house in a real town and not live in a nasty old broken airship. Jackass."

A minute later, they found themselves on Nidra's doorstep, so to speak. The domed tent was identical to every other one in Pontequest. Nothing at all to indicate its owner might be willing to proffer food to a willing buyer.

The tent's flap was already pulled open, so they assumed they could freely enter. When they did, they discovered that Nidra was already tending to another customer.

Their mysterious figure.

The person was indeed no taller than Puk, and just as wide, though it was difficult to tell whether that was due to their body or the puffiness of the coat. They turned their head slightly to see who had entered the tent behind them, but their face was completely dark, obscured in shadow by the brim of their hat.

"One moment," Nidra said, showing them more warmth and politeness in those two words than anyone else in the town had. To the hatted figure, she said, "Three potatoes, six cactus ribs, and ten packets of cactus flower tea. Need anything else this week?"

They shook their head and handed over the requisite crescents, which Nidra exchanged for a sack full of the listed items.

"Glad to do business with you again," Nidra smiled. "See you in a few days!"

The figure nodded and turned to leave. As they shuffled by, Puk still couldn't make out any features in the darkness of their face.

As soon as the person was gone, Nidra's mood shifted considerably. "What do you want?" she asked them, that previous warmth now entirely missing from her voice and replaced with cold steel.

"Uh...food," said Puk, unable to form more words, taken aback by the abrupt change in the woman's demeanor and still shocked by the appearance of their quest's subject.

Kali was peering out of the tent, watching as the stout person waddled away back toward the bow of the *Pontequest*. The same question on Puk's mind was surely on hers as well: *Why is no one confused or alarmed by that person?*

He immediately figured what Kali's answer would be: red magic. Either the townspeople were seeing the person with a different appearance, or they forgot about them after seeing them, or any number of ridiculous magical explanations. With a red mage living there, nothing made sense, and Puk just needed to accept that.

Nidra glared at him and said, "What kind of food?"

"Food to eat," he blurted out, weary of every interaction being such a chore. He wanted some meat after last night's unfulfilling roasted cactus dinner, but at this point he would gladly accept some cactus ribs if it meant he could rush through the conversation. Still, he figured he'd try. Calming himself, he said, "If you've got any sort of meat…"

The woman huffed, then said, "I've got two salted lamatka shanks left. That's all. I can't give you both, because I want one. I want both, as a matter of fact. Do you have money?"

"Yes, I have money. I am trying to buy things from you with it."

Kali still said nothing, watching Kleus's minion disappearing into the ship's entrance, the same one they'd used the day before.

"If you give me fifteen crescents, I will sell you one of my lamatka shanks," said Nidra. She placed her hands on her hips, awaiting his payment.

"Fifteen crescents for one slab of meat is nonsense," he said, refraining from swearing at the woman. "How much are your cactus ribs?"

"Fifteen crescents."

"For six ribs?"

She thought for a second, then said, "For two ribs."

It was an absurd price. "I take it that's not the rate you gave our buddy who just left, is it?"

Nidra remained silent.

It was no use. If he was going to pay fifteen crescents for something, which was still a deal compared to what Paul wanted to charge them for sharing his food—ten crescents for a measly portion of cactus that had not been tasty nor filling—then he wanted the lamatka shank. He handed over the money and Nidra reluctantly relinquished the meat. Puk thanked her, and they departed.

"I thought Vence was a bullshit village, but Pontequest is on a whole other level," he grumbled as they circled around the dead bonfire pit. The slab of meat was thick and wet in his hands, wrapped in thin paper. They were heading back toward the storage room to tuck away his meat for later, when the fire was roaring.

"That was interesting," said Kali, finally finding her voice.

Puk knew what she meant. "Yeah," he agreed. "I think I've got an idea, too."

"What is it?" she asked, her voice high and excited.

"I'll tell you in the room."

He'd initially been distracted by Nidra's salesmanship, but with a minute or so to think about everything, a plan had come to him.

Though he wasn't sure how Kali was going to react.

- -

Kali stared at the bottle in Puk's hand, flip-flopping between pride and anger.

Pride for the qarm's trickiness and ingenuity, which might actually, against all odds, save their asses.

Anger for blatantly lying to her.

"You told me you didn't have any left," she said.

"I lied," the qarm said, his tone meek.

The slender, corked bottle was slightly less than a third of the way filled with cordol spit. He had indeed *not* consumed it all back when he'd foolishly downed it in Eva's bathroom.

It took a minute or two to get the outrage and vulgarity out of her system before she was able to calmly ask, "Have you been drinking it this whole time?"

"No! No!" Puk assured her, frantically waving his hands. His eyestalks seemed to rise even higher in alarm. "Haven't touched the shit, I swear. If I had been, it woulda all been gone by now, I can promise you that. And you probably would've had to pull my head out of the sand or stopped me from throwing up all over Zenib or something. No, I didn't lie when I told you I'd stop."

If it was true, then that was a relief. The temptation must have been great, carrying the vial around with them for so long. But Kali had to wonder why he'd kept it, giving himself an easy opportunity to relapse.

She asked him, "Why do you have it? Why'd you keep it even after you told me it was gone?"

The qarm shrugged, genuine regret on his face. "I dunno," he answered. "It was an impulse. At the time, I...didn't want to let it go. Just in case." He hastily added, "But I haven't even been tempted by it! I swear."

Kali's eyes narrowed to slits, observing Puk for any sort of tell. Anything to tip her off that he was being untruthful. Nothing jumped out at her.

She truly wanted to take his word for it that he hadn't been drinking the spit. She didn't want to assume the worst about him. They had shared so many enjoyable nights together since that unfortunate incident in Restick, and she wanted to maintain that trust in him.

A part of her considered cursing at him again, but it would gain nothing. And, truthfully, he'd been nothing but helpful and kind ever since she found him splayed on Eva's bathroom floor.

Knowing he had lied about keeping the vial irked her, but she believed he had been true to his word about not indulging in it or any other form of fire-spit.

She decided she could forgive the transgression. Especially if it got them out of this mess.

"What's your idea, then?" she asked. She had a suspicion, but wanted to hear him vocalize it.

Puk blinked. "Oh," he said. "Sorry, I thought it was obvious. The guy's little pal was buying tea packets, yeah? Meaning he drinks tea. Sneak into his place, pour some of this—" he waggled the vial of viscous spit in the air "—into his tea, and then let him froth on the ground while we steal the book. Won't be able to cast any spells on us if he's gooped outta his gourd."

"So your plan is to drug him."

"Yes. Unless you've got a better way of dealing with a mind-bending red mage that can tear us limb from limb or whatever."

She didn't.

But that didn't mean Puk's plan didn't put her ill at ease. Yet another step of this whole journey that did not sit right with her. She had to tell herself it would all be worthwhile.

With no retort, she asked, "How do you propose we sneak in?"

Puk sighed. "That's the part I ain't crazy about," he said. "The best way I figure is that I ambush Ear-Boy up on the deck and slip into his coat and hat as a disguise so I can get into the ship wherever our mage is. We're both the same height; I wouldn't be surprised if they were a qarm. Should be able to trick him for at least as long as we need, which ain't too long. I can make him his tea, like I'm sure his dutiful little servant does for him every morning after their sunrise stroll, and find the book."

It wasn't a horrible idea.

Highly risky, with several opportunities for utter failure, but not horrible.

And it was also the best they had.

"You'd be in there alone," she said. An obvious statement. "You wouldn't have me for backup."

The qarm grinned. "We both know I'm the better backup anyway." He was never going to let her live down being knocked unconscious back in Myrisih. "I'll be fine in there. I've learned to handle myself in shitty situations over the years."

Kali was quiet a moment before saying, "I don't like it."

"I don't either," said Puk.

"This whole operation was probably a huge mistake." A sense of dread had been building up since departing Myrisih, but she felt too entrenched in the scheme to pull herself out of it now.

Puk clearly felt the same way. He said, "Probably. But we're here, so…"

So we might as well.

"We're doing this tomorrow?" she asked. They were now incredibly low on funds, especially with his earlier meat purchase. Paul's boarding fee would ruin them soon.

Puk nodded, his head moving but his stalks staying trained on her. "Bright and early."

The qarm's idea seemed more and more manageable with each passing moment. The book might actually be within their grasp, as much as it shocked her.

"At least we've got a plan now," Kali sighed, allowing a grin to spread across her face.

"Of sorts."

They both chuckled. Her heart was racing in her chest, and she could feel it pounding in her neck. The sooner this endeavor was over, the better.

The lush forests of Atlua awaited her.

CHAPTER XVIII

FLICKS OF THE WRIST

They awoke even earlier than the previous day, which made Puk miserable, but he knew it was essential. While he mentally prepared himself for his upcoming monumental task, Kali fed Bella and promised her they'd be leaving soon.

The plan was to grab the book and bolt out of Pontequest immediately thereafter. No time for Kleus or his crony to give chase.

It was still dark and cold outside when the two quietly crept through the broken ship's innards, toward the upper deck. Puk found himself wondering where Kleus and his pal could possibly be living as they snuck through the passenger deck.

A harsh breeze blew topside and rattled Puk's bones. He stood stationary, his entire body shivering. Kali laughed at the sight, then reminded him that they should hurry and hide.

There were not a ton of great places to do so. They chose somewhere on the lowered side of the bow, given that each day the duo had spied the person standing on the opposite end, so they hoped that wherever Ear-Boy appeared from was somewhere near there.

Part of the deck on the front end was raised on a slight platform, presumably so that guests would feel like they were getting an even better view as they stood there, overlooking the world inching by below. A foolish reason, but regardless of the intent, the designers had built a thick wall separating the raised platform from the rest of the deck, perhaps acting as a countertop on which guests could rest their cocktails while they chatted with each other. The deck's innumerable niceties were now battered and piled against said wall.

Getting tipsy on a luxury airship was not a scenario in which Puk could even begin to imagine himself. He would absolutely love it, that was guaranteed, but with his dire funds he couldn't afford a ticket on the worst airship of the lot. It seemed fitting to him that the closest he would likely ever get to being on a luxury airship was standing on the remains of one crashed and long forgotten. All he needed now was a cocktail.

That thought brought him to the vial of cordol spit tucked away in his pants pocket. He slipped a hand inside to feel the smooth glass, paranoid that it had fallen out somewhere between the storage room and his imaginary flight. The plan, feeble as it was, hinged on that vial. His chest was still tight, his heartrate accelerated, but he let out a small sigh of relief at the vial's touch.

He and Kali were ducked down behind the wall. For Puk, it meant only that he retracted his eyestalks a little and otherwise stood at his full height while Kali crouched. She eyed him fingering the vial in his pocket.

"You alright?" she asked him.

"Sure," he replied, absentminded.

"I'm serious. If you're not up to this, we can figure something else out. If you think—"

"I'm fine," he cut her off. "A little nervous, sure, but I'm fine. This was my idea, after all. I'm fine." The more he repeated the words, the more they sounded like a lie, but he needed her to believe it. Needed himself to believe it.

Kali cast a doubtful look, but did not prod further.

Puk slowly curved his left eyestalk around the corner of the wall to keep an eye on the deck.

The sun was starting to crest the horizon. Their target should be making an appearance soon.

"Should we work out some kind of signal?" Kali then asked.

Keeping one eye on the empty deck, Puk turned the other to address Kali. "What do you mean?"

"For if something goes wrong with Kleus."

"Based on what you've told me about red magic, I'd assume 'something going wrong' would mean 'my torso being torn in half' or 'being turned into a bulloko's ass' or something, so I dunno if a signal would be particularly effective."

"Well, it doesn't hurt to be prepared."

"You're right. If I get morphed into a bulloko's ass, I'll be sure to let out a gigantic fart, so be listening for that. The smell will knock him out too, so you shouldn't have any issues infiltrating his base."

"I'm being serious," she said.

"I am too," said Puk. "You're gonna be way up here, and we still don't know where I'm gonna end up within the ship. I don't think there's any signal that would get through to you. I'm gonna be on my own."

Saying it made his throat dry up like he'd swallowed sand. He pressed his fingertips harder against the wooden wall.

Kali had no rebuttal. She leaned her forehead against the wall, staring down at the floor. Puk could tell she was frustrated, but there was nothing to be done.

He wanted to lighten the mood, but the knot in his stomach would not allow it.

All he could think about was the plan. About being ripped to shreds by red magic. Or turning into an animal's ass. If the mage didn't drink the spit quickly, Puk was going to die.

So I might die today, he thought.

Voicing that worry made him want to throw up. If he had eaten any breakfast, he might have.

The two shared another minute of silence before the strangely-dressed person popped into existence in the corner of Puk's eye. They had materialized near the railing, a foot or two away from the broken mast. He made a mental note of the spot.

"They're here," Puk whispered. Kali didn't reply, but her breathing grew more staccato. She looked to him, awaiting his move. Letting him take the lead for his plan.

Puk watched the short figure walk to their usual place on the deck to view the sunrise. He then realized he didn't know what specifically he was going to do to knock this person out. Tackle them? Bonk them on the head? And with what, his tiny little sticky fist?

"What should I do?" he asked Kali, immediately relinquishing his leadership position.

"Take them out," she said.

"I don't wanna fuckin' kill 'em!"

"I did not mean *kill* them," she grumbled. "Just get out there and do something!"

Shit.

The rest of Puk's body caught up with his left eyestalk as he clumsily slipped around the corner of the wall. His shoes beat against the wooden deck and he figured there was no use trying to sneak, so he rushed the mysterious figure.

They turned to face Puk as he raced forward, but all they did was raise their hands and wave them pleadingly, urging him to slow down and stop.

Puk ignored the gesture.

He collided with the person, sending them both tumbling onto the floor. Their head smacked against the hard wood, knocking the ridiculous pointed hat off their head.

Their face was not at all what Puk had expected, because it was like nothing he'd ever seen before.

The reason their features had been so caked in shadow was because there was no actual shadow—their head was total blackness. It was rounded, smooth, and completely pitch black. Its skin was fuzzy and soft like felt. The only feature on their face was two misshapen circles acting as eyes, sewn with thin red yarn. Strangely, there were also X's sewn across the eyes.

Puk could not comprehend what sort of creature he was looking at, nor could he figure out why the impact hadn't knocked them unconscious. It had not been a gentle landing.

Without a mouth to protest, the peculiar thing struggled underneath Puk's weight to push the qarm off its body.

"I don't wanna hurt you," Puk told it, "but I might need to hit you on the head or something."

He raised his fist to strike them, but couldn't bring himself to do it. Instead, he gazed morosely at the creature's blank expression as it writhed beneath him.

"Signal!" he then called to Kali.

She stood up from behind the wall and said, "*That's* your signal?"

"Just come here, please!"

Kali jogged over to where the two diminutive figures were struggling on the ship deck and gaped at the thing's face.

"What...?" She couldn't form the question.

"I dunno," Puk said, "but it ain't got a mouth, so it ain't gonna yell for help. You stay here with it while I go downstairs."

She nodded and grabbed the thing by the arms while Puk awkwardly slid off its body. He was thankful that he would not need to harm it any further—if it had gotten hurt at all in the first place.

"Is it a doll?" Kali wondered.

Puk shrugged. A doll was probably the closest approximation he could think of, especially with its yarn eyes. Kleus Saix's red magic had to be manipulating the thing somehow. It hadn't been knocked out because it was not actually a living being.

Underneath its green coat, the doll was wearing a rumpled tan shirt, similar to what Puk himself was wearing. With Kali's help, he removed the coat and hurriedly slipped into it. He then waddled over to the discarded hat and picked it up, immediately realizing a fatal flaw in the plan.

"Okay, I fucked up," he groaned loudly.

"What's wrong?"

"The only way I can wear this is if it goes over my stalks," he explained. With eyestalks jutting out from the top of his head, there was nowhere he could traditionally place a hat and still see.

"That is a problem," said Kali.

"Yes. I would like to be able to see things while I am dealing with the mage and looking for a book, if at all possible."

"Understandable. How much can you retract them?"

"Not much more than they were a minute ago," he said. He could comfortably retract his eyestalks to around half their normal length, but any more than that was painful. Definitely not sustainable for the amount of time he would need.

"Try tearing some eyeholes into it," Kali suggested.

As soon as Puk pinched two parts of the hat and began to tug, the previously docile doll began to flail in Kali's arms. Puk immediately stopped, feeling too guilty about ruining the thing's prized possession, no matter how ugly the hat was.

A half-baked idea came to him. He swooped his stalks down, creating smooth curves like hangers on a coat rack, and placed the hat on top of them. The hat's brim pressed against the backs of his eyes, his stalks cradling it in place.

"How do I look?" he asked.

"Insane."

"Will it work?"

"Probably not."

His eyeballs were very clearly poking out from underneath the hat. He'd been planning for the brim to shade his face and obscure it enough to fool Kleus. Fool him just long enough to spike his tea, in any case. Sporting two very-real eyeballs where there should be zero might give him away, though.

"I don't think there's anything else I can do," he said with a defeated shrug.

"We can cut them off and glue the eyeballs to your face instead."

"Do you have scissors and paste?"

"Unfortunately not. I have my dagger, but no paste."

"Dang. And it was such a solid idea."

The situation was far from perfect, but he would have to adapt.

He instinctively wanted to turn his stalks to face the doll, but being constrained by the hat, he had to turn his whole body. It felt awkward and uncomfortable. The thing stared at him, yarn eyes unblinking. He had also been planning to demand it tell him where to find Kleus, but without a mouth, that was not in the cards. And he couldn't politely ask it to escort him to its home.

Great work, you fuckin' idiot. Plan's going great, he berated himself.

Puk took in a deep breath, felt his heart pounding in his tiny chest, and let it out slowly. He was sure he'd suffer a heart attack before the day was done.

Kali handed him her sheathed dagger and said, "Just in case."

He took it, gripping the hilt in his sweaty palm. He thanked her.

There was nowhere to strap the weapon to himself without it being visible to Kleus, so he opted to stuff it into one of the countless oversized pockets in the absurd coat he now wore. He took the opportunity to transfer the spit vial to a coat pocket as well, for easier access. As he did so, it clinked another object already occupying the pocket.

Puk dug past the glass vial and grasped the other item. It was cold and small.

What he pulled out was an iron key.

"Well, that's helpful," Kali grinned.

He agreed. The key was rough, its stem slightly bent. There was no decorum to it at all, strictly utilitarian. His immediate thought was that it was nowhere near fancy enough for a luxury ship like the *Pontequest*.

"This looks like an engineering key to me," he said.

Kali nodded and said, "Yep. Too ugly for a passenger room key."

The doll remained unfazed. It had long since given up its struggle, sitting limp in Kali's arms. Watching the proceedings.

Puk didn't know if it had any awareness of what was going on. Though it must, if it was cognizant enough to know Puk was going to rip its hat. Did it have any affinity for its master? Were they friends?

He shook the thought. It didn't matter. They were here for the book, and they were going to get the book. Simple as that.

"Guess I'm going to the bottom deck," Puk said. "See you on the other side."

She offered a weak smile. "Good luck. I'll be here with our new buddy."

"Don't wish me luck!" he groaned. "That's gonna guarantee I get liquefied or jellified or something!"

"Good luck!" she said, with extra enthusiasm.

"Thanks."

The disguise was set, key in hand.

Puk wandered toward the area where he'd seen the doll suddenly appear less than five minutes earlier. Anxiety nipped at him and it felt as if so much more time had passed since then, like it was crawling by.

The spot was empty, nothing more than some wooden planks and open air. Clearly there was magic obscuring an entrance, so Puk took a step forward—

402 · travis m. riddle

—and nearly tumbled down a set of hidden stairs. There was a square hatch in the ship's deck, hanging open and exposing a stairway that seemingly led straight down to the bottom floor of the vessel. A magical cloak hid the entrance from any onlookers, and Puk had nearly careened downward to the fate of a broken neck.

He had almost let out a creative swear, but refrained in case it carried down the stairwell into wherever Kleus lived.

It had to be uncomfortable, living amongst—well, admittedly Puk didn't have the faintest clue what sort of machinery an airship operated on, but whatever it was, it couldn't be cozy living amongst it.

The sun was barely peeking over the Gogol's dunes. The day was still fresh. Maybe Kleus was still curled up against a boiler (or a steam engine or whatever was down there), sleeping peacefully, dreaming of waking to a mug of warm, delicious tea.

Puk regained his footing and descended the staircase.

Each step groaned with his footfalls, conjuring images of humongous splinters jutting out from the splitting wood and piercing through his skin. He shuddered.

There was hardly any room to move, aside from up or down. Puk was a small individual, and yet his shoulders almost grazed the walls on either side, even without help from the over-padded coat. He guessed this acted as a service corridor for workers, allowing them to move between decks without being seen by the paying customers. Because it would truly be the end of the world if they saw a lowly worker on their pleasure cruise.

A door soon appeared on his left. Jiggling the handle revealed that it was securely locked. Puk tried inserting the iron key just in case, but its teeth would not fit within the keyhole.

He resumed his downward march.

More doors appeared during his descent, one for each layer of the ship, but the key did not work for any of them. Finally, he reached the bottom of the staircase and stood before the doorway leading to the engineering deck. He inserted the key, smiling lightly at the gentle, satisfying *click*, and pulled it open with caution.

There was no mage inside.

What he discovered was a small, empty room with an unmarked door on each of the walls that flanked him. The walls were pockmarked with holes from the crash, and in the intervening years sand had spilled inside onto the floor. Across from him on the far wall was a door with the simple word ENTRANCE etched into it. That had to lead to the portion of this deck they previously explored, one of the many locked doors that had impeded their progress. He bet that if he stuck the newfound key in there, it would open without a hitch.

Glancing at the doors on either side of him, the decision of which to try first was made for him. One hung slightly ajar, inviting the room's dim light provided by a few stray holes in the wall to impose on its darkness. Being so utterly dark and open to the world, Puk knew Kleus was not inside.

The other, however, was shut tight.

Just begging for a key, Puk thought, tiptoeing toward the imposing doorway.

Nothing about its outward appearance was sinister, but knowing what it held inside put Puk ill at ease. Even without breakfast, he gurgled up something in the back of this throat.

The lamatka shank, threatening its resurgence. He swallowed it down, vile and burning.

Standing before the doorway, Puk was less confident than ever in his disguise.

He looked like a buffoon. There was no way Kleus would be convinced that he was the black, red-eyed doll.

Regardless, he slid the bent key into the hole and turned.

It was time to put on a performance.

The thick metal door swung open away from him, slow, like it was pushing through molasses. No one was standing directly on the other side, so his cover wasn't blown quite yet.

However, the room was certainly a sight.

Puk had an albeit small understanding of the *Pontequest*'s layout, but it was enough to know that the room he entered was far larger than the ship could accommodate.

It was vast, stretching far off in every direction from the doorway. It easily had the floorspace of Shiar's Slumber, if not more. Several walls were erected throughout the space, dividing it into numerous separate rooms.

Kleus Saix had conjured himself an entire house in the miniscule engineering room. For all Puk knew, this had once been a broom closet.

Once he grabbed *Malum*, he needed to scan the table of contents for these spells and rip them out, then find a jeornish friend to cast them on the cheapest, shittiest house he could buy in Trillowan.

He shook himself from his daze. There was no time to get distracted by the abstract red and gold wallpaper, the massive paintings hung on every wall, the ornate furniture—what he had to find was a teakettle.

Kleus was still nowhere to be seen, but Puk needed to stay on his toes. Falling out of character could literally be the death of him.

Doing his best imitation of the doll's awkward gait, he closed the entryway behind him and apprehensively sauntered through the home toward one of the open doorways. He could spy a dining table and chairs through the opening and had to assume the kitchen was through there.

The gamble paid off as he entered the room and was greeted by the sight of a dented silver kettle already nestled on the stovetop, filled with water. Just waiting for heat.

Weird that he didn't magic-away the dent, Puk thought, searching for an empty mug. He had to stand on the tips of his toes, but he managed to pull one down from a cabinet and snatched a teabag off the countertop. Kleus had already gone through a couple since the prior day's purchase.

Puk flicked on the heat to bring the water to a boil. While waiting, he extracted the vial of spit from his coat pocket and popped the cork off.

It would not take much of the substance to debilitate Kleus. Puk knew all too well that the raw stuff packed a hell of a punch.

He carefully tapped the vial, sending a few droplets dripping into the mug; not quite enough to cover the bottom of it, but more than he remembered ingesting back in Restick, to ensure that the dosage would render Kleus unconscious. The liquid was thick but clear, hardly noticeable unless one was specifically looking for it. He then dropped a teabag into the mug, letting it cover and soak up some of the animal saliva while the water finished boiling.

Part of him wanted to further explore, but he knew he shouldn't push his luck. Just isolate himself in the kitchen until Kleus made an appearance.

Mere moments after the teakettle began whistling, there came a frantic shuffling from another room. Puk's heart dropped through his stomach and down to his ass. He drummed his fingertips on the counter nervously, but quickly stopped himself.

The doll would not be nervous.

The doll would be still.

So he was still.

He stood motionless for a few seconds, waiting for the mage to appear and say something. But Kleus was still knocking about in his bedroom, so Puk loosened up a bit and poured the hot water atop the waiting teabag. Water sloshed against the saliva, mixing with the viscous liquid, and the dried leaves began steeping.

And then he was still again. Staring dumbly at the kettle.

"What are you doing?"

Puk immediately stiffened. The voice was raspy, croaking. A throat throttled by age.

The doll could not speak, so Puk did not speak.

Or could it speak, but hadn't wanted to speak to him?

He swore internally.

He also refrained from turning to face the mage, who then addressed him again.

"You know I don't like my tea until well after I've awoken. All your racket stirred me."

Shit, Puk cursed. *Why did this fuckin' guy have the kettle all set up and ready to go so early? Hasn't he heard of procrastination?*

"Face me," said Kleus. "Why are you just standing there?"

Shit. His one recurring thought throughout this entire operation.

He glanced down at the tea. The water had slightly browned from the leaves, now more of an amber color.

"Vosk," said Kleus authoritatively. "Turn around."

Deep down, Puk had known it would come to this. The plan was faulty from the start.

He was no burglar.

He was no Vosk.

He was Puk, a failed musician.

But he had hoped the ruse would last a little longer than half a minute, at least.

Puk turned, and his eyes widened at Kleus Saix's appearance. The mage's did likewise upon seeing the qarm.

Kleus had to be somewhere in his fifties, though his voice had aged faster than his body. His skin was tan and wrinkled, deep creases up and down his arms and face. The platinum white hair of his jeornish people was absent from his head, either shaved clean or long since fallen out. He stood slightly hunched in the doorway of the kitchen, wearing a long, velvet red robe cinched tight around his skinny waist.

What had startled Puk was the man's scars.

Ustrel symbols carved themselves into the flesh of mages when they cast spells, and depending on the type and severity of the magic, sometimes it was harder for them to fade. Red magic, being the most volatile and earth-shattering of all the magical disciplines, had mottled Kleus's flesh.

Scars covered the man from head to foot. Every piece of skin Puk could see was scarred, white fibrous symbols covering up his darker skin with years of magical abuse. In many places,

408 · travis m. riddle

new symbols had been recently carved, leaving behind cuts and scabs.

And what had startled Kleus were Puk's stupid, bulbous eyes.

"Who in the hell are you?" the man demanded. "What did you do to Vosk?"

"Okay, well, the—"

Puk was interrupted by his arms and legs snapping to his side. He stood stiff as a plank, his breathing beleaguered as anxiety gripped him.

He was about to attempt talking himself out of the very bad situation he suddenly found himself in, but swiftly realized he had far bigger concerns: his flesh was melting together.

His arms and legs somehow sifted through the layers of clothing he wore, pressing hard against his body until they started melding. He tried to let out a scream, but his lips had fused together as well. A stinging sensation prickled through the length of his body as his limbs morphed into one lump of flesh, and he fell onto the ground, unable to keep himself upright. The big, useless hat tumbled off his head and under the nearby table.

The mage ambled over to where Puk lay prostrate like a slug. He pressed his heel to Puk's back and rolled the qarm over so that he could look up toward his captor.

Puk blinked his stupid eyes stupidly at Kleus.

The man said, "I'm going to unbind your mouth. Before I do, I want you to understand that I can kill you in an instant, and I have no qualms about doing so. The only reason you are not already dead is because I want answers from you. If you irritate me, though, I will kill you. Are we clear on that?"

Well, this does not bode well for me.

Puk nodded, his cheek scraping against the floor.

With that, Kleus gestured with his hands and the flesh of Puk's lips began to tear apart.

"Can't say I care too much for how my body feels right now," said Puk, smacking his lips to get some feeling back in them. A chill ran down his spine; he could still *feel* his arms and legs, but was unable to move them. It was an unpleasant and unsettling sensation.

Kleus mercifully ignored the quip and asked, "Where is Vosk? Did you kill him?"

"He's up watching the sun. He's fine. I just took his clothes."

The mage eyed him suspiciously, but accepted his answer for now. "Why are you here, sneaking into my home? As you've no doubt realized, I've gone through great lengths to ensure I do not receive any visitors. This is most unwelcome."

Puk wasn't sure what the right move was. Would it be detrimental to simply state the truth, that he wanted to steal *Malum*? Was there even a believable lie he could churn out if he wanted to?

"I'm here for your red magic book," he decided to say.

The longer he talked, the longer he stayed alive.

The longer he stayed alive, the more time he had to concoct a new plan. Hopefully one less catastrophic than the first.

His response made Kleus laugh. A bitter, amazed laugh.

"So, they've finally tracked me down?" the man muttered. Puk didn't know who he meant, but he went on. "Those shit-brained High Mages figured out where I was and sent *you* after me?" He let out another barking laugh. "I knew they'd never give up the hunt, but...I admit, I thought their hunters would be a bit more formidable."

Puk shifted on the floor. He did not appreciate being a slug. He also did not appreciate this old, battered mage cackling over him.

"Yeah, well," Puk mumbled, "what can ya do?"

Kleus quietened himself and took a seat at his table. He would have been out of sight if not for Puk's ability to twist his stalks to track the man.

"Where are the High Mages now?" Kleus asked.

"Not sure," Puk said. Lying was coming naturally now that he had stumbled into a scenario that Kleus could buy into. "They sent me in ahead of them to try stealin' the book, keepin' it simple and clean. Said if I don't come back, they would storm the place. Cause a ruckus."

"Well, I'm not going to hand the book over," said Kleus, "so it seems there's no real difference between holding you hostage and simply killing you, right? Either way, they'll be coming."

Shit.

"I guess you're right," said Puk.

Not his best piece of improvisation. Vick would be ashamed.

Kleus laughed, a nasty, phlegmy sound. He said, "You know, this development has riled me up, I must say. The blood's pumping. Maybe I *will* have that tea to soothe my nerves a bit." He gestured again, and the red wooden chair beside Puk morphed itself into a cage that housed the qarm on the floor. As if he would get anywhere fast in his current form.

Oh shit! Puk thought gleefully, pleased his plan was finally spurring into action, before remembering he was now a slug-person.

Kleus stepped past the debilitated Puk and picked the mug up off the countertop. It was still steaming.

He gingerly blew on it, then said to Puk, "It amuses me seeing you like this. It's been so long since I've done it to somebody, you know. Hiding myself away in here was vital, but it *does* feel lonely sometimes. Thank you for bringing me some entertainment. And thank you for the tea, though I'm sorry your charade did not fool me like you'd hoped."

"No problem," said Puk, eyeing the mug. Waiting to see what happened.

"I take it your simple brain thought that a convincing disguise, and you fancied distracting me with tea and perhaps my early morning read while you searched for the book, impersonating Vosk?"

"That about sums it up, yeah."

"A pity it didn't work out for you."

"A real pity," Puk agreed.

"Of course, you might as well die. I have no need for you, and it'd be as simple as a flick of the wrist."

"Naturally." He tried making his anxiousness not so apparent in his tone. It was difficult not feeling anxious when one's arms and legs retracted into their body. Nearly impossible.

Drink the fucking tea, he thought.

"And one more thanks to you again, for alerting me about the High Mages' upcoming assault. I should have ample time to prepare now. Knowing they're on their way, it should not be terribly difficult to mount a defense. Just more flicks of the wrist, really."

"Happy to help."

Kleus blew on his hot tea again. Puk thought more rambling might follow, but the man had evidently said his piece.

He took a wary sip and then, deeming the temperature adequate, gulped down more.

Puk watched as the man's face puckered up, that foul sweetness of the spit finally hitting his tongue. It was immediately obvious that something was wrong with the tea.

"Whun—?" Kleus asked, which was not a question.

Kleus took a step backward, slipping on nothing and collapsing to the floor. He mumbled nonsense to himself, each word getting louder and louder, which Puk could not help but giggle at.

At least that part of the plan had worked.

What Puk had not anticipated, however, was whatever gesture Kleus was making with his hand before he fully slid into unconsciousness. Plus, he was still a slug-person, which was far from ideal and put a huge damper on the rest of the plan and his life in general.

"Shit," he finally got to say aloud.

The mage was still spouting gibberish, but his words grew softer and softer until they eventually ceased. Puk watched his eyelids flutter shut.

Silence, but for Puk's haggard breaths. The room was still. Until it wasn't.

The chair-cage enclosing Puk suddenly burst into splinters that rained down on him. He closed his eyes so as to not be blinded. He then felt a bubbling on his sides, an intense vibration in his flesh. His arms and legs began to re-form, oozing out from his abdomen.

Disgust quickly faded and he was instead awash with relief. He wanted to scream to the heavens, he wanted to get down on his knees and pray, he wanted to kiss the next person he saw.

But the next person he saw was Kleus, and that feeling instantly dissipated.

He spied fresh, deep markings on the man's hands from the two spells he had cast, still dripping with blood. For a second, Puk wondered why those two spells had been broken by the man losing consciousness while the illusion of the home hadn't.

But he dismissed the thought, not wanting to waste any precious time trying to parse the various qualities of red magic. He chalked it up to the scars not having yet settled on the flesh. A good enough explanation for his simple brain.

It was then that Puk was cognizant enough to notice a swirling vortex of dark, cool colors floating by the stovetop, and he remembered Kleus had actually cast a third spell as he tottered to the floor.

Rich blues and purples and greens twisted and shimmered, a surreal sight, which Puk could not understand how he had previously missed. His stomach sunk at the thought of what spell the mage might have cast.

He needed the book.

Now.

No one besides Puk was stupid enough to drink raw cordol spit, so there was no frame of reference for how long Kleus would be knocked out. There was also no telling what the beautiful, horrific vortex was about to do or produce.

He needed to act fast and get the hell out of Pontequest. Thankfully, Bella would have a load of energy stored up and ready to exert. Their party being cooped up in Paul's storage room would soon pay off.

It didn't help, though, that he didn't have a clue what the book looked like.

414 · travis m. riddle

He darted out of the kitchen and twisted his stalks in every direction, until he landed on a single towering shelf over in the corner.

The shelf held various items. There were multiple jars of unidentified liquids, packets of dried herbs and cured meats, golden sculptures, and much more, but what interested Puk was the pile of books resting on the bottom shelf.

If they had been even three rows higher, it would have presented a problem for the short qarm.

But they were well within reach, so Puk dashed toward the shelf and tossed all the books onto the floor so that he could read their covers. All of which, he then discovered, were blank.

He dared a glance behind him, rotating a single stalk around to eye the kitchen, and was met with some disgusting, otherworldly creature slithering out from the vortex Kleus had summoned in his final moments.

The creature's front half was similar to that of a human man, though its skin was a pale blue and riddled with spiderwebs of oozing cuts all over its flesh. Wispy white hair hung in clumps from its misshapen head, hanging past the yellow orbs of its eyes. Its mouth hung open abnormally wide, with countless rows of tiny, razor-sharp teeth.

The back half of it was no better. Just past the monster's pus-filled bellybutton, its flesh turned dark and scaly, coming to form a point at its end.

It swiveled its head around, the bones in its neck cracking with every movement, searching for the prey it had been summoned to hunt.

"Oh for fuck's sake," Puk sputtered, panicking even more.

The heart attack was coming, he was sure of it.

He flipped open each book to a random page, and every single one was a spellbook of some kind. All of the language and symbols were foreign to him. Nothing distinguished a Fire spell from a Turn A Man Into A Slug spell in his mind.

"Fuck it."

He slammed the books shut and gathered them all in his hands. One of them had to be *Malum*. They could let Haratti figure out which and throw the other three in the trash.

The sound of him closing the books alerted the snake-monster to his presence. It loosed another ear-splitting scream, its voice shrill and wet, and it darted toward him. The yellow eyes gleamed hungrily.

The monster shuffled hastily over Kleus's unconscious body, aiming for the small qarm.

Puk, with his one free hand, grasped the bookshelf he'd plundered and attempted to knock it over to delay the monster's charge, but it was too heavy. He swore loudly and raced forward, toward the metal door back out onto the engineering deck.

But the snake-man could move much faster than Puk's stout qarmish legs could carry him.

It coiled itself then sprung into the air, crashing into Puk's back, sending him sprawling onto the ground. He managed to keep ahold of the books, slamming his stomach into them as he landed on the ground, winding him.

The creature's clammy palms pressed against his back, its sharp, broken fingernails digging into the doll's coat. Vibrations rippled through the floor as it gleefully slapped its tail against the ground, happy to have caught its snack.

Dagger, Puk thought to himself. His mind could not presently formulate more than a single word.

He wriggled his arms out from underneath his torso and elbowed the monster in what he assumed was its face. It let out a screech but did not loosen its grip on his coat.

The creature then bit down, its teeth tearing into the thick fabric but not breaking through to Puk's flesh. He was silently thankful for Vosk's insane fashion choice, which had undeniably just saved his life.

He struggled to reach his hand into the pocket containing Kali's dagger. It was difficult maneuvering his limbs with the snake-man writhing around on top of him, but it was too heavy for him to shove off.

After a few agonizing moments (during which the monster continued feasting on Vosk's now-mangled coat), Puk successfully grabbed the hilt of the weapon and pulled it free of the pocket, conveniently leaving the sheath behind as well.

At his current angle, the dagger's blade was pointing upward into the air, so he swung his arm backward, nearly popping it out of its socket, and jabbed the blade into the monster's arm.

It screamed again, the only noise it knew how to make, and flopped off of Puk like a floundering fish.

Puk scrambled to his feet while he had the opportunity and stared down his attacker. Its eyes were slits, glaring at the weapon embedded in its arm as it roared, and Puk briefly considered grabbing the books and fleeing then and there. It was the easiest option.

He would be pursued, though. Of that he had no doubt.

If the beast didn't merely kill him and return to its master before he even had a chance to escape the ship, it might also reach Kali and kill her.

"Fuck me," he groaned, knowing he had to put a stop to it or die trying. Most likely the latter.

Puk hopped forward and grabbed the dagger's hilt again, immediately being flung backward by the monster. But it was enough momentum for the weapon to slide out of its arm, and Puk was careful enough in his rough landing to not stick himself with it.

Before he had a chance to rise again, the snake-man was charging toward him.

He sat up, his back against the bookshelf. His eyes widened as the monster grew nearer, its rank mouth open wide and eager.

Without thinking, Puk held the dagger straight ahead of him then remained still.

The snake-man had already built up too much momentum to stop itself in time and careened face-first into the blade, which pierced one of its yellow, yolky eyes.

It instantly slumped to the ground, its head smashing into Puk's right leg. He let out a yelp of pain, though he was relieved to see the monster lying motionless.

Kleus was still fast asleep on the kitchen floor when Puk pushed past the metal door back out onto the engineering deck. He turned and raced up the stairway, banging his shoulders against the walls as he clumsily ascended. He gripped the collection of books tight to his chest, pressing them against the torn, ooze-covered green coat he still wore.

He zoomed past the different doors on his way up the stairwell until he finally burst out into blinding sunlight. Kali loosed a sharp yelp at his sudden appearance.

"Let's fuck outta here!"

"What?"

He was feeling loopy from the spell and anxiety and exhilaration. He didn't have the mental capacity to form coherent sentences. He shoved the four books toward Kali, who let go of red-eyed Vosk to grab them.

Puk removed the dagger from its pocket again then shouldered off the coat and returned it to the ink-black doll. "Sorry for ruining your morning," he said. "And your coat, too, I guess."

Vosk, predictably, said nothing. The thing slipped its arms back through the coat sleeves and pointed to Puk's head, which was distinctly lacking a hat.

"In the kitchen," Puk said.

Vosk nodded and moved past him, walking calmly away as if nothing out of the ordinary had transpired.

"Watch out for the snake-man," Puk told Vosk as the doll disappeared down the invisible hatch.

"Excuse me?" said Kali.

"I'll explain later. Let's go."

"Which of these is the book?" Kali asked, accepting his answer.

"Don't know," Puk replied. "Let's just go before he wakes Kleus up. I don't wanna see more of his spells."

"Wait!" Kali shouted. "How can you be sure one of these is it, then? Did you search the entire place? What happened?"

"There's no *time* for all this," Puk said. "I dunno how long he's gonna be out for, and I don't wanna be here when he's back on his feet!"

He was tempted to just jump over the edge of the ship and take his chances landing in the sand, but he made the smart choice and started toward the main staircase that would lead them back below deck.

Kali grabbed him by the arm before he got too far. "We need to be sure, Puk," she said, her voice grave.

"If you can figure out what any of that shit is," he said, exasperated, "then be my guest. But I don't know what any of it means, and I don't want my bones melted or whatever the fuck it is Kleus wants to do to me when he wakes up. I didn't see no more books down there, so I say we *leave*. We aren't gettin' another chance either way, so either the book's in that batch or it ain't."

He let out a heavy, uneven breath. His body shivered, and Kali let go of him.

"Okay," she said. "If you're really sure, then I trust you."

Puk closed his eyes a moment, sighed, and opened them again. "Thank you," he said.

They shot down the staircase, racing through the different levels of the ship. When they reached the bottom floor again, a chill swept through Puk as he thought about Kleus's scarred flesh and his terrible magic.

Bolting through the door and back into sunlight, with the shifting sands at his feet, was a sweet relief. He had never been so happy to feel the sun on his skin.

It was not a long run from there to the storage room where Bella awaited them. Kali loaded up a sack with the four books, and soon they were navigating the lumbering ayote through the hall and back out into the desert.

Kali hoisted Puk up onto Bella's back, then saddled herself atop as well. She double-checked that all of their possessions were either strapped to their bodies or Bella's, then said, "Let's get out of here."

"Not a moment too soon."

She urged the ayote, and Bella took off like a bullet.

It was the best ride of Puk's life.

CHAPTER XIX

ONE STEP TOO FAR

The ride to Weynard felt beautifully short after their multi-day ordeal in Pontequest. Both Kali and Puk were relieved to be done with the village, and Kali was sure that Bella more than anyone was thankful to be out of the confined storage area.

Kali slowed the ayote down to a more reasonable jaunt once they had fled a great distance from the crashed airship and could be certain Kleus was not in pursuit. Without the wind whipping at their ears, she asked Puk what had happened within the red mage's lair. His recounting of the spell Kleus used on him horrified her, as did his description of the snake-man hybrid, and she profusely apologized for being topside and unable to lend assistance. He assured her it was fine, but his voice was still somewhat shaky. By the time they reached their destination several hours later, the qarm seemed more like his usual self, albeit faintly more reserved.

Once again the pair found themselves seeking shelter at The Restful Oasis. The elderly owner, Grace, accurately predicted their preference for the Ayote Room, the inn's cheapest available lodging. Funds were nearly dried up, so it was a good thing they had successfully obtained *Malum*.

Probably.

After getting settled in their room, the first thing Kali did was scan the pages of the texts that Puk had stolen. All bore unmarked covers, and all contained pages upon pages of spells. None of her family had traveled the path of becoming any type of mage, but growing up in a jeornish household, there was still some amount of magic discussion. Kali hoped that meager knowledge would come to her aid now.

While Puk relaxed on the bed, a well-earned minor comfort after such a long and challenging day, Kali planted herself on the floor with all four books spread in front of her.

The first book she went for was the obvious choice, one with a red leather cover. As she flipped through the pages, she was glad that Puk hadn't made a similar assumption under pressure and solely grabbed it while leaving behind the others, because it was definitely not *Malum*.

As far as Kali could tell, it was not actually a spellbook, but rather Kleus's journal. There were scribblings of spells—their functions, how to cast them, different forms they could take—but those were supplementary to the primary text. The book detailed Kleus's life on the run, its oldest entry dating back nearly forty years, to when he was studying magic at Allinor University.

The man had not partaken in daily journaling, but it seemed significant moments of his life garnered entries. Big social events, discovering new magic, things of that nature. Kali skipped around until she found an entry from the spring of 1102, the period in which Kleus and his ally Michio Loz had first stolen the red magic spellbooks from a vast library in an Atluan city called Bral Han. His script was neat, with thin inkstrokes and pleasant, swooping curved letters.

I'm finally starting to figure out a basic illusion spell. The book starts you off with something small, like making someone think a cup is on a table, then working your way toward turning a room into an enormous desert. I haven't quite cracked the cup yet, but I'm getting there. I was able to make Michio see an item on his desk, but he said that if he tried to use the misshapen thing as a cup, water would be spilling all over the place.

These countless attempts at something as simple as tricking someone's mind into seeing a cup are really taking a toll. I can tell Michio is hurting from his practice, too. Our hands are practically slashed to ribbons with red magic symbols that sometimes take over an hour to stop bleeding. Maybe we'd be able to staunch that if we were studying white magic during the day, but alas. We've started wearing gloves to cover up our fresh markings. Letting Professor Nonyai see these would be the end of us.

Despite the pain, I think we're both having a ton of fun with the magic. I'm excited to put Michio in that fake desert eventually. I never imagined having power like this. I feel so strong, finally. Even if all I can do so far is make a shoddy cup.

She needed to figure out which book was the one Haratti sought, their big payday, but Kali found herself fascinated by the man's notes. She flipped ahead through the years, skimming entries about Kleus and Michio splitting while on the run, how Kleus made his way westward through Atlua and eventually down through Gillus, where he lived for a number of years. All the while he continued practicing his red magic, growing more and more skilled with the techniques.

By 1115, when Kali was merely a three-year-old puttering around her newly adoptive parents' home, Kleus had mastered the ability to not only trick a person's mind into seeing something that wasn't there, but a method in which he could genuinely create something out of nothing. That had to be how he'd created the living quarters Puk spoke of, maintaining the illusion even while unconscious, which Puk had expressed confusion over during his telling of the tale. As it turned out, it was no illusion at all. It also explained why Kleus's strange servant—whose name she now knew was Vosk—had not suddenly ceased living while she kept ahold of him up on the deck. There had to be some highly complicated spellcraft at work on that doll, stuff far beyond her own limited comprehension.

Eventually Kleus made his way to Herrilock, and he wrote a small section on the *Pontequest*'s crash, which was big news when it had happened and quickly spread throughout the country. He later wrote about the rumor of some nomads who were traveling to the crash site to build a home, which sprouted an idea in his mind.

Kali read through the details of his scheme, which involved entering the newly-formed town and pretending to blow up the ship. Up to that point, he had remained out of the High Mages' grasp, but his journal was filled with paranoia about being caught as well as anger toward the mages for, as he put it, attempting to "stifle his growth." He figured his best course of action was to hole up in the airship.

To remain undetected, he would fake an explosion, which worked twofold: the first benefit was that it would create a rumor to spread through Herrilock, leading no one to bother visiting Pontequest if they believed it to be destroyed and therefore not finding him; the second being it would cause the current residents to not want to enter the place where he'd be shacking up. A life of solitude was his for the taking. Kali scanned through the next few pages to see if the man had written anything about altering the townsfolks' personalities and how he intended to deal with visitors who did stumble upon the intact ship. Either he never committed those parts to the page, or they were written elsewhere in the book.

But with all these safeguards in place, Kali failed to deduce how Haratti had discovered Kleus's whereabouts. The man must have an impressive web of connections. A tingle ran down her spine.

She was trying to flip around and find an entry about Vosk, to read the origins of the doll, but that thought about Haratti and his connections kept nagging at her, clawing at her focus.

What does he really want Malum *for?*

Kali closed the journal and picked up the next book. It didn't take her long to deem it a black magic book, and a fairly rudimentary one, at that. Most of the spells discussed within were lower-level versions, with only brief explanations on the complex conjuring required for the more intense flames of Fire or the cyclones of Aero. There was not anything at all for Bio or Demi spells, either, which Kali knew were for more highly advanced mages. She guessed the book was a holdover from Kleus's hasty exit from school so many decades before, though she could only wonder why he had not discarded the tome long ago.

The third book's cover was black leather, faded with age. Kali gently opened it up, and right there on the very first page was the word MALUM.

She held the book up to show Puk with an exasperated look on her face.

"You didn't think to just check the title pages of these?"

Puk squinted at the page, then shifted his gaze to Kali. He said, "We've only known each other a short time, but based on everything you've learned about me, do you think I read fuckin' books? Enough to know that they have 'title pages'?"

"Alright, fair enough." She hadn't thought to check the title page of the first two books either.

The two both groaned with relief at confirmation the book was in their possession at last. All they had left to do was transport it to Haratti.

The title was not intricately drawn with large, fancy lettering like in many books she had read. It was simple, small, and in the precise center of the yellowed page. Totally unsuspecting for anyone who stumbled upon the book and was unaware of what horrible spells it contained.

Kali's curiosity got the better of her.

Like Kleus had described in his journal, the first few spells in *Malum* were relatively tame, but they wasted no time ramping up. She read about the spell for conjuring a cup—both tricking a person into believing they were seeing one, and also genuinely creating one out of thin air—which was the most incomprehensible jumble of words she'd ever read. It seemed to her like one of the most difficult spells to pull off, and yet Kleus's home was filled with items and amenities he had crafted for himself out of magic.

The man is clearly powerful. Or at least he was in his youth, anyway. Puk got off lucky. That plan of his was a stroke of genius.

The book then detailed transmogrification, and given that such a horrific practice was merely the second or third spell taught in the book, Kali shuddered at the thought of what else the illicit volume contained. She imagined Puk's body morphing, his limbs disappearing into the flesh of his body. Such a terrible thing to inflict on a living being, and yet it was evidently a simple task for Kleus. No more effort than cracking an egg.

Only fifteen or twenty pages later was a spell that allowed the user to choose a target and manipulate the most basic foundations of its tissue. In other words, the spellcaster could gesture with their hands and instruct a person's arm to separate from their torso.

Kali was starting to feel nauseous and did not want to know what other foul secrets the book held. She had no interest in learning how the man had conjured some sort of monster to attack Puk. She slammed the book shut, awash with guilt for merely having it in her possession.

Puk looked up from his duraga, which he had spent the last few minutes tuning, and asked, "You okay?"

She shook her head.

He set the instrument down on the bed's rumpled sheets and asked, "What's wrong? Read something messed up in there?"

"'Messed up' is putting it lightly," she grimaced. "Obviously spellbooks are structured going from the least complex

428 · travis m. riddle

spells to the most, and in less than thirty pages this one is teaching you how to rip a person's head off their neck. Can you imagine what the *last* spell in the book could be?"

"Maybe attaching their head again?" the qarm offered.

Kali rolled her eyes. Usually she enjoyed Puk's jokes, but the pit in her stomach soured her mood. "I'm being serious," she said.

He apologized, then went on. "I mean, it's bad shit. We knew it was bad shit. That's why it was outlawed however long ago. That's why the mages want that thing destroyed," he said, pointing dumbly at the book before her.

She nodded. Of course she'd known red magic was vile, but getting a chance to see it for herself made it all the more real. Before, it was only an abstract concept. She was kept at enough of a distance to separate herself from the reality of it.

But now the book was here, in her hands. Tangible.

Her thoughts returned to Haratti and whoever his unknown employer was. If they possessed the resources to find Kleus Saix after being in hiding and eluding the most highly-trained mages in the world for thirty-eight years, there was no telling what else they were capable of.

Doubt pierced her.

She said, "I don't know if we should do this."

"Do what?" Puk had just been about to pick up his duraga, but moved his hand away from the slender neck again.

It felt stupid, but she had to say it. "Give the book to Haratti."

Puk laughed, bending his eyestalks backward before shooting them up straight to glare at her. "The hell are you talkin' about?" he demanded. "I *just* told you the story, but maybe you need a refresher on the bullshit I went through this morning to *get* that book. The reason I did that was so we could give it to Haratti for a lot of money. I need that money." His skin was still slicked with sweat from their hasty retreat.

"I know. Trust me, I know. It's *my* money that we've been using for this whole trip, in case *you* need a refresher. But…reading this shit, doesn't it make you uneasy? Knowing that we'd be handing off such a powerful, nasty resource to someone so shady?"

"His boss might not be shady. We don't even know who it is."

"That's what makes them shady."

"Well, either way, we don't know what they wanna do with it. Maybe they're some sort of weird pervert who wants to add it to their personal library. Or maybe they just wanna sell it too, for an even bigger profit. Who cares?"

"Yeah, that might be what they're doing, but who are they selling it to? That's what we should care about!" She realized she was shouting, and quickly lowered her voice. "Remember those Varedan ships we saw docking in Myrisih? There have been rumors floating around of Vareda trying to start a war, sinking ships and shit. What if Haratti's selling the book to them? I bet they'd be willing to pay a giant mound of crescents for a book like this. It would be a pretty solid investment to help themselves win a war, don't you think?"

"I don't think nothin'," said Puk. "I don't know what the Varedans are doin', I don't know what Haratti and his goons are doin'. All I know is what *I'm* doin', and that is *going the fuck home.*"

Kali wanted to throw a book at his head. She resisted.

"I wanna go to Atlua too," she said, keeping calm. "That's what I want more than anything right now, and I've done a lot of questionable shit to make that happen, which is something I'm gonna have to wrestle with. But I think this is one step too far. I'm not sure I could live with myself knowing that I helped some piece of shit get this book. There's too much bad that can be done with it."

"I dunno how you've deluded yourself into thinking that's not what we were doin' this entire time, but you're a moron if you wanna throw away everything we've done now. If we do that, we'll both be broke fucks stuck in this huge, horrible desert."

Without warning, he jumped off the bed and stormed out of the room.

Kali remained on the floor, her stomach aching, staring down at the black void of the book's cover.

- -

Puk's feet automatically glided him down the stairs and out the inn's entryway. He wasn't sure yet where his tantrum was taking him.

He marched straight across the town's circular path, through the thin treeline, all the way down to the oasis shore. A good ways away on either side of him were people enjoying the water or lounging on the beach downing bottles. But he was alone in his little patch of sand.

He dropped down onto the sand, sinking in, the warmth of it irritating him further. He wanted dead leaves crunching underfoot. The rustle of greenery in the breeze. Dirt between his toes. Real dirt, not this poor excuse for dirt they called sand. He leaned back on his hands, fanning his fingers in and out to feel the grains.

"Idiot," he muttered to himself, aghast at Kali's sudden turn.

After numerous dreadful days traveling across this dreadful desert, finding not one but *two* mythical towns, wrangling with wild cordols, and so much more...now she wanted to give up their reward? All that hard work wasted?

The prospect infuriated him. He wanted to go back to Atlua. That was that. It was all he had been striving for, ever since being unceremoniously booted from the Rusty Halberd.

That felt like ages ago. He tried and failed to mentally map out where the troupe might be by now. Maybe they were in the east, traveling along the mountain ridge, performing in centript hives. Or taking a break to explore the southern beaches now that he wasn't weighing them down.

"Idiots," he muttered this time, thinking of his old comrades that had abandoned him back in Seroo's Eye. He'd thought they were his closest friends, ones who would never turn their backs on him. Now he had no idea where in the world they were, and they would likely never see each other again.

I should find out the schedule for their next tour and go to every stop and heckle them. Maybe I'll even buy a tomato or two to throw at the stage. Or maybe something harder, like a pumpkin.

The petty thought made him chuckle, brightening his mood a little. He then pictured Dern, with his unending appetite, attempting to catch a tomato in his mouth as a snack. Then Hin catching a pumpkin to the head.

Puk sighed. He watched as a couple waded out into the water, flirtatiously splashing each other. The sound of the water began to calm him down.

With his mind clearing up, he tried to really reflect on what Kali was suggesting. Deep down, he knew she was right to not trust Haratti or anyone the haggard man worked with. That was obvious just from speaking to the guy. Even just from looking at him.

But all those crescents...

The money was a huge motivator. One that he could not entirely ignore, no matter what his conscience was screaming at him about his selfishness. He couldn't survive without crescents, let alone get back home to hear that breeze, feel that dirt. A sacrifice might have to be made.

It was unfortunate, and he did feel selfish, but it was the truth.

The red mage's snake-man was horrific. It would give Puk nightmares for years to come, he imagined. But it was not what had bothered him most in that ordeal.

All day he had been forcing himself to think about anything other than Kleus Saix altering his body, but now the memory wouldn't leave him alone. Writhing on the man's floor, being able to feel his limbs but unable to move them.

Dammit, Kali.

He had felt so constrained, so trapped. So utterly helpless.

Beyond that, something he had kept thinking, limp on the floor while Kleus taunted him, was that he'd never be able to play his music again.

The disconnect he experienced with being able to feel his limbs—to feel their presence, their existence, yet them no longer being physically part of the world—was the worst thing Puk had felt in his entire life. It was like a tingle he couldn't get out of his back, or trying to vomit with nothing coming up.

Constant struggle and discomfort. Trying to do nothing more than wiggle his fingers.

If that was only a basic red magic spell, Kali was justified in fearing the more complex spells at *Malum*'s disposal. Kleus had kept himself secret, either content to learn the spells to make himself feel powerful or too concerned with whatever the High Mages' punishment might entail were he caught.

The book could easily fall into more sinister and ambitious hands, though, and havoc could be unleashed on Ustlia.

Puk didn't want to envision living a life in that sluglike state, nor did he want to think about others suffering a similar fate, let alone something worse.

They were far from Myrisih. And as far as they knew, no one was following them. They could easily slip away, never to be seen by Haratti or his cohorts again. The stupid qarm and the naïve faif could have easily gotten themselves killed on their way to or within Pontequest. An entirely plausible scenario.

But Puk had to dismiss that notion as soon as it had entered his mind. He knew it was too idealistic.

They were able to find Kleus, and he's nowhere near as big an idiot as me. Haratti's people could find me in a day. Probably less, if I'm in a loud mood.

Haratti doubtless had innumerable connections throughout Myrisih and beyond.

But I've got connections too, Puk suddenly thought.

And connections were invaluable.

I've got Voya, and Voya's got even more. He's nowhere near as influential or all-reaching as Haratti and his boss are, but...

Puk tried to connect some dots in his head.

On one hand, relinquishing the book to Haratti could potentially invite doom for many innocent people, even inciting all-out war if Kali's prediction regarding Vareda was correct.

But all that money...

Maybe we can get the money and also keep the book, Puk pondered. He had since grown used to the sand's warmth and was enjoying it while he watched the setting sun. He was reminded of Vosk's morning routine.

"Idiot," he said aloud again, this time referring to himself.

None of his plans thus far had gone smoothly. Why would this one be any different?

All of 'em worked in the end, though. They got royally fucked first, but in the end...

Perhaps it was worth a shot.

He lifted himself off the ground, then left the oasis and headed back toward the quaint inn to inform Kali of his newest harebrained scheme.

- -

"You wanna steal the book again," Kali said, clarifying that was indeed what Puk intended.

The qarm stood before her, nodding fervently. His eyestalks bobbed back and forth as he did so. The motion had to be disorienting.

While he'd been sulking outside, she had tidied up the room a bit, stacking their new collection of books on a table near the window. She then sat on the bed and leafed through Kleus's journal, once more searching for entries about Vosk, and had been surprised to find Kleus once had a wife and son, back when he lived in Gillus. Puk returned before she'd had the chance to learn what happened to them.

"Voya knows lots of people around Myrisih, and I know for a fact he's acquainted with some mercenaries, because I've gambled with and lost a lot of money to them," said Puk, pacing. In spite of all he had been through that day, he was suddenly brimming with energy.

"I just don't think it's feasible," she murmured.

His intentions were noble, but she doubted their viability. When he reappeared in the room, he had breathlessly pitched a plan to go along with Haratti as normal and sell the book, obtaining the precious crescents they both so desperately required, then use some hired hands to turn around and immediately nab the book back before any harm could be done with it. At that point, they could burn it to a crisp or dispose of it in some other way.

"What's not feasible about it?" Puk wanted to know. It was not irritation in his tone or expression, but disappointment.

Kali wanted the plan to work. She truly did. It would be perfect if they could somehow keep the money while simultaneously safeguarding the book. But she could not bring herself to see it happening.

She said, "It's just the fact that we have no idea what Haratti's intentions are. He or whoever he sells it to could hop on a boat that day or even half an hour later and sail away to kill some people with it. We just don't know the timing of it all, so it's difficult to hatch a plan."

Puk stopped pacing and considered her concern for a minute, his stalks bunching up in thought. Finally, he said, "I think it's unlikely that whatever they wanna do with the book will be done in Myrisih, right? They've got no reason to fuck up that place, it's their headquarters. They don't wanna destroy it or draw any attention to it."

"Right," Kali said with a nod.

Puk nodded as well. "So I agree with you that they're likely gonna be getting it off the island as soon as they can. The solution's easy, then: we can get to Restick whenever, but we'll ask Zenib to take us over to Myrisih on the last day the port's open. Only a few hours before it closes, even. That way, we can go meet with Haratti, get our hard-earned money, then grab the book and scram. Plenty of time for us to snatch the book and sail through the port right as it's closing so no one can follow."

The qarm stood in the middle of the room with a hopeful grin plastered on his face like a fool. Kali chuckled at him.

"I wouldn't call 'a few hours' *plenty* of time," she said.

"But it'd be enough."

"That's…" she started. She almost didn't want to say it, because the idea made her nervous, but she went ahead. "…not a bad point. It…uh, it *might* be feasible."

Puk's face lit up.

His enthusiasm was infectious, and Kali found herself smiling too.

The plan made her incredibly anxious, letting *Malum* slip into Haratti's hands for even a second. If they didn't pull it off, then the fallout could be disastrous. Every life lost to red magic would be blood on her hands.

But all of their previous plans had made her anxious too. And now here they were with the book.

It was entirely possible that they were not an awful team.

Certainly not a good one, but not an awful one, either.

"Are we doin' it?" Puk asked hopefully.

Kali sighed, glancing over at the table where *Malum* rested. It looked so unassuming, sitting there amongst the other innocent texts.

"Okay," she finally said. Puk whooped in celebration. "But only if we get the best of the best working with us. We can't afford even the tiniest misstep on this."

Puk sported a smug look and said, "Don't worry about that. The best of the best are the only people Voya knows. I'm a prime example."

Kali burst out laughing at this.

"Oh, so we *are* totally fucked," she teased.

"Hey now," said Puk, "Lookin' at all the shit we've accomplished, I wouldn't bet against us."

"You don't have any money to bet anyway."

"Not yet, I don't."

CHAPTER XX

MEETINGS

Their journey from Weynard to Restick was largely uneventful, aside from Puk eagerly overextending himself during dinner at a travelers' outpost and unburdening his upset stomach outside by the stables. Neither the ayotes nor the stablemaster were especially thrilled with his behavior.

Conversation atop Bella's back was peppered with ideas for what to do with *Malum* once they stole it back from Haratti's crew. They bandied about a few different scenarios, but what seemed easiest and most reasonable was simply burning the book. Removing all trace of it from the world.

In Restick, they sought Zenib and requested another ride to Myrisih on the last day of its port being open. The centript agreed, and they arranged to meet by his boat's hiding spot the following night after he secured another passbook and directions from his unnamed source.

After leaving the centript's home, Kali recalled reading a few pages in *Malum* about altering an individual's memory, and she wondered how such an effect was placed on Myrisih's entrance. However it was possible, there was no denying the spell was effective; she could not recall even the smallest detail about how to reach the city. She felt violated, having her memories erased.

Soon the trio was once again huddled together on the diminutive *Fiery Lass*. Their escort looked different somehow from the last time they'd seen him, and it took Kali a few minutes to realize what the change was: he was missing a new segment of his carapace. The mold had taken more of him.

On the boat ride over, Kali took the time to explain their situation to Zenib. She was careful to leave out the exact details, just in case the man decided to get a little greedy and steal the book to sell for himself, but she mentioned that they would be looking to get out of Myrisih with haste.

I've gotten to visit all these bizarre, interesting places, and yet we're always trying to leave as soon as we can, she lamented. The innate traveler in her yearned to spend more time exploring the ins and outs of Myrisih, of Weynard—of Pontequest, even.

"When you tryin' to leave?" Zenib wanted to know. They did not have an exact answer for him, so he said, "I'll try to be ready at a moment's notice, then. For a few extra crescents, of course."

"Of course," Puk muttered. Kali never appreciated having every possible crescent squeezed out of her when she was haggling with other merchants, but sometimes that was the name of the game. It was not an unreasonable request, coming from Zenib. He held quite a lot of leverage.

So he agreed to post up somewhere near the docks upon their arrival, awaiting their retreat at an unspecified later time.

"If we're leaving tonight, though, make sure to get back before the ports close," he reminded them. As if they needed to be told.

With that problem solved, the next step would be hiring a friend of Voya's that could be trusted. Kali did not have what she would describe as "a lot" of faith in the type of company the ujath kept, but Puk insisted it would be fine.

To her surprise, she found that she still trusted Puk, regardless of his lie about the spit vial. Even with the drug in his possession, he had kept his word about not consuming it, as far as she had been able to tell—if he'd ingested any, it hadn't affected their quest or relationship. And, of course, it had been an invaluable asset when it came to dealing with Kleus. It was probably the sole reason they had succeeded. All of her initial anger toward him had fully faded.

The Myrisih port was full when they sailed in through the cavern's canals. There were plenty of small vessels similar to their own bobbing in the gentle waters, but there were also bigger ships with Varedan architecture. Their presence strengthened Kali's assumptions and resolve; they could not screw up this last job. If she was correct about Haratti's intentions with the book, she would not let herself incite a war.

After checking in, Zenib bade them farewell. "I'll be here," he said in his scratchy voice. Kali appreciated his lack of inquiries into their plans. If they were to succeed, his cut of the profits would be a hefty chunk of crescents, so maybe that was motivation enough to wish them good fortune.

Myrisih's tunnels were bustling with activity. Kali had to swerve and dodge hurried passersby, tightly squeezing between those unwilling to modify their paths in the cramped walkways. There was a dull roar within the Mass, a conglomeration of footsteps, bartering, and food sizzling. The hidden city was much more active at night than when they had previously navigated it during the morning.

Without discussing it, Kali knew that Puk was leading them down the Mass's outermost ring to Voya's home. It was clear how fucked their situation was when visiting the intimidating ujath's house was the part that worried her the least.

She just hoped he would be willing to lend them a hand.

- -

"Thuck off!" came Voya's bellowing voice from the recesses of his home, an unfortunate echo of their first visit. The man's irate shouts were followed by the sound of something very expensive shattering.

But Puk pounded on the door again and said, "It's Puk!"

"What do you not underthtand abou' thucking off?"

No one could say Puk was not persistent. He continued whacking his fist on the rough wood until his old companion eventually flung the door open.

"I thaid thuck off!" Voya roared in his face. The ujath's massive tongue slid carelessly on the ground, specks of dirt sticking to the wet, pink flesh. It flicked toward Kali, picking up her scent.

"That's no way to treat a friend," said Puk. "Especially not after the gift I gave you on our last visit."

"I'm thick of you and your githt," said Voya, his wiry, spidery limbs clacking on the floor as he retreated into his home. Puk took this as an invitation inside, and Kali followed, taking care not to accidentally step in the trail of saliva left in his wake.

"How are you even alive thtill?" Voya asked him. "I thought wha'ever job you took would kill you."

"I'm resilient," Puk replied.

The house was much messier this time around. There were still boxes everywhere, but several were toppled, with their contents spilling out onto the floor for Voya and them to crush underfoot. Much to Puk's disgust, there were also tiny white droppings scattered all over the place, granting the house a sharp, tangy stench.

And soon the mess's culprits came into view.

Two baby cordols darted into the room, one chasing the other. They sped across the span of the room like tiny red bullets. Both slammed into the side of a box, its contents jangling inside. Only then did Puk notice bits and pieces of pale orange eggshells littering the floor.

Voya started a low growl that turned into a frustrated scream.

"I thould have nether taken thothe thucking eggth from you!" he thundered. "I hate cordolth!"

"Aww, but they're so cute!" Puk grinned, watching the two babies run around in a circle, biting after each other's tails. Being so young, their skin was hairless and smooth, and they glided across the floor with ease. Must speedier than the lumbering ujath. It was no wonder he could not keep up with them.

Behind Puk, Kali laughed. He joined in.

"Thut up," Voya grimaced. He slammed the end of his tongue on the ground like a fist. "Take them back."

"I don't want 'em," said Puk. "I ain't a paternal type like you."

"They thit all over the plathe, and my tongue ith *alwayth* on the gwound. It'th not thunny, Puk."

"It's a little funny."

Voya growled again. For a moment, Puk thought the ujath might finally enact his revenge for being unceremoniously thrown off a boat. Better not to instigate further.

"Okay, look. I'll make a deal with you. I don't know why you think raising these little tykes won't be worthwhile with all the profit you'll make off their nasty little mouths when they're older, but I'll take 'em off your hands. As long as you help us with something first."

The ujath was plainly desperate. "Name your prithe," he said without hesitation.

"The price is this: we need to hire some mercenaries, and I know you know the best in town. Am I wrong?"

"Not wong," said Voya, "but what do you need them thor?"

"Something important, which is why we need your most trustworthy. No backhanded deals where they'll turn around and fuck us over right when the job is done. Or if you don't know anyone like that personally, at least point us in the direction where we can maybe find some."

"If I find thomeone you can twutht, you'll take thethe thingth?" Voya wanted to verify, using his tongue to gesture toward the energetic cordols wrestling on his floor amongst debris.

"Yes," said Puk, lying to his friend's face. His face split into a grin and he almost broke into a laugh, so it was lucky for him Voya had no eyes.

"How many do you need?"

"I dunno. Four? Five?"

Voya pursed his lips as much as he could around his hulking tongue. He said, "Thine. Le'th go." He scuttled past Puk and Kali then out the door, not bothering to wait for them.

They slipped out into the Mass, closing the door behind them while the cordols banged into more of Voya's precious possessions.

The ujath led them a few rings deeper into the Mass. As they navigated the crowd, Kali asked Puk, "Where's he taking us?"

"I'm not sure exactly," he answered. "I know there are a few mercenary crews in the city and they all have their own bases, but I dunno where any are 'cause I've never needed one. The ones who work solo tend to just hang around bars and shit. I figure he's takin' us to one of the bases he's got connections to."

The building Voya stopped in front of identified itself as the home of The Ziolo's Tusks. He lifted the end of his tongue into the air, waving it around the sign, checking that it was the correct place.

"Here," he then said, reaching to open the door.

The three entered, and every person inside turned to get a good look at them.

The base had the feel of a travelers' outpost, though with more modern and higher quality furnishings. Various monsters' heads were mounted on the walls, their mouths hanging open in vicious snarls. Men and women were lounging on sofas in the middle of the room, while others stood in an open kitchen area cooking and chatting. Exasperated grunts and groans of those training could be heard from another unseen room.

"Hey there, Voya," said a tall, thick man sporting a scar that ran down the length of his neck. "Who're your friends here?"

"'Fwendth' is a bit of a thtweth," said Voya sourly. "That'th Puk, and the'th...well, I don' remember her name."

"Kali," she introduced herself to the man.

"I'm Jon Hoskings, head of the Tusks. Pleasure to meet you, ma'am." He bowed, which Puk found exceptionally off-putting.

Voya cut to the point. "I atthume you have four or five people you could par' with for the nigh'?"

Hoskings nodded, flashing a smile at Kali. "Sure do. What's the job?"

The ujath allowed Puk to speak for himself. "You know Haratti?" the qarm asked.

"Sure."

"Great. Well, we're about to go sell him something, and we wanna steal it back right after. We need some brawn to jump his goons after we make the exchange and grab the item for us."

Voya's jaw would have dropped if it were possible. "Oh, thuck off," he muttered. "You can' be theriouth. You're gonna double-crotth Hawa'i?"

"Yes."

"I thould not have bwought you here."

Hoskings cheerfully laughed at the exchange. The man was unperturbed by the arrangement. "Haratti's got a hell of a rep-utation," he said, a faint frown etching onto his face. "Everyone in Myrisih is smart enough to let him and his crew operate with-out any pushback. They ain't the hardest crew on the island, but screwin' with them ain't the smartest choice."

Puk frowned as well. Getting the mercenary band on board was vital. He and Kali had narrowly escaped a few scuffles, but they were no match for Haratti.

"You're a thtupid man," said Voya to Puk.

The qarm shot him a sarcastic smile, which Voya reciprocated, exposing a row of jagged, discolored teeth hanging above his massive tongue.

"Voya's right," Puk went on, "I am a stupid man. But…"

He trailed off, not sure if appealing to Hoskings's moral code would do them any favors. He did not know the man at all, so it was entirely possible he had no moral code beyond "whatever gets me paid is good."

But he decided to give it a shot. "Haratti's dealing with some bad shit here. I know that's his whole thing, but this is badder shit than usual, I'd wager. Like 'start a war' type of bad shit."

Hoskings grinned. "Truth be told, wars are good for the mercenary business."

Shit, Puk thought before muttering it aloud.

Kali piped up. "Fair enough," she said. "But you know what else is good for business?"

"What's that?" Hoskings asked her.

"Business."

They all waited for her to elaborate.

"Puk's not wrong. This stuff that Haratti's dealing with is really bad, and in all likelihood it could start a war. But it also might not. And even if it *does* start one, it might end it just as fast. It's some devastating shit that could maybe wipe you out in an instant. It's not something you wanna go up against." She did not tear her gaze from Hoskings, her voice strong and confident. "So maybe you'll get that war business later, or maybe not. Or maybe you'll get it and be killed before you ever get to spend the crescents. There's the potential for a big payday, sure, but there's the potential for none at all too. What we're offering is a guaranteed one. *Today.*"

Hoskings absorbed everything she had said and scoffed, the grin returning to his face. He asked, "If what he's peddling is so dangerous, why should I risk goin' up against it today? You're making a convincing argument to stay the hell away from whatever this is."

"He and his people don't know how to use it yet," Kali answered swiftly. "It's gonna take them—or whoever ends up with it—a lot of time to master it. Seems smart to me to take it from 'em before they can do a damn thing with it."

"Sounds like something my crew could use," said Hoskings.

"Doubt you want to," Puk said. "It's red magic. Nasty shit."

Hoskings shuddered at the mention of such magic. Its reputation preceded it. That fantasy was effectively shut down.

"Look," the man began, "you make a compelling argument. Like I said, Haratti's got a hell of a reputation in this city. But so do we. And between you and me, I don't like the man. I'd be happy to lend our swords to the cause and fuck him over."

"I was hoping you'd lend some guns, maybe," said Puk.

"Well, either way. For one night of work, four mercs will run you two thousand crescents. Five-hundred more for a fifth. That's with the friends and family discount," he winked.

"Money is no object," Puk said. "Voya said he'll handle all that. We'll take five."

Voya groaned, but did not object. The baby cordols had to truly be making his life hell for that price to be worth getting rid of them.

"Five it is," said Hoskings.

"Who've you got in mind?" Puk asked.

Hoskings held up a finger indicating for them to wait, then disappeared into the back room where others were training. He returned a minute later with four mercenaries in tow: one woman and three men.

"Beatrix?" said Kali.

The mercenary woman's face lit up at the sight of Kali. "Hey, it's you!" she shouted joyfully. "The girl who laid that scumbag out at the outpost!"

Kali laughed, and Puk rotated his stalks to eye her quizzically. He could not fathom how Kali possibly knew someone in Myrisih, but there would be time to expound on that story later.

"You two know each other?" Hoskings asked, precisely as confused as Puk.

"We've met," said Beatrix. "This girl can hold her own in a fight. Stabbed a guy in the arm who was trying to rob her in an outpost. Really fucked him up. I've still got his gun!"

The coincidence amazed Puk, and he couldn't keep quiet. "She was there when you stabbed that guy?"

Kali nodded with a smirk. "So this is your retirement?" she said to the woman.

"I told you it doesn't suit everyone," Beatrix winked.

"I told her she shoulda stabbed that guy in the dick," Puk told Beatrix.

The woman laughed heartily and said, "I would've enjoyed that, too."

"Tho," said Voya, "I take it they're twuthtworthy enough for you?"

"Yes," Kali answered confidently.

If Kali had faith in her buddy and the rest of the mercenaries, then that was good enough for Puk. He nodded as well.

Beatrix and the three men by her side asked Hoskings what the job was, and he quickly explained it was a simple bash-and-grab. Beatrix beamed and asked, "Where's this going down?"

Kali spoke up. "We want it done fast," she said. "Like, right when they carry it away from the meeting spot. Do you know where Haratti holes up?"

Hoskings shook his head. "He tends to keep his operation pretty well under wraps. Especially from mercs like us."

"It's a place down the alley behind the Rabid Dog," Puk explained. He described the building as best he could, then added, "If your guys are positioned somewhere near there, they should be able to spot us being led to the right place."

"Got it."

Kali said, "We'll go in, sell Haratti the item, get our money, and leave. Then I assume some time later, he'll need to transport it somewhere else, at which point you guys can swoop in and take it back. Or if they don't leave, would you be able to bust in and get it?"

"Sure," Hoskings nodded. "Doesn't make a difference to us so long as we're getting paid."

Voya was still flabbergasted by what he was hearing. "You're okay with thucking him over? You know he'th par' of—"

"I know perfectly well," Hoskings said, cutting him off. "You don't need to lay out the risks. I know what consequences there'll be. We'll do it."

"Please no killing, though," said Kali, surprising Puk. "Only if it's *absolutely* necessary, I guess. But I'd rather this not lead to bloodshed, if at all possible."

"Seems like a tall order, but we'll do our best," said Hoskings. "What's this object we're looking for?"

Kali replied, more to Beatrix than anyone else, "A book. Black, no title on the front."

"Ooh. Cryptic," Beatrix chuckled.

Hoskings wanted to know when they intended to make the sell, and Puk told the crew that they were planning on going over to the Rabid Dog right when they finished here. He said, "Our goal is to get the hell out of Myrisih tonight."

The man clucked his tongue. "That timing's gonna be tight. No exact schedule, but the port probably won't be open more than another hour or so. Maybe two."

"Are you sure you wanna do this tonight?" asked Beatrix.

"Or maybe not at all?" suggested Voya.

Kali was resolute. "Cutting it close is risky, but good," she said. "Honestly, we wanna give Haratti's crew the smallest window possible to catch us."

The mercenaries raising that concern made Puk somewhat apprehensive, however. He turned and asked Kali, "You sure?"

They could lay low for a few days, sort out the timeline more precisely. Though staying at Voya's free of charge was not an option, and he suddenly remembered their previous encounter with Thom, who might still be on the lookout for them.

"No," Kali said, "but I haven't been sure about any of this shit up to this point, so why switch things up now?"

Hoskings guffawed. He was a fan of Kali's gusto. Once again, Puk found the man repellant, but he certainly wanted his help in a tussle.

"Well, then tonight it is!" Hoskings declared. "We'll trail behind you over to the Rabid Dog. We'll keep our distance and station ourselves behind the bar to wait. We can all rendezvous back here afterwards."

Beatrix had a different plan in mind. "Why not meet down at the docks?" she proposed. "Seems like the best course of action, if they're trying to sail away before the city's closed. No time to waste."

Her leader nodded, and the plan was sealed.

All eight of them stepped outside, and Puk felt energized. Part of him was scared out of his mind, but the adrenaline spiking through his small body was giving him a nice kick.

"Before you go see Hawa'i and get yourthelf killed," said Voya, "come back to my houthe and take thothe damn cordolth with you."

"Sorry, bud, but I can't!" said Puk, jauntily skipping away. Kali took the cue and raced after him. "No time. We've got a meeting to catch!"

- -

On their route to the Rabid Dog, they passed countless lively bars, all of which had been closed the last time she'd walked the streets. She gazed in wonder at the different signage posted on each ramshackle establishment.

One particularly derelict place was named Kalganax's, with a squat rectangular sign hanging above its doorway with a crude painting depicting a man smashing a bottle over another man's head. Not the most enticing image, in Kali's opinion. She knew based on the name that the joint was owned by a centript, and her guess was that there was some kind of cultural misunderstanding and Kalganax figured, after observing many breaking out for little to no reason, that bar fights were a symbol of comradery and fun nights drinking with friends.

Another pub a few buildings down was named Crown & Anchor, with the two objects painted in loving detail on its door. It appeared to be more of a dining establishment, with chef's specials posted on a board outside.

Yet another was humbly named Bar, and not for the first time Kali found herself questioning how so many places to consume alcohol and eat greasy food could remain profitable in one city.

Soon they came upon the Rabid Dog, with its ferocious snarling sign and blood-red letters. The text on its sign felt ominous to her now. For a split second she thought the letters might be dripping with fresh paint, bleeding onto the path below, but it was only her imagination.

Keep your cool, she told herself.

Up ahead, Puk looked to be unfazed by their current errand. Either he had much more confidence in Hoskings's crew and the plan than she did, or he was more adept at hiding it. She could practically feel herself shaking in her boots.

If she was this nervous regardless, she could only guess how much of a wreck she would be if Beatrix wasn't involved. She hardly really knew her, but from their brief interaction back at the travelers' outpost, she felt a warmth and kindness from the woman. Something implicitly told Kali that she could be trusted.

Puk held the door open with his scrawny arm and grinned, saying, "After you."

But Kali did not enter the building. Puk stood there holding the door with a befuddled look. She said, "Are we sure about this? Like, *really* sure?" The prospect of handing over the book and subsequently failing to retrieve it never stopped gnawing at her.

"I thought so," Puk replied. "Are you not now? I thought we were pretty keen on getting paid a lot of money and also savin' the world or whatever. That sounds like a win-win to me."

"But we could just walk away right now, burn the damned book, and not endanger anybody. If we slip up and don't get it back…"

"We will," said Puk. "Not slip up, I meant we will get it back. Have a little faith in us. Let's go in there and cheat these sacks of shit. Don't that sound fun?"

She broke into a weak smile. "It does," she confessed.

People shuffled between them and into the bar, momentarily confused by a qarm holding the door open for them. Kali attempted to swallow her doubt and followed the patrons.

Inside, she shuddered at the violent murals adorning the walls all around her and scanned the animated room for their previous escort, Niska. The rail-thin woman with her spiked green hair would be easy to spot amongst the other ruffians, a collection of ujaths and rocyans and scarred jeorns. There was a woman sat at the piano in the back corner of the bar, banging on the keys and drunkenly crooning. Someone in the crowd yelled at her to shut up, and in turn, she informed them where they could shove their criticisms.

Niska was not behind the bar, which sent a pang of worry through Kali's chest. She wanted this business over and done with.

The constant anxiety was killing her. It had been for years, the unending concern over whether she could provide for herself and make something of her life. But over the past several weeks, the feeling had been compounded tenfold. The minute she reached Atlua, she would make her way to the prettiest beach with the clearest water and relax for a week straight. She needed to finally rest.

"There," she just barely heard Puk say behind her. She followed the line of his finger and spotted Niska attending to a group of centripts seated at a round table. They remained standing near the doorway (much to the irritation of a man who stumbled inside, tripping over his own feet and nearly toppling Puk), watching the woman work until she returned to the bar.

When she finally did, Puk was the one to initiate conversation. They stepped up to the counter, Puk hoisting himself onto a stool. His eyestalks curved downward and he shot Niska a smile.

"What?" she asked him, in no mood for any foolishness.

"Oh," the qarm mumbled. "Kinda thought you'd remember us. We ain't the most typical duo."

"I do," said Niska. She stared blankly at him.

Puk sighed, then asked, "Do I really gotta say it again? We gotta go through the song and dance?"

"The codes and precautions are in place for a reason."

"But you *know* us. You just said so."

"We're Voya's dipshit friends," Kali blurted out, wanting the exchange to hurry and proceed.

Puk irritably rolled his stalks back, and Niska grinned toothily. Her teeth were surprisingly a gleaming white.

"I'm goin' on a break!" she shouted to her fellow bartender, then led Kali and Puk outside. In the alleyway behind the Rabid Dog, their guide dropped an unexpected tidbit. "Haratti's gonna be shocked to see you," she laughed. "He thought for sure y'all were never gonna come back. Thought you'd get lost and die in the desert, or *not* get lost and die wherever he sent you. Where *did* he send you, by the way?"

"Out to some shitty town," Puk grumbled vaguely.

"Sounds about right. Shitty towns are where people like Haratti flourish. The guy he sent out there before you two came back a few days after y'all left, actually. Didn't receive a warm welcome."

Kali had no interest in being on the receiving end of Haratti's displeasure.

Conversation dried up after that. Niska brought them to the nondescript building Haratti used as headquarters and unlocked the door, ushering them into the darkened hallway. Down at the end on the left, the man's office was closed. Niska rapped her knuckles on the door and said, "Sir? The qarm and the faif are back."

There had been the faint sound of scribbling, which immediately stopped at Niska's words. "Let them in," came Haratti's croaking voice.

Niska pushed the door open and stood aside.

Like before, Haratti was sitting behind his impressively carved desk, jotting away in several opened notebooks. He looked more like an accountant than a crime boss.

Maybe that's all he is, really.

Haratti rubbed a gloved hand over his bald head and greeted his guests. The man's gray goatee was longer and messier than when they'd last met with him.

"You may leave," he told Niska. The woman said nothing and stepped out of the room, yanking the door shut behind her. "Take a seat," he then said to the pair.

They did as instructed.

No one spoke. Kali and Puk stared at Haratti, and his gaze shifted between the two of them. A shiver coursed through her.

"So," said Haratti, "I take it you have good news for me. I should hope so, anyway. Our previous hired hand did not bring good tidings, and, well…" He trailed off, leaving the rest to their imagination.

"We do," said Puk, always taking charge in Myrisih. Places like this were his domain. "We got the book."

Haratti's eyebrows shot up, his expression one of incredulity. His face wrinkled into a wry smile. "I would like to see it, please."

Puk motioned toward Kali, who swiftly extracted the book from her knapsack. She tossed it onto the desk in front of her and it landed with a thud, sending up a spray of dust.

The old man reached toward its enticing, mysterious black cover and pulled it closer. He opened it to the title page and his foul grin grew wider.

"I am impressed," he said, proceeding to flip through the first few pages. His eyes flicked up and down as he read the different disturbing spells and Kleus's notes scribbled in the margins. "Quite frankly, I did not anticipate you returning at all, let alone so soon."

"Yeah, well, we're impressive," said Puk. "Now, about the payment…"

She appreciated the qarm's boldness. Her leg bounced up and down, though she kept her heel from tapping on the floor. If Haratti noticed how nervous she was, he clearly did not care.

"A quick transaction. I can respect that," the man said, closing the leather-bound book. He made a quick note in his records before continuing. "First, I would like to ask you how Kleus Saix was disposed of."

Kali blinked. "We didn't 'dispose' him," she said. "He's still alive. We just stole the book from him."

Haratti considered this, then wrote something else down. "Okay," he said, drawing the word out. "That is good to know."

"Killing him wasn't part of the deal," Puk said. "It was ten thousand to get the book. You didn't say anything about having to kill the guy."

"Don't worry, little one," Haratti said, finishing his scrawling. The jab clearly annoyed Puk. "You will receive your full payment. I simply wanted to know the mage's current status, for my boss's sake. If he is going to have a skilled red mage seeking revenge on him, then that is information he would like to be privy to."

Puk shook his head and said, "Won't be any revenge. Not on y'all, anyways. I told him the High Mages sent me. Didn't mention you guys at all."

"That was wise. But why would the High Mages employ a qarm in hunting down a renegade mage?"

"I didn't completely flesh out the fiction," Puk said irritably, "but it was enough for him to believe. He's probably been paranoid thinkin' the mages would find him any day now for the past forty years, so he'd believe anything. Obviously. Can we get paid now?"

Kali piped up with a question of her own, though. She couldn't help herself. "What is your boss doing with the book?"

Puk's stalks shot to the left, wide-eyed in shock at her indiscretion.

Haratti laughed, the sound akin to a chicken being strangled. "That is none of your concern."

It was the ambiguous answer that she had expected, but still, it was a disappointment. In actuality, the only answer that would not have disappointed her was "He's going to destroy it," so she would have been let down no matter what Haratti said.

"Niska!" the man then called. The door creaked open and the woman peeked her vibrant head inside. Haratti held up *Malum* and said, "Please bring this to Banwe and have him and his people transport it. I take it you two will be able to find your way back without our lovely Niska's assistance, yes?" he asked Puk and Kali.

They both nodded.

Niska glided past Kali and grabbed the book, then disappeared once more. Kali listened as her footsteps grew quieter, eventually giving way to the opening and closing of a door.

Ideally, they would have been paid and long gone before Haratti sent the book off. His boss had to be pretty eager to get the ball rolling on their plans. Perhaps they already had a buyer on standby.

But that meant—

Kali swallowed. *Shit is going to get bad any second now.*

"Money," she sputtered.

Puk jumped in to support her. "Money," he echoed.

"Yes, yes, of course," said Haratti. He made another note, then called out, "Ilyi!"

A few seconds passed, then a muscular, green-and-orange faif with a shaved head burst through the doorway. "Yes?" he asked, his voice meek and wavering.

"Please fetch the payment for job code 111300. And be quick about it; our guests are in quite a hurry, it seems." He sneered.

Ilyi repeated the job number then scampered away. Maybe Haratti was not a glorified accountant after all, and this man was the person in charge of the finances.

Kali hoped the man was fast.

Every second felt like an eternity, sitting in Haratti's office waiting for Ilyi's return. Waiting to hear hell break loose in the alleyway as Beatrix and her squad descended on Banwe and his.

Why do none of our fucking plans ever go right?

Haratti stared at the two of them, his expression placid. It made her uneasy. The silence was worse than anything he could've said. Suddenly, he broke into a smile, and Kali was sure he suspected something was up.

But before her own suspicions were confirmed, Ilyi popped back into the room with a small pouch in hand, wound tied tightly shut. Haratti gestured toward Kali, and the buff man handed over the pouch.

"Twenty five-hundred crescent notes. Ten thousand crescents in total, as agreed. You may count them, if it would make you comfortable."

Kali untied the bag and peered inside. Her leg was shaking uncontrollably now as she failed to accurately count the money. Based on a quick glance, it all seemed to be in order. Given their current circumstances, that would suffice for her.

"Looks good," she said, her throat dry. She slipped the pouch into her own bag with an unsteady hand.

"Excellent," said Haratti, clapping his hands together. "Well, it was a pleasure doing business with you. Maybe we'll meet again someday."

Puk scooted off his chair and said, "No offense, but I hope not."

Kali stood as well and turned to walk out the door, where Ilyi stood dumbly overlooking the room. She imagined he was the type of underling who required strict instruction, and he had not been explicitly told to leave yet.

Suddenly there came a crash outside the building, and then chaotic shouts. Haratti perked up, glancing in the direction from which the sound had come, then back to the pair standing before him.

"What is that?" he asked them.

Neither answered.

Instead, Puk opted to climb back up on his chair, turn to face Haratti, and then leap forward over the desk, yelping like a crazed animal.

CHAPTER XXI

HARMLESS

Puk collided with Haratti's bald head, propelling the man backward and slamming him into the wall. The two tumbled to the ground, a streak of blood left behind like an arrow pointing down at the man's slumped body.

"Humph?" Haratti tried pushing out words, but they were muffled and incomprehensible. Puk was sprawled on his chest, with his eyestalks wrapped like a sticky blue noose around the old man's thin, wrinkled neck. Haratti then managed to ask again, "What is happening?" Blood dribbled from his split lip.

"Gotta go," Puk said, unwrapping himself and hopping up off the ground. He went to take a step, but Haratti was cognizant enough to seize his legs.

The qarm was sent tumbling to the ground, reaching his hands out to break his fall, when a *pang!* screeched through the small room.

He had not managed to catch himself, instead smashing his face on the dirty carpet. There was a stinging pain in his left hand, intense yet dulled somehow, like something prevented him from fully feeling it. With his face still planted on the floor, fluffs of carpet sticking to his lips, he curved his stalks upward to look at his hand.

There was a hole in it.

Puk rolled onto his back and held his battered hand above his head. The wound was ragged, with bits of flesh hanging down into the hole, which dripped blood onto his face. He could see the ceiling through his hand.

"Blood," he murmured. Then, *"There's blood here!"*

Haratti pounded a fist into Puk's torso, winding him. Another gunshot rang out, and Puk suddenly realized he was unaware of Kali's location or living status.

"Kali!" he wheezed, just before Haratti punched him in the gut a second time.

"Busy, Puk!" came her curt reply.

So she was still alive. That was something.

Next, there came a thump and a clatter, which Puk prayed were noises associated with Ilyi being tackled and Ilyi dropping his gun.

Haratti landed yet another punch, and Puk decided he should probably start moving if he wanted to make it out of this room alive. He sat up and lurched forward, hole-hand first, slapping it directly onto Haratti's face.

The man let out a startled, disgusted scream as Puk rubbed the bloody wound all over his cheeks, his eyes, his mouth.

Is his nose in my hand hole?

The thought chilled him and he removed his hand, rising and stumbling backward while Haratti was preoccupied with wiping the red grime off his face.

Puk clumsily made his way around the desk and saw Kali straddling Ilyi's body, repeatedly punching him in the face as he struggled to shove her off. She glanced over her shoulder and asked, "Little help?"

Without hesitation, Puk raced toward them and started rubbing his bloody hand on Ilyi's face as well, streaking the man's bright green skin with muted red. Ilyi immediately let go of Kali and started swatting at Puk, who laughed.

He had to find pleasure in the situation while he could, because he was all too aware that once the shock wore off, the pain would be incredible.

From behind the desk, Haratti let out a roar and pulled himself up off the ground. Blood covered the front and back of his head, and the old man's breathing was stilted.

"You're worthless, Ilyi!" he shouted, observing his lackey flailing on the floor while a qarm made a grisly finger-painting on his face.

Haratti yanked open a drawer in his desk. The sliding sound of the wood on its track alerted both Puk and Kali, who knew he could only be reaching for one thing.

Sure enough, Haratti leveled a gun at them and fired almost instantly.

But the man was dazed and angry and his aim was shaky. The bullet pierced the right side of the doorframe, whizzing past Puk's head.

Now that Ilyi's nose had also penetrated his hand hole—as well as the fact that Haratti was shooting at them—Puk decided it was now well past time to split.

He stood and darted out of the room, trusting that Kali was following his lead and still had possession of her knapsack. As he sprinted down the unlit hallway, he rotated one stalk around to see that she was close behind and indeed had her bag strapped over her shoulder. Their money was secure.

Puk, being somewhat delirious from his shock and blood loss, temporarily forgot that knobs needed to be turned in order to open doors, and so he careened into the exit at full speed and promptly crumpled to the floor in a foolish heap.

His vision darkened, and he willed himself not to black out. He had experienced his fair share of blackouts in the past, and they were all in good fun, but now was not the time.

Kali tugged him up off the dingy carpet as Haratti staggered out of his office. This time around, he did not bother stopping to make a proclamation or ask a question. He simply fired his gun.

But his aim was still poor due to the blood dripping from his brows and obscuring his vision. Wood splintered above their heads and rained down on them.

For a moment, Puk felt proud of his ingenuity and improvisation skills, but then the pain set in.

He screamed loudly.

He then clutched his hand to his chest and screamed loudly again.

Kali ignored his cries and pushed the door open, accidentally stepping on his foot when he did not move out of the way. She apologized amid the chaos, but then grabbed him by his shirt and jerked him out of the building. Ilyi appeared beside his boss, aiming his gun at the pair with what was surely much greater accuracy.

Things were no less hectic outside.

They burst onto the scene to find Hoskings and his crew of Tusks still brawling with Banwe and his men, of which there were six, including Niska. The woman always acted nice enough, so it was unfortunate she had been pulled into their mess, though Puk had to remind himself that anyone who willingly worked with Haratti couldn't be all that great of a person.

"Don't draw attention to us," Kali whispered. "Wait. But move."

She stood on the other side of the door, the side it would open from, and Puk stared blankly at her. His dizzied mind could not comprehend what her contradictory instruction meant or what she was waiting for.

"Move," she urged him again, but stood still herself, and so Puk remained still as well.

After a few seconds, the door swung open. The unforgiving wood connected with Puk and sent him careening toward the ensuing scuffle, effectively drawing attention to their presence. As he flew through the air, Puk remembered that was the opposite of what they wanted to happen.

Kali stuck to her plan, though, and got the jump on Ilyi, who emerged from the building with his pistol drawn. She hit the man in his already-swollen face and latched onto his arm. He impulsively pulled the trigger, sending a bullet digging into the cavern floor. She wrestled the gun from him and smacked its grip into his nose. The appendage crumpled and leaked profusely.

A shot rang out from Haratti's gun, but it pierced Ilyi's backside. The faif screamed in agony. It was a bad day to be an accountant. Kali then pushed him backward into the hall, sending him tripping over himself, and slammed the door shut again.

"Fuck?" Puk sputtered on the ground, gazing up at the drab cavernous ceiling above with its dangling stalactites, unsure why he formed the word as a question.

Every single part of his body ached, but if he had to make a top three list, third place would go to his foot, then his face, and the top prize would be his hand. It was a bad day to be a failed musician.

And then Niska appeared seemingly out of thin air and kicked him in the side, sending him rolling over from his back onto his stomach. His torso might soon overtake his foot on the list.

I wish I had a gun, he thought, *so that I could shoot people with it.*

He shakily rose and was instantly kicked in the back by Niska. His thought as he flew through the air for the umpteenth time that night was that her dirty boot surely left a print on his shirt.

Puk skidded along the ground, scraping his eyes on bits of rock. He then finally relented, giving in to the inviting dark.

- -

There was nothing with which she could barricade the door.

Kali floundered for several moments, trying to find anything at all that might work, but had to give up. Ilyi and Haratti would inevitably be joining the fray, and she would not be able to pull off a second surprise attack.

She turned in time to witness Niska landing an impressive kick in Puk's back, sending the qarm springing forward and thumping face-first onto the hard ground.

Kali raced forward, tackling the green-haired woman to the ground. She pinned Niska's arms with her knees, rifling through her knapsack while the woman struggled underneath.

She had just grabbed the dagger and pulled it from its sheath when Niska spit on her. The action flustered her and she almost instinctively backed off the woman, but she caught herself and flashed the blade of her antique dagger. Niska's eyes widened in terror.

No part of Kali intended to murder anyone. She had participated in many dicey activities as of late, but that was a line she was unwilling to cross.

She was not above stabbing someone if needed, though. Jeth could gladly attest to that.

A swift slice downward, impaling one of Niska's upper arms, followed by the other. Removing the blade from the flesh took more effort than Kali anticipated. The blade desperately needed to be sharpened.

Niska screamed, and Kali hoped the two wounds would be enough to impede her mobility and efficiency in the fight.

Kali left Niska to flail on the ground and ran over to where Puk lay prostrate. She flipped him over to find he was unconscious. His left hand was completely caked in blood.

She heard footsteps fast approaching and swiveled her head to see Niska racing toward her. The woman could barely lift her arms, but Kali had seen the damage she could do with a swift kick.

And that was precisely what Niska intended to do. She stopped short and raised her leg in a wide swing, but Kali was ready and held up the sharp side of her blade. Niska's leg plowed right into it, cutting through the fabric of her pants and tearing into her skin.

She yelped and crashed to the ground, drawing her leg up to her chest, rocking back and forth. "You bitch!" she shouted, hoarse.

Kali shrugged.

A ways away on her left, the door to Haratti's headquarters opened and the old man tottered out, waving his gun frantically in search of a target. Ilyi's body was slouched by the doorway, unmoving.

"Kill them, you incompetent fucks!" Haratti screamed as he observed the alleyway clash taking place. This had to be the most chaotic his business had ever been on his home turf.

Kali took a moment to check in on the fight as well.

None of the Tusks were dead, though Hoskings was sporting a nasty bullet hole in his right shoulder. That did not stop him from swinging his mace into a bulky jeorn's gut, however. One of the male Tusks also appeared to be missing a finger, but Kali could not be sure if he'd entered the fray like that or if it was a result of the battle.

Beatrix looked a bit roughened up, but was otherwise uninjured. Her face and clothes were speckled with dirt and blood that Kali ventured to guess was not her own.

The woman noticed Kali staring and ran toward her, gun drawn. It looked a lot better in her hand than in Jeth's. As she reached Kali, she raised the pistol and cocked it, aiming at Niska's head.

"No!" Kali shouted without any thought. "Don't kill anyone! Please! Just—"

She did not need to say any more. Beatrix kneeled down and whacked Niska on the head, knocking her out cold.

"Yes," Kali said. "That."

"What about him?" Beatrix asked, bobbing her head in Haratti's direction. "Can I kill him? Would do the world a lot of good, I'd wager."

Kali shook her head. This whole mess was her fault, and she did not want any more blood on her hands. Even Warren Haratti's.

Beatrix shrugged, not caring either way. She was simply happy to revel in the violence. She barreled toward Haratti, who was still mesmerized by the bedlam between his men and the Tusks. At the last second, he faced Beatrix—who was charging with the ferocity of a wild lamatka—and got off one round before the massive woman sent him crashing back into the building.

Kali winced watching the old man's frail body twist and crumple as he rolled backwards over his henchman and through the hall.

Beatrix stood upright, closing the door once again before examining the wound in her leg. Haratti truly was a terrible shot.

She ran past her fighting brethren and crouched beside Kali, who was amazed by the woman's resolve in spite of the gushing wound in her leg. "You two should get out of here," said Beatrix.

"Where's the book?" Kali asked. One problem at a time; she could figure out how to get Puk to the docks after.

Beatrix didn't know. Kali crawled toward Niska's unconscious body and rummaged through her belongings, but the woman didn't have a pocket or anything else sufficiently big enough to carry the tome. She had to have already handed it off to Banwe or one of the others.

She peered at the raging battle and saw that two men lay unmoving on the ground. It was impossible to tell whether they were passed out or dead. Either way, neither of them was her ally.

"Puk's knocked out," she told Beatrix. "I think he's too heavy for me to carry. I'm sure you could, but your leg…"

"I'll be fine," the woman said, waving away the thought. "Let's get to the docks."

I need the book.

"You get going," Kali told her. With the injury and Puk's added weight, it would take her a considerable amount of time to reach Myrisih's port, and every second counted. Preparations might already be underway to close them off for the next few days. There was also no time to wait for the fight to cease and for Hoskings to bring the book to her.

With that, she sprinted forward. Beatrix called to her from Puk's side, but the woman obeyed her and did not follow, lifting the qarm's limp body in her arms and taking off down the opposite end of the alley, back toward the Rabid Dog.

This is a bad idea, Kali told herself, adding it to the ever-growing list of bad ideas she and Puk shared.

She did not have a real plan. She sped past Hoskings, who was wrestling a bald faif woman to the ground, and leapt onto the back of a grizzled, bearded oaf who was reloading his gun. The man fumbled around, trying to shake Kali off his back, but failed. She stabbed her dagger into the man's shoulder, again and again, cringing with each roar of pain he unleashed.

The bear of a man seemed the most authoritative to Kali, due largely in part to how obscenely massive his body was, so she assumed that maybe he was Banwe. Banwe the Bear had a nice folktale sort of ring to it.

"What in the—?" the man bellowed, finally flinging Kali from his back. Her dagger remained upright in his shoulder. He reached for the weapon and turned to face his attacker, a demented glare in his eye.

He bore down on her, dagger in one hand and gun in the other. Kali hoped against hope that he had not gotten the chance to finish reloading.

The bear raised the dagger and flung it through the air like a throwing knife. It swiped past Kali's head, bouncing harmlessly off the cavern floor. Before she could reach for it, the man pounced on top of her, squeezing all the air from her lungs.

She could not move an inch under the man's colossal weight. He leaned down only an inch or two from her face, and she inhaled the rancid, rotten stench of his breath as he panted over her.

"You're wily," the man said with a grin. He was missing two of his upper teeth, and the others were a color somewhere between yellow and brown.

"And you're Banwe?" Kali coughed. She tried recovering from the man's horrid breath, but it was not easy.

In response, she received a harsh slap in the face. Her cheek flushed and her vision doubled for a second before coming back into focus. "Don't matter who I am," the man growled.

"Yeah, I guess you *don't* matter," Kali taunted.

Predictably, he raised his arm to slap her again. The shift in his weight gave her just enough room to wriggle underneath his hulking body and bring a knee to his groin.

The man groaned and keeled over, freeing her. She scrambled for her dagger and jabbed it into the bear's hand before he could fire off a round. He dropped the gun with a clatter, which she picked up and aimed at his clenched face.

"Give me the book," she ordered him.

"Ain't got the fuckin' book," he grumbled.

Kali cocked the gun. The man laughed at the faint click.

He said, "Don't matter if you shoot me or not. Not gonna change the fact I ain't got the fuckin' book."

She groaned and went to smack him in the head with the hilt, but he rushed forward and brought her back to the ground. In the struggle, her finger pulled the trigger, and the gunshot blared in the man's ear as it fired into the ceiling. He yelled angrily, clasping his injured, bloody hand to his ear, and fumbled backward.

Kali took the opportunity to jump up and run away. She saw Hoskings had finished dealing with his faif assailant, and Kali breathlessly asked him, "Do you have the book?"

He flashed a smug grin and pulled *Malum* out from a pouch slung across his chest. Kali quickly snatched it from his possession. She was about to take off without another word, but Hoskings stopped her to ask, "Have you seen Beatrix?"

"She's bringing Puk to the docks. I've gotta go. Thanks for—"

"She's hurt," Hoskings interrupted. "I saw Haratti shoot her. Give her this." He reached into his pouch again and handed her a small glass vial filled with a bright blue liquid.

Kali wordlessly took the potion and stuffed it along with the book into her own knapsack, then raced toward the Rabid Dog. Over her shoulder, she saw Hoskings rearing up to square off with the bear.

Sounds of the battle echoed through the otherwise unoccupied alleyway. Kali soon reached the back door of the bar, and took a second to check that no one was on her tail.

The coast was clear.

All of Haratti's goons were too worried about the vicious Ziolo's Tusks to bother chasing after some harmless, unassuming faif girl.

She dashed through the crowded bar, shoving past agitated patrons and cantankerous drunks on her way out the door. She thought someone might have called after her, but she ignored them and pressed on.

It was then she realized her understanding of Myrisih's geography was spotty at best. If she was currently in the Mass, then the docks would be...

This way, she hoped, mentally charting her course. Her sense of direction couldn't fail her now.

She turned down the next outer ring and spotted Beatrix limping not too far ahead, with Puk bouncing on her back.

"Beatrix!" she yelled. The woman stopped and turned, beaming. She waited for Kali to catch up.

"Did you get the book?" Beatrix asked once Kali reached her. She still held Puk aloft.

Kali nodded. "This too," she said, extracting the potion vial from her bag. "Special delivery from Hoskings."

"Thank you," said Beatrix, popping off the cork and chugging the luminescent liquid. "Certainly helps with the pain. What do I owe ya?" she joked.

"That one's on the house," Kali grinned.

Together, they ran the rest of the way to the docks. The potion vastly improved Beatrix's pace, though it was not strong enough to fully close the wound and stanch the bleeding. Kali let the mercenary lead the way, and soon they were clambering down the makeshift pier toward a panicky Zenib.

"Took you long enough!" the centript shouted. "The fuck's going on *here*?" he then asked, spying Puk on Beatrix's back.

"No time," said Kali, rushing past him.

"You're tellin' me!" Zenib grunted, scampering to keep up with the two women. "They're closing the place down any minute now. I already signed all the paperwork to get us out, but they still said—"

Whether or not Zenib finished his rambling sentence, Kali didn't hear it. Her heart was pounding in her ears, drowning out all else. She was almost to Zenib's boat, and that was all that mattered.

The *Fiery Lass* had never looked so beautiful, bobbing in the water.

She came to a skidding halt before the boat. While Beatrix eased Puk into the vessel, Kali unclasped her knapsack and double-checked that *Malum* was inside. A downright deafening groan of relief escaped her lips at the sight of the black leather book.

She could positively not wait to get rid of the damned thing.

Beatrix stepped back out of the boat once Puk was safely positioned, and Zenib lumbered in next. He looked up at Kali expectantly.

"Tick tock," he chittered.

"I have to go," Kali said to Beatrix.

"Get going, then," the mercenary smiled.

"Thank you for all your help. Really. And please tell the others, too." She then added, "Even Voya, though I doubt he wants to hear anything about us again for as long as he lives."

"No, he does not seem especially fond of you two," Beatrix laughed. Her expression then turned grave and she said, "He needs to get to a doctor, like, an hour ago." She nodded toward Puk.

"Another reason to *tick tock*!" said Zenib.

Kali ignored his nonsensical urging, though he was right. She leaned forward and wrapped Beatrix in a tight hug.

"Thanks," she said again.

"No problem." They separated and Beatrix told her, "If you're ever in Myrisih again, come find the Tusks and hang out a while."

Kali couldn't stop herself from laughing at the prospect of ever returning to Myrisih. It still wasn't even a guarantee she would make it out alive this time around. She wouldn't take her chances coming back.

"Maybe we can meet at an outpost somewhere instead," she suggested.

Zenib was chittering anxiously to himself when Kali finally ducked into the boat. With her help, he pushed off and the *Fiery Lass* was on its way out of Myrisih at long last.

They drifted past the floating Varedan ships and into the entry channel. Kali's heart raced and she unconsciously held her breath as they swerved through the winding canal, finally reaching the end.

Ahead, all she could see was blackness.

Blackness blanketed with stars that glimmered sweetly, reflecting in the gentle sea below.

The gate was open.

Zenib worked the oars tirelessly until they passed through the archway and out into the open waters of the Loranos Gulf.

"We made it," Kali uttered, finally breathing again, not totally believing it even as she said it aloud.

"I can't wait to get paid," Zenib said behind her. Then, "Is he gonna be alright?" Kali was mildly surprised by the concern in his tone.

She looked down at Puk, who lay battered at the bottom of the boat, dripping blood onto its planks from his injured hand. But for now, he was still breathing steadily. That was promising.

"I think so," Kali answered. "We just need to get back as soon as possible."

"That's what I've been saying," said Zenib, "but you two sure took your time getting back to the boat, didn't you?"

Kali nodded. "We had a bit of a hiccup," she said.

As they coursed through the waters and the dark night, Myrisih's winding canals faded from her memory. Shortly, she would be unable to remember anything about what the island looked like, or where it was in the vast Loranos Gulf.

And that was fine by her.

CHAPTER XXII

THE FLOWER AND THE FROG

It was early morning, the moon still hanging longingly in the sky, when they knocked anxiously on Eva's front door.

To her credit, the woman did not immediately scream at the sight of Kali, battered and bruised, propping up a bloodied and unconscious qarm with the help of a mold-ridden centript.

Instead, she asked, "Kali, are you...? What's—?"

"He needs your help," Kali said, nodding her head toward Puk. "He's lost a lot of blood and he might have a concussion, I don't know."

"Come in," said Eva, moving aside.

Kali and Zenib rushed in, navigating to the living room and gently placing Puk down to rest on the couch.

The two moved aside and Eva stepped closer, lifting the qarm's bloody hand. She began to gesture with her own, and the dried blood liquefied, dripping down onto Puk's dirtied clothes. Eva then began casting a new spell, which slowly sealed the hole in his limp hand.

It had been several years since the woman had practiced white magic in a clinic, but she had clearly not lost her touch.

"Is he going to be okay?" Kali asked.

Eva frowned. "It's a bit soon to tell," she answered truthfully. "He seems alright for the moment, but there's no telling for sure until he regains consciousness."

There came soft but audible footsteps from above, and soon Eva's wife Violet appeared on the nearby staircase, a powder blue robe wrapped around her slim figure.

She was much more taken aback by the sight than her wife had been. "What in the hell is all this?" she demanded to know, before nodding at Kali and saying, "Hi, Kali. It's been a while."

"Yes," Kali said, offering a weak smile. "I'm sorry to intrude…"

"Speaking of," said Zenib, "I should…leave here." He scuttled back toward the entryway, but stopped to tell Kali, "You can bring me my payment tomorrow. Or make Puk do it when he wakes up." She could sense a tinge of sad hopefulness on the centript's words. He nodded his crimson head in farewell to them, then ducked outside.

Eva waved her hands over Puk's body, wiggling her fingers and gesturing wildly to cast more spells on the beaten qarm. When she finished, she said, "This doesn't look like the result of a normal business trip."

Kali sighed.

"You're not wrong," she admitted. There was no reason to conceal the truth anymore, least of all after banging on the woman's door in the dead of night pleading for help.

All three of them had been jolted into wakefulness, so Violet prepared some coffee and they seated themselves around the kitchen table. With a warm mug in hand, Kali set to regaling the entirety of their scheme, starting with the egg heist.

The women were shocked by the confirmed existence of Myrisih and Pontequest, and Violet particularly enjoyed the portion about stealing Bella from the too-forward jeorn at the outpost. They gasped in awe at her prowess in the night's scuffle, which already seemed a world away. Kali could scarcely believe it had been mere hours before.

At the conclusion of her story, Eva assured her that they could stay at the house for as long as needed. She would continue watching over Puk and administer any necessary treatments until he awoke.

"Thank you," Kali said, her voice cracking. "You two are far too generous. Really, I don't deserve this, but I truly appreciate it."

"Nonsense!" Eva smiled. "You're always welcome here."

Less than five minutes later, the boys were racing down the stairs, demanding they be fed breakfast. Eva and Violet got to work cooking, with which Kali offered to assist.

"You're exhausted," Violet said, chuckling. "You've been up all night. Go upstairs and get some sleep in the guest room. It'll do you a world of good."

That much was true. Her muscles ached and her head was pounding. She could collapse and sleep soundly right there on the kitchen floor. A nice bed sounded better, though.

She thanked the two women again, said goodbye to the boys, and marched upstairs to the guest bedroom. She practically threw herself onto the bed and was asleep before she could even pull herself underneath the sheets.

The next day saw no change in Puk's condition.

Kali had slept through most of the day and enjoyed a nice dinner with Eva's family that night, unaware of how hungry she'd been. She then slept again until morning, and the first thing she did upon waking was check on her companion.

She fretted over him for a few hours before Eva suggested that getting some fresh air might do her some good. "I'll keep a close eye on him," she assured Kali with a kind smile.

It probably was a good idea for her to get out, so Kali made herself presentable then left the house to wander for a while. Her hair was pulled taut in a high ponytail, swinging carefree with each step she took.

The ocean waves lapping against the docks could be heard from where she walked in Restick's arts district, heading north toward the gulf. It was then she realized she had not gone outside at all since appearing at Eva's doorstep, and the sunlight on her skin was amazingly refreshing. She felt reinvigorated.

Kali zoned out while walking the streets, letting her feet automatically guide her wherever they saw fit. When she snapped out of her daze, she discovered they had brought her to the docks. Already eager to travel. Never resting.

I wonder...

The thought had come to her out of the blue. She was planning on resting the entire day, waiting for Puk to finally awaken, but she was already at the docks.

It wouldn't hurt to look. Just in case.

She walked over to the nearest worker, a man lugging unmarked crates off a ship and onto the pier one by one. With some trepidation, she asked, "Excuse me? Do you happen to know a merchant named Zara?" She hoped she was correctly remembering the name Vonoshreb had given her so long ago.

The man grunted and shook his head no. She moved on to someone else, asking the same question. The process repeated up and down the docks, until finally someone perked up at the mention of Zara's name.

"Oh, sure," the girl nodded. She couldn't be more than twenty years old, but already her skin was weathered by the sun. "Her ship's the *Yawning Cat*. Flag's pretty much what you'd expect it to be."

Kali exuberantly thanked the young woman and set to peering at every flag she could spy at the docks. She wandered down the glistening bones of Seroo's tail, which swayed gently in the calm waves, seeking out some sort of feline flag fluttering in the sea breeze.

Finally, near the end of the dock just short of where the aeon's bones dipped downward into the water, she spotted it.

A modest but mighty ship floating in the gulf, with a green flag flying proudly at the top of its mast. On it was stitched a white cat with blue eyes and its mouth stretched in a satisfying yawn.

Kali's heart momentarily stopped beating. Part of her couldn't really believe that she was standing there, before Zara's ship, with the crescents she needed to embark on a voyage to Atlua.

Back in that Yspleash inn, the whole concept had been little more than a dream. Something far off, something intangible, always an inch out of her grasp.

But now she clutched it. Tight.

It was real.

She spied a woman up on the ship's deck, authoritatively shouting orders at men and women scurrying about. Some were tending to the ship, others were hefting boxes to and fro.

The woman had to be Zara. She had short, white hair that hung down in front of her face, with the sides shaved close to her scalp. Kali briefly wondered whether she could pull off such a hairstyle. Zara was absolutely making it work for her.

Kali apprehensively sauntered across the gangplank, sliding out of the way of Zara's employees as they huffed past her. She stopped when she reached the deck, staring creepily at Zara a few feet away.

It did not take long for the jeornish captain to notice her. "Can I help you?" she asked Kali. "Sorry to say most of our stock's accounted for already, but I might be able to find you what you need." Her voice was silky and strong.

Kali stood blinking like a fool for a second before finding her voice. She coughed and said, "I'm not looking to buy."

Zara gave her a curious look.

Why are you being so awkward? Calm down, act normal.

The past couple weeks had all been leading up to this moment. In truth, nearly her entire adult life had been. She was simply at a loss for words. Once more, she reminded herself this wasn't a dream.

She said, "I heard you travel to Atlua."

Zara nodded and smiled. "That's right," she said. As if reading Kali's mind, she asked, "You lookin' to book a trip?"

Kali nodded, saying nothing.

"Well, I think you can buy a ticket somewhere over there," Zara said, pointing off in the distance at the other end of the dock. "Plenty of Herrilockian ships coming and going."

"I was hoping to specifically ride with you," Kali said, only recognizing after the words escaped her lips how creepy they sounded. "I—sorry—the thing is, I'm a merchant too. Nowhere near your level, but..." she trailed off. Finding her footing again, she continued, "I was talking with someone who bought from you, a centript named Vonoshreb, and he—sorry, okay, I'm rambling, sorry—the point is, I would love to ride with you and learn from you. And, more than anything, I'd love to see Atlua."

She held her breath, watching the woman's reaction. Zara's face was a blank slate as she processed the faif's inane words.

"You—"

"I can pay my own way," Kali cut her off. "That's no problem."

Zara grinned. "You're weird, but I like you. What's your name?"

You didn't introduce yourself first, you idiot?

"Kali," she said, embarrassed.

"I'm Zara," said the woman, holding out her hand. Kali shook it and smiled. Her tension eased ever so slightly.

"I know," she said, doing nothing to help assuage the assumption that she was a creep.

Zara brushed the comment aside and said, "I'd be glad to have you on board. We're leaving in two days, if that works for you. Two hundred crescents should be able to cover food and everything else for you, assuming you can help carry the load around here and work a bit. Sound fair?"

"Totally fair," Kali beamed. One part did not work for her, though. "I need to make a trip first, though," she said, frowning. "I can't really leave in two days." The errand was an idea that had occurred to her during her walk to the docks, and she couldn't shake it. But she needed to run it by Puk when he awoke.

The captain shrugged, blowing her hair out of her face. "No big deal. We'll be back again in a few weeks and you can hop on then. How's that sound?"

"Perfect," said Kali. With her confidence somewhat boosted, she said, "Can I ask one more thing?"

484 · travis m. riddle

"I'm all ears."

"I've got this friend who's trying to get to Atlua too. Is there enough room on board for him?"

"If he's got two hundred crescents and can clean dishes or scrub decks, then he's welcome aboard."

Kali hadn't stopped smiling. Soon she would strain her facial muscles. "Thank you so much," she exhaled.

In that moment, it was as if all the stress of her life suddenly rushed out of her body and crashed into the sea. Washed away, indistinguishable from the water lapping up against the *Yawning Cat*'s hull.

"I should get back to barkin' orders," said Zara, "but I'll see you in three weeks, yeah?"

Kali nodded. "Definitely."

The sun beat down on her, sinking into the pastel swirls of her skin. She caught herself nearly skipping down the gangplank.

- -

When Puk awoke, his eyelids fluttering open with drowsiness, he found himself in a distressingly familiar environment.

"Why the fuck am I here?" was the first thing he said once he found his voice again.

He was propped up with his head on a pillow on Eva's lavender velvet sofa. The fabric was amazingly soft against his skin, and he felt as if he were laying on a cloud. He felt absurdly comfortable, but had intended never to enter this woman's home again.

"Because you needed to rest," came an answer from a woman Puk had never seen before.

She was sitting in a plush armchair nearby reading a novel, which she bookmarked and placed closed on the side table. Her hair was long and luscious, a slightly wavy brunette. Her face was thin with sharp features, her skin dark in contrast with the powder blue robe she wore.

"And please do not use coarse language," the woman added.

"Sorry," Puk apologized. "I guess you're, uh…" He was ashamed to have forgotten Eva's wife's name.

"Violet."

"Right. Where's—"

"Kali and Eva are in the kitchen, preparing lunch. I'll go fetch them." Violet stood and disappeared around the corner.

Puk attempted to sit up and it was as if a sharp spike stabbed through his lungs.

He felt, simply put, like garbage.

It was then he remembered that the last time he was conscious, there had been a hole in his hand. He raised the rubbery appendage and was pleased to discover nothing more than some scar tissue in the center of his palm. His next question was how much blood he'd gotten all over Eva's immaculate home. No matter what he did, he was fated to ruin the woman's house.

The three women then entered the room. Violet was still mostly apathetic, but Kali and Eva's faces lit up at Puk's improved condition.

Kali hurried to his side and slung her arms around him, which hurt terribly, but he refrained from mentioning it. He embraced her, and they stayed that wait for a moment.

When she pulled away, tears were welling up in her eyes. Puk did not know how to react to that. So instead he asked, "Did we do it?"

She wiped her eyes and gave him a devious smirk, then nodded.

His eyes widened and he laughed heartily. "Fuck me! How the hell did we manage that?"

"Language," Eva and Violet said in unison. Puk could hear the boys playing in the next room, definitely not out of earshot.

Kali acted affronted by his question. "What do you mean 'how'? Did you think we wouldn't? You were talking a big game back there when we got to the Rabid Dog. *I* didn't stop believing in us."

"Yeah," Puk said, "but that was before I got the sh—*stuff* kicked out of me," he self-censored.

She shrugged and grinned wider. All trace of sentimentality had by now been erased from her features. "You know what this means, right?" she asked him.

"What?" He dreaded whatever the faif was about to say.

"You can't rag on me anymore for being knocked out in that mage fight. *Ha!* You passed out in a fight too, and *I* saved *your* life this time!" She cackled heartily. "We're even now."

"Fine, fine," Puk conceded. "We both passed out. We're both wildly incompetent at this whole business."

"That's true," Kali agreed, "but we won in the end, huh?"

He had to laugh. It was insane that they had managed to succeed. A few weeks prior he couldn't even hold his own in a poorly-made card game, and yet he had somehow pulled this off.

"Oh, by the way," Kali added, "Zenib's waiting to see you so that you can pay him."

"I was hoping he forgot," Puk confessed.

"You really think he'd forget collecting his fee? Not a chance."

They both laughed.

Eva prescribed Puk a few more days of rest, which he gladly accepted.

He was stationed on the sofa with his duraga, plucking along to half-mumbled lyrics throughout the days. Violet was usually off working; Eva stayed at home alternating between tidying up and reading a book while her sons were at school; and Kali sat on the floor, leaning her back against the sofa, listening to Puk play.

"I know it's long overdue," he started, "but I took your advice."

"Oh, yeah?"

"Yep. I came up with a metaphor for myself to go with 'the flower.' You ready for this? 'The frog.'"

"How creative!" she giggled.

"Hey, it's apt," he said. "I've been reworkin' the song, too. Wanna hear?"

Kali nodded wordlessly.

Puk began to play, strumming mostly the same chords as the last time, though some had been changed and refined. In between some plucks he smacked his hand on the duraga's face like a drum beat.

"For days they searched, each night a hopeless slog
Years and dreams long lost, the Ribroad pierced the sky
Each night of his far gone with spit and song
And hers far trod along the path well-plod
Their paths converged, the flower and the frog.

488 · travis m. riddle

He stumbled through the streets, seeing no one, like a ghost town

His vision blurred, steps uneven, one then two into a swerve
Pockets hollow as he fell, the same inside, an empty shell
In his eyes, there spoke a ghost who said he's right
That it was true, he was accursed."

Puk abruptly stopped strumming, stopped beating the makeshift drum, and blurted out, "That's all I've got."

"You wrote one more half-verse than last time."

"And I revised all the rest! I'm makin' progress over here!"

Kali chuckled. "It's good!" she said. "Kinda sad, though. Is that verse true? Did you really think you were 'cursed' or something?"

Puk shrugged. "I mean, I'm exaggerating for some dramatic effect," he said, "but maybe it's true to an extent. I dunno." Speaking on his feelings was awkward. Even with Kali. Though there was no one else in the world he would feel more comfortable opening up to. He said, "I guess I just forgot for a long time that I was worthwhile. That the things I can do are worthwhile."

He didn't dare glance at Kali as he said this. It was too uncomfortable, opening himself up so unabashedly.

"Well," she said, "I'm glad you remembered."

Puk curved his stalks to look at her. She was leaning back on the plush lavender, her red hair spilling over the cushion, her eyes closed and facing toward the ceiling. He smiled at her.

--

It was great seeing Puk finally up and about. Another small victory to add to the list. Unfortunately, it seemed their list of victories was much shorter than the list of screw-ups, but at least it wasn't utterly empty.

Later that night, while Eva and Violet were busy cooking dinner for everybody, Puk asked her how it had felt to burn the book.

"I didn't," she replied, surprised it had taken him this long to ask about *Malum*. She hadn't wanted to broach the subject before he was ready, before he'd recovered his strength. She scooted away to retrieve her knapsack and returned a minute later, showing him the untarnished book.

"Why the fuck not?" he hissed, keeping his voice low so as to not invite the women's wrath. "That was the plan. Let's light a fire and get rid of that thing once and for all. Go throw it in the stew, for all I care!"

"Well," she started, "I had a thought about that…"

"Ah," Puk nodded. "You've been enticed by the idea of limitless power. I get it, it's fine. Won't hold it against you. When you become a malevolent overlord and commit a qarmish genocide, are you gonna let me live?"

"No," Kali laughed.

"Harsh."

"I mean no, no enticement. I think we should bring it to the Repository."

She had the idea when she was walking around Restick before encountering Zara, and had been considering it ever since. She had devised a way to tell Puk about it while counting up the crescents they'd gotten from Haratti, splitting it into two piles for herself and the qarm.

Kali wanted to make up for the wrongs she had committed in pursuit of her own selfish gain. While thinking up ways in which to do that, she had recalled what Lissia told her when visiting the Repository; about how closely guarded the centript scholars kept the knowledge within, and how they tirelessly worked studying texts from all over the world, countless years old, concocting methods in which to improve society, both magically or otherwise.

It was possible the scholars at the Repository could study *Malum* and formulate ways in which some of its magic could be beneficial to the world. The book would be confined to the centripts, who would not be tempted to indulge in the darkest aspects of the tome, given that they were unable to cast magic anyway. And if nothing came of their studies, or if the magic was deemed too dangerous to work with in any capacity, they could simply destroy the book like Kali and Puk had planned to in the first place.

As Kali explained her thought process to Puk, he stared at her on the couch, slack-jawed.

"We went through all that trouble—I got turned into a slug and got a hole in my hand, and we had to steal the book *twice*—and you just wanna turn around and give it away again? Keep it in the world?"

"Well, yeah," she nodded. "Something positive might come from all this. Wouldn't that be nice? For people besides us to benefit from all this nasty business we've endured?"

"'People' didn't endure that shit. *We* did! Why not just us benefit?" Kali was about to protest, but Puk spoke first. "Look, I ain't gonna lie and say I totally get it, but I'm behind you on it. If that's what you feel is best, then I trust you. Let's do it."

"Really?"

"Really. When have you ever let me down?"

"Oh, probably never," she grinned.

It was a relief that Puk was on board with her idea. She was thrilled by what they had accomplished, and excited for what they were still to do. Maybe it wasn't quite the same as studying for years and years like her sister, but it was something, and she was proud of it.

She couldn't wait to deliver the book and finally set foot on the shores of Atlua.

"But how far is the Repository?" Puk asked. "I ain't tryin' to go on another grand adventure so soon," he grumbled.

"It's not close," Kali laughed.

"Well, at least we've got Bella, I guess. Unless you're still plannin' on setting her free and buying that dumb ayote back home or whatever you said before."

Kali shook her head. "Nah. Bella's staying with us."

She had grown awfully attached to the spunky animal over the course of their journey.

"But we've gotta go to Seroo's Eye first, anyway. We can relax at the inn for a while. I'm more than ready to get to Atlua, but I sure could use a week in bed too." To her surprise, the idea of taking a break did not consume her with guilt like it usually did.

"A week of bed and free food sounds perfect to me," said Puk.

"Who said anything about 'free' for you?" Kali teased him.

"You and I are a team!" Puk objected. "A package deal!"

"Nah," Kali said, tossing him a pouch filled with his share of the job's profits. "I know you've got the money for it."

- -

A few days later, Puk was feeling well enough to travel, although he was severely not looking forward to it.

Kali had told him she'd secured voyage on a ship bound for Atlua in a few weeks, after their jaunt to the Repository, but that he'd have to work onboard during the trip.

"Can't I just pay more and do nothing?" he complained. "I just want to lay down. For the love of all things Waranexian, please just let me lay down."

"You've been laying down for almost a week straight. You were asleep for, like, two days."

"And yet I crave more."

They said goodbye to their gracious hosts (with Puk being sure to profusely thank Eva again for not letting him die on the street), then headed to the Restick stables to pay for and retrieve Bella.

Puk uselessly stood by and watched Kali saddle up the ayote and attach all their belongings to her. With Bella's outrageous speed, the Ribroad would take them practically no time to traverse. It might be his last ride with the trusty ayote. He would miss her.

That realization struck him. He really liked this ayote.

Maybe they ain't all the same.

"You ready to go?" Kali asked, tightening the strap on her knapsack that held *Malum*. It would be a terrible irony if, after all this time, the bag slipped and was swallowed by the desert for any chump to stumble upon.

Puk nodded, standing up on the tips of his toes to scratch Bella behind her ear.

The shade of the Ribroad was a welcome reprieve from the open-air desert travel they had undertaken on their journey to and from Pontequest. Puk felt a pang of sympathy for the miserable people stuck there, brainwashed by Kleus into keeping themselves in and keeping newcomers out. Being stuck in that wretched town was a fate worse than being transformed into a sapient slug.

"We should tell someone in the Repository about Pontequest, right?" he said. "So that maybe someone can be sent there to, I dunno, knock everyone's brains loose? Get 'em out from under Kleus's thrall?"

"That's...a very good idea, actually," said Kali. "I'm embarrassed that it did not occur to me. I bet the scholars there would be thrilled to learn that the town still actually exists, too."

Puk was pleased with himself. They rode on down the Ribroad, with Bella moving at a nice clip but not fast enough to send him flying like usual. Her gait was calm enough to maintain conversation at a reasonable, respectable volume, for which he was grateful.

"You're gonna be doin' a lot of traveling once you're over in Atlua, aren't you?" Puk asked. His arms were wrapped tight around Kali's waist to keep him on the ayote's back. He bounced up and down with each of the animal's bounds. Even with her slower pace, he was a small creature, and he was worried about falling.

Kali nodded. "Yeah, of course," she said. "I'm gonna try to see everything I can. Take in all the beautiful sights, the different cultures, the tasty foods...the best part is that it'll not only be fun, but also really good for my work. I think this is gonna finally help my business take off, if I can start importing and exporting some goods exclusive to each country. I'm sure I can learn a lot from Zara and her shipmates." She then added, "I need to find some noxspring, too. Bryieshk will want me to cut him a good deal. And maybe I can cut Vonoshreb a bad one."

Puk didn't have the faintest clue who Bryieshk or Vonoshreb were, but the scenario Kali had just painted in his head sounded marvelous.

"You don't think you'd..."

He felt nervous asking. He didn't know why; he was perfectly comfortable around Kali at this point. But still, he didn't know how she'd react to his question.

He started again, "Once we're over there, you don't think you'd maybe need some help, do you?"

"Help?"

"Sure. With, like, carrying shit or haggling with stubborn idiots or whatever. If you think you'd need some help, I, uh..."

"I don't need help," Kali answered succinctly.

"Oh," Puk whispered. "Alright."

It made total sense. Kali was fully capable of operating her business on her own. On this adventure of theirs she had repeatedly proven how capable she was, how well she could handle herself. And regardless of all that, she had been a merchant for a while now; she was only looking to expand outward. She already knew how to barter, how best to transport goods, how to—

"You can come along if you want, though," she said, knocking him from his daze.

He blinked, curving his stalks up to look at her. She was peering down over her shoulder at him, grinning.

"You don't wanna work for me. I know you don't," she said.

"You're right," Puk confessed, laughing. "Bein' a merchant sounds shitty. No offense."

"A little taken. But I'd be glad to have your company, if you feel like tagging along."

It sounded nice. There was no denying that.

"I've been thinking about maybe starting to write some more," he told her. "Now that I've got my own duraga, and all. There'll be plenty of bars and inns on the road looking for some nightly musicians to play, I would think."

"Undoubtedly," Kali said. "I think that sounds like a great idea."

Puk nodded. "Maybe we can make that work," he said. "Travelin' the roads together, you sellin' shit to people while I sing 'em songs. The flower and the frog, on the road together again!"

Kali laughed merrily at the moniker. Puk knew she would love the cheesiness of it, and he joined in her laughter.

"Back on the road," she said. "But before that, a week in bed."

"Hell, let's shoot for the stars. Make it two."

ACKNOWLEDGMENTS

First, I'd like to say a long overdue thank you to my stalwart beta reading team who have been with me since the first book; without Jenna Jaco, Tyler Gruenzner, and Emily Cummings, none of these books would be what they are today. As well as Dave Woolliscroft, Steven McKinnon, Cat Skinner, and John Bierce for providing their feedback and insight into how to make Puk and Kali's adventure the best it could be. Of course I'd be remiss not thanking Tim Simmons, Barry Riveroll, and Dean Thomasson for their input on previous books. How have I not done acknowledgments before? What is wrong with me?

A special thank you as well to the bloggers who have helped champion my work and have brightened my days on more than one occasion: Calvin Park from Fantasy Book Review, Ella from The Story Collector, Jordan from Forever Lost in Literature, and the countless other kind souls who have spread the word and left reviews on their blogs or r/fantasy, my favorite place to hang out.

One of the best aspects of joining the indie writing community has been getting the opportunity to become acquainted with so many great, friendly authors. People like Jon Auerbach, John Bierce, Angela Boord, Josh Erikson, Barbara Kloss, Devin Madson, Steven McKinnon, Richard Nell, Kayleigh Nicol, Carol A. Park, Clayton Snyder, Aidan Walsh, Phil Williams, and Dave Woolliscroft. Thank you all for your endless advice and support and for being great people to vent with when this whole venture gets to me, as I'm sure it does every author.

And finally, thank you to everyone who has bought this book and any book in the past. I'm thankful for the opportunity to share these stories with you, and grateful every time you leave a review, tell a friend about the book, or gift a copy to someone in your family. Your support and encouragement mean the world to me, and I hope I can continue sharing these weird stories with you for as long as possible.

ABOUT THE AUTHOR

TRAVIS M. RIDDLE lives with his pooch in Austin, TX, where he studied Creative Writing at St. Edward's University. His work has been published in award-winning literary journal the Sorin Oak Review. He can be found online at www.travismriddle.com or on twitter @traviswanteat.

Made in the USA
Middletown, DE
28 October 2022